Coe

Coe

The Preacher's Sons 3

Mary E. Hanks

www.maryehanks.com

Suzanne D. Williams Cover Design

www.feelgoodromance.com

Cover Photo:

VGstockstudio @ shutterstock.com

Visit Mary's website:

www.maryehanks.com

You can write Mary at

maryhanks@maryehanks.com

To Gary and Kathy

Thank you for your friendship and encouragement,

and for sharing your love of plants with us.

He has made everything beautiful in its time.

Ecclesiastes 3:11

Chapter One

Chest heaving and breathing ragged, Coe North collapsed into the first-class seat next to Skye Tamarack, who was also gasping in short breaths, and thanked God they reached the plane before the door closed. After Skye was detained by airport security for no other reason than being Liam Tamarack's daughter, they'd found themselves in a race against time. They rushed through the Dubai terminal, fleeing past shops, dashing through the maze of travelers, and barely making the final boarding call.

No doubt, the influential Tamarack Foundation CEO had called in a favor to keep Skye in India, but his efforts failed. So, despite Coe's pounding heart and Skye's pale features, they were on a jet that would soon depart for New York. After two years away, he was eager to return to the United States and see his family again.

Liam's long arm can't reach us now. The thought barely crossed his mind when two muscular men wearing opaque sunglasses and black apparel charged onto the plane. They were the same guys who dragged him off Liam Tamarack's property after he caught Coe kissing Skye a week ago. They were the same ones who followed him the past few days, threatening that he'd be sorry if he didn't leave the country. Skye's gasp confirmed she recognized them, too.

To prevent Liam's men from spotting her, Coe did the only protective thing he could think of. He shifted in his seat and drew Skye into his arms, and even though they hadn't kissed in a week, he pressed his lips to hers with some heat. At first, she didn't react. And no wonder. They were on a public plane, and his romantic overture was over the top. But moments later, Skye's lips warmed to his, becoming pliant and sweetly responsive. She wrapped her arms around his neck, drawing him closer to her, and for a few seconds, he almost forgot where they were and why they were here. Heat pounded through his veins despite his initial subterfuge.

Hearing the rumble of jet engines as they pulled away from the boarding bridge, Coe broke their kiss and checked the aisle behind them. Liam's intimidating brutes weren't in sight.

"It was them," Skye whispered. "Is that why you kissed me?"

"Yes." However, their presence wouldn't be the reason he kissed her like that again.

"What should we do now?"

"Nothing to do until we land in New York other than pray." He relaxed in his seat as the jet rolled down the runway. "I've hardly stopped doing that since you came to my door last week and we talked about leaving together." Her cheeks turned rosy. Was she embarrassed about their passionate kiss that got them into trouble with her father? Or how they'd discussed getting married?

"I am sorry for getting you involved, Coe." He loved how she said his name softly. It made his thoughts scramble to their first daring kiss that started the whole run-for-their-lives situation. And imagining that kiss made him long to kiss her again. "Thank you for saving me from a life of misery. I'll never forget what you did for me." She was referring to his vow to get her away from an arranged marriage and even marry her himself. But at that moment, he was too captivated by the memory of her soft, pouty lips pressed against his to talk about Liam Tamarack's efforts to force her into a union she opposed.

"Father pressured me about marrying Edmund all week, telling me how the arrangements were all made. Why did he think he could plan my marriage, and I'd go along with it?" She stared out the window as if speaking more to herself than him. "I'm thirty. This isn't the eighteenth century."

"Too bad he didn't arrange for you to marry me."

"If only." She glanced back at him wistfully.

He stroked his fingers down her warm, soft cheek, still enjoying the newness of touching her skin. "Who would have guessed one phenomenal kiss would lead to us fleeing together and discussing marriage?"

"Yeah. Who would have thought?" She cringed slightly.

"Having second thoughts?"

"Maybe."

"I'm not. If it takes us getting married to get your dad to call off his flunkies, I'll do it." He gazed into her glistening eyes and felt a magnetic pull to take her in his arms again and show her how serious he was about his pledge and his hope for a happy future with her. He was attracted to her. The rest should be simple.

"Was it worth it?" she whispered.

"Our kisses? Oh, yeah."

"Good." She kissed his cheek, her eyelashes fluttering against his face, and his heart pounded.

The chemistry between them felt so powerful that sparks were surely flashing around them. He could picture a lifetime of kissing this woman he found adorable and one who also loved Jesus. He'd always wanted to marry a woman whose faith was as vibrant as his. Was he getting his wish?

What about love? Love would come. He was sure of it.

Skye settled back into her seat, and the delicate dimpling of her cheeks made him ache to touch his mouth to hers again. Why was he so incredibly attracted to her? Was it due only to her beauty? Or was it her compassionate heart for serving others that he'd witnessed in their humanitarian aid efforts and was fascinated by? He'd seen how cute she looked with mud caked on her cheeks and brows after they'd been digging ditches all day. And how beautiful she looked when she helped hungry children get in a food line and went the extra mile to ensure they had enough food.

And the way she kissed him? Whew. They'd surely have a deeply romantic marriage. *Slow down, North.* If they got married right away, it would be platonic in the beginning. They'd be pledging themselves to Skye's freedom and safety. But a marriage in name only? *Impossible, right?*

Watching Skye in profile, he admired her long eyelashes, chocolate irises, and tanned skin tone. Her nearly black hair brushed her chin and curled under slightly. She had a habit of tucking both sides behind her ears, something he'd like to do for her. She had cute ears, too.

"What?" She met his gaze.

"Nothing. You should get some sleep."

"After seeing my dad's bodyguards on the plane and us kissing like it was the end of the world, you think I can drift off to sleep?" Her dimples widened again.

"I'm glad thoughts of kissing me will keep you awake. Wanting more, perhaps?" He was flirting, but he also wanted to know what she thought of him, despite the threat of her father's men being on board.

"Don't push it." She nudged his arm with her elbow. "I don't think we should kiss anymore until we're certain of our future."

"Like you think we're going to die or something?"

"No, silly. No more kissing until we're sure about our feelings for each other."

Oh, he was certain about his feelings.

"Does this mean you want a marriage in name only?" His tongue stumbled over the question, but he thought he should ask. After the way they kissed, he didn't think she'd want anything less than a normal marriage. But what would a regular marriage be like for two people who weren't in love yet?

"Will that be any better than the arrangement Father planned for me?"

"How can you even ask that?"

"I'll still be marrying a stranger. A nice one, but still."

"We aren't strangers, Skye. We've volunteered and worked on projects together for two years and went to the same church."

"I know. But I don't want you to feel trapped into marrying me." She ran her fingers over the edge of the window. "Helping me get on this flight fulfills your promise to me."

"Skye—"

"I mean it."

"We'll figure out how to make it work."

"Work?" She swiveled toward him, eyes wide.

"Not work as in *work*. I mean—" What did he mean? Their escape across Dubai, the mad dash through the airport, and the breathless kisses made him want to take risks to get her back to the U.S. and keep her safe. The only way he knew how to do that was to marry her and give her his last name. But was that God's plan for their lives? Or was his solution selfishly forged by his desire to have Skye as his wife? "I meant marriage is a lifelong journey. If we decide to marry before we fall in love—"

"*If* we fall in love."

"We will," he said confidently.

"How can you be so sure?"

"My parents married before they were in love. And they're still crazy about each other thirty-five years later." He'd explained a bit of their story to her already.

"So, you thought you could pull this off?" Tip, Liam's menacing redheaded security guard, asked gruffly from the aisle, a silver front tooth adding a sinister edge to his sneer.

Coe tensed and pivoted in his seat, positioning himself as a barrier between Tip and Skye. He was prepared to do whatever it took to keep her safe, even if it meant confronting this ruffian head-on.

"Leave us alone," Skye said.

"Not until you're back with your father. You know how this works." Tip's voice sounded scratchy like he used it to yell a lot. "We're bringing Liam's princess home."

"I'm no one's princess. And I'm not going anywhere with you."

"Wanna bet?"

"Enough!" Coe undid his seatbelt and stood, glaring at the other man, his right fist clenching and unclenching. His ribs were still tender from his last altercation with Liam's men, and he didn't want to experience that again, but he wouldn't back down and do nothing, either. He was prepared to fight for Skye's honor and safety. "You should return to your seat and mind your own business."

"Make me," Tip said tauntingly.

All right. But before Coe could respond, a flight attendant approached them. "Sir, please return to your seat. The captain still has the remain-seated light turned on."

A few passengers were watching with interest, and some looked uncomfortable with the exchange. Coe tried to relax his stance to put them more at ease, but the tension in the air was palpable as he and Tip scowled at each other.

"We aren't finished here." Tip ground his fist into his palm, eyeing Coe darkly, then trudged down the narrow aisle.

Great. Coe dropped into his seat with a long sigh. All thoughts of getting some sleep or flirting with Skye on this flight were gone.

Chapter Two

Skye glanced toward the cabin behind them several times without spotting Rhett or Tip. Where were they seated? And what would stop them from doing something terrible to her or Coe if they fell asleep? She wouldn't put it past her manipulative father to have told his security team to do whatever was necessary to return her to his fortified empire, and he'd pay double or triple for a job well done. And all for what? So she'd marry a man of his choosing, someone who'd contributed a ton of money to his foundation? A feeling of unrest and anger churned in her stomach.

Father had no right sending his goons after her. She was an adult. She could marry anyone she wanted. And she could make her own decisions about where she lived.

How had he discovered she was leaving India? Rhett and Tip had followed her more than usual this week, obeying her father's orders to keep her away from Coe, no doubt. It had taken her sneaking out the back of the house under the cover of night to get away. One of them must have been trailing her when she entered Coe's bungalow last night and reported it. Nothing happened, but she imagined her ex-military father's volcanic reaction when he heard about her staying overnight with Coe. Look how irrationally he responded after finding them only kissing!

She shuffled in her seat, trying to get comfortable and failing, her thoughts flitting over her father's past offenses. How often had he paraded some wealthy older guy before her like a prized treasure? *Some treasure.* What kind of fantasyland was he living in, where he thought he had the right to sell her off to the wealthiest man he knew? Just because he was the founder and CEO of the Tamarack Foundation, a private organization dedicated to helping people in natural disasters and crises, and had worldwide notoriety for his philanthropic work, it didn't give him the right to control her future. And just because men like Edmund Lung gave a huge amount of money to the foundation, it didn't mean she had to marry any of them.

All her life and more so since Mom died, Father had told her he would choose her groom, that he knew best who would make a good husband and partner for her. At first, she hadn't taken him seriously. An arranged marriage in modern society? He was joking, right? She even laughed about it. But then, she realized he was seriously planning to choose her spouse. No wonder he insisted they live in countries where such a practice might be more accepted or tolerated.

Thanks to Coe, I'm almost free.

But was she willing to marry a man she didn't love to get the freedom she coveted when she vehemently refuted the idea of an arranged marriage? Even if Coe was a friendly guy, whom she admittedly had a crush on, would she agree to be his wife? What if she was exchanging one prison for another? She moaned.

"You okay?" Coe asked.

"I guess." Her vague reply probably didn't satisfy him, but he didn't push for another answer.

Why did Father consider her trustworthy enough to assist flood and hurricane victims with building homes and nursing wounds, but not intelligent enough to pick a life mate? And why would he choose an old grump like Edmund Lung for her?

Returning to the States and even marrying Coe was a smart move—her only option, considering the alternative. However, with Rhett and Tip on board, how would they get away? Was New York City large enough to stop Father from using every resource to hunt her and Coe down?

If Rhett and Tip found them and dragged her back to Dubai, would Father try to force her to marry Edmund again? She felt a rush of anxiety. What would they do to Coe? Beat him up? Threaten his family? She couldn't let those things happen. He didn't deserve the garbage her power-wielding father would make him suffer. Despite the heroic image he portrayed in public, Liam Tamarack had a tyrannical side that made even her afraid of crossing him. His power had cast a long, dark shadow over her life, making her feel like a bird trapped in a cage. But with Coe's and God's help, she was breaking free. However, she was still concerned about what Rhett and Tip might do.

Dear God, please protect us. Keep Coe and his family safe. Don't let any harm come to them because of me. Help us to know if we should get married.

A marriage of convenience was an outrageous, preposterous idea, right? But what if it wasn't? What if marrying Coe was the most excellent decision she would ever make?

She mentally relived the kiss he gave her minutes ago, dwelling on its every detail. Even though it was a ploy to keep Rhett and Tip from seeing her, she enjoyed it immensely. And last week's kisses on her porch were sweet and tenderly passionate. For a few seconds, the stars seemed to dance above them. Even now, imagining Coe's lips pressed against hers caused pings of lightning to race up her middle. But did their kisses mean anything beyond fantastic chemistry?

Was Coe a man she could spend her whole life with?

She glanced at his profile, her gaze lingering on his features. His dark, slightly long, wavy hair could use a haircut, but it only added to his charm. Shadowed whiskers covered his cheeks and chin, which dipped inward, making a handsome dimple. She was drawn to him and wanted to stroke his face and feel his whiskers like she did when they were kissing and get better acquainted with him. Could she marry Coe based on how wonderful she felt in his arms? Were unforgettable kisses enough to build a marriage on? She released a long sigh.

"Something bothering you?"

"Other than wondering how we'll get out of our predicament?" She couldn't explain her thoughts about kissing him.

"Uh-huh." His eyes looked glazed.

"If we were to marry, what would you expect?"

"Expect?" He sat up straighter, his eyes widening.

A heatwave of emotions flooded her, but she forced herself to look him in the eye. "Would you want everything?"

He cleared his throat. "After the way we've kissed, I'd say I'm looking forward to everything about our marriage."

"Before we fall in love?"

"Not necessarily." He gave her a slow smile. "But if we were married and one thing led to another, it would be okay, wouldn't it?"

He made marriage and intimacy sound easy. But she knew people who married, divorced, and were in second marriages, proving relationships weren't all that simple.

"My life has been about rules."

"I'm sorry." Coe clasped her hand. "Let's make it a point not to live by any human's rules except the ones the two of us agree on, okay?" He drew closer to her in the limited space, his gaze locked on her lips as if he were going to kiss her again.

Everything within her wanted his kiss. She licked her lips in anticipation, then realizing what he said, she tugged her hand free.

"Which rules are you referring to? Are you talking about wives submitting to their husbands?" Father quoted that one to her several times. Only he used it to describe her submission to the husband he chose for her, the one who would supposedly make her future secure.

"How about doing to others what you would want done to you?"

"Oh. You mean the Golden Rule?" She relaxed a little.

"Mmhmm. How about loving your neighbor selflessly? I'm rephrasing based on things my grandmother used to say to me and my brothers." Imitating an older woman's voice, he said, "You boys should live a life filled with grace and kindness. Love the Lord with all your heart, and your heart will be pure. Be holy." He chuckled. "Can you imagine telling nine rambunctious boys to be holy?"

"No, I can't." She loved hearing his stories about his big family and how much his parents and grandmother meant to him.

"Would you hate being married to me?" He met her gaze with a soft, yearning look that made her want to lean closer for that kiss she pulled away from. "I wouldn't want you to claim my last name and then regret it."

Would she regret marrying Coe North?

Chapter Three

Coe awoke with a start. He hadn't meant to doze off and was glad to find Skye sitting beside him, her cheek resting against his arm. Enjoying the feeling of her being close, he shut his eyes again. Her gasp nearly shot him to his feet. He glanced up and saw Tip peering down at them. *Not again.* "What do you want?" Coe clasped Skye's hand instinctively.

"I want steak and eggs," Tip said in a raspy voice. "What matters is what the boss wants." His gaze homed in on Skye. "Come with us peacefully, and your friend here will be okay. Or we'll take you by force, and he'll be sorry."

"Look, chum." Coe set their clasped hands over his heart. "We plan to be married. So leave us alone."

"Not happening." Tip lifted his chin toward Skye. "Mr. Tamarack has a marital arrangement lined up for you that doesn't include this loser. He demands that you come home immediately."

"He's not getting what he wants this time." Skye released Coe's hand and jabbed her index finger at Tip. "I'm making my own decisions. I'm marrying Coe whether my father likes it or not." Coe grinned at her adamant words and tone.

"Run if you can, but we'll find you every time." Tip's jaw tightened. "We are taking you back to India."

"No, you aren't!"

"Yes, we—"

"Enough!" Coe stood abruptly. "We don't want any trouble."

Tip made a disgusted snort. "You don't know what trouble is until you've seen Rhett and me in action. We have men on the ground waiting to take care of you."

Coe bit back a groan. Additional guys following Liam's directives in New York meant getting away from them would be more challenging, but not impossible. God had been with him during his entire time in India, and *He* was here with Skye and him. *He* would help them.

"Why don't you head back to your seat?" Coe nodded toward the rear of the plane.

"Make me."

"Fine." He'd had enough of Tip's bullying.

"Is there a problem here?" A first-class flight attendant with short-cropped curly hair and a nametag of Casey stopped next to them, peering between Tip and Coe. "Is there something I should report to the captain?"

"Nope. No problem." Tip gave her a fake smile.

"I'd suggest you return to your seat, then. The captain still has the seatbelt light on."

"Yes, ma'am." Tip grimaced at Skye. "Don't forget what I said."

Coe waited until Liam's bodyguard was halfway through the plane before dropping into his seat. "Does your father have recruits in the U.S.?"

"Everywhere, no doubt." Skye pushed her hair behind her ears. "What are we going to do?"

"We'll come up with a plan." The fact that Rhett and Tip were on the plane with them was troubling enough. It'd be more challenging in New York if what Tip said about others waiting for them was true. How would he keep Skye safe?

"Maybe this escape attempt was a mistake." She twisted her hands agitatedly.

"It's going to be okay." He smoothed his hand over hers. "We'll figure out something together." He liked saying *together* as if it already had special meaning.

The flight attendant returned and took their meal orders. They chose chicken curry dinners with rice, salad, and a peach cobbler, then the woman moved on to other first-class passengers.

"Why can't we just report those guys to the cops and get this over quickly?" Coe asked, resuming their conversation.

"Because my father is a conscientious humanitarian who has done a ton of good around the world."

"Does that excuse his wrongs?"

"Never." Skye shuddered. "However, I won't be the cause of bad publicity or harm coming to the work he and all the volunteers have accomplished with the Tamarack Foundation. I feel protective of what we've done over the years, don't you?"

Coe heaved a sigh. "I guess."

"If you can't go along with getting me away from his bodyguards without police involvement, I understand. We can part ways in New York City."

"Not on your life. But I don't see—"

"Please. Can we just get out of the city as soon as possible?" She gave him an imploring look that twisted knots inside him.

"Okay. Fine." Even though he'd worked for Liam for two years and knew he was a demanding boss, Coe didn't understand Skye's need to defend him. Even great leaders had to be held accountable for their personal actions. But his unwavering commitment was to keep her safe and fulfill his vow to her, no matter the cost, even if he didn't understand her relationship with her father.

While they ate their dinners and drank coffee, they discussed ways to disembark from the plane without Rhett, Tip, or any other employees of Liam's spotting them and leaving New York. They discarded many of their ideas due to the lack of cash it would take to pull off an elaborate scheme. Escaping in a hot air balloon seemed absurd and too costly, even if it might have been adventurous. Renting a car and driving twenty-five hundred miles to Thunder Ridge, Idaho, was doable but time-consuming and exhausting. Just the gas and rental costs were too expensive.

One escape plan had the most potential for success, so they reviewed its details until they ironed out every imaginable scenario and route from JFK Airport to one of five hotels in New York City. Coe picked five because he wanted options in case Rhett and Tip followed them. They agreed to flee to another city if their plan was compromised or became too dangerous.

"If we were married, this might be easier," Skye said after the flight attendant took their trays and cups.

"I agree. But would marriage stop Rhett and Tip from trying to take you back to your father?"

"Nope," a man's gruff voice said.

Coe nearly jumped out of his seat, and Skye groaned as Rhett, Liam's black-haired, muscular bodyguard, leaned over Coe with a fierce grimace, reeking of onions and garlic. "Marriages are so easy to annul these days. My boss wants you out of the picture. Know what that means?"

Coe had an idea after the way Rhett and Tip dragged him off Liam's property last week.

"Don't follow us in New York, or we will report you," Skye said.

"Like anything you say will affect what we do once we land."

"If we report you to customs, the agent will be interested to hear your plans to off me and kidnap Skye." Coe met Rhett's steely gaze without flinching.

"Just doing my job."

"Not according to U.S. law." Coe tapped his phone. "Research how long you'll be incarcerated for kidnapping in New York. Is doing Liam's dirty work worth a mandatory prison sentence?"

Rhett coughed hard.

"Sir? Are you okay?" Casey asked. "Do you need assistance?"

"Uh, no."

"Why don't you head back to your seat? I'll tell my coworker to bring you some water."

"Thanks." Rhett stared hard at Coe and Skye. "You will be picked up in the terminal. This is the end of the line for the two of you."

"You're wrong. Skye and I are getting married," Coe stated firmly.

"We'll see about that."

"Yes, we will!" Coe and Skye said together.

Chapter Four

After going through customs without any problems, Skye slipped into a narrow stall in the women's bathroom at JFK. Luckily, she and Coe disembarked ahead of Rhett and Tip, but they didn't know who might be waiting for them ahead. Was Tip possibly lying about other men being present to capture them? What if she and Coe couldn't camouflage themselves well enough, and those men took her by force? She groaned, thinking of other times she'd futilely tried to leave her father's household. But worrying wasn't helping anything. She had to have faith. God was helping her, and this time she had Coe, too.

They each had one carry-on bag, and they planned to change clothes and ditch their bags. According to their getaway scheme, they'd be dodging in and out of places, so hanging onto luggage would only slow them down.

Footsteps scuffed outside her stall. Tip or Rhett? She doubted either would observe the niceties of remaining outside the ladies' restroom. She tugged on a large pale blue sweatshirt with a giant word "Live" written across the front in white. Gray leggings, running shoes, and a pastel pink knit hat—clothes that didn't scream she was running from men who planned to kidnap her—completed her disguise. She tucked her hair under the hat and put on pink lipstick.

Ready. Coe's text flashed on her phone. The single word meant they wouldn't see each other until they met in the city.

Lord, help us. Strapping her slim purse, with her ID, Uber fare, and emergency funds inside, snugly around her body, Skye exited the stall cautiously. No one was in the handwashing area. She emptied her bag into the trash, located another garbage can, and threw the travel bag in.

Ready, she texted back.

She pushed her phone into her leggings pocket, wanting her hands free if it came to a struggle or trying to outrun Father's men. If Rhett, Tip, or anyone else grabbed her, she'd fight, claw, scream, and make the noisiest scene possible, ensuring they regretted capturing her. Hopefully, her hair tucked in her hat, the change of apparel, and being alone instead of with Coe would take them off guard, and they wouldn't notice her. *Lord, please.*

She sauntered out of the restroom and joined the crowd, heading toward baggage claim without seeing Rhett or Tip. She exhaled. She'd made it through phase one.

"Act like you're a disembarking New Yorker," Coe told her. *"Don't run or behave nervously. Act like you don't care who sees you. Blend in with other travelers."* It sounded easy when they talked about it on the plane, but would it work?

A little girl ran past her, and Skye gasped. *Ugh.* She wasn't supposed to be jumpy or draw attention to herself, and in the first minute out of the bathroom, she did just that. She forced herself to breathe normally and continued walking with a casual stride. She even smiled at a young mom who was corralling twin boys.

Her next objective was to get beyond the exiting passengers and through the doors to the street where she'd search for her ride. Had Coe made it out yet?

As she descended the ramp, she did what he suggested, grinning and waving at an imaginary person in the crowd like she was eager to meet him. She scanned the group briefly. Five guys dressed in black stood in a row, looking tense and ready to grab someone—her, no doubt. But their gazes were locked on the ramp beyond her, not at her. *Thank You, Lord.* She veered toward the exit without making eye contact with any of them and meshed with the moving group.

She'd completed phase two.

Outside the terminal, she didn't peer around wide-eyed like a tourist, and didn't let down her guard, revealing she had no idea where she was going. *"Look for a gray sedan in the taxi and rental waiting area,"* Coe told her after he scheduled their pickups on an app. *"Your driver's name is Clancy."* He suggested she memorize the vehicle license. *"Unless your life is in danger, walk. Don't run to the vehicle."*

Easier said than done. Heart pounding, she faced a sea of taxis and Ubers, and everything within her urged her to race to one of them and jump inside. Firm footsteps sounded like someone was running up behind her. The back of her neck itched. She walked faster. Where was the gray sedan?

"Skye!" Tip's voice. *Oh, no.*

She sprinted down the pedestrian-filled sidewalk, zigzagging around travelers, frantically searching for her ride. She was on the brink of freedom, her escape within reach. She couldn't get caught now.

"Skye! Stop!"

There! She waved frantically at the driver of a gray car, barely checking the license number, before leaping into the back seat. "Go. Go."

"Skye?"

"Yes. Hurry. Get out of here fast!"

Tip yanked on her door handle. "Open up!"

Thankfully, the door was locked. "Please, just go."

"Is that man—"

"Yes. He's trying to kidnap me. Get out of here!"

"You've got it." Clancy steered sharply into the next lane, tires squealing as he veered into a slot in the slow-moving traffic.

Tip ran alongside the car, pounding on the window. "Stop the vehicle! Pull over!"

"Don't stop. Go faster," she said through gritted teeth. "Faster!"

"I can't drive faster." The driver glanced back nervously toward Tip, who was still running beside them. "Do you want me to pull over so you can talk to that man?"

"No!" Couldn't he see she was in danger? "Don't stop for any-thing." Tip pounded on the window, but Skye didn't make eye contact with him.

"Miss?"

"Keep driving. I beg of you, get me out of here." *Lord, help. Be with Coe, wherever he is.*

Finally, Clancy got the vehicle moving beyond Tip's ability to keep up.

Skye slumped against the back seat. *I'm not out of the woods yet, but I'm in the U. S.* She checked her phone for texts or messages from Coe. Nothing.

Had he made it out of the airport? Or did Father's men detain him? Skye trembled at the thought of what that might mean if they did.

Chapter Five

After leaving the men's room, Coe secretly trailed Skye, making sure she reached the ramp safely before he pursued his escape route. They'd agreed about going through customs and exiting the secure area separately, then getting rides into the city alone. But letting her go into New York City by herself was driving him crazy and he hadn't left the airport. What if Liam's security team captured her and put her back on a plane for Dubai? What might they do to make her submit to their wishes?

Coe groaned. He needed to think positively and prayerfully, not imagining the worst-case scenario, but tension raced through him. If anything happened to her—

Skye left the secure area without anyone noticing her, and his breathing normalized. *Praise God.* There was some crowd shuffling at the bottom of the ramp. A child ran toward a grandparent, shouting in Spanish. A young couple kissed fervently, blocking some foot traffic. Family members called out greetings and stopped to hug and chat. The chaos and congestion improved Skye's chances of getting out the door without anyone spotting her.

Coe figured he'd have more difficulty since the departing group had thinned. If Liam's brutes realized Skye eluded them, they might be more determined to catch him. Angrier, too.

He waited five minutes before heading down the ramp, which felt like an eternity. Everything within him compelled him to follow Skye through baggage claim and onto the street, but he fought the urge, waiting and praying around the corner. *Lord, be with her. Help her make it to our checkpoint. Help me, too.*

He tried to act normal as he strolled down the ramp, not like he was about to run for his life, which he would do if Tip and Rhett came after him. He tugged his baseball-style cap with a Gonzaga basketball team logo low over his forehead. He'd donned a dark green pullover sweatshirt, jeans with a hole in the knee, and worn-out shoes. His other possessions went in the trash.

His phone vibrated. It could be one of his brothers, or it might be Skye. She wasn't supposed to contact him unless she was in trouble. He yanked his cell from his pocket.

Safe was her one-word text.

Thank You, Jesus. He stuffed the phone in his pocket, melded into the crowd whistling "Amazing Grace," and scanned the area. Three guys in black clothes, wearing glowering expressions, stood side by side like a wall of muscle. Coe veered left. So did they. He veered right. They did the same. He groaned, realizing he hadn't fooled anyone with his minimal disguise. Where were Rhett and Tip?

"Where do you think you're going?" the most muscular of the three demanded.

"I'm a tourist. I want to see the sights. Doesn't everyone in New York City?"

"Tourist," the guy spit out. "And I'm Matt Damon."

He wasn't the actor, but Coe went along with it. "I'm glad to meet you, Matt. Now, I have to get going."

"Not so fast." The three thugs surrounded him, one pulling his arm hard enough to leave bruises. Coe's heart pounded, his throat went dry, and swallowing was difficult. Another guy prodded him with his fist, shoving him toward the exit. "Let's go, chump."

"Where are you taking me?" Coe frantically scanned the crowd, searching for airport police or security. If he didn't find someone soon, this might be the end of the line for him. How bad would Liam's ruffians beat him up before they tossed him in a garbage receptacle or threw him into the Hudson River? He tried not to give in to fear or panic. *Lord, You are my strength. Please make a way of escape. Help Skye.*

"You are going to take us to your girlfriend."

"Girlfriend?" Just then, he spotted a guy wearing an official uniform. "Help! Help!" He yanked against the bad guys' hold like he told Skye to do if she got caught and made as much noise as possible, jerking and kicking at them. "Let me go!"

"Stop! What do you think you're doing?" The biggest guy squeezed his arm. "I can have you dead in seconds."

No doubt. Still, Coe's chances were better if he made a scene. "I'm being kidnapped! Someone, help me!"

"Shut up." One of the guys attempted to pick him up like a sack of potatoes, but Coe squirmed and resisted.

"Stop!" an airport security guard with a nametag of Bruce shouted. Two other uniformed officers joined him, and the three approached Liam's men. "Put this man down." *Finally.* "Why are you restraining him?"

"I'm a U.S. citizen," Coe said as the guys dropped him like a chunk of wood onto the floor. He scrambled to his feet, rubbing some sore places on his arms. "These men are roughing me up on account of the woman I plan to marry."

"What's this?" Bruce demanded, eyeing the brutes.

"They want to take her back to India against her will."

"It's all a misunderstanding," the most muscular guy said in a fake, contrite tone.

Coe tried moving away, hoping to mesh with the crowd, but the other hoodlums grabbed his arms, pinning him in place between them. The clutch of their hands around his limbs felt like tourniquets, stopping his blood flow. Twice, he started to talk, and they squeezed harder.

One of the airport security guys spoke into a walkie-talkie, then asked, "Where is this woman you speak of? Is she a U.S. citizen?"

"Yes, she is," Coe said, despite the ruffians' grip on him. He didn't want to say where Skye was, so he yanked against their hold. If they let go for a second, he'd dash outside and find his ride.

"Take your hands off this man," one of the airport security guards commanded.

Liam's henchmen glared defiantly at him, then, after a final squeeze, released Coe with a shove. He rubbed his wrists and stepped back, putting some distance between himself and the men who seemed intent on doing him harm.

"Where is she now?" the third officer demanded.

"That's what we're trying to find out," the biggest guy said. "If this moron would answer our question, none of this would be happening."

Two more airport security guys joined the group. Five against three? The odds of Coe emerging from the airport alive were improving. *Thank You, Lord. Please, help me get to Skye.*

"Gentlemen, show me your passports or identification," Bruce said firmly, holding his hands out toward Liam's men.

Grumbling and badmouthing the officers, the three reluctantly pulled out their wallets. While they were preoccupied with showing the officers their IDs, Coe inched backward, melding into the crowd like he'd imagined doing, and prayed he wouldn't attract any attention. He ducked behind a group of men hauling oversized suitcases toward the exit and moved alongside them. He'd almost made it outside, when he heard, "Where is he? Find him now, you fool!"

Coe dodged through the double doors and out onto the sidewalk, racing around travelers to reach the ride-hailing cars. He searched for a navy blue Prius. He was late. Hopefully, the driver Paulo was waiting. Was that his navy car? Wrong license number. He read the first two letters of another navy vehicle's license plate as it pulled into traffic. *That's it!* He ran after it. "Stop! Stop!" Paulo pulled over. "I'm Coe. Sorry, I'm late," he said as he leapt into the back seat.

"No problem." Paulo glanced at him in the rearview mirror. "You in trouble?"

"Just go," he shouted as Tip ran up to the vehicle, yelling about retribution. "Keep going. Don't stop, no matter what."

"You've got it." Paulo gunned the car into a slim opening of traffic.

"You won't get away with this!" Tip waved his fist. "Rhett is already following Skye."

"Please, go faster," Coe urged the driver. *Lord, be with Skye. Protect her.*

"Look at this congestion. How do you expect me to go faster?"

"Sorry. Just try."

Paulo finally merged into a faster flow of traffic, and Coe exhaled a sigh of relief. He was safe, for now. But what about Skye? Was she still safe?

Chapter Six

Skye had been waiting half an hour in a coffee shop across from the motel where she and Coe were supposed to meet. But since Rhett's driver had been hot on their tail and Clancy screeched to a halt in front of the motel and ordered her to get out, she ditched their plan and darted into this coffee shop.

Had Coe managed to get out of JFK? It took every ounce of determination she possessed not to check her cell. They had agreed to maintain silence, fearing that someone like Nimrod, one of Father's more sinister employees, might have hacked their phones. She had to either keep her phone turned off or risk checking it, turning it off quickly, and then making a mad dash for safety.

What would it take for Father to tell his men to stand down? Her promise to marry Edmund? Would a quick marriage to Coe even stop Father's attempts to control her? Rhett implied there would be a forced annulment. Would her dad go that far?

She peered around the edge of the window. A black car pulled in front of the motel across the street. It was Rhett's driver again. Nimrod must have hacked their phones as they feared. How else would Rhett know where Coe had made their reservations?

Rhett jumped out of the vehicle and ran into the motel. Moments later, he was back on the sidewalk, peering intensely down the row of businesses. His gaze swung in her direction. She jerked away from the window, heart pounding.

What if he came in here? The restroom didn't have a window—she'd already checked—so there would be no escape from there. According to the signage, an emergency exit would set off an alarm. Did she dare go through that door?

She peeked around the window frame again. Another black car pulled behind the first one. Tip got out, and Rhett pointed in her direction. Adrenaline shot through her like waves of ice. If she ran out the front door, they'd see her. Tip peered down the street intensely, but Rhett continued staring beady-eyed at the coffee shop. Skye pulled back, weighing her options. Should she make a run for their next checkpoint or stay and possibly get caught? Either was risky.

When she checked again and saw Rhett and Tip talking and gesturing vehemently like they were arguing, she figured this was her chance. She dashed out the door, ducked down, and walked stealthily alongside another woman, trying to stay invisible to the two men if they happened to glance her way. The woman eyed her strangely but didn't comment.

The next motel on Coe's list was a few blocks south. She could reach it on foot, but what if she couldn't find a haven from her pursuers? She needed to contact Coe but didn't dare use her cell. What if she borrowed someone else's phone?

"Sir, do you have a phone I could use?" she asked an elderly man. He shook his head, barely glancing at her. She asked a middle-aged woman and received a similar response. A third person glared harshly at her without answering. She probably looked disheveled and close to hysteria. Was it any wonder they didn't want to offer help?

Just ahead, she spotted a public telephone sign but didn't have any coins, and thanks to Father's meddling and manipulation, she couldn't use a credit card. She dashed into a jewelry store. "Do you have a phone I could use?"

"Sorry. Customers only."

"Can you make change for a twenty?"

"I'm not allowed to open the register without a purchase."

"Thanks anyway." She ran back onto the street, staying close to the compact storefronts, and the scent of hotdogs cooking on a grill made her stomach growl. Head down, staring at the sidewalk, she accidentally bumped into someone. "Sorry."

A woman who appeared to be in her seventies offered her a small smile. "That's all right. The entire world is in a hurry these days."

Skye glanced over her shoulder and saw Rhett sprint into the jewelry store where she'd just been. "Do you have a phone I could borrow? I need to make one call."

"Sorry. It's on the blink."

"That's okay." Skye looked furtively behind her. How much longer until Rhett caught up with her?

"Are you all right? Is someone following you?"

"Yes. And I don't want to get caught."

"Come with me, then." The woman waved her wrinkled hand toward an alcove in front of a store. "Over here."

Could she trust the grandmotherly-looking woman? What if she was conspiring with Rhett and Tip? *Ugh.* Now, she was acting paranoid.

"Come quickly. Hurry."

"Okay." Skye followed her. "You seem kind, but I don't want to get you involved in anything dangerous." And she had to keep moving, staying ahead of Rhett.

"I've been in danger before. What do you need?"

"Some change to make a call would be helpful." Although, she hated asking her for anything.

"That's easy enough." The woman withdrew coins from her pocket and held them out, her hand shaking. "Here."

Skye clasped the change to her chest as if it were a hundred dollars. "I can't thank you enough."

"Sure, you can. Offer a kindness to someone else."

"I will. Thank you. God bless you."

The older woman shuffled into the shop, and Skye thanked the Lord for sending a kindhearted person right when she needed help. She tried to meld with the crowd, searching for another public phone sign, but couldn't help peering over her shoulder to see if Rhett was following her.

After several blocks, she spotted a public phone. Fortunately, Coe had insisted she memorize his number. When his voicemail picked up, she said, "Plan A failed," and hung up.

If anyone other than Coe were listening, they wouldn't know what the message meant. But according to their Plan B, they would meet in Washington D.C., a three-hour train ride away.

Would Coe be there when she arrived?

Chapter Seven

Coe spotted trouble when Paulo turned onto the block where he was supposed to rendezvous with Skye, and Tip stood like a sentinel in front of the motel entrance. At least, that must mean he hadn't found Skye. But how did Tip know to look for them here? Was this the work of Liam's hacking whiz?

"Keep going." Coe ducked so Tip wouldn't see him.

"Where to this time?" Paulo asked with trepidation in his tone.

Coe gave him the address for the next motel. Would Skye be there? He was tempted to check his phone but wouldn't risk putting her in danger. When he came up with the idea of leaving the airport separately, he thought it was the best way to sneak past Liam's men, but his plan had a significant flaw. Severing all communications with Skye felt horrible. New York City was enormous, with people everywhere. He wouldn't be able to get to her swiftly if anything bad happened. And if either of them veered off-course, what then?

"This is it." The driver pulled up to the motel, which looked run-down compared to its online photograph. "Are you getting out here?"

"Yes." Coe grabbed the handle, but the muscular guy from the airport marched out of the motel's front door, his lips curled in a scowl. "Go. Go!"

"You don't want to—"

"No. Leave. Now!"

Paulo gunned the engine, his tires squealing as he pulled out. The muscular guy ran after the car, shaking his fist. "Stop! This is it for you."

No, it isn't. With God's help, Skye and I will be together soon.

"Where to now?" Paulo asked.

Coe was about to give him the address of the third motel on the list when another idea came to mind. "Pull over at the first parking lot you come to, will you?"

"What about the guy following us?"

"What?" Coe swiveled around. A black vehicle was following closely. "Try to lose them."

"I'm a good driver, but I don't do evasive driving."

"Do your best." That's all anyone could do.

"*Aye, yi yi.* He's right on my bumper."

"Can you dodge into traffic like you did last time?"

"No openings. But I'll—" Paulo turned sharply onto a side street, drove around several apartment buildings, and cut through an alley, proving he was more proficient at tactical driving than he realized. "Didn't help. You should hop out."

"What?"

"If you get out and I zip in and out of traffic for a few blocks, they'll assume you are still in the car, right?"

"That might work. But it could be dangerous for you."

"Either way, I am ready for you to leave my vehicle." Paulo gave him a sharp look in the rearview mirror. "No offense."

"None taken. Sorry for dragging you into this. Can you find a mall or somewhere crowded to drop me off?"

"Will do." Paulo veered into a narrow space between two moving cars. Another slot opened, and he swerved into the next lane, then made a fast right. Moments later, he stopped abruptly in front of a convenience store. "Goodbye. Farewell." He didn't add "good riddance," but by his tone, he could have.

"Thank you." Coe jumped out and ran into the store. He'd leave a positive review for Paulo on the company's app later.

He rushed up and down the short aisles, searching for anything to use as a disguise. He grabbed a knit hat, scarf, sunglasses, and an extra-large NYC T-shirt and paid with cash. "Mind if I put these on here?"

"No problem," the clerk said, looking him over suspiciously.

Coe pulled the tags off, threw the T-shirt over his sweatshirt, and donned the other items. "Thanks." He ran out of the store and dodged around the corner of the building, planning to do one more thing before he sprinted away. He pulled out his phone and waited while it powered up. If someone were following his phone signal, they'd know he was here. As soon as he checked for texts or messages, he'd put a dozen blocks between him and this place.

"Come on," he coaxed the phone. The screen came to life, and he found a voicemail message from Skye confirming she was safe and moving on to their next location. *Hallelujah.* He quickly tapped in, "*Remember our kiss,*" which was code for "I'll see you soon," shut off his phone, and raced toward the train station.

Chapter Eight

Skye's first stop in Washington, D.C. was a secondhand store, its sign barely noticeable among the bustling shops on a busy thoroughfare of nonstop traffic. She was pleased to have found this boutique with a wide range of clothes, shoes, and accessories in a compact space. She had to make her selections quickly, but hoped to be so creative that Coe wouldn't even recognize her. She kept glancing over her shoulder due to a creepy feeling that someone was watching her. But each time she looked, she didn't find anyone observing her.

She fingered a pile of wigs. Which color would work best as a disguise for her? Short and black? Long and red? Barbie blond? She chose a long, pale blond wig that differed the most from her chin-length dark hair. In women's apparel, she picked out a simple light blue dress, which was her favorite color, and grabbed a purple sweater and black leggings. She tried on several pairs of shoes before choosing some comfortable but dressy-looking slip-ons.

The store was well stocked with a variety of vintage makeup. Deep blue eye shadow would complement the dress, and cherry red lipstick would go well with her wig. In the jewelry section, she searched for the gaudiest necklace on display. A bronze owl with a winking green eye should work to draw attention away from her face.

Lastly, she hunted for wedding and engagement rings, then paid in cash. "May I change into these here?" she asked the cashier.

"Sorry. That's against store policy."

She suppressed a groan. Now what? She hurried outside, clutching her bag and perusing the street for any shady characters who might be looking for her. Where would she find a public bathroom in D.C. on this busy street? Following the crowd, she walked several blocks before spotting a public bathroom sign. *Thank goodness.* The three stalls weren't too shabby for a free facility. There was a line, but she didn't mind waiting, since it gave her time to consider whether to check her phone. She decided it was too risky.

Ten minutes later, she trashed her other clothes and exited the bathroom, all dolled up. With long blond hair, a bright purple sweater, bangle bracelets, an owl necklace, Marilyn Monroe red lips, deeply shadowed eyes, and a fake diamond engagement ring and wedding band, she barely recognized herself. Tip and Rhett wouldn't know her even if they were staring right at her. *Perfect.*

Determined to play the part, she swayed her hips and tried to act casual as she strolled toward the National Mall, attempting to get lost in the crowd of tourists. Glancing over her shoulder, she couldn't stop checking for Rhett and Tip. A lot of people milled about, taking photos of monuments and buildings, but none of Father's men were following her, much to her relief and worry. If they weren't pursuing her, were they currently going after Coe?

She watched a little boy running circles around an older man, who appeared to be his exasperated grandfather, and grinned at his antics. What would raising a kid with Coe be like if they were married and managed to figure out a real relationship? On the flight, he shared more stories about his childhood and being raised with eight brothers, including how his mom, dad, and grandmother worked together to raise them. The idea of a supportive, close-knit family was far from her isolated, international upbringing. Nevertheless, a simple family life sounded appealing.

Inside the National Air and Space Museum, Skye tried staying in character as she went through security, smiling and walking confidently. She paused by a display of the original 1903 Wright Flyer, according to the placard, and admired the ingenuity of its creators. She skimmed the information about the exhibit's popularity, the brothers Wilbur and Orville, and their determination to succeed at air travel. She tried to act extremely interested in the display and photographs in case someone was watching her. She also kept a discreet lookout for Coe.

"Nice model," a male voice that wasn't his said.

She turned and found a younger man grinning at her. She said the first thing that came to mind. "Are you a fan of this historical aircraft?"

"Definitely." He looked her over like he wasn't discussing the plane at all.

"Excuse me." She strode toward the other side of the room, not swaying her hips or trying to bring any attention to herself. The click of the guy's shoes falling in step with her caused tension to race up her spine.

Suddenly, a warm hand on her waist brought her close to a man sporting a dapper hat, a beefy mustache, and a wide grin, his eyes twinkling with mischief. *Coe?* She could have hugged and kissed him. "I thought you'd never get here."

"I'd cross the widest sea and slay dragons to get to you, my love." He was playing a role, but his words and how he caressed her with his gaze were convincing enough to make her heart palpitate. He lifted her left hand and pressed his lips to her rings. She felt giddy and almost forgot the other guy until she heard him groan. Coe kissed her cheek, and his slight touch set her heart racing even more. "Shall we go?"

"Definitely. Can we find some food?" Her stomach had been growling. "I'm starving."

"Anything you want, darling." Coe's stony stare at the other man sent a clear message of protection, and Skye couldn't help but smile. He kept his arm around her waist as they left the museum and walked down the street a block.

"How did your escape go?" she asked.

"We'll talk when it's safe."

"Are we being followed?" She glanced at the people behind them.

"Maybe." He held her hand, and they strode faster along the busy sidewalk.

"Should we hail a cab?"

"Let's keep walking." His gaze skimmed her outfit. "I like your getup. It's classy. Except for that owl necklace. I can't tell if it's winking or laughing at me."

"Good. It's part of my disguise. How did you recognize me so easily?"

"Who said it was easy?" He chuckled, and she appreciated the lighter mood between them. "I made three passes through the exhibit before realizing it was you."

"I'm glad to hear it." She smiled, pleased with her efforts. "If Rhett and Tip are as easily fooled, we're in the clear."

"Here's hoping." He led her across the street, using the crosswalk but sticking close to others moving in the same direction.

A little while later, they sat across from each other at a small table in a dimly lit, crowded café. "How did you get away from the airport?" she asked.

"With some difficulty." He stared intently toward the front of the restaurant.

"You keep watching the entrance. Are you expecting company?"

"Possibly. There's a back exit if we must leave in a hurry." He'd obviously paid more attention to their surroundings than she had.

Their server arrived with water glasses and took their orders. After he left, Coe stroked his fake mustache. "This thing is barely staying on. I'm tempted to rip it off."

"Do you need some help?" She reached out to assist him, thinking how nice it would be to touch his face and initiate a soft kiss, but he shook his head somberly, and she pulled her hand back.

"I saw Rhett at the train station."

"You did?"

"He scanned the platform without looking directly at me, so I assume he didn't notice me. But he's in D.C., lurking somewhere."

"And where Rhett is, Tip isn't far behind."

"My thoughts exactly." Coe squinted around the room, as if expecting to see her father's bodyguards here. "We'll eat, head to our hotel room, and make more plans. And we should get rid of our phones in separate locations." He was making all the decisions without asking her opinion, but considering the circumstances and the risks he was taking for her, she tried not to let it bother her.

"Is that how Nimrod knows where we are?"

"How else would Rhett and Tip keep following us?"

"I wondered about that, too." She patted her phone in her pocket, already feeling the loss. "I hate the thought of losing my contacts and the ability to text you. How soon can we—"

"Let's not discuss anything pertinent in case the phones are bugged audibly."

"Do you think that's what is happening?"

"Maybe." He glanced tensely around the restaurant, and she didn't ask any more questions.

Chapter Nine

After they had deleted all contacts, messages, and photos from their cell phones, Coe dropped his into a trash receptacle a few blocks from the café. Skye disposed of hers in a garbage can at an art gallery farther down the street. They'd uploaded their photos from India to their cloud storage so they wouldn't lose those. Still, he felt bad tossing out such expensive items and was frustrated with his need to do so in the first place. But they were just things, nonessentials. Skye's safety was what was important, and they had to focus on that.

He clasped Skye's hand and drew her close as they walked, playing the part of a doting husband, but also enjoying being near her. "Too bad you didn't buy me a ring."

"Who says I didn't?" She smiled coyly. He wasn't used to her flirty blond routine but liked it.

"Did you now?" He pulled her to the sidewalk's edge, letting others pass, and smoothed his fingers down her soft cheek, circling her dimple. His heart pounded rapidly, and his thoughts replayed their previous kisses. Skye smiled and set a simple band on his palm. It was part of his disguise, but since they'd been discussing marriage and his thoughts were taking a personal direction, the gesture also felt like it meant something significant. "Thanks, darling." He pushed the silver ring onto his left finger. "We should do something to commemorate this."

"Such as?"

"A kiss?" He grinned, feeling his fake mustache tug against his upper lip.

"I don't know," she said with a lilting voice. "Someone might see us."

"I'll take the chance if you will."

She smiled softly. "I will."

Even though they were on a busy sidewalk in D.C., he drew her to him and kissed her gently. She responded affectionately, kissing him back and running her fingers through his hair. He loved Skye being in his arms, and he deepened the kiss with all the emotional intensity he felt after their race for safety, the fear of being apart, and the overwhelming joy of reuniting, until someone's clapping rudely intruded, shattering the tender bubble they'd created.

"What a cute couple," a woman said.

"Get a room," a guy grumbled.

Coe leaned back, and Skye wiped her thumb gently around his mouth, which felt like a fire against his skin, making him yearn to kiss her again. He barely breathed because of the sensations rushing through him. He attempted to wipe some red smudges from around her mouth, but his fingers fumbled with the task.

"Our kissing helps us play the part of being a loving couple, right?" She gazed at him adoringly and with some vulnerability.

"I wasn't playing a part just then, Skye."

"Good. I got caught up, too."

"Glad to hear it." He held out his hand to her. "Shall we?"

"We shall," she replied, taking his hand with a smile.

He loved the feel of their hands touching and with the memory of their recent kisses strumming through his brain, he walked beside

Skye toward their hotel, feeling almost like a regular couple. Unfortunately, his thoughts were also racing with the possibility of Rhett and Tip following them. He glanced back a couple of times, unable to shake off the worry.

Their room was on the sixth floor of a nice motel. It had taken a chunk of the money he had left from what he borrowed from Lake, but it would give them a safe place to rest for the night. As soon as they entered the room decorated in blues and greens, he inspected every possible hiding space, then peered out the window through the slit between the curtains. He didn't spot Rhett or Tip outside, which made him breathe easier.

"What now?"

Coe jerked at Skye's nearness. She stood beside him, peering out the window, too. Her arm brushing his sent him reeling with thoughts of their recent kiss and his longing to kiss her again. Needing space and a measure of self-control, he took off his hat and coat and hung them over the back of a chair. Then he ripped off his fake mustache that was barely fastened, the slight pain bringing his senses back to reality. "We'll order room service and get some sleep."

"And that's all?" Her dark, expressive eyes gazed at him so intently, he had difficulty pulling his attention away.

He tugged off the necktie. "We aren't married. So, yes, that's all." He raked his fingers through his damp hair, pressed down by the derby hat. "After the way we've kissed, it's tempting to want to take things further. But you don't have to worry. I'm an honorable man, or trying to be."

"I appreciate that. It's good there are two beds." She nodded toward the queen-sized beds.

"Yep. Otherwise, I'd be sleeping on the floor."

"No need. I trust you, Coe."

He swallowed hard. Had his promise to help her escape her father and marry her helped her put her confidence in him? He wanted to be worthy of her trust. But there were times—

Skye pulled off her wig and tossed it on the nightstand. She thrust her fingers through her hair and moaned, making him wish he was the one running his fingers through her hair. *Get a grip, North.* "I'm going to shower and wash my face," she said. "I wish I'd bought more comfortable clothes to change into."

He tried clearing the cotton ball from his throat. "We'll have to make do for now."

"That's okay." She went into the bathroom and shut the door.

He exhaled a long sigh and tried to focus on what he needed to do next, which was to contact Lake. He'd purchased two cheap, disposable phones at a convenience store before they arrived at the hotel, yet hated operating his, even to contact his brother. Was there any chance Nimrod would find a way to track these phones? Still, he'd have to take the chance.

Hopefully, Rhett and Tip hadn't followed them here. He'd registered the room under Mr. and Mrs. Coe Dupont, his mother's family name, in case Liam's hacker tapped into the hotel database. But considering the uniqueness of his given name, would Nimrod spot it, anyway?

He slipped from his shoes, sat on the bed, phone in hand, and texted Lake. *This is Coe. We made it to the U.S. Will keep you posted.*

Where are you, man? Lake's text came back swiftly.

Can't say.

Are you in trouble?

How should he answer? Telling his family what he'd been through would only cause them more alarm. *Trusting God to get us home safely.*

If you need more money, say the word. Stay in contact. Love you, bro.

Ditto.

Remembering one other thing, he tapped in a quick review on the app for Paulo's excellent driving and customer service. Then he shut off the phone and prayed for God's wisdom and protection.

Chapter Ten

Skye cleaned the gunk off her face and showered under the hot stream for a while, grateful for soap, shampoo, and conditioner amenities. "Are you ready to order some food?" she called as she entered the bedroom area wearing her blue dress and leggings and found Coe asleep on top of the bedding. Poor guy. He was exhausted, and she'd taken a long time in the bathroom.

"Coe?" She leaned over him and nudged his arm. "Do you want to order—" His eyes shot open, and he gazed at her with a glassy look. "Coe?"

He stared at her for several long seconds, his gaze searching her face and lips as if he was thinking about kissing her. Suddenly, he pulled her into his arms. "Oh, Skye," he whispered huskily. Her heart pounded chaotically. Was kissing like this a good idea? Then, just as abruptly as he held her, he turned her on her side, tucked her head against his shoulder, smoothed his hand over her damp hair, and sighed like he was already asleep. *What in the world?* She didn't know whether to be outraged by his tender behavior or forget about it and fall asleep beside him. She was exhausted. Sighing, she closed her eyes.

At two a.m., she awoke alone on the bed. The room was dark, other than one dim light shining from the bathroom. "Coe?" She spotted him near the door.

"Shhhh," he whispered.

"What are you doing?" When he didn't answer, she crawled to the end of the bed, watching him peer out the peephole, his body tense. "Is someone out there?"

He waved his hand in a shushing gesture. Undeterred, she crept over to him. He jerked like she burned him when she touched his arm.

"Hey," he barked. "What are you doing?"

"What are you doing? Who's out there?"

"Someone tried to get in."

Fear slammed through her. "Are you sure? Did you see who it was?"

"No. Someone messed with the door handle and woke me." Coe strode back to the other side of the bed, his gaze wary and intense. "They're gone now."

"Good. Maybe they had the wrong room."

"Possibly." He squinted at her. "Mind telling me why you were curled up beside me?"

"Why I—"

"Kissing is one thing. Sharing a bed is out of—"

"Coe North, I ought to belt you!" She clenched her fist. How dare he assume their cozy position was her fault?

"Sharing a bed with a woman is something I'm saving for marriage."

"Likewise. You're the one who—"

A forceful pounding at the door interrupted her.

"Get in the bathroom and put your wig on."

"Don't tell me what to do." She glared at him.

Three strong raps sounded again. "Mr. Dupont! I must speak with you."

"It's the clerk." Coe lifted his chin toward the bathroom. "Go."

Skye scowled at him. "Don't we have to keep up the pretense of being married?"

"Not if it means sharing a bed," he growled.

"Then keep your hands off me until we're married."

His jaw dropped two inches. "I didn't—"

"Are you awake, Mr. Dupont?"

"Just a moment!" Coe turned to Skye. "Hurry up, will you?"

"I said—" *Oh, forget it.* "Put your mustache back on." In jerky movements, she dashed into the bathroom and stuffed her hair into the wig, grumbling about Coe's bossy attitude. She returned to stand tensely by him and noticed his slightly askew mustache. "Wait." She tried to adjust it over his shadowy facial stubble, then ran her fingers through his hair, messing it up. "There." The touch of her fingers gliding through his silky strands was unnerving. Coe's expression softened toward her as he opened the door, making her think he was more affected by her touch than his gruff demeanor implied.

"I apologize for the intrusion." The clerk looked them over, eyebrows raised. Did he notice their apparel and wonder why they were fully dressed at two a.m.?

"What's this about?" Coe asked.

"There's been a security breach."

"You're kidding." Coe's muscles tightened where his arm touched hers. "What kind of breach?"

"Someone accessed your room details. I apologize for the inconvenience, Mr. and Mrs. Dupont. Our entire system is locked down."

Nimrod. Skye groaned.

"Thank you for letting us know." Coe shut the door. "Grab your stuff. We'll exit out the hotel's rear door."

This time, she didn't grumble about him telling her what to do.

Chapter Eleven

Coe chose the back seat of the bus for their ride to the Baltimore airport so he could have a discreet view of the boarding passengers. So far, no one resembling Rhett, Tip, or Liam's other ruffians had entered. He and Skye had left the hotel in the dead of night, hailed a cab, and waited in the bus station for the next bus to Baltimore without being followed, as far as he could tell.

He was hoping for a direct flight to Spokane or Seattle from Baltimore, preferably Spokane, since that would get them closer to his hometown of Thunder Ridge. But the continental distance from Baltimore to Seattle was about as far as a traveler could cross in the U.S., making it easier for Skye and him to disappear from Rhett and Tip's radar. At least, that's what he prayed would happen.

"Where to next?" Skye asked as she settled into her seat.

"Washington State. Then Idaho."

She gave him a probing look, and he wondered why. He still felt awkward about what he awoke to back at the motel. Why had she been sleeping so close to him? How long was she burrowed against him like she already belonged there? He couldn't remember anything about it other than being extremely tired and closing his eyes. After the bus had been moving for a few minutes, he figured he'd put off the topic long enough. "Did I do something last night?"

"Don't you remember?" She tipped her head, eyeing him.

"No. I don't. You acted weird when I asked why you were sleeping beside me."

"No kidding. You were being bossy and unreasonable."

He didn't pause to unpack her accusation. "I flipped out when I awoke and found you hugging me."

"Hugging you?" She pegged him with a lethal glare. "Were my arms wrapped around you?"

"Well." He scratched his forehead, trying to reflect on how they'd been resting together. "Uh. Maybe not. I was sort of—" He cringed as recollection hit. "If anyone was hugging anyone, it was probably me." He swallowed hard.

"Exactly."

Heat bled up his face. He'd been quick to blame her. Too quick. "What did I do?"

"You were sleeping and—" Her eyebrows lifted. "Do you do things in your sleep?" What was she implying?

"Such as?"

"You grabbed me and pulled me to you." She held her finger and thumb nearly together. "This close. I thought you were going to kiss me. Or more than kiss me," she added quietly.

"Skye, I—" The dryness in his throat nearly choked him. "I don't know what to say, other than I'm sorry. My brothers used to joke about me talking or walking around in my sleep. I thought I'd outgrown that." A flush crept across his face. "Did I do anything unwanted?"

"Not really. You stared at me intensely, then nestled me beside you and fell asleep. That's all."

"Okay. Good." He heaved a breath. "It must have been due to all the stress recently. Still. I'm sorry."

"It's okay. I felt safe beside you and fell asleep, too."

He sagged against the seat. It was hard to believe he pulled her onto the bed when he was shocked to find her beside him when he opened his eyes. He'd have to be more careful and not let that happen again. He thought of another subject he wanted to mention that might be touchy. "Can you call your dad and ask him to tell his men to back off? And remind him you are an adult who can make your own decisions?"

"I tried that before. Didn't work."

"Try again."

"Stop telling me what to do!"

"All right." A couple of travelers looked their way, and he lowered his voice. "I'm only expressing my concerns. What's the harm of having a conversation with Liam? He's tough, but he's got to see you're capable of making up your mind about important things."

"And if I marry you, will I get a say in the important things in our lives?"

"Of course."

"Don't say, 'of course,' like any idiot should know." She lifted her chin. "Where would we live if we were married?"

"In Thunder Ridge."

"See. You made the decision like that." She snapped her fingers. "How can you decide where we'll live as a married couple without including me in the decision?"

"As my wife, I'd want you to be where I am, and I'll be—"

"You can't decide for us. I want an equal partnership, or nothing."

"Okay. Sorry." He had been a bachelor for a long time and was used to deciding where he was going and what he would do next, sometimes on the spur of the moment. If they got married, including Skye in the decision-making would take some getting used to, but he was determined to try. "Do you have a hometown for us to go to?"

"No. But that isn't the point." She sighed and gazed out the window. "I've lived my entire life with someone else deciding everything and dictating how I'd live. I won't accept you or anyone else telling me what to do. I'm going to make my decisions or at least have an equal say about them."

"Okay." He exhaled a lengthy sigh that felt like it came from deep within. They barely knew each other. He needed to try to understand her better. Had he even paused to consider her likes and dislikes? Her wishes? "I've lived in Thunder Ridge most of my life, but that doesn't mean we have to live there." He shuffled in his seat, trying to get comfortable and formulating his next words. "Is it okay with you if we visit my family? I've been gone for two years, and I'd like to introduce you to them. Hopefully, we would be safe there." She didn't answer for so long, he wondered if she would. "Skye?"

"I guess," she finally said aloofly.

After a while of not talking and relaxing with the rhythm of the moving bus, he felt himself nodding off.

"Coe?" Skye touched his arm.

"Hmm?" He forced his eyes open and fought a yawn.

"I haven't made many decisions in my life," she spoke quietly, like she didn't want anyone else to hear. "Father was relentless about picking my husband, as if he were the only person capable of deciding who my spouse would be and how I would live my life." She took a stuttering breath. "His controlling nature is one of the reasons I don't want a husband."

Not even me? "Look. I'm sorry for not being more sensitive to your feelings. I've been a bachelor for a long time. But I'm sure I can figure out how to communicate better and include you." How difficult could it be to become a good husband? Dad made it look easy.

"It's nice of you to say that." Her dark eyes glistened at him. "I need to know the person I marry wants to hear my opinions and will let me be involved in making decisions. It's a deal breaker."

"I understand." Something else came to mind. "Is that why you're determined about not calling the police?"

"And about where we'll live *if* we get married."

He didn't comment on her use of "if." "What bothers you the most about going to Thunder Ridge? Other than me being bossy? Again, I'm sorry about that."

"Your family sounds overwhelming."

"They can be." There wasn't any getting around that. With nine boys in the family, there had always been something going on that turned out wrong or was loud and chaotic. He hoped his family wouldn't seem like too much for Skye to handle.

"And they'll find out we married for the wrong reasons and hate me."

"Not all wrong." He imagined their kisses and how it felt like she was the only woman in the world when she was in his arms. "And no one is going to hate you."

She leaned closer, gazing at him like she was investigating his face. "What are you thinking about? You have a funny look on your face."

"I was thinking about kissing you."

"Oh." She huffed. "What will your mother say?"

"That wanting to kiss you is normal and—"

"Not that, silly. What will she say about you marrying someone you don't love?"

"Maybe that isn't entirely the case."

She quirked an eyebrow. "Are you saying you love me like a man loves a woman he's going to marry?"

"No." He slipped his hand over hers, linking their fingers. "But I am saying I'm infatuated with you, Skye. And when we kiss, I am in awe of you and the strong emotions I feel."

"So, maybe there's hope for us, after all?" Her smile was adorable.

"Maybe there is."

Chapter Twelve

After eight hours of being stuck in the corner of the Baltimore Airport, Skye was going stir-crazy. They passed on the first two standby flights because there weren't two seats available together. But the more hours she and Coe spent waiting here, the more probable it seemed that Rhett and Tip would find them, which caused her more stress and worry. Maybe they should have gone on one of the other flights and sat apart. Would that have been so bad?

She wanted to take another walk to the coffee shop, the restroom, or anywhere away from the stiff chairs facing a sea of travelers moving both ways in the corridor. Coe had chosen this location so he could keep watch. But Skye ached from sitting around and doing nothing all day, other than contemplating her adversaries finding her and dragging her back to Father. She needed to get up and move, especially considering they still had a cross-country flight with many more hours of sitting and contemplating. She groaned.

"What's wrong?" Coe asked.

"I need to stretch. Maybe get some coffee? Or a pastry?"

"We have to be careful and keep an eye out."

"I know." Hadn't they been doing that for eight hours? "Do you mind if I head to the restroom?" *Preferably by myself?*

"I'll walk with you." Coe stood, wincing like he was stiff from sitting, and Skye fought a groan.

"Why don't you keep resting? We haven't seen anyone suspicious since we got here. I'll be fine."

He gave her a serious look. "I'd prefer we stick together."

"Come on, Coe. You don't have to escort me to the ladies' room. It's not that far." She was protesting too much, but she itched for some independence. "I am a grown woman."

"I am aware." His smile bordered on flirtatious. "I'll feel better staying near you. Okay?"

"Fine," she grumbled. "Do you really expect Rhett or Tip to whisk me away from you in front of all these people?"

"It's possible they are waiting for you in the bathroom."

"Seriously?" His pointed look stole her skepticism. "You're not kidding, are you?"

"I'm not. Let's take a stroll but stay together."

"Okay." She heaved a breath.

They walked silently, melding into the crowd. Coe's gaze roamed the corridor, while Skye focused on the delicious scents of coffee, cinnamon buns, and hamburgers cooking emanating from the small shops.

After they both used the facilities, Coe agreed to get more coffee but said they needed to return to their seats afterward. He was such a worrywart. He dropped into his seat and sipped his coffee, his features looking strained. "I saw Rhett in the men's bathroom."

"What?" She sat down abruptly. "Why didn't you say something sooner?"

"I don't think he saw me. But what you said about them grabbing you?" His forehead wrinkled with his frown. "If someone were to inject me with a sleeping drug or something, you'd be more vulnerable."

"That isn't going to happen." They were safe at this airport, right?

"I'm not saying you couldn't fight them off, but—"

"I get it." She took a drink of coffee, and the flavor of her vanilla creamer didn't taste as satisfying. "I didn't mean to make light of our situation." *Or label you a worrywart.*

"I know." The shadows around Coe's eyes and the tension on his features screamed of exhaustion and anxiety. He was doing all of this for her, which made her feel deeply indebted to him and sorry for the trouble she'd caused. After that first time they kissed and Father's men roughly threw him off the property, she'd gone to check on Coe. They'd talked, and that's when she mentioned the idea of them fleeing together. He said he needed to think about it and pray about it. Was he regretting his decision to get involved with her now?

She glanced over her shoulder and saw a man dressed in black walking by, his face averted. Was that Rhett? Suddenly, Coe pulled her close, wrapping his arms around her protectively. "Did you see who it was?" she whispered.

"Sorry. False alarm." He expelled a breath and released her. "I thought I saw Rhett. When I realized my mistake, I was enjoying having you in my arms and didn't want to stop."

"Coe—"

"Sorry." He stroked a finger down her cheek, making her skin tingle. "How do you feel about marrying me, Skye?"

"Do we have to talk about that now?" Even though she had a crush on him, whenever the topic of marriage came up, she thought of Father's plans for an arranged marriage and didn't want to discuss it. If they married right away, would that push Father into making more rash decisions about Rhett and Tip chasing them?

"Liam's men might back off if they knew we were sincere about getting married." Coe fidgeted with his ring. "I wonder about getting married on the plane."

"Be serious."

"I am being serious. It's possible in special situations. But we couldn't pull it off without getting preapproval and such."

"It's just as well." She held up her hand with the thrift-store rings. "These haven't kept them from stalking us."

"True. Once we reach Seattle, we'll rent a car and head for Idaho. We could be married the same day."

"There you go, making the decisions again."

"Just suggestions. Too bad we didn't get married in D.C. since there's no waiting period. It's a three-day wait in Washington State."

"Where is all this wedding talk coming from?"

"I want you to stay safe, and I can think of only one way to make that happen."

"And?" She pushed for whatever he wasn't saying.

"And I don't like bringing trouble to my family's doorstep."

"Then leave me in Seattle and visit your family by yourself." She heard the defensive tone in her voice but didn't try to calm it.

"That's not what I meant." He set their drinks on a short table beside him, then clasped her hands, smoothing his thumbs over her palms. "Skye, why don't we get married tomorrow?"

"I don't want you to feel forced into marrying me."

"I don't."

"I'd feel terrible if anything bad happened to your family because of me." She drew her shoulders up, tucking her elbows into her sides, and took a deep breath. "I'm responsible for getting you into this mess. So let me release you from any feelings of obligation."

"I don't feel obligated. Now, can we discuss our marriage?"

"This isn't the time or place."

"I think it is since we have a few hours to kill." He gazed into her eyes with a sweetly charming expression and adjusted her hands between his. "Skye." *I love it when he says my name softly.* "I've been attracted to you for a while. I want to be with you as your husband."

Heat rose in her veins. Would he be a kind husband? Would he grow to love her? Would she love him like she longed to love the man she chose to marry?

"If Rhett or Tip approach us, let's show them our rings and profess our commitment to getting married and loving each other. That will send a clear message they can share with your father."

"What message? That we are in a fake relationship?"

"Not fake." He gave her a wounded look, and for a moment, she wanted to take back the words.

"They'll see through our charade, Coe." She pulled her hands away and clutched them in her lap.

"All the more reason for us to get married as soon as we enter Idaho."

"Why are you taking these risks for me?"

"You came to me for help. I kissed you and—"

"I may have kissed you first." Thoughts of how and why they kissed swirled in her brain, creating a mix of tantalizing and worrisome imaginings.

"Regardless, I promised to help you escape your situation, and that's what I'm doing."

He was such a good guy, trying to keep his word to her. Had she met a more thoughtful, authentic man than Coe? She'd never met anyone willing to stick his neck out for her or stand up to Father. Or anyone that she thought she could love like a wife loves a husband, someday, anyway. She felt her heart warming to him and was almost convinced of their future happiness until she recalled why they were running from Rhett and Tip and how badly this trip across the country could still go.

"Father won't accept anything but a real marriage with all the bells and whistles." Her face heated up, but it needed to be said. "You heard what Rhett declared about an annulment."

"That's not happening. But I like the sound of the bells and whistles." He brushed his mouth softly against hers, his breath tasting of vanilla and coffee. "Can you picture yourself falling in love with me, Skye?" The sweetness of his words and kisses momentarily stole away her worry about Father's plans and Rhett and Tip being nearby.

"There is a slight possibility I could fall deeply in love with you," she whispered.

"Only slight?" He dipped his chin, eyeing her.

"I might need more convincing."

"How's this?" He kissed her longer and more tenderly, and despite the noisy setting, she kissed him back, relishing the shared moment of closeness and warmth.

After their romantic interlude ended, he handed back her latte, and she took a sip. "We don't want these to go to waste." He drank from his cup, his gaze lingering on her with admiration or longing, and she couldn't help but wonder if he was as attracted to her as she was to him.

Suddenly, he slouched over, his chin slumping against his chest.

"Coe? What's wrong?" She shook him. "Coe!"

"So you thought you could get away from us?" *Rhett!*

Icy shivers raced up her spine. "What have you done to him?"

Chapter Thirteen

Coe awoke with a painful kink in his neck and his head throbbing. Why was he sagging in his chair? He peeled his eyelids apart. The room blurred, focused, blurred. *Skye?* She wasn't in her chair. "Skye?" he called, but his voice came out garbled. He remembered them kissing. What happened after that? Stumbling to his feet, he nearly toppled over. The room swayed, then righted itself. Did Rhett drug him and take Skye? Coe staggered forward. He had to find her.

"Did you see the woman I was with?" he asked a mid-twenties woman in the next row, hoping his words came out clearly enough for her to understand.

"You mean the other guy's wife you were making out with?"

"She's not anyone else's wife." What was she talking about?

"The guy said you stole his wife, and he was taking her back." She glared at him like he was the criminal. "Seemed fair to me."

"She's not his wife!" Coe raked his fingers through his hair, searching the corridor, and trying to make sense of all this. Where had Rhett taken Skye? "How long ago did this happen?" When was the next flight to Dubai? He'd have to find a flight board, if he could even read it in his stupor.

"Five or ten minutes."

Five or ten minutes? He must not have had much of the drug in his system to be out only that long. Still, that was too long for him to be away from Skye. "Which way did they go?"

The woman bunched her lips together like she refused to answer, but then she gave a brief nod toward the left corridor.

"Thanks." Coe stumbled in that direction, praying the fuzzy sensation and the pounding in his head would stop. Why would Skye go anywhere with Liam's men without making a horrible racket he would have heard? Had Rhett given her a sedative or whatever, too? Coe remembered setting their coffee cups on the table and kissing Skye. Was that when Rhett spiked their drinks?

I'm sorry, Skye. I promised to keep you safe. Where are you?

He searched for any nooks and crannies where Rhett might be holed up with her. If she was unconscious, Rhett couldn't risk roaming through the airport with her slung over his shoulder.

A woman screamed. *Skye?* Coe forced himself to move faster toward the sound.

"Let me go!" *It was her.*

"Put her down," an authoritative voice said.

"She isn't well," Rhett spoke persuasively. "She's my wife. I'm taking care of her. We're about to board our plane." *No, they aren't!*

"I'm not his wife," Skye spoke in a perturbed tone.

"Put her down!" Coe demanded as soon as he spotted Rhett carrying her in his arms like an invalid. He wanted to yank Skye from the brute, but the room swayed like he was on a boat in rough seas, and his legs weren't fully cooperating.

"Coe?" she called weakly. "Coe!"

"Let. Her. Go." He panted between words.

An older, stern-looking airport security guard held out his hands toward Rhett. His nametag started with a B, but Coe couldn't focus on deciphering it. "Sir, put the woman down."

"I'm marrying that man." Skye pointed at Coe, but her finger bobbled between him and Rhett like she wasn't seeing normally, either. "I choose him."

"That's right. We're getting married tomorrow."

"They are not getting married," Rhett said adamantly. "I am bringing her back to her father."

"No, you aren't," Coe shouted.

"No, he's not." Skye swung her foot and kicked Rhett, who groaned. "This man stole me and drugged me."

"No, I didn't!" Rhett cursed.

"I told him I don't want to return to India, but he wouldn't listen."

"Put her down!" Officer B demanded. "I am detaining you for questioning."

Teeth clenched and looking mad enough to put his fist through a wall, Rhett lowered Skye to the floor. "You're making a grave error. I have the authority to bring her back to her father."

Skye swayed, and Coe reached out and caught her before she fell.

"By whose authority?" the officer asked.

"She's Liam Tamarack's daughter," Rhett said as if announcing a king's daughter.

"Tamarack, you say?"

"That's right. He's the CEO of the Tamarack Foundation." Rhett nodded like he was silently communicating something. Was he implying that Liam would pay Officer B grandly if he went along with his abduction scheme? Why wasn't airport security hauling Rhett's lying, conniving backside to airport jail or wherever they took criminals?

The officer squinted at Skye, then talked rapidly into his walkie-talkie. Rhett grinned cockily, rocking on his feet as if he thought he'd get away with his rotten scheme.

"I think I'm going to puke." Skye bent over and retched on Rhett's shoes.

"Stop that!" He stomped and cursed. "Why, you little imp!"

With Rhett and Officer B distracted, Coe made sure Skye could walk without assistance, whispered, "Run," and nudged her toward their boarding area. She glared back at him and opened her mouth like she was about to protest. "Go," he said. "Get on the plane. I'll meet you there or in Seattle." She gazed at him uncertainly. "Don't worry. I will find you. Wherever you are, I won't be far behind." Nodding, she disappeared into the crowd. *Attagirl.*

"Where'd she go?" Rhett demanded.

"Nowhere that concerns you." Coe grabbed him, locking him in a wrestling hold, just barely stopping him from following Skye. He was glad he had enough strength and inner fortitude to hold on.

"Let me go!" Rhett yanked against Coe's restraint. "She's going back to Liam."

"No, she isn't. She's marrying me."

"What's going on here?" Bill—Coe could read his nametag now—questioned after ending his call.

"This man has been stalking us," Coe said above Rhett's demands to be released. "Please detain him until my fiancée and I can board our plane."

"Show me your ID." Bill thrust out his hand, palm up. "And let him go."

"If I do, he'll run after her. He's dangerous and should be locked up. We haven't done anything wrong, yet he continues to pursue us."

"You call stealing Liam Tamarack's daughter nothing?" Rhett asked snidely.

"Is that right?" Bill stared at Coe. "Did you force that woman to come with you?"

"No, sir. Skye is thirty years old. She came to the U.S. of her own volition. We plan to be married tomorrow."

"As if Liam's daughter would marry someone like you." Rhett spewed a string of curse words.

"Enough!" the officer shouted. "IDs, now."

Coe almost lost his grip on Rhett while he withdrew his wallet. Still clinging to the lowdown snake's arm, he held out his Idaho license for Bill to see.

"You're heading to Idaho?"

"Yes, sir."

"Do you want to press charges?"

"Absolutely."

"You'll have to come to our office and complete the paperwork."

"I don't have time for that." Coe was determined to catch up with Skye. His promise to keep her safe was a commitment he would not break. He eyed the man, who, in his mind, deserved to rot in prison. There was no proof Rhett tampered with their drinks, a fact Coe found hard to accept, even if he believed he did. But all he wanted was to get on the plane with Skye. Had she made it on board? Where was Tip? His absence was highly suspicious. "Please hold this guy until our plane leaves. Better yet, put him on the first flight to India."

"Bill!" Another officer marched over, pointing at Rhett. "Let him go."

"What? Why?" Coe demanded.

The two officers conferred quietly, which frustrated him even more.

"See how it works when Mr. Tamarack is your employer?"

Coe ignored Rhett's snide remark and tried to get Bill's attention. "This man inflicted personal harm on my fiancée and me. He should be charged with criminal activity."

"We can't hold him," Bill said. "Rest assured, someone will investigate this matter."

"I told you." Rhett chortled. "Liam's influence is far-reaching."

"I beg you to do your job regardless of Liam Tamarack's status." Coe shoved Rhett toward the officer, then sprinted for the departure gate, praying he wouldn't follow him.

Please, God, let Skye be safely on the plane.

Despite his unkempt appearance, he made it through the checkpoint and onto the plane. When he found his seat, he fell into it next to Skye. She was already sleeping, probably due to the aftereffects of the sedative or some other unknown substance that caused their sudden sleepiness and lethargy.

Sighing, Coe closed his eyes. They were safe, but for how long?

Chapter Fourteen

Skye had never been to Idaho, where she and Coe were heading in a rental car that ran so smoothly it lulled her to sleep. She still wore her wrinkled blue dress and would need a long, hot shower to get rid of the grungy feeling of sleeping in her clothes for a couple of nights. Or some delicious coffee would make her feel better. "Can we stop somewhere for coffee?"

Coe navigated the car around a semi-truck on I-90. "We should put as many miles between us and the airport as possible before we stop."

"Do you think Tip is following us?"

"I think he was on the plane with us."

"Really? Why didn't you tell me before?"

He changed lanes again. "You were sleeping. I didn't want to worry you."

Their gazes met briefly. "Were you able to sleep also?"

"Some." Not much, by his tone.

"If you need a driving break, I can spell you."

"I'm awake and eager to cross the Idaho line, but thanks. How do you feel about getting married today?" His broad smile made his chin dimple widen, which made her itch to touch his whiskers, smooth her fingers over his face, and kiss him. But marrying him? She still had doubts.

"Why do you want to marry me? We barely know each other." He was too nice of a guy to tie himself down to a woman he didn't love. Granted, their chemistry was undeniable. But what if that lost its power and died a woeful death of lost hopes and dreams? What if they never fell in love? Wouldn't it be better never to marry than to marry and fail at love?

"Not true. We worked together on many humanitarian efforts, so I already know some things about you and your kind heart for helping others. My dad would say you have a servant's heart." What would his dad say about him marrying a woman he didn't love? Would Coe's mom and dad despise her like Father despised Coe?

"You weren't aware of my father's overbearing nature until we kissed."

"True."

"Are you sorry you kissed me?" She searched for doubts in his expression, wishing she could read his thoughts. "Or that it caused us to be on the run?"

"I'm not sorry about any of our kisses." Another generous smile crossed his mouth. "And being on the run with you has had some delightful parts."

Her heart melted a little. "Okay. So why do you want to marry me?"

Coe took his time answering, probably due to negotiating traffic, but she imagined him mulling over his thoughts. "I promised to keep you safe. If that includes marriage, I'm fine with it. I can't say I love you yet. But between our time together and our spectacular kisses, it's been a pleasant beginning with someone I admire and care about already."

"You are nicer than most men I've met." She noticed the deep green, lush evergreens they were passing on the hill, which reminded her of the efforts made in Dubai to increase the number of trees and provide more green spaces. With all the rain in the Pacific Northwest, the whole area appeared carpeted with green. As if on cue, Coe turned on the windshield wipers. "But marriage? Promising to stay together for our whole lives?"

"You don't think you'll fall in love with me?" He sounded like he was feeling vulnerable. "Even with my being 'nicer than most men' and having good kissing abilities?" He chuckled lightly.

"Your kisses have me almost wanting to run to the altar with you."

"See there. First stop, the courthouse."

"I said almost." She drew in a shaky breath. "I have to be certain of my decision about something as big as marriage."

"Both our decisions, right?"

"Sure. So why would you choose to marry me?" She was being repetitive, but she had to know if his request went beyond his feelings of duty to protect her.

"There's my attraction for you," he said, and her heart kicked up a beat. "And yours for me." He smiled in that teasing way that made her smile back. "How could we kiss like we have without feeling some fascination for one another?"

She was fascinated with Coe. But was that enough to tie her to him in a lifelong commitment? "Aside from our romantic feelings, do you picture us as a loving couple, growing old together and not hating each other because we jumped into marriage without being in love first?" She stared at him while he remained focused on the road.

"I told you about my parents having the kind of marriage I'm proposing. My mom was pregnant with my oldest brother, Lake, and my dad had reasons for getting married quickly. Along the way, they fell in love, had five more kids, adopted two of my cousins, and when I was twelve, they adopted a newborn. They've had a great life together." His chin dipped. "I kissed you in India because I was interested in you. I'd noticed your devotion to the Lord and your heart for helping others, so it wasn't like I was kissing a stranger."

"I adored our first kiss. But I still feel leery of dragging you into all the danger with my father's men." She rubbed the back of her neck. "Father creates trouble for anyone who crosses him. He is wealthy enough to be ruthless about manipulating what he thinks belongs to him."

"Including you?"

"Especially me." An emotional ache burned in her chest. "How can you want to be involved with someone like me?"

Without explanation, Coe turned on his blinker and veered toward a pullout alongside the freeway. He stopped the car and faced her, his expression warm. "Skye, this is how I feel about being involved with someone as incredible as you." He leaned over the console, gazing at her with a deep, heart-stirring look, and kissed her softly. His butterfly kisses sent her emotions soaring. Vehicles rumbled past, but it felt like they were in a safe, cozy cocoon.

He cupped her cheeks with his palms, his eyes locking with her gaze. "I want to get involved with you, marry you, and love you for the rest of my life." She could hardly believe he was this serious, but she wanted to believe his every word. "And it's not just because of the last days of being on the run and all the adrenaline spikes, but because I have feelings for you. And while it will take time, I expect us to fall deeply, crazily in love with each other."

Her heart pounded, and she felt a fluttering in her stomach. Would they fall madly in love? Would it last forever? "If we get married, I'd want you to treat me as an equal partner."

"Of course I will." He linked their fingers. "If you agree to marry me, I am in this relationship for the long haul. You can count on me and trust me."

"I wish we'd fallen in love the regular way."

"Me too." He kissed her again, their lips seeking each other's with warmth and desire. "Can you marry me despite the unique circumstances we've found ourselves in while vowing to be faithful and live together for the rest of our lives?"

Was she ready to promise him all that?

Chapter Fifteen

"Welcome to Idaho," Coe said to himself since Skye was asleep in the passenger seat. Finally, he was back in his home state and eager to see his family. Mom and Dad were on a Caribbean cruise that Lake and Irish had given them for their thirty-fifth anniversary, so they wouldn't be home. He'd heard Hud and Trista were going on a honeymoon in Montana. Maybe he'd catch up with them before they returned to Alaska. Spur and A.W. were in other parts of the country. But he was excited to introduce Skye to everyone else as his wife. *Wife!* How would his brothers take that news?

Thinking of their old defunct pact and how his two older brothers ignored it and got married to access a time-sensitive inheritance made him chuckle. Some of the younger brothers had been downright rude and indignant about it. Fortunately, according to their emails and texts, Lake and Hud had fallen in love with their wives, and their marriage arrangements, although uncommon in modern society, were working out well. Their tales of marital bliss had inspired Coe to believe a marriage of convenience could work for him and Skye, too. How hard could it be to fall in love with and stay married to someone as beautiful and thoughtful as her, and someone he enjoyed kissing so much?

He believed God had brought Skye into his life for a reason. For years, he'd asked the Lord to direct him to the person who would be an excellent match for him and one he would also be a great match for. Who better than Skye Tamarack to fulfill that wish and prayer?

But what if the rush of emotions he felt fleeing from Liam's men and racing back to Idaho made him look at her through rose-hued lenses that weren't entirely accurate? Was his desire to protect her impacting his judgment about his feelings for her? About their compatibility? Was it possible he was trying to save her just to be heroic? *No, that's not it.* But what if Liam didn't give up? What if his men didn't stop chasing Skye? What if they came after his family? Coe groaned.

"Troubled?" Skye yawned. "Where are we?"

"Post Falls, Idaho."

"Already?" She gave him an analyzing look. "What's bothering you? Homecoming blues?"

"Maybe." Why was he suddenly questioning his decisions and doubting himself? Surely, he and Skye could make a beautiful marriage from their unusual beginnings. Mom and Dad had. Lake and Irish were doing that. So were Hud and Trista. If Coe and Skye committed to staying together, they would honor their vows and, with God's grace, figure out how to live together and love each other through all the ups and downs of life, right?

"Coe? Could you pull over somewhere? Some coffee would be nice." Skye took a deep breath like she was gathering her courage. "And I want to talk with you about something."

"Okay. I'll take the next exit. Are you all right?"

"Yeah. I had a weird dream."

"Oh." Is that what she wanted to talk with him about? He took the next exit and drove to a familiar coffee shop on the south side of the interstate. "Care to take a short walk and stretch our legs before we hit the road again?" he asked after they had their coffees in hand. He'd keep a lookout for Tip, but he hadn't noticed anyone tailing them.

"Sounds good."

They walked a block without speaking, both lost in their thoughts, as they sipped their drinks. The air smelled clean and fresh, so much like home, that Coe felt tempted to skip Coeur d'Alene and continue north. He glanced over his shoulder several times but didn't see any suspicious activity.

"Yes," Skye declared without preamble.

"Yes?" He stopped walking and met her gaze.

"I've been contemplating us getting married." She smiled, her dark eyes shimmering. "My answer is yes. I will marry you, Coe."

"You will?" His heart seemed to stop and start. "That's great. I mean, uh—"

"If you are still willing, that is." A look of panic raced across her features.

"I'm willing. But considering no one appears to be following us, we aren't under any pressure to get married right now." *Talk about sounding like I'm backpedaling.* He groaned inwardly.

"Are you backing out? I get it if you are."

"No. I'm not." Yet he raked his fingers through his hair. Were fatigue and worry the culprits behind his hesitancy? Hadn't he already decided that he would marry her? *I like Skye. I love kissing her. I long to protect her. And always be there for her.* "I am ready to marry you."

"You are? You scared me for a second."

"Sorry. Just tired. Do you want to marry me today, Skye?"

"I'm ready if you are."

"Then let's get married!" He pulled her close for a hug, and she giggled. "We're officially engaged."

"Yeah, we are." Skye patted his back. "Uh, Coe? Did you notice the car parked behind us in the lot?"

"No." He swiveled around, his breath catching. A grayish-green sedan was parked close to their rental's bumper. "Did you see the driver?"

"No. I didn't."

"We don't know if it's Tip. Still, we should get going." Coe forced himself to breathe normally and not assume the worst. "What changed your mind about us getting married?" he asked as they walked faster toward the rental car.

"That dream I mentioned? It was about our kiss on the porch, my first kiss."

"I had no idea." That he'd received her first kiss pleased him, and he wished he could have also given her his first kiss.

"Are you being chivalrous?"

"No. You are good at kissing, for never having done it before." He teasingly added, "But you might need more practice."

"It's not very gentlemanly of you to mention it." She nudged his arm. "However, kissing someone I like for the rest of my life sounds like I'd be getting a good deal."

"The same goes for me." He met her gaze and clung to it for a few moments. "But if I'm the only one you've kissed, you have nothing to compare it to."

"It's hard to imagine anyone competing with your kisses." Her eyes twinkled like she was trying to tempt him, and he couldn't resist drawing her into his arms again, if only briefly.

"We'll make a fine duo as husband and wife." He lowered his lips to hers, his thoughts whirling with what it meant to be her husband, and their kiss lengthened.

"Hey!" a raspy male voice shouted, and they jerked apart. About thirty feet away, Tip marched straight toward them.

"Oh, no," Skye said.

"I need a word with you two."

"Run!" Coe grabbed her hand, and they dashed across the parking lot. Behind them, Tip's threats only fueled his resolve to get away. Ignoring the ruffian's command to stop, they jumped inside the rental. Coe turned the key with one hand, secured his seatbelt with the other, then drove to the freeway and merged into traffic without spotting Tip's car in the rearview mirror.

"That was close," Skye said. "When will he stop chasing us?"

"Not until your dad recognizes our marriage. Which makes me think you should call and explain things to him."

"He won't listen or give his blessing. Are you going to call your parents?"

"Yes." Coe thought of the phone calls he needed to make. "I want my parents and Gran to know about us getting married. It's important to me."

"Even if it's fake?"

"How can you say that after the way we've kissed?"

"Sorry. It's just so sudden."

He pulled back into the right lane and wondered how he would convince her they were going to have a real marriage if she already felt it was fake. "Do you have feelings for me?" It was challenging having this conversation while driving. "Do you, Skye?"

"Yes."

"I have feelings for you, too. So it isn't fake for either of us, all right?"

"Yeah. Okay." After a silence, she said, "I don't have a wedding dress or any clean clothes to wear. The judge will take one look at us and deny our marriage."

"I don't think it works that way. But I'm sorry I didn't consider a wedding dress. Is it crucial that you have something nice to wear?"

"Yes. The dress doesn't have to be fancy or white, but I don't want to get married in this rumpled thing." She scowled at the wrinkled dress fabric.

"We'll find something, then." He took the next exit toward Coeur d'Alene, determined to find his wife-to-be a dress she'd be proud to wear when she married him.

Chapter Sixteen

Skye loved the soft, delicate fabric of the pale pink, knee-length dress she found in a thrift store in downtown Coeur d'Alene. When she put it on, the fabric caressed her skin so delicately and comfortably that she didn't try on any other dresses. She was grateful Coe understood about her wanting to pick a special outfit for the occasion. Even if she wasn't having the wedding of her girlish dreams, she was marrying the man she hoped to spend her whole life with, and she wanted to be dressed up and have fond memories of their ceremony.

"How's it going?" Coe met her in the shoe section.

"Fine." She kept her dress under her arm so he wouldn't see it.

"I found a gray sport coat and dark pants that fit."

"That's good. What color is the shirt?"

He fingered through the pile. "White or light blue? I can't decide."

"You'll look handsome in either."

"Yeah?"

"Oh, yeah."

He smiled warmly, and she wondered if he was thinking about the secret they shared, like she was. They were getting married today, and only the two of them knew about it, other than God. Skye longed to wrap her arms around Coe's neck and kiss him for an hour or so. *Goodness.* They wouldn't be doing what newly married couples expected to be doing on their wedding night, yet her thoughts were leaping to a gloriously happy future with this man who said he believed they would fall in love.

Did she deserve such happiness? A twinge of conscience stole some of her giddy anticipation. *I didn't mean for things to happen this way or go this far.* Yet Coe said he wanted to marry her and spend his life with her. Maybe he wasn't feeling as trapped as she feared.

"I'll choose white to better match your dress." He winked. Did he notice the light pink fabric she was trying to hide?

She clutched the dress tighter. "When are you going to call your mom?"

"Right after we get the license."

"Okay. I'm not going to call Father until after we're married." She wasn't letting him say something awful about Coe and trying to influence her decision before their ceremony. She turned toward another rack, fingering some sweaters so Coe wouldn't argue with her about it. Thankfully, he didn't.

If Mom were alive, Skye would have included her in their wedding, perhaps setting up a video call for her to watch the civil ceremony. Did people get to witness special moments, such as weddings, in heaven? *I wish you were here, Mom. I miss you.*

She might not have kissed Coe like she did or begged him to help her escape if Mom had been alive. Of course, Mom wouldn't have allowed Father to go through with his threat of an arranged marriage. She would have been appalled by the grumpy, domineering parent he turned into.

But why was she dwelling on that? She was on the brink of marrying Coe North, the man she enjoyed kissing and laughing with, who made her feel safe. For a moment, she thought back to his lips meeting hers for the first time, his hands tracing a slow path over her back, and how she responded eagerly to his kisses. The heat of a blush crept up her neck as she relived the intensity of her feelings toward him.

"Skye?" He waved his hand in front of her face. "Are you all right?"

"Uh-huh." She needed to focus on getting ready for their wedding, not kissing Coe. Yet a part of her wanted to stand here and live in that romantic daydream.

"Do you still want to go through with this?" Why did he sound uncertain when she felt more confident about their marriage?

"I do. How about you?"

"Yes. But we should hurry." He nodded toward the exit. "I don't want to stay in one place too long."

He was right. Tip and Rhett could show up at any time. "Do you mind if I pick out a few items for later?"

"Later?" His eyebrows lifted.

"I need something to change into after the wedding." What did he think she meant?

"Oh, right. Grab anything you need."

"Thanks. Are you going to get a few things, too?" She felt awkward inquiring, but that was the sort of thing married couples would ask each other, right? Hopefully, they'd be more comfortable asking each other personal questions soon.

"I probably should." He turned back toward the men's section.

Skye selected a stack of casual wear, including jeans, a blouse, a sweater, some underwear, and modest pajamas. She resented the need to depend on Coe's finances, especially when he was relying on his brother's inheritance. She'd pay him back when she had access to her funds again, if Father gave her access. She grumbled about her dad's control over her inheritance, over her life, and felt some tension building up inside her. But this wasn't the time for stressing about things she couldn't change. She'd done enough of that. With God's help and Coe's friendship, she was making some critical decisions. And today she was marrying Coe.

Skye North. How would she feel taking his name? Was she ready for the commitment and promises that came with taking that step?

After Coe purchased their clothes, they hurried to the rental and went directly to the Kootenai County Marriage License office. They filled out the paperwork, showed their IDs, and paid the fee. They didn't have to find witnesses for their ceremony since Idaho didn't require any. Putting on their wedding clothes and exchanging vows at the courthouse was all they had left to do, and then they'd be married.

"Where are we going to change?" she asked.

"The library bathrooms." He rubbed his chin. "There's a coffee shop across the street where we can get coffee and snacks after the ceremony. I still need to make a couple of calls first."

"Right. Are we going to use these?" She held up her hand with the rings she bought in D.C.

"I forgot about rings." He smacked his forehead with his palm. "Do you mind if we use them for now? Later, we can get new ones."

"That's fine." She gazed into his eyes. "Thanks for being willing to do this with me, Coe. You're a sweet guy."

He leaned over and kissed her cheek. "I hope you'll always think I'm sweet."

Tears filled her eyes, and she couldn't fathom why, other than his gentleness touched her heart.

Chapter Seventeen

Coe checked his cell phone. He had only a few minutes to make two calls and text Lake. Would his family understand his brief explanation about marrying Skye? *Lord, please help everyone accept my decision to get married.* He'd put a lot of thought and prayer into whether they should take this step, so he wasn't committing to Skye lightly. But he wanted his family's support and acceptance. He swiped Mom's name on the phone screen, feeling some apprehension about telling her the news.

"Hey, Mom. It's Coe," he said because he had a new number, and she wouldn't recognize it.

"Coe? Honey, are you all right? Are you using someone else's phone?"

"I'm okay. This is my new number. I, uh, have something to share with you."

"Is that right? Ever since I got your email, I've been praying for you."

"Thanks. I've needed it." His thoughts zipped through some of his recent close calls with Rhett and Tip, and he thanked God for a praying mom.

"What's going on? Are you okay?"

"I'm all right."

"Are you sure? You sound troubled. We're here for you if you want to talk or need us to pray with you about anything."

Tears moistened his eyes, and he blinked fast. "That means a lot, Mom. Thank you." He had to hurry this conversation along. "What I'm about to tell you may come as a shock."

"Oh, dear. Something is wrong."

"Who is it?" Dad asked in the background.

"Coe," Mom whispered.

"Hey, Coe," Dad called.

"Hey."

After a rustling sound, Mom said, "We're on speaker phone. Dad can hear, too."

"That's great. I have to rush this call, but I'll talk with you more another time."

"What's going on?" Dad asked.

"I'm going to—" How could he explain in a way they'd understand? Gran used to tell him that speaking the truth, even if it came out wrong or was misunderstood, was better than talking himself out of a lie. Still, telling his parents what he was about to do and how it would impact all their lives challenged his inner peace. He hated disappointing anyone, especially Mom and Dad, whom he respected deeply. "I'm sorry if what I'm about to say disappoints you. I love you both and never want to cause you distress."

"You're scaring me," Mom said. "Just tell us what it is."

"I'm getting married!" He exhaled a breath and some tension with it.

"That's great, son," Dad said jubilantly. "We've been praying about that very thing."

"Coe?" Mom said in a thin voice. "What aren't you telling us?"

"I'm getting married today." The line went silent. "Mom?"

"I heard you. Just processing." She made a gulping sound.

Please don't cry. He was already fighting some emotional upheaval himself.

"What's her name?" she asked.

"Skye."

"How did you meet?"

"We volunteered together in India. She's Liam Tamarack's daughter."

"The philanthropist?" Dad asked.

"That's right."

"So, you're marrying the boss's daughter?" Dad sounded like he was smiling, which was comforting to imagine.

"I guess I am."

"Where are you now?" Dad asked. "How about getting some counseling before you make such a life-changing decision?"

"There isn't time. I wanted to call and let you know about our wedding." Coe took a deep breath, rallying his determination. "I feel like I must do this, but also, I want to do it. Skye is an amazing, compassionate woman. You're going to love her."

"Oh, Coe," Mom said.

"Son, we respect your decision and will stand by you, no matter what," Dad said. "But are you sure about this?"

"I'm sure."

"What led you to choose to get married today?" Mom asked, like she was trying hard to understand.

"I'm out of time, but I will tell you everything when you get back. Can you trust me in this?"

"Yes," Dad answered promptly.

"Of course," Mom said. "God has been leading you your whole life. We trust you to listen and follow Him."

"Thank you. Love you guys."

They said they loved him, too, and he ended the call. Skye stepped into his line of sight, eyebrows lifted, as he swiped Gran's name on the screen, and he tried to give her a reassuring smile. When Gran answered, he quickly explained about getting married and promised to see her soon. She sent her love and said she couldn't wait to meet Skye.

Lastly, he sent a text to Lake. *In Idaho. Getting married. Will be in touch.*

Then he shut off his phone. Marriage was a leap of faith in any scenario, but with the one he and Skye were about to embark on, he sensed there would be some unique challenges. He took a minute to pray that their marriage would be blessed and filled with love and longevity, no matter its beginning.

Chapter Eighteen

Skye smoothed her hands down her pink knee-length wedding dress, straightening out wrinkles and frowning at her messy hair in the reflection of the library bathroom mirror. At least her tanned skin, from a bazillion hours of outdoor work, contrasted nicely with the pale color. She ran her fingers through her dark strands, then grabbed the makeup she'd previously used as a disguise and put on a few light strokes of lipstick and blush. Her eyes gleamed like they held mysteries. Would Coe try to unravel those mysteries? Her heart pounded, and she yearned for a deeper understanding of the man she was marrying.

What would he expect from her on their wedding night? Her hands trembled, and she clutched them together to still them. She and Coe should have spent more time discussing their expectations for marriage. But he was an honorable and trustworthy man. She could trust him, right?

She took a deep breath, then exhaled slowly. Coe had stood up for her, taken personal risks on her behalf, and aided her in coming to the States. Didn't his noble actions prove he was a man of integrity and honor?

But when they were married, would he consider her opinion about everything? Or would he assume his decisions would prevail when it came to sex, money, living arrangements, and family matters simply because he was the man? Heat flushed through her body. He'd better not think that way! And what about having kids? They hadn't discussed that part of their life together. Did he want a big family? He'd better not expect her to give birth to six babies like his mother had. *Ugh.* Why was she fretting about all these things now?

Skye, you're about to marry a man you chose. She attempted a few calming breaths and stared at herself in the mirror, her reflection mirroring her uncertainties. *If problems arise in our marriage, and they probably will, we'll manage them together and with faith. We can do anything with Jesus's help*—she recalled her mom telling her that several times when she was a child. *Lord, help me remember that You are always with me. Thank You for caring about what I'm going through, and what Coe and I are going through. Please be with us.*

A few minutes later, Coe's palms felt warm and moist as they held hands before a white-haired judge in his chambers. Did Coe notice how desperately she was clinging to him?

"Are you both in agreement about this marriage?" The official who had introduced himself as Judge Clark eyed them. Did he doubt their marriage would last? Could he tell she was nervous?

"Yes," they both answered.

"No duress?" Judge Clark looked straight at her.

"No duress." She was marrying Coe because she chose this avenue for her peace and safety, although she hoped and prayed for a loving future with him.

"Do you, Skye Tamarack, take Coe North to be your husband?"

"I do." The words came out more breathily than she intended.

"Coe North, do you take Skye Tamarack as your lawfully wedded wife?"

"I do," he said strongly, as if he didn't have a single doubt.

Judge Clark kept the ceremony brief. "By the power vested in me by the state of Idaho, I declare you husband and wife. You may kiss your bride."

Her groom lifted his eyebrows like he was asking if it was okay for them to kiss. She nodded slightly, her heart pounding with excitement and nervousness. His lips touched hers with a soft but brief kiss far from a Cinderella and the Prince kiss, but befitting a judge's chamber. She felt a surge of attraction for him, but also a pang of uncertainty about their future together.

They signed the marriage license, and Judge Clark shook their hands. "I wish you the best. Good luck." And with that, the short ceremony was over.

"That was quick," Skye said, exiting the courthouse.

"Yeah, it was. Come here." Coe tugged her under his arm and, withdrawing his phone, snapped a couple of selfies of them. "Some photos to show our kids someday." So he was contemplating having children on their wedding day? She wondered again about the size of a family he hoped to have.

"What now?" she asked when the impromptu photo shoot ended.

"Celebrate?" He rocked his eyebrows.

She stiffened. "What did you have in mind?"

"Food and coffee. Hey. What's wrong?"

"Nothing. Sorry." She mentally shook herself. She needed to give Coe the benefit of the doubt and stop being suspicious of him. "When you said celebrate and your eyebrows danced, I thought you meant, well, you know what I thought." Her cheeks heated up, and she tried swallowing down her embarrassment.

"Ahhh." He nodded slowly. "You don't know me very well yet."

"Not really."

He held out his hands, palms up. After a moment's hesitation, she set her palms on his and forced herself to meet his gaze with more certainty than she felt. "I promise not to push for anything you aren't comfortable with, okay?"

"Okay." She heaved a sigh. "Thank you."

"Now, Mrs. North, shall we get some food and have a private party to celebrate the beginning of our forever together?"

Forever sounded like a long time, but she said, "Sure. Let's do that."

Hand in hand, they walked to the bakery and coffee shop, and somehow, that closeness of walking beside Coe and holding his hand felt reassuring and hopeful, symbolic even. Each step they took seemed like an exclamation point on their new beginning and this chapter in their lives.

"Did you two just get married?" the lady behind the counter asked with a grin.

"Yes." Coe smiled broadly. "About fifteen minutes ago."

"Congratulations!"

"Thank you. How did you know?" Skye asked.

"Your beaming faces. The way you act together. And you are all dressed up." The barista smiled knowingly. "It's simple. You're madly in love and couldn't wait to get married, right?"

"Something like that." Skye exchanged amused glances with Coe.

They ordered two coffees and chocolate croissants. Every time their gazes met, Skye felt sparks flashing between them. *Settle down, my heart. Just because he's my husband doesn't mean anything has changed.* Who was she kidding? Everything had changed. They were married. She was Skye North, Coe's wife.

They'd barely sat down at a table for two when she spotted the person she didn't want to see, especially now. "It's Tip." She groaned.

"Where?"

"There." She nodded toward the window, where he stood outside, hands over his eyes, peering back at them with his smirky "gotcha" look. Why did he have to find them now? Why couldn't he have waited thirty minutes, so they could have enjoyed the newness and happiness of being married?

"Come on." Coe drew her close to him. His protective arm around her shoulders felt like a shield from Tip's gaze. "Let's get out of here. We'll leave through the adjoining building."

"Okay." She picked up her coffee and dessert, and Coe grabbed his. Then they scurried through the other business, ran outside, and raced for the rental car.

Welcome to married life, Skye.

Chapter Nineteen

Coe sped out of the parking lot, frustrated that Tip had found them so quickly and annoyed at himself for letting his guard down. He should have been more aware of the possibility of Liam's bodyguard showing up and interrupting their celebration plans. He'd been preoccupied with the wedding ceremony, hopeful their marriage might fix things with Liam, and forgot about the henchman still hot on their trail.

"Where are we going?" Skye glanced toward the back window.

"Farther north. I'll pull over at Hayden Lake so you can call your father and talk privately."

"I almost forgot about that." She heaved a sigh.

"Are you okay with telling him about us getting married?"

"It's the only way he'll know I mean what I say about choosing a husband for myself. Although I still don't think it will be effective." Her defeated tone made him wish he could call Liam and tell him what he thought of his treatment of his daughter. Why couldn't Skye's dad appreciate the wonderful person she was instead of trying to control her?

Coe pulled into the parking lot at the end of Honeysuckle Avenue, glad to find it empty, and parked as close to the beach as he could. "You might as well finish your croissant. No reason to let it go to waste." He took a swallow of his tepid coffee and grimaced.

"Coe? What is your plan for us?" Skye's dark eyes held unspoken questions.

"Plan?" His voice hiccupped on the word.

"Like, where are we going to stay tonight?"

"I don't know." His thoughts hadn't traveled much farther than how to get away from their foe. "I hoped to get a room near Lake Coeur d'Alene, since it's so beautiful. But now that Tip knows our location, I'm uncertain." He glanced over his shoulder, making sure they hadn't been followed. "Maybe you'll convince your dad to call off his guards. Then we could drive back and spend one night at the resort." Any more than that would dip too far into his funds. He had a small emergency buffer on a credit card, but did a nice room, beach walks, and a wedding dinner for two warrant using it? Perhaps it did, although he'd felt strongly about not using it for the last two years.

Skye nibbled at her pastry, looking introspective, while he wolfed down his chocolate croissant, savoring the sweetness, and cast a couple of glances at her. Was she concerned about sharing a room? Or troubled about calling her dad?

"What did your parents say?" she asked.

"That they supported and loved me, that sort of thing. But my mom—" He sighed, regretting how he'd abruptly told her the news and how she took it.

"Did she cry?"

"It sounded like she was sniffling or about to break down."

"No wonder, after you dashed her dreams of seeing her son get married."

"Hey. It's not that tragic." He wiped his hand over his chin, making sure he didn't have any croissant crumbs on his whiskers. "Besides, she'll forgive me when we give her a grandbaby."

"Coe! That might not happen for a long time."

"Just saying." He chuckled, feeling awkward about the topic since she'd responded so intensely. "Babies have a way of changing people's opinions about things." He wondered what she thought of having kids when she was silent for a few minutes. They should have talked about that before, but he didn't want to bring it up if it was a touchy subject.

"Maybe we could do something special for your mom and grandmother to make up for them not being invited to the wedding," she said quietly.

"That's not necessary."

"Will they hate me?"

"No." He reached over and squeezed her hand gently. "Mom and Gran will love you no matter how we got married or what led to us making that happy decision."

"Happy?" She moved her hand and peered at him like he'd grown horns. "What did your grandmother say?"

"That she can't wait to meet the woman the Lord sent me to India to meet."

"She said that?"

"Yep. Gran believes God is present and always working in our lives. She says we can talk to Him about everything, including asking for something as mundane as gas. I've tried to follow her example, but I don't always succeed." Thinking of Gran made him miss her and wish they were already in Thunder Ridge.

"I envy you having a grandmother like that." There was heartache in Skye's tone. "Your family sounds wonderful."

"I have some impish brothers. Don't make any assumptions about how wonderful my family is until you've met them all."

"Father's uncouth methods are far worse than being called impish."

That sounded like a perfect segue. "Are you ready to call him?"

"I guess." She rubbed her palms over the fabric of her pink dress. "Would you do something for me first?"

"Anything."

"Will you pray with me?" Her desperate look melted his heart.

"Of course, I will." He clasped her hands loosely, smoothing his fingers across her palms, and closed his eyes. "Lord, we know You have been working in our lives for Skye and me to meet and be together. Our marriage is unconventional, but we are grateful for every step of the journey that has brought us to this point." He opened his eyes and found Skye watching him, a tender smile on her lips. "Thank You for giving me a beautiful, compassionate woman to be my wife. Please help Liam understand about us getting married and give Skye peace about calling him. In Jesus's name."

"Amen." She let go of his hand and opened the door. "I'll make the call. Then, should we discuss what we will do next?"

"Absolutely. I'll keep watch for Tip."

"Okay. I'm going to walk on the beach." She stepped out of the vehicle.

"Skye? If you need anything, let me know."

"I might need you for the rest of my life." Her eyes sparkled back at him, unshed tears glistening, and his heart somersaulted.

"I'm glad to hear it. Really glad." He spent the next few minutes praying for his wife and their marriage.

Chapter Twenty

Skye had already entered Father's number into her new phone, but she didn't immediately tap his name. She strolled along the damp, sandy shoreline, trying to release her worries to the Lord and gather some courage for the resistance she anticipated from Father. He wasn't going to like her telling him she got married. No doubt, he'd yell, curse, and cast blame at her. But she still had to call him. It was the right thing to do, even if she felt anxious.

"Yeah?" Father answered gruffly when she made the call.

"It's me, Skye."

"Skye Tamarack, what are you thinking, leading my men on a wild goose chase across the States?" He bellowed at her like she was an unruly teenager. All the feelings of fear and anger toward him merged, and she felt herself shaking. "Are you ready to come to your senses and get back home where you belong?"

"No, Father."

"No?" His voice blasted in her ear.

Gritting her teeth, she forced herself to speak calmly and rationally, despite her trembling. "I'm calling to ask you to tell your men to back off. Please, order your hounds to stand down and leave me alone."

"Back off? Stand down? Leave you alone?" His voice got louder and more demanding with each question. "After you took off with a stranger, you expect me to leave you alone? After you spent the night with him and disgraced me, you think I don't have a right to send my faithful workforce after you?" *Faithful workforce? Unbelievable.* "And to top off your offences, you got Rhett detained?"

"No doubt you've had him released." She didn't acknowledge his claim about spending the night with Coe.

"Of course, I did." Father growled a swear word. "Now, when are you coming home?"

"I'm not. I'm an adult," she said firmly but with as much respect as she could muster. "Don't you think it's time for me to make my decisions? For you to let me grow up? I'm thirty years old."

"I don't care how old you are. You are my daughter. I make the decisions for our family." The phone seemed to vibrate with his intensity. "You won't see a penny of my fortune if you don't do as I say."

"This isn't about money, Father." Even though she disagreed with him keeping Mom's legacy from her, she wouldn't take his emotional bait. "If I'm a pauper for the rest of my days, living in a hovel in the mountains, it will be worth it to have the freedom to do what my heart leads me to do."

"Your heart," he scoffed. "Who's filled your head with nonsense? With lies? Was it that potato farmer? That nothing from Idaho?"

"His name is Coe." She squeezed the phone tightly. "No one is filling my head with nonsense. I'm doing what's right for me. And I don't believe God would have me marry Edmund."

"God," he muttered.

"That's right. I'm still following *Him* like Mama taught me to."

"Don't bring her or Him into this conversation," Father said, grinding his teeth. "Your mother wouldn't condone your sneaking off with a man, an aid worker, no less."

He was such a hypocrite. While he relied on volunteers from all over the world for the Tamarack Foundation, he considered them contemptible when it came to her befriending or, heaven forbid, forming an attachment with any of them. They'd fought that battle enough times over the years.

"I will marry whomever I choose," she said, even though she hadn't found the courage to tell him she already had. *Lord, give me strength. Please help Father understand.*

"What matters is trusting me to know what's best for you, like you have in the past." His groan sounded like a roar. "Now get your backside on the next plane to Dubai before I lose my temper."

"I won't." Standing up to him made her limbs shake and her heart pound erratically. She clenched her jaw to keep her teeth from chattering but wouldn't let fear stop her from expressing herself. "I'm not coming back."

"Yes, you are. So help me—" A voice in the background was garbled like Father's hand covered the phone while someone else spoke with him. "I'll forgive you," he resumed the conversation with her more amicably. "And this rebellion will be forgotten if you return in the next twenty-four hours and promise you'll wed Edmund."

Didn't he hear anything she said? "I'm not marrying him. This isn't a rebellion. It's about me choosing how I live and who I spend my life with, and that isn't with Edmund Lung." She took a swallow of air. "I'm not returning to India for you to control my life."

"Think again. Tip is watching you as we speak. He's there to bring you home."

"What?" She swiveled toward the rental. Coe leaned against the driver's side door, gazing toward the lake. She scanned the area without spotting Tip. "He's not here."

"Yes, he is. One word from me and that kidnapper's life won't be worth living."

Skye felt the blood drain from her face. "Don't you dare touch him! Coe isn't a kidnapper. He's helping me because I asked him to." She stomped through the sand toward the car. "Leave him out of this, you hear me? I left India of my own will. I stopped your plot for my life. I chose Coe North to be my husband."

"Husband?" Father shouted so loud that Skye had to yank the phone from her ear.

"That's right. I married him today."

Something crashed like Father threw an object against a wall, and it shattered. "You married that money-hungry scoundrel?"

"He's a good and honest man. He doesn't care about money. I beg you to accept me as a full-grown woman who can pick the man she wants to marry." She swallowed hard, knowing it was a lot to ask of Father.

"Are you telling me you love that drifter? That pathetic speck of humanity?"

A fire burned in her chest, and her desire to stick up for Coe increased rapidly. "Coe is a kinder, more empathetic person than *any* man I've ever met. He is loyal and would die defending me."

"He might have to," Father growled.

Skye gasped. "Don't you dare sic Tip or Rhett on him again!" If she'd thought Father might make things worse for Coe, she wouldn't have made this phone call.

"I'll do as I please," he said gruffly.

"As will I. Even if you have them tie me up, drug me again, and haul me to Dubai, I will never marry Edmund or any man of your choosing." She shook so badly that every word came out tremblingly, but she was determined to speak up for herself and Coe. "I am legally married to Coe. I am Skye North."

"No, you're not!" Father roared like an injured lion. "I will never accept that. Have you consummated this pretend marriage?"

"That isn't your business." She clenched her jaw, tempted to end the call.

"So the answer is no." He sounded pleased and smug. "Edmund is the best match for you. When he dies, you'll inherit a fortune. Can't you appreciate the pearl I've picked for you?"

Pearl? Her footfall froze in the sand, and she glanced at the sky, wishing she could see her mother's face. "Is he the man Mama would have wanted for me? Is he the prince she said would kiss me one day?"

"I told you not to mention her!" Father pounded on his desk or a table. "Your dalliance and running away like a child is over. Tip will bring you to the airport. He's there to get you now. What happens to Cole depends on your actions."

She was going to correct him about Coe's name, but footsteps crunched on the sand, and Tip strode toward her with a mocking grin. "How could you?" she shouted into the phone and sprinted toward Coe.

"Because I love my daughter. I'll see you tomorrow."

"No, you won't! And this manipulation has nothing to do with love." She ended the call and shouted, "Get the car started! Tip's here!"

Eyes wide, Coe jumped into the rental, started the engine, and flung open the passenger door in time for her to leap inside. "Go. Go!" she urged.

Tip ran up to the car and pounded on the hood, yelling for them to stop, but Coe sped out of the parking lot.

Chapter Twenty-one

Coe checked them into a budget motel in Sandpoint using the Dupont name again. It was late. They were exhausted. Anywhere to rest for the night was fine.

The drive from Hayden to Sandpoint had been tense. He'd been consumed by worry, every set of headlights approaching from the rear a potential threat. He was tired of running from Liam's men and wished they'd leave Skye and him alone. He had dared to hope Skye's conversation with her dad might change his opinion about pursuing them or his need to have his men drag her back to India. Obviously, it hadn't.

During their drive, Skye recounted the conversation with her dad, her voice tinged with hurt from the exchange. "He knew Tip was watching me, so they were communicating all along. I'm shocked by how far he is willing to go to get me married off to a wealthy person. Even when I told him that you and I are legally married, he said awful things and demanded I return, as if he could snap his fingers, and I'd follow his wishes." She groaned like she felt deeply emotional about it. "I've never cared much about our family's wealth. But there's something heartbreaking about him withholding Mom's inheritance, her last gift to me."

"I'm sorry." Coe felt bad about her situation but was also deeply frustrated with Liam's choices. It dawned on him that Skye's father was now his father-in-law, a concept that was difficult to grasp.

"Thanks." She sniffled, and he wished he wasn't driving so he could hug her and offer his support.

After a few minutes of silence, and with his thoughts wandering, he asked, "Do you think money influences how people live?"

"What do you mean?"

"Take wealthy people, for instance. They can be self-focused and greedy, like my maternal grandfather was, or generous and caring, like Lake has been with his inheritance." Coe shuffled his hands on the steering wheel and glanced in the rearview mirror, keeping watch. "Likewise, someone who doesn't have much wealth can be selfish or preoccupied with their problems, or they can be generous with whatever they do have. Right?"

"I think so." She told him about the lady who gave her money to make a call in New York City and how grateful she was for her kindness.

"So, what matters is that we care about others and do what we can to help with whatever opportunity or means we have. You know the love-your-neighbor-as-yourself thing?" Their gazes met in the light of an approaching vehicle, and Skye nodded. "Does the widow next door have provisions? Is the hurricane victim sleeping on the street? Is the kid without a dad going to bed hungry?" He felt the passion for his beliefs building up, inspiring him to act if he could. "If I were blessed with a fortune, I'd want to use it to help others."

"Who taught you to have a caring heart like that?"

"Gran and Mom, I suppose. And Dad, who was also my pastor."

"Father cared about people after horrific acts of nature swept through a village, or people were facing extreme hardships. His philanthropic leadership proved that, or I thought it did." Skye sighed as if questioning everything about her father, a man she previously admired. "But loving his neighbor like himself? Caring for others like he cares for himself? Have those thoughts ever crossed his mind?" She laughed mirthlessly. "He's ex-military and unrelentingly rigid in his views. I've rarely questioned him, except in this area of him choosing my spouse. I couldn't tolerate that."

"Is that why you call him Father, instead of Dad or Pop or something more casual?"

"Yeah. He places extreme value on titles and demands respect."

With nine boys in the North household, his parents expected them to act respectfully, but they also gave lots of love and grace. While Coe had some difficulty relating to Skye's situation with a regimented parent, he was also determined to better understand the woman he married.

"What did he say about our marriage, other than wanting you back?" When she didn't answer, he asked, "What is it? You can tell me."

"It's embarrassing."

He clasped her hand gently. "What did he say?"

"He wanted to know if we—" She pulled her hand away. "To him, we aren't married unless we've, you know, been together."

"I see." He swallowed hard.

"Not that having done so would have made a difference. No doubt, he'd send Rhett and Tip to do something worse." She groaned. "I'm sorry to mention that."

"What do you mean by worse?" Dread filled him. Her father's bodyguards had already gone to extreme measures to take Skye back, including trying to inflict pain or do him harm.

"Cause an accident for you? Force me to go back? I won't marry Edmund."

"Of course not. You chose me." He grinned despite the topic's serious nature and his worries about keeping her safe and staying safe himself.

"Yes, I did. But Father won't accept our marriage unless we—"

"Are you saying we should make that distinction official?" His thoughts flashed like a movie on fast forward through what kissing his wife beyond what they'd already experienced would be like, but he reined in his thoughts. He was determined not to rush into anything, and for love to grow naturally between them.

"Not really. However, we are going to share a room, right?"

"Yes."

"Even if we don't—"

"Even then. You and I will be spending the rest of our lives together, which means sharing everything. However, if you want me to sleep on the floor until we get to know each other better, I will." He gulped. "You can trust me, Skye."

"I told my dad you are a great guy."

"Did he believe you?"

"Not even slightly."

Coe glanced at the rearview mirror. Another set of headlights was getting closer, and more apprehension hit him, forming a knot in his gut. "I want you to promise me something."

"What's that?"

"Whenever you're sure you are falling in love with me, no matter how long it takes, will you tell me?" He wanted to gaze deeply into her eyes, but he kept his attention on the road. "Hearing those words coming from you will mean the world to me. Will you?"

"I will," she said softly. "And will you tell me when you fall in love with me, too?"

"You'd better believe it." He didn't suppress his wide grin.

In their hotel room, two queen-sized beds covered with floral prints looked inviting. Coe felt like he could fall into bed and sleep for a week. He checked the deadbolt and set a chair snugly beneath the doorknob. If Tip and Rhett tried anything, he wanted to be alerted immediately.

"Mind if I wash up first?" Skye asked.

"Go ahead. Take all the time you need."

He heard the shower running as he thumbed through some texts. Lake had sent him a message following his earlier text. *Congrats, bro. I can't wait to see you. Stay safe.*

Thanks. Can we meet for coffee at Featherly's tomorrow? Ten a.m.?

I'll be there.

While Coe waited for a turn in the bathroom, his thoughts skimmed through the day. They were married. Coe and Skye North. He liked the way their names sounded together. *Skye is my beautiful bride, and I am her husband. Someday, her beloved husband.* He smiled. He'd told her she could trust him, and he meant it, but he was also eager to become her husband in every way.

Chapter Twenty-two

Skye crept into the silent motel room and wondered why the TV wasn't on until she saw Coe lying on his back, eyes closed, and his face completely relaxed. *Good for him.* One of them ought to get some rest after their chaotic and tiring day. She, for one, was emotionally and physically exhausted. The thought of snuggling up beside Coe and resting her cheek against his chest was tempting. But she couldn't forget how he came unglued when she slept next to him the last time.

His long, dark lashes fluttered against his sun-darkened skin. His lips looked soft and attractive, reminding her of how it felt when they were kissing. Did she have the right to a sweet good night kiss on her wedding day? One tiny kiss should be okay. She brushed her mouth whisper-soft against his. "Good night, husband." He didn't stir.

She settled into the other bed and prayed for a few minutes, as was her custom, before drifting off. She told the Lord about how troubled she was about her talk with Father. She confessed her worries and fears about the men he'd sent to get her, and how fatigued she was of running from them. Then she thanked Him for safely bringing them to Idaho and not letting Tip and Rhett's plans succeed.

Her thoughts drifted to replaying her exchange with Father. *"I will never marry Edmund or any man of your choosing. I am legally married to Coe. I am Skye North!"*

"No, you're not! I will never accept that." Why did Father have to act so unyieldingly pigheaded about letting her live her own life? Why couldn't he accept her choice of a spouse?

Undoubtedly, it had been shocking for him to catch Coe and her kissing last week. And when he found out she'd run away with him, Father must have been outraged. But he took outrage to a ridiculous level when he sent his bodyguards after them. Didn't he fathom the trouble he could get into with the actions of his employees, who were following his directives? In the past, he'd bragged that his wealth could buy him out of any scrape. If his ruffians found a way to abduct her and drag her back to Dubai, would he evade blame then, too?

Her discussion with Father made her feel more certain she'd made the right decision by marrying Coe. But then, like unwelcome guests, doubts crept into her thoughts. What if they never fell in love? What if, after a few years, they came to despise each other and how they married so quickly? She groaned. Why did she have to ponder such things on her wedding night? Couldn't she hope for the best, believing God would guide and help them in whatever situation they faced? And that they'd come to love each other eventually?

Lord, help me to trust You. I'm sorry for my doubts and misgivings. She turned from her back to her side, then did the reverse, making a mess of her blankets and sheets, and groaned again.

"Skye?" Coe croaked. "Can't sleep?"

"No."

"Are you hungry?" He leaned his chin on his palm, supported by his elbow, and his tired gaze met hers. "I wonder what's open this late."

"I can wait until morning. My mind keeps whirring with stuff about Father and some other concerns, that's all."

"Why don't you turn on the TV? Find an old movie to distract you."

"It wouldn't bother you?"

"Not at all." He propped two pillows behind him. "Do you want to sit over here by me?"

"Yes." She leaped off the bed, bounced onto his mattress, and settled beside him with her pillows behind her. "Thanks."

"Sure. We're married. You can sit by me anytime you want." His smile warmed her heart.

"I'll keep that in mind." She imagined the goodnight kiss she gave him and felt self-conscious about it. But a wife could kiss her husband before falling asleep, whether they loved each other or not, right? "What kind of shows do you like?"

"Old ones. Westerns, mostly."

"I like those, too." She flipped through the channels until she found a John Wayne movie. "*McLintock?*"

"Perfect. I laugh every time I watch the best mud fight in movie history. But I'll probably fall asleep again."

"No problem." Just being near him made her feel safer, relaxed, and less troubled. After a few minutes of watching the show, she felt him staring at her. "What?"

"You're so beautiful." He stroked her cheek with his fingers, circling her dimple with the briefest touch. "Thank you for marrying me, Skye." He said her name so softly her gut tightened. She was the one who should be thanking him.

"You're welcome. And thank you for going along with our ruse."

"It's more than a ruse. I care about you."

"I don't deserve someone as wonderful as you. My convenient husband?" She meant it teasingly, but emotion thickened in her throat.

His eyes sparkled, and another smile creased his lips. "I don't know how convenient I'll be. But I'm happy to have played a small part in your escape." He settled his arm over her shoulder. "Is this okay?"

"It's okay." *So, very okay.*

"Happy wedding day, Skye." He stroked a few strands of hair back behind her ears, causing her cheeks to tingle in every spot he touched. "Can we share a kiss?"

"Yes," she whispered.

She closed her eyes, and his mouth brushed hers with an ethereal beauty that made tears burn in her eyes. She didn't deserve his sacrifice in marrying her. But she hoped and prayed she'd genuinely love him one day, as he deserved to be loved, and that he'd love her. She smoothed her fingers over his bristly cheeks and dimpled chin, getting more acquainted with the sensation of touching her husband's face. He ended the kiss abruptly and coughed like he was covering some emotions.

"We should watch John Wayne's attempts at romance. Maybe I'll learn from his mistakes, huh?"

"Maybe." She leaned against his shoulder and sighed.

Along with being a sweet kisser, Coe was an honorable man. It would be easy for them to keep kissing and let their wedding-day euphoria prematurely take them down a road of marital bliss. Coe was keeping his word about not pushing for anything beyond what she was ready for, and she was deeply grateful for his patience and understanding.

How long would it take until she truly felt ready to be his wife?

Chapter Twenty-three

Coe took his shower early the following day and slipped out of the room to find some breakfast before Skye woke up. He'd turned off the TV in the middle of the night and fell asleep beside her as if they'd been doing that for years. But he could hardly believe he was married to Skye, and they would be partners by vows and love for the rest of their lives.

He already felt so many things for her. Every time they gazed into each other's eyes and kissed, he experienced a depth of emotion for her that he'd never felt with anyone before. Was that the beginning of love?

He also felt some caution. While he was strongly attracted to Skye, a lot had happened in a short amount of time. What if their romantic feelings were built on the adrenaline rush of adventure and their extraordinary flight from Liam? Would everyday life after that be boring or lackluster? Groaning, he tried ridding his mind of negative thoughts and turning them over to God. Their escape from Liam's men was part of their journey together. Someday, they might even laugh about their escapades. For now, he glanced over his shoulder every few steps, fearful of seeing the men he didn't want to see in Sandpoint and prayed for the Lord's protection.

At the deli, he purchased breakfast burritos and coffees for the two of them. He didn't dally, since he was in a hurry to get back to Skye. Without waking her, he entered the motel room and set the drinks and food on the table. She must have been wiped out to still be sleeping.

"Hey, Skye? Good morning." When she didn't stir, he sat on the edge of the bed and rubbed her shoulder gently to wake her up. "I got some coffee for you."

"Hmmm?" She groaned softly. "What?"

"I have coffee and a breakfast burrito, I'm sure you'll love."

"Coffee?" She sat up, her hair looking messy and gorgeous. He reached for her drink and handed it to her, distracting himself from wanting to pull her into his arms. "Thank you, Coe." She sipped from the to-go cup and purred, "This is amazing."

Chuckling, he moved to a chair at the small table by the window, unwrapped their burritos, and swayed his hand toward the other chair. "Care to join me for our first breakfast as a married couple?"

"Sure. Thanks." She carried her coffee over and sat down, their gazes meeting.

"Mind if I pray?" He reached for her hand.

"That would be great." She breathed deeply and exhaled before placing her hand in his as if she felt cautious about holding it. What was that about?

He closed his eyes. "Lord, thank You for the food and the fabulous company. We pray for wisdom and safety for this day. Amen."

"Amen." Skye lifted her cup to his in a toast. "To our future."

"And our love." He tapped his cup against hers, and her face paled. "What's wrong?"

"It's nothing." Obviously, it wasn't nothing.

"Did I say something stupid? I have been known to do that." He smiled, trying to prompt a smile from her that didn't materialize.

"I've never held a man's hand and prayed with him before yesterday, let alone talk with him about falling in love. It feels a little intimate. And weird." She huffed. "Not that falling in love with you would be weird."

"Well, Mrs. North." He drew her hand to his lips and brushed his mouth over the middle of her palm, feeling like he'd got a glimpse into his wife's thoughts. "I plan to hold your hand, pray with you, and talk about our love often, if that's all right."

"It's all right." She sipped her drink. "Father didn't want me to hold hands with boys. Even in junior high, when we were required to square dance, he forbade me from touching the boys, like they might give me a disease by our palms touching."

"Pretty extreme?"

"You have no idea. So, if it takes some time for me to adjust to us holding hands and talking about love, it isn't you. It's me."

His heart warmed at the tender look she gave him. "I'll wait as long as it takes for you to get comfortable with me touching you. Honestly, I don't know much about women since I grew up with eight guys." A wry grin crossed his lips as he thought of something else. "Although, you didn't seem averse to my touch during our kisses."

"True." Her cheeks turned a delightful pink. "Kissing you is a different matter altogether."

"How so?" He hoped to extend their flirtation and wanted to know more about her thoughts.

"I wanted to keep kissing you and kissing you."

His breath caught. "I wanted that, too."

"Why didn't you last night?" She stared at her uneaten burrito.

Surprised, he countered, "Why didn't you?"

She lifted her gaze to his. "If I'd wanted that, you would have gone along with it?"

"You are a lovely woman I'm attracted to, and we are married." He smoothed his palm over his heart. "However, while being with you as your husband is tempting, we should wait until we fall in love before we share a closer relationship. Intimacy shouldn't happen because we're riding an emotional high after being chased across the world. Don't you agree?"

"In the light of day, I do." She nibbled at her burrito. "You are a temptation to me, too."

"Good." He hoped to be much more of a temptation to her in the coming days.

They ate their breakfast and drank their coffee in relative silence, their gazes occasionally dancing with each other's in a way he found riveting. His thoughts zigzagged between wanting to find out how much of a temptation he was to her and what he'd said and believed about waiting for love.

Chapter Twenty-four

Coe held Skye's hand as they hurried toward Featherly's Bakery, a small establishment he and his brothers had visited when Dad brought them to Sandpoint, or later, as teenagers, when they hung out together. The place looked more run-down than he remembered, or else he was looking at it with the passage of time, and after having traveled to other countries. He chose a table near the window to keep watch for Lake and, possibly, Tip. He was eager to see his brother. But if Tip approached, he wanted some warning. He glanced around the shop and didn't recognize the server behind the counter or the young lady pushing a broom around a few tables, which was unusual considering he used to know everyone here.

"Do you think Lake will be against us getting married?" Skye pressed her lips together, which he accepted as her thoughtful pose.

"No. Why would he?"

"Since he's the oldest, will he have a negative opinion about me?"

"If anyone understands our impromptu marriage, he will." Coe glanced out the window. "The brothers you have to be concerned about are Spur and Wilks, the more mischievous duo. However, Spur is temporarily living in Hawaii."

"Why is he there?"

"Dad thought he needed some guidance in his life."

"Like an intervention?"

"More like a nudge to help him find purpose." Coe's gaze shifted to the door before returning his attention to Skye. "Remember what I told you about our names?"

"That your dad wanted you named after men of faith?"

"Yes. Especially the people who inspired him. We often talked about that with him when we were growing up, you know, about living lives of purpose."

"And Spur didn't have that?"

"After Stone left, I think Dad was worried about him."

"And Wilks?"

Before he could answer, someone entered the bakery, and he turned in that direction. "Lake." He stood as his brother strode toward them, smiling broadly. "Coe!" They hugged, clapping each other on the back.

"Good to see you, man."

"You, too."

They sat down, and Lake thrust out his hand toward Skye. "Hello. I'm Lake, Coe's oldest brother." He grinned like being older was important, even though there was only one year difference between them.

"Hi." She shook his hand. "It's nice to meet you."

"This is Skye, my wife." Coe's heart swelled with pride over his first introduction of her as his wife, and that he was the third North brother to get married recently.

"I've heard a lot about the Norths." Skye gave Lake a timid-looking smile. "I've been anxious about meeting you and the others."

"What concerns you about us?"

"Whether you'll hate me. Considering Coe gave up the chance

of a normal relationship for one like we have, it might not be popular with your family."

"You'd be surprised." Lake chuckled. "You had your reasons for getting married, like Irish and I had ours. You are a North now, so we'll treat you like our sister." Lake rubbed his hand over Coe's hair, messing it up like he did when they were kids. "Although there might be a pesky brother or two who will try some juvenile tricks on you, no one will hate you."

"Tricks?" Skye glanced at Coe.

"Well—"

"The North brothers are notorious for pulling pranks and trying to one-up each other." Lake shook his head. "Poor Irish had to put up with their shenanigans. Trista, too."

"Shall we order?" Coe asked, hoping to move beyond their introductions and any discussion of pranks. He hoped none of his brothers would do anything to cause Skye more worry about the family's acceptance of her.

After they had drinks and pastries, Lake leaned forward, facing Coe. "Are you guys safe? You keep looking out the window."

"Our trip has been fraught with danger, fleeing, and constantly checking over our shoulders." Coe briefly explained the situation that led them to leave India and the ensuing pursuit by Liam's bodyguards. "Someone might be watching us now." He nodded toward the window.

"Is that so?" Lake peered outside. "If you're married, what will they do? Try to return you to India?"

"That's exactly what they plan to do," Skye said solemnly.

"Really?" Lake cast a long look around the room.

"My father is outraged that I left with Coe. He doesn't accept our marriage, or him. He wants to force me into doing what he requires, which is marrying a wealthy supporter of his foundation." She gripped her coffee cup, her knuckles turning white.

"We hoped if we got married, Liam's thugs would leave us alone."

Coe heaved a sigh. "That hasn't happened. Who knows what their next move might be?"

"You have me to help now, and our brothers." Lake lifted his mug to his lips. "How many guys are we talking about?"

"Two of her father's men. A few others were at the airport in New York." Coe shifted in his seat to see the door beyond Lake better. "We don't know how many followed us here."

Lake asked Skye a few questions about her life in India and how she stayed in her father's household, knowing his expectations of her. She gave him some background details that Coe hadn't heard before. Like the lineup of eligible men Liam brought to dinners, showing her off like a prized heifer and how awful she felt about that, and whittling down the group to Edmund Lung, a leering creep, according to her. She shared her experiences of failed attempts to leave India and how heartbreaking that had been. Her explanation made Coe more thankful that the Lord had used him to help her get to America and soon, to his loving family.

He shifted the conversation to inquiring about their parents' house. Lake said he and the others were working on the place, painting walls and installing new appliances while Mom and Dad were away. Since Lake and Hud were footing the bill, and Coe couldn't help financially, he was interested in volunteering with the renovation.

"Count me in. I look forward to helping." He patted Lake's shoulder. Skye glanced sharply at him, and he wondered why, but another thought took precedence. "I can't thank you enough for the loan for the plane tickets and the money it took for us to get here. I appreciate it, man."

"We both do." Skye nodded. "Your help made all the difference."

"I'm glad the finances were useful." Lake raked his fingers over his hair, looking uncomfortable with the topic. "Let's call it a wedding gift from Hud and me, okay?"

"That's too much. I want to pay it back."

"So do I," Skye added.

"If it helped you get home safely, the money was worth every cent. Please accept our gift with all the love it was given from Hud and me. I mean that."

"I don't know what to say, other than thanks." Coe hugged him, feeling grateful for his brother's generosity. "I appreciate it. Thanks, man."

"You're welcome. Have you noticed the guy across the street?" Lake lifted his chin toward the window. "That muscle has been standing by his car, glaring in this direction like he's got an ax to grind with someone."

"Me, no doubt." Coe followed Lake's gaze. "It's Rhett."

"He's here?" Skye groaned.

"His partner won't be far behind." Coe's chest tightened simultaneously with his right fist. "We need a plan to get out of here."

"How about a diversion?" Lake smiled like he already had one in mind.

"That would be great. We could use the help."

"Leave it to me." Lake stood and dropped a tip on the table. "I'll catch up with you later." He exited the building, his shoulders back and stride confident.

Coe met Skye's gaze. "Are you ready to run again?"

"Yes. But I hate that Lake is sticking his neck out for me, too."

"You're my wife, and you are a North now. When someone is against us, we stick together and fight, if necessary."

"Is Lake going to fight Rhett?"

"Nah. He said a diversion."

"Coe—"

"It'll be okay." He clasped her hand and led her out the door. He paused under the awning and peered around the alcove's corner, watching Lake approach Rhett.

"You must be Davis," Lake said boisterously. "Sorry, I'm late." He extended his hand, but Rhett didn't accept the handshake.

"Any second now," Coe whispered.

Rhett glanced toward the bakery, and Lake jerked, grabbing his head and staring at the sky like a rock had fallen and hit him. "What was that? Am I bleeding?"

"Our cue," Coe said. "Come on."

They crept away from the building and ran to their rental while Lake begged for Rhett's assistance and kept calling him Davis. His theatrics gave Coe and Skye time to jump in the car and drive away before Rhett caught on to what was happening.

Skye glanced back. "I thought Rhett might hurt Lake."

"He's good at coming up with creative ideas for getting out of scrapes. That came in handy when we were growing up."

"You two seem close."

"We are." Coe glanced in the rearview mirror as he drove, thankful not to see anyone following them. "Lake, Hud, and I were like three peas in a pod. Sometimes Stone, who is two years younger than me, wormed his way into our circle."

"But you left the pod?"

"We all grew up and moved on." He took a left turn in the direction of Thunder Ridge. "Lake's life revolved around his dogs. Hud moved to Alaska. I left for aid work. Stone took off for who knows where." It felt good to talk about everyday things and not be overwhelmed with fear about Rhett and Tip knowing where they were or following them. Hopefully, Lake would detain Rhett long enough that he couldn't catch up to them. However, it wouldn't be difficult for Liam's thugs to discover the location of the Norths' house in the small community. And it was still possible that Nimrod had found a way to hack their disposable phones.

"Aren't you worried about Lake? Rhett is a trained bodyguard." Skye cast an anxious glance out the back window.

"Lake works with his dogs and lives on twenty acres. He's muscular and capable."

"Runs in the family, huh?" Her voice softened, and Coe caught her gazing at him appreciatively, which made his heart pound. "I had to check out the man I was marrying."

"Oh, yeah?" He would have flexed or puffed up his pecs if he wasn't driving and feeling tense. "It's from all the work I did under the Indian sky," he said semi-modestly.

"Wait." Skye stared at a road sign. "Are you bringing us to Thunder Ridge now?"

"Yes. What's wrong?"

"Shouldn't we have talked about it?" She shot him a glare he intercepted between watching the road and checking the rearview mirror.

"Well. We are running from Rhett. But you're right. I should have mentioned it. When Lake said everyone was helping at my parents' house, I thought—"

"That you'd decide where we would stay tonight?" She shook her head like she couldn't believe it. "I would have questioned it at the bakery, but I didn't want us to argue in front of Lake. Aren't we going to make decisions together? Isn't that what you promised?"

"Yes. That's what I said and meant. I'm sorry." If they weren't heading to Thunder Ridge, he'd have to turn around and drive through Sandpoint again. But where could they go with the little money they had left? He hated using his emergency credit card when he didn't have a job lined up. "Do you mind if we head to my parents' house?" When she didn't answer, he pulled onto the gravel shoulder and parked without shutting off the engine. "You knew we were heading this way eventually. We talked about that."

"Eventually doesn't mean right now." She rubbed the back of her neck. "Are we going to stay at your parents' house when we haven't gotten used to each other yet? We just got married."

"I know. Are you saying you don't want us to continue north?" He tried keeping annoyance out of his tone but was feeling somewhat exasperated. They couldn't keep staying in motels, eating at restaurants, or paying for gas if they had to flee from Liam's men. He should have explained all that before now. A regular husband would have, but they were far from being a normal couple.

"I'm saying we should have discussed it."

"You're right. I apologize." He tapped the steering wheel with his ring. "So, what do you think about us staying in my parents' house for a few days?" He kept his tone light, trying not to sound bossy like she'd accused him of previously. "We could help update my childhood home, have free room and board, and lay low for a week or two." He hoped she understood his unspoken nuance about their limited finances.

"Will we be alone there?"

"No. A couple of my brothers live in the house. They'll move if my parents decide to sell."

"Then where would we go?"

"We'll figure it out together." He'd make sure of that. There was something else he ought to bring up. "Also, if my brothers are a nuisance, we can crash on my grandmother's couch. She lives in a small house behind my parents' place."

"Nuisance, how?" She gazed at him suspiciously.

"Pulling pranks like Lake talked about."

"Coe—"

"I just thought I'd mention it."

"And if Rhett and Tip show up, what then? Weren't you the one who was worried about bringing danger to your family's doorstep?"

"I was, and still am. I hope that doesn't happen."

"But it might."

Yeah. But he hated thinking about what that outcome might mean.

Chapter Twenty-five

They arrived at the Norths' white farmhouse-style home, and Skye was impressed with the beautiful hydrangea, clematis, and rose bushes in front. When all the blossoms opened, it would be a magnificent sight. Everything looked green and lush, and she was eager to check out the apple orchard that Coe told her was in the back. In those first moments at his childhood home, she tried to imagine him as a kid, running and playing here with Lake and the other brothers she hadn't met.

Three of Coe's siblings, Wilks, Sunday, and Finn, were working in the kitchen, pulling up old tiles, when they walked in on them. They looked shocked when they saw Coe and Skye and heard the news of their marriage, yet they exchanged backslaps and hugs with Coe and shook her hand pleasantly. The trio remained polite and friendly throughout the introductions and subsequent conversation. But Skye sensed a tense undercurrent, like an explosive discussion was coming that they wouldn't bring up in front of her. Would they argue after she went upstairs? Were they angry with Coe for marrying a woman he didn't love and bringing her to their parents' house? Their tension amped up her nervousness.

On her way up to get a bath and rest, she heard their voices clearly and paused on the stairway. She shouldn't have continued listening, but she felt frozen to the step.

"What's the deal, Coe?" Wilks's tone reeked of sarcasm. "I thought you, of all people, would marry for love, not for convenience."

"Who says I haven't?" Did he mean that? Skye held her breath, waiting for him to continue.

"Did you?"

When Coe didn't respond, she exhaled. Of course, he didn't love her.

"Is her dad wealthy, too?" That sounded like the youngest, more dramatic brother, Finn.

"Too?" Coe echoed.

"Lake and Hud married to take Grandfather's money, though they promised never to do so. Maybe you married the girl to get her money, huh?"

"No, I did not." Coe sounded agitated.

"Then why the speedy marriage? How could you do this to our family?" Finn's voice rose.

Skye's heart pounded in her temples. She hated being the cause of this strife among brothers.

"We trusted you," Finn said, like he wasn't letting the offense go.

"Yeah," the softer-spoken Sunday said. "Why not marry a nice girl here in Thunder Ridge?"

"Skye is a nice girl." *Coe thinks I'm nice?*

"Why did you get married without telling us?" Wilks demanded. "Why the secrecy? We didn't even know you were coming back today."

"And the place is a mess. Not somewhere to bring your lady love, if she is that," Finn muttered.

Skye yearned to be the one Coe loved, yet knew she wasn't.

"Look. What matters is I'm home. I brought my wife to meet my *loving* family. So behave like respectable Norths and welcome her like the polite people you were raised to be."

"Fine words coming from the guy who broke our pact," Wilks said.

"Yeah," another brother agreed.

"Just let it go, will you?"

"Are you going to make us, big brother?" Wilks asked.

"Maybe I will." *What?*

Some grumbles, groans, and scuffling sounds reverberated through the house. They weren't fighting, were they? Skye's heart pounded.

"Knock it off!" Coe shouted. *What in the world?*

"Back off, old man." Wilks yowled.

"That's the way to show him," Finn cackled.

More scuffling. Something crashed! Should she go down there and check on Coe?

"Now, you broke the chair," Sunday accused.

"It was worth it," Wilks said.

"You'd better fix it."

A silence followed. What were they doing? Glaring at each other? Sending silent signals of rage? Skye leaned over the wooden railing to try to see Coe, but the floorboards creaked, so she stood motionless.

He said something so quietly she couldn't make it out. Then there was an explosion of laughter, guffawing, backslapping, and the abrupt sound of a door slamming shut. Their raucous banter continued outside.

What just happened? What was with these North brothers?

Chapter Twenty-six

Coe wandered upstairs to check on Skye. She'd been in the guest room for a while, and he was concerned that she might feel uncomfortable coming downstairs after the commotion she must have heard and was probably troubled by. He hadn't meant to roughhouse with Wilks. But his infuriating, seven-year-younger brother kept egging him on, so he used some wrestling maneuvers on him. Surprisingly, Wilks gave as good as he got, not letting Coe take him down quickly. However, the skirmish ended amicably, with laughter and camaraderie, and the air felt clearer between him and his brothers.

"Skye?" He knocked on the door. "Can I come in?" If his brothers heard that, they'd wonder why he felt a need to ask. "Skye?"

"Come in."

He opened the door, and she sat on the bed, leaning against the headboard, a golden haze from the bedside lamp splayed over her. She looked relaxed and beautiful, and her soft smile made his heart race. She was his wife. And they were married. He stepped into the room and closed the door, wishing he were already the husband he wanted to be and had all the liberties that entailed. *But you're not. And don't. So tone down the emotions, North.*

"Are you okay?" she asked. "You look pale."

"I'm all right. I thought I'd check on you." He felt slightly out of breath, like he'd run up the stairs at full speed. "How are you doing?"

"I'm fine. Taking it all in."

"The Norths are a lot to take in, aren't they?" He sat gingerly on the edge of the bed.

"Kind of." She swung her feet down and scooted beside him as if she were unaffected by the complex feelings he was experiencing. "So, what's the plan?"

"Plan?"

"Food. Figuring out what's next." She squinted at him. "Were you fighting with Wilks?"

"Not fighting. I put him in a headlock."

"As in wrestling?"

"Yeah. It's something we used to do. Still do, sometimes." He cringed, realizing how juvenile that sounded when he wanted her to see him as a man, her husband.

"Aren't you a little old for that?"

"No doubt. Lake and I still like to show our younger brothers we are tougher and wiser." Grinning, he flexed his arm.

"Your family is a strange and intriguing group."

"We play hard and love—" He barely stopped himself from saying "passionately."

Her face turned rosy. "Are we going to get something to eat? I'm hungry."

He wasn't just hungry but aching with a hunger that felt close to starvation. He yearned to take Skye in his arms and kiss her until she knew how much he cared for her and wanted her for his honest-to-goodness wife.

"Coe?" She waved her hand in front of his face. "Is there any food around here?"

"Right. Food. Wilks is ordering pizza."

"Good. I hope he orders two."

"I like that you appreciate fine food." He chuckled.

"I wouldn't call pizza *fine food*."

"No? Pizza is a fine dining experience in this household, especially if it's from Singers' Pizzeria." Coe held his arms in a wide circle, glad for their discussion about food, which took his thoughts off kissing her. "They make the largest family-sized pepperoni pizza you've ever seen. With our huge family, size matters."

"My dad and I didn't need a large pizza."

He imagined how overwhelming being around his rowdy brothers must be compared to her sedentary home life with Liam. "If things seem too weird here—"

"They'll get better?"

"I was going to say sorry." He shrugged, recalling the roasting he got from his brothers about bringing an unexpected wife home.

"I am wondering about something."

"What is it?" He wanted to clasp her hand, but after his intense feelings of longing to kiss her, he didn't trust himself to stop at just holding her hand.

"I heard what you guys were talking about. I shouldn't have been listening, but your voices got louder, and my curiosity got the better of me."

"I should have made them go outside for that conversation."

"Or had it while I was present?" She gave him an annoyed look. "I can answer my own questions. Your discussion made me feel more like an outsider." She picked at a nail. "If we plan to make this work, I need to feel like I'm becoming part of your family."

If we plan to make this work? He felt her words like a slug in the gut. Did she doubt his intentions even after they said vows and he'd stood up to his brothers?

"I didn't want you pelted with awkward questions right off." Coe lifted his chin toward the door. "They bombarded me about why I married you."

"Why is that? I could tell our marriage bugged them, even more than I imagined it might."

Coe hated digging up old history, but Skye should hear the truth from him. "It goes back to us brothers pledging we'd never marry for any reason other than love." Heat crept up his neck at the admission.

"You did?" Her face blanched.

"Just kids' stuff."

"That's what Wilks meant about a pact. No wonder he despises me."

"Hey, now. No one despises you." He tipped up her chin until their gazes met. "We chose each other, didn't we? That's what matters."

"But there's so much we don't know about each other."

"So, we'll learn." He kissed her cheek. "I'd marry you again tomorrow if I had the opportunity." She squinted at him doubtfully. "I mean it."

She didn't comment, and he didn't push to find out what she was thinking

Chapter Twenty-seven

With a fluttering in her stomach, Skye followed Coe along a narrow stone path toward a cottage behind the Norths' house. She was about to meet his eighty-eight-year-old grandmother, a family member he spoke highly of and with much admiration. What would the woman who helped raise him think of his unexpected bride? Skye breathed deeply, taking in the fresh spring air, and the scent of apple trees drew her attention as Coe knocked on the door. The cluster of trees in the Norths' orchard, coming out of dormancy and with all the new buds starting to open, seemed like a promise of good things to come. *Please, God.*

"Don't worry," Coe said before entering. How could she not worry? "Gran?"

"Coe, is that you?" A white-haired woman with a broad smile and sparkling light green eyes shuffled from a room to the side of the living room.

"It's me, Gran." He rushed over and clung to her in a long embrace.

"My dear boy, it's so good to see you." Coe's grandmother sniffled and patted his shoulder. "I'm thankful beyond measure that you made it home safely. Praise God!" She leaned back and set both wrinkled hands along his cheeks, gazing affectionately at him. "I've missed you, and I've missed our late-night talks and brownie baking sessions."

"Me too, Gran."

At Coe's and his grandmother's words of love and affection for one another, Skye's eyes welled with tears. She couldn't help but feel emotional and a bit jealous of the childhood moments she had missed while imagining Coe as a young boy embracing his grandmother.

Coe turned toward her. "Gran, this is Skye, my wife." A wide grin crossed his face, and she felt in awe of the genuine warmth he extended toward her. Maybe he meant what he said about them falling for each other and staying together forever.

"Oh, my goodness." Coe's grandmother held out her arms, and Skye also melted into her embrace. "Welcome to our family, my dear. I'm so thankful the Lord brought you and Coe together and helped you get home safely. *His* plans are marvelous and wondrous, aren't they? I'm Trish, Gran, or Granny Trish, whichever you feel comfortable calling me."

"Thank you." Skye stepped back, feeling overwhelmed and cherished at the same time. "And thanks for the heartwarming welcome. I've missed a woman's hug since I lost my mom when I was ten."

"I'm sorry for your loss." Trish smoothed her palm over Skye's hair lovingly. "I admire your name. Skye is poetic, isn't it?"

"Maybe. My mom loved the color of the sky."

"Me too." Trish's grin spread out the fine wrinkles around her mouth. Her warmhearted personality made her even more beautiful. "What we need in this family are more women. I was grateful to the Lord for sending Olivia to Smith." Trish shuffled toward an easy chair, and Coe assisted her as she sat down. "How would my boy have gotten his wish of a big family otherwise?"

"They were meant to be together." Coe's wink in Skye's direction made her heart flutter. Was he saying they were meant to be together, too?

"Indeed, they were." Trish nodded at a large family portrait on the wall, featuring nine boys of varying ages, from young children to older teenagers. Each boy's grinning face looked either mischievous or playful, yet Skye noticed something warmly irresistible in their expressions, too.

Coe waved for her to join him on the couch, and she did. He put his arm over her shoulder, and she experienced a rare feeling of belonging and contentment. Did she belong with this man she married? Would she always feel connected with him? She hoped he wasn't putting on a show for his grandmother, trying to make her believe they were already in love. Despite her apprehension, the coziness of resting beside him and the familiar scent of his spicy deodorant pleased her, even comforted her. She listened as Coe told Trish about their race across the country and why, although he noticeably left out the more dangerous aspects of their journey.

"So your father is a bit of a rapscallion?" Trish asked.

"Yes. He takes being an overprotective parent to a herculean level."

"Can you blame him for wanting to protect you?"

Was Trish taking Father's side? Did she imagine all parents, Liam Tamarack included, were caring parents who doted on their children and raised them to follow God's ways? Skye tried shoving down the irate feelings that surfaced too rapidly. Trish didn't mean anything offensive.

"I'm sure your father loves you no matter what he feels about your leaving his household." Trish palmed her chest, her gnarled-looking fingers curling. "If I overstepped, I apologize. I have no right to comment about your challenging circumstances." She sighed. "It's been my pleasure to raise one son and help raise his brood, but I don't mean to sound like a know-it-all."

"Now, Gran. You have been a wealth of wisdom and love to us guys. We all appreciate what you've done and how you prayed for us and guided us through our growing-up years." Coe looked compellingly at Skye like he hoped she'd say something positive or affirming.

What could she say? How could either of these two, who enjoyed a loving family dynamic, understand the pain she had gone through with Father, who was not as kind and caring as Coe's grandmother?

"What a privilege it has been." Trish wiped her eyes with a purple floral hanky.

"It's been a privilege to be raised by you and Mom and Dad." Coe clasped his grandmother's hand and smiled affectionately at her. "When I was in India, I felt your prayers. It was comforting to know you were thinking of me and praying."

"Aww, Coe." Trish patted his cheek like she did earlier.

Skye had missed so much family support without a mom or grandmother for the last two decades. After listening to Coe and Trish chatting and laughing about their family news, she worked up the courage to mention what he'd skimmed over before, intentionally or not. "I'm sorry to say my father will stop at nothing to force me to return to him, which makes me fear for your safety."

"Skye—" Coe shook his head.

"She needs to know the truth."

"What's this?" Trish glanced between them. "Is our family in danger?"

Coe flicked a sharp glance at Skye. What? Wasn't he obligated to warn everyone in his family of the potential risk? She couldn't bear the thought of Trish being in the dark about it. Was he planning to explain it more thoroughly to her when she wasn't present, like he did with his brothers? Was that how he thought their marriage would work? With him talking about important matters behind her back and making all the decisions? Her chin hiked up, as if a string were attached to it.

"Yes, the threat is real," she spoke firmly.

"But hopefully, nothing will happen," Coe countered.

"There will likely be an attempt to kidnap me." Skye stared at him stubbornly. "Others could get hurt."

"But God has been watching over us every step from India to Thunder Ridge." He nodded toward his grandmother. "*He* will protect us."

Skye didn't like him silencing her, although she understood his desire to reassure Trish and help her feel safe. Still, the older woman deserved to know the whole truth, not just the comfortable one.

"I believe that." Trish clasped Coe's hand. "But you think there might be trouble?"

"Yes," Skye said.

"I hate to cause you alarm." Coe gave his grandmother a concerned look.

"My ticker can take more vexing news than you think." Trish wagged her finger at him. "Hearing the entire story is better than hearing half-truths. Understood?"

"Yes, ma'am," he said contritely, and Skye bit back a chuckle at his crestfallen expression. "Skye's dad sent some mean guys to follow and detain us. They used force to stop us, but with God's help, we escaped."

"Force? Escape? Oh, my dear boy. Were you injured?"

"Not—"

"Only slightly. Father will stop at nothing to get me back and wants payback for Coe helping me."

"Payback?" Trish gasped. "Coe, what are you going to do about this?"

"I'm going to protect my wife and family the best I can." His muscled arm tightened around Skye. Even though she didn't need a man taking care of her, his arm wrapping her in a cocoon of safety, if only symbolically, felt reassuring and overrode some of her irritation with him.

She set her hand over Trish's gently. "I promise that Coe and I will do everything we can to keep you safe."

"I can tell you are going to be dear to me. Like I said, our family needs more women."

"What am I, chopped onions?" Coe asked in faux offense.

"I wasn't going to mention the smell I detected when you came in." Trish put her hand over her mouth and chuckled.

"What?" Coe sniffed his armpits.

Skye giggled. Her introduction to the matriarch of the North family had gone better than she expected. Someday, would she feel comfortable enough to call her Gran, too?

Chapter Twenty-eight

.

Later that night, Coe stood indecisively outside the guest room door. Should he sleep in the same room as Skye when his brain kept replaying their kisses and how he felt when he was holding her? The house had enough beds, so they didn't have to share a room. However, if he chose one of the other bedrooms, his brothers would be more suspicious about their marriage's legitimacy. Besides, he wanted to be near Skye if Rhett and Tip tried breaking in. He'd explained the safety concerns to his younger brothers, so Wilks volunteered to crash on Gran's couch. The other two were watching a movie in the living room, supposedly keeping watch.

"Skye?" He knocked. He could always sleep on the floor.

"I'm awake."

His heart pounded in his throat as he opened the door to the darkened room, seeing only a dim night-light shining near the floor. "Are you okay?"

"I'm all right. Wilks saying it was easy to climb a ladder and get into this room was troubling."

"I'm sorry. He likes to tease." He eased onto the side of the bed closest to the door, staying as far as he could from Skye and remaining on the mattress. If an intruder entered, he'd be the first to see him, but the window was on her side. "Are you okay with me sleeping on the bed?" He scooted against the headboard, fully dressed.

"I guess. You said we'll take our time getting to know each other, and I believe you."

He wanted to be worthy of her trust and someday, her love. "Would you feel better if I slept on the floor?" He sat up, planning to move if she said yes.

"Do you want to sleep on the floor?"

"Not especially."

"Then stay where you are and go to sleep."

Sighing, he rested against the pillows and turned so he wasn't facing her. Telling his heart to stop racing and that this was no different from when they slept platonically at the motel, he closed his eyes. He planned to pray silently for a few minutes before falling asleep. Only sleep didn't come quickly.

"May I ask you a question?" Skye asked.

"Sure."

"Why did you kiss me back at my father's house?"

"You want to talk about that now?"

"I would if you don't mind."

He groaned and inched closer to the edge of the mattress until he nearly rolled off.

"I was lying here thinking about how all this came to be—you and me on the run, getting married, and sharing a bed, but not really." She made a gulping sound.

Even with two feet between them, he wasn't in the right frame of mind to talk about anything personal, especially not about kissing. "I'll answer your questions about anything you want to discuss, but can this wait until morning?" Did she hear the desperation in his voice?

"Okay. Good night, then."

"Good night." He sighed in relief.

"One other thing," she said after a minute.

"What's that?"

"It seemed you didn't like me telling your grandmother the truth about Rhett and Tip's persistence in trying to take me back."

The reminder renewed his tension, which distracted him from wanting to kiss her. "I didn't want Gran to worry."

"I figured. But she deserved to know what might happen. Good night."

"'Night."

After a while, he heard her soft breathing like she'd fallen asleep. He listened for any unusual noises downstairs. Sunday and Finn trudged up the stairs, and their bedroom doors closed. The next hour ticked by gradually. Coe alternated between praying and listening to the sounds in the house until he finally felt himself relaxing.

He awoke with morning light streaming across the empty bed. *Empty?* He sat up abruptly. Was Skye taking a shower? Had someone managed to slip past him and snatch her away? He jumped up and ran into the hallway. The bathroom door stood ajar, the light off. His heart pounding, tension rushing through him, he jogged downstairs. "Skye? Skye!" He flung open the front door. "Skye!"

"Coe?" He spun around at the sound of her voice. With an apron tied around her middle and flour smudges on her cheeks, she emerged from the narrow pantry door with a bag of powdered sugar. "What's all the commotion? I'm making breakfast." She'd cleared some counter space, and the electric griddle was set up. Only then did he notice the aroma of sausage and eggs in the air. He should have paid attention to the room's delicious scents before rushing to the door.

"Nothing." He exhaled his feeling of panic. "I'm glad to see you're okay." He crossed the room and embraced her.

"What's wrong?" She leaned back, peering at him.

"I woke up, and you were gone. I feared the worst."

"Aww. You are my knight in shining armor."

"Am I?" Gazing into her dark, shining eyes, he wondered what she really thought of him. A knight in shining armor sounded good, but he wanted to be so much more to her. He tipped her back slowly, and her inviting smile seemed to beg him to do what he'd wanted to do since their last kiss. He brushed his lips across hers, kissing her tenderly and sweetly, and sparks of electricity raced through his sensors as she kissed him back.

"What's going on here?" Wilks slammed the back door.

Coe and Skye jumped apart, her face turning pink and his heart pounding like a runaway train. He set his arm over her shoulder and drew her to his side. "Just some marital affection, if you don't mind." He glared at his brother, giving him a visual warning.

"Maybe you like each other a little then, hm?" He sniffed the air. "What smells so good?"

"Egg and sausage casserole." Skye moved away from Coe. "French toast will be ready shortly."

"You can cook?" Wilks sounded astonished.

"What's that supposed to mean?" Skye set a fist on her hip and squinted at him.

"Just that I'm surprised a pampered princess like you knows how to cook. I'll get the coffee going." Wilks crossed the room to the coffee-making ensemble, and Coe was tempted to put him in another headlock.

"Sorry," he mouthed to Skye.

Rolling her eyes, she returned to working with the food on the griddle.

After Coe ran back upstairs and freshened up, he returned and helped arrange a buffet on the island, setting out plates, silverware, and condiments at one end. While he worked, he thought about Skye's kisses and how he'd like every morning to begin like that, minus the part about his brother intruding.

When the food was ready, he piled his plate high, ready to eat before they started working on the house. Sunday and Finn joined them, and they discussed the tasks they needed to accomplish before Mom and Dad returned—painting the cupboards, updating the flooring, and replacing the appliances.

"Lake's picking up a fridge and stove in Spokane," Wilks said. "Why don't you and your wife do the painting? Finn and I will finish ripping up the tiling."

"No can do." Finn stuffed a forkful of casserole in his mouth. After he chewed, he said, "I'm working with Lake and Irish's dogs today. Then I have practice for *Robin Hood*."

"Oh, right. Are you the lead in this one?" Coe recalled he'd been the lead actor in several local theater productions while he was away.

"Yep. I won't be available to work much this week. You all have fun with the manual labor."

"Way to wimp out," Wilks said.

"What about you?" Finn challenged. "Why aren't you working at the coffee shop?"

"No comment." Wilks stuffed several bites in his mouth.

"So, you clam up if we badger you about stuff when you question us about everything?"

"I have some unexpected time off, that's all."

"Meaning you lost your job?" Sunday asked pointedly.

"Leave it alone." Wilks pierced his younger siblings with a stern look. "End of discussion."

"And if I don't?" Finn's eyebrows shot up.

Wilks stood abruptly. "Then we have a problem."

"Guys." Coe palmed the air. "Let's focus on what needs to be done here. Skye and I are available to help. If you need to head back to your jobs, go."

"Seriously?" Wilks tossed a scant glance at Skye. "Other than cooking, what can she do?"

Skye leaped to her feet, scowling at him. "I'll have you know I've worked in unbelievably poor conditions, repairing and rebuilding houses and roads."

"That's the truth," Coe said, feeling proud of her.

"I've assisted in installing or repairing anything that needed to be fixed or replaced in a house." She jabbed the air with her finger with each point. "I've also shoveled mud and rock, nursed the injured, helped birth babies, and hauled heavy water buckets that would make you cry in pain by the end of the day. Have you done anything like that?" Wilks's jaw dropped. "Don't you dare look down on me because I'm a woman! It didn't go well for the last man who underestimated me."

Coe stood and put his arm over her shoulder. "My wife is a diligent worker. I'd watch what I say if I were you, Wilks."

"I apologize for implying you can't do some things. You're obviously—"

"What? Weak? Female?"

"No. I was going to say you're tougher than I thought." Wilks plopped back into his seat.

"And don't forget it." Skye sat down, her eyes flashing with defiance or frustration, and picked up her fork, jabbing at chunks of French toast.

Returning to his seat, Coe chuckled inwardly. Skye was gritty and determined not to let anyone, including his brothers, tell her what she could or couldn't do. *Bring it on, Skye North.*

Chapter Twenty-nine

Skye finished painting a second coat of a deep ocean blue on the kitchen's upper cupboard doors and climbed down the ladder. She had been at it for hours and was ready for a break. She still trembled whenever she contemplated how courageously she stood up to Wilks at breakfast. Where did that boldness come from? She'd never spoken to Father so insistently, and he was the ultimate chauvinist. She should have called him on his arrogant attitude long ago. Hopefully, she wasn't taking out her frustration with him on Wilks. *Was I?* She groaned.

"Are you okay?" Coe was kneeling on the floor, painting the lower edge of a cupboard door.

"I could use a walk. What do you think of getting out of here for a while?"

"That sounds good." He stroked the paintbrush across the wooden surface a few more times. "Let me finish this, then I'll be ready."

"Are you hungry yet?"

Their gazes met, and the air seemed to crackle with palpable tension. She meant a hunger for food, but her thoughts raced back to the fervent kiss they shared, and her heart pounded like a drumbeat she feared Coe might hear. And the look of anticipation or desire he gave her? If a fire could ignite based on such a look, they'd have to run out of the house.

"Sure," he said huskily.

She wrapped her paintbrush in plastic wrap to use later, staying busy and trying hard to avoid contemplating kissing her husband again. Thinking of him as her husband and the closeness they would eventually share stirred something tender in her heart toward him, but also made her a little nervous. She hurried into the bathroom to wash the dried smudges off her hands, leaving the door ajar.

A few moments later, he came up behind her and met her gaze in the mirror. "Mind if I have a turn at the sink?" He held up his blue-speckled hands.

"Go ahead." She moved out of his way and playfully flicked a few water droplets at him.

"Hey, now. If I splash you, you'll have blue freckles."

"No thanks." She grabbed a paper towel and dried off her hands but secretly wished he would do something to flirt with her, especially after the glances they'd exchanged and the thoughts she'd been thinking.

"We should stick close to the house today." He turned on the water and grabbed the soap.

Should? Her thoughts of flirting fled. "Why?"

"It's safer here." He lathered his hands, the suds turning bluish. "I want to put off Rhett and Tip finding us for as long as possible."

"Oh." Some of her tension eased away. He was trying to keep them safe, not telling her what she could and couldn't do. But the lack of freedom to do what she wanted grated on her, a conflict she couldn't ignore. "I still need some exercise."

"We can walk over to the church and back. It's not far."

"Any chance of getting some lunch, too?" Despite her big breakfast, she was feeling hungry.

"Uh. I need to talk with you about our money situation."

"Sounds ominous. Does that mean getting lunch is off the table?"

"Probably. We can eat anything in the fridge." He grabbed a couple of paper towels and gave her a look she couldn't decipher. "While we walk, we should have one of those married discussions about finances."

Ugh. Had they burned through Lake's funds already? Did Coe think that was her fault?

Their walk through the neighborhood, with the ornamental trees starting to bloom, their delicate spring buds a beautiful sight, and the tiny wildflowers emerging through the grass, painted a delightful scene that did wonders for her senses and relieved some of her inner tension. After a couple of blocks of silence, she thought of a topic that might lighten the mood between them before Coe brought up finances again. "What did you think of us sharing a bedroom last night when we aren't in love? Should we discuss that, too?" She wanted to burst out laughing over his dropped-jaw expression.

"Let's not overly complicate things."

"Isn't it already complicated? The second we left Dubai, our lives became more complex."

"I'd say it did as soon as we kissed." His voice softened like he was mentally reliving their momentous kiss that started this whole thing between them.

Hearing the tenderness in his voice, she tempered her tone. "Even before our lips touched, I wanted to get to know you better."

"I wanted to know more about you, too." He clasped her hand, and she felt more of her frustrations easing, and she realized how comfortable she felt with Coe holding her hand.

"Why didn't you ask me out or flirt with me, then?"

"You were the boss's daughter. Wouldn't you have had to ask Liam for permission to date me?"

"Either that or sneak around."

"Then Rhett and Tip would have chased me away sooner."

She groaned. "I don't like imagining what they'll do if they come after us now." She glanced back, relieved to see an empty sidewalk behind them.

"Let's hope they've given up."

"We both know that isn't happening."

He drew her to a stop and stroked some hair off her cheek, his fingers barely grazing her skin, and her heart raced. "I want you to feel safe here with me. I will protect you." He spoke confidently. Yet Skye knew what Rhett and Tip were like and what they were capable of doing.

Coe's gaze locked with hers, and intense feelings like she'd felt back at the house rushed through her, making her long to forget about Father's bodyguards and focus on her husband. She wished Coe would kiss her like he did earlier, removing any doubts about their marriage or their chances of falling in love. But why was she waiting for him to make the first move? She could start something romantic with him. "Coe?" A warm, inviting look filled his gaze, and she took a chance, pressing her lips to his, initiating a slow, lingering kiss that made her heart pound with anticipation and desire for more. He engaged with her, kissing her deeply and affectionately.

"Sweet Skye," he whispered and wrapped his arms around her, and the sound of a passing car scarcely registered.

"Was that okay? Me kissing you, I mean?" She hated feeling even slightly insecure.

"It's more than okay." He kissed her a few more times, toying with her ear and hair, his eyes sparkling. "You can kiss me anytime you want and as much as you want."

"I'll try to remember that."

"I hope you do." He clasped her hand again, and they walked farther down the street. She sighed contentedly, feeling a sense of belonging with Coe, a connection that seemed to transcend their physical touch. "If anyone comes after you, I will do everything in my power to protect you. So will my brothers." His words were like a splash of icy water after all the warm feelings she'd been experiencing.

"I don't want anyone getting injured because of me." She tugged on his hand, bringing him to a stop again. "How can you act calmly about what might happen if Rhett and Tip show up at your parents' house?"

"I haven't forgotten about that. But I'm mostly focused on what's before me. And what is before me is my lovely wife, whom I'd like to get to know better." His radiant smile and the way his chin dimpled were irresistible, and her insides turned to mush.

"I'd like to get to know you better, too, Coe."

"I'm glad." He brushed butterfly kisses along her cheek, ending with some delightful kisses on her mouth that sent her thoughts spiraling toward a real marriage and future with him.

"Shall we continue our walk, Mrs. North?"

"If you promise me one thing, Mr. North."

"What's that?"

"That you'll always kiss me." She was navigating unknown territory but kept going, trying to share her heart. "Even if we quarrel or have hurt feelings toward each other, let's find each other and kiss like we just did."

"I promise."

Chapter Thirty

As they neared his home church, Coe felt the lingering warmth of their shared romantic encounter. The glances they kept sending each other, the way their fingers were linked, and the powerful emotions he was feeling, knowing Skye was his wife and he was her husband, were like a comforting fire in his heart. However, the impending discussion about their financial situation loomed over him, threatening to dampen his upbeat mood.

It was hard for him not to feel a twinge of inadequacy, knowing Skye had been raised with every luxury. The prospect of discussing their financial situation was daunting, but as a husband, facing uncomfortable talks was part of his job, wasn't it? But that wasn't a part of married life he looked forward to, especially considering the stark contrast in their backgrounds.

He'd been raised in a household of twelve, so stretching their money and resources was a way of life. Mom and Gran made their family's meager budget reach farther by growing a vegetable garden and small orchard, buying local meats and produce in bulk, and making the kids wear hand-me-downs. How would Skye do with a limited income after her cushy lifestyle as Liam Tamarack's daughter? He groaned inwardly.

"Thunder Ridge Fellowship. Pastor Smith North," she read from the sign on the church's manicured lawn as they approached it.

"Dad has pastored here for thirty-five years. I cut my teeth on the wooden pews, so to speak." A troubling thought, other than their upcoming money talk, crossed his mind and must have shown on his face.

"Is something wrong?"

"My dad wants to chat with me when he gets back."

"About us?"

"It's probably nothing." No reason to worry her. Still, he said, "There's a chance he wants me to apply."

"For what?"

"The pastoral position."

"Here?" Her eyes widened toward the large old church building.

Before he could explain, a woman with stylishly short hair and a friendly smile strode down the church steps toward them. "No way! It can't be Coe North."

"Jazzy?" He grinned at his old friend and childhood playmate. "It's good to see you."

"You, too." They shared a hug, then Jazzy stepped back, glancing between him and Skye.

"Skye, this is Jazzy Martin. We grew up together."

"So much so, I thought I was a North, switched at birth, or something." Jazzy laughed in a way that sounded as familiar as his brothers' laughter.

"I'm Skye North." Skye extended her hand before Coe had a chance to finish introducing her. "Coe and I recently got married." Coe kicked himself for not jumping in and saying that part right away.

"Married?" Jazzy's jaw dropped, and she shot Coe a shocked look as she shook Skye's hand. "Why am I the last to find out? Congratulations!"

"Thanks. No one knows outside the family. It's a long story, but it's hush-hush, especially about where we're staying."

"You have my curiosity piqued. Does Irish know you're back? She hasn't mentioned anything." Jazzy glanced at her phone as if checking for messages.

"Lake knows, so I assume she does."

"And the brothers approve of you two?" Jazzy's gaze ricocheted between them. "Even Wilks?"

"He almost threw me out last night." Skye rolled her eyes. "So, I wouldn't say he approves."

"You know Wilks," Coe added.

"Don't I, though? One day, a strong-willed woman will put him in his place." Jazzy patted Skye's shoulder. "Don't worry. You'll get used to the North brothers and their pranks."

Skye groaned.

"Hopefully, they've outgrown that," Coe said, trying to sound reassuring.

"Not according to Irish." A somber, nervous-looking expression crossed Jazzy's face. "Any chance you've heard from Stone lately?"

"No. Have you?" The mention of the brother who'd wandered far from the family and faith sent sharp arrows of concern to his heart, stirring up a mix of worry and regret. Why hadn't he been more aware of Stone's struggles and tried harder to help him before he left the country?

"Not in seventeen months." Jazzy twisted her purse strap around her fingers, her gaze homed in on the church. "I wish he'd call and tell someone he's alive."

"Me too. If I get the chance, I'll let him know you're concerned about him."

"Please don't." She cleared her throat, her eyes widening as they met his. "I'm nervous about what trouble he might have gotten himself into, that's all." Coe wondered why the mention of Stone made her seem so tense. She nodded toward a dark green car parked nearby. "I have to get to work. It was great seeing you, Coe. Nice to meet you, Skye. Good luck with the North brothers." She nearly ran to the vehicle.

"Thanks. I might need it."

"Hey, Jazzy. I forgot to say congratulations," Coe called. "I heard you had a baby."

"Yes, I did." She pivoted back, smiling proudly. "At eight months old, she's a darling and a terror. But she's the best thing that's ever happened to me."

"If you need anything—"

"We're good. I work at the animal shelter with Irish and live with my grandmother." Jazzy jumped into the car and drove away, waving.

"She's lively," Skye said. "I don't get why your brothers play tricks on each other, though."

"You'd have to experience life in a household of nine rowdy boys to understand. Jazzy was a girl we knew from church and school who fit in with our crew."

"Did you and her ever—?"

"No. She was a fellow baseball player and snowball fighter, that's it." Coe linked his fingers with Skye's the way they'd been before and checked both sides of the street for any sign of Rhett or Tip. "We should head back."

"Did she have a thing for any of your brothers?" Skye asked as they walked.

"I don't know. Why are you asking me about this?"

"She seemed so happy to see you." Skye gave him a probing look.

"We were all friends." Had Jazzy ever flirted with any of his brothers? She and Hud dated briefly. He heard her and Stone arguing once. "Jazzy is Lake's age, and our moms have been friends since they were babies. Her grandmother was Dad's secretary."

Skye nodded like she was contemplating what he'd said.

They walked silently for a few minutes before he recalled the topic he still needed to bring up. "Skye? We, uh, the thing is, we don't have much money left."

"Oh." She shrugged. "I have plenty if Father would let me have it." Her tone revealed her frustration with the matter.

"I have an emergency credit card if things get too tight. However, I'd rather not have to use it."

"I understand. I'm willing to do anything to help."

"Thanks. We'll have to look for work soon. God will provide." He felt relieved she took the news so well, better than he'd imagined. His phone vibrated. "Yeah?"

"Rhett is asking around town about you and Skye," Lake said without preamble.

Shivers raced up Coe's spine. "Thanks for the heads-up. We're on our way to the house." He stuffed his phone in his pocket.

"What is it?" Skye asked.

"That was Lake. Rhett's in town, asking about us." He held out his hand to her, and she clasped it. "Let's get back quickly."

"Okay."

They took off, jogging along the familiar street from the church to his childhood home, the comforting sights and sounds of Thunder Ridge surrounding them. Only the awareness of Rhett and Tip being in town, and possibly, watching them, made Coe's heart pound harder.

Chapter Thirty-one

Why were they sitting in Trish's house when Skye would rather be checking train schedules or talking with Coe about taking a long drive out of state and getting as far away from his parents' and grandmother's houses as possible? But he insisted they come here before making any decisions.

How long would it be before Rhett and Tip arrived at the Norths' house? She shuddered at the memory of other times Father's men caught up with her and restrained her, forcing her back to the Tamarack fortress—not that it was a fortress. Still, it had sometimes felt like it, especially with his bodyguards always on duty. She couldn't shake off the worry about Rhett and Tip's pending arrival, which only added to her anxiety. What kind of force would they use to achieve their objective this time?

"Are you going to confront them?" Trish asked after Coe explained their situation.

"Liam's security team is aggressive. They still want to take Skye back to India."

She heard the tremor in Coe's voice, and his gaze met hers with a panicked or worried look. Was he afraid of Rhett and Tip dragging her from him and beating him up to capture her? Was he concerned about his family, his grandmother?

If those two degenerates did their worst and she never saw Coe again, how would she feel? Of course, she'd kick, scratch, and punch them to avoid being taken. There was no way she'd accept their actions passively. But how would she feel if they succeeded, and she never saw Coe again? She was growing accustomed to his gentle touch and kisses. More than growing accustomed to them, if she was being honest. She yearned for his affection with an unquenchable longing. She couldn't let Father snuff out what had barely started between them.

"Isn't your father's wish to choose a husband for you a moot point?" Trish twisted a hanky between her swollen-looking fingers. "Can't you explain that you are already married?

"I did, but he is still demanding my return."

"I've never heard of anything like this." Tears welled in Trish's eyes, and she clasped Skye's and Coe's hands loosely. A knot formed in Skye's throat at the endearing look she gave them. "But I know the One who can take care of every problem and injustice we ever experience. *He* can change things and make even bad situations turn around for our good."

Skye met Coe's gaze, and he nodded, smiling slightly. Is this why he wanted to come to his grandmother's house? To get Trish's spiritual guidance and prayer?

"Dear Lord." Trish raised her teary eyes toward the ceiling and smiled radiantly as if she were gazing right into heaven or at Jesus. "We need You now more than ever. We're bringing our cares and concerns to You, because You love us so much and know what we are going through. Help us, today. Help us to walk in Your footsteps and carry Your love like a treasure."

"Yes, Lord Jesus," Coe whispered.

Skye's heart turned prayerful, too. *God in heaven, help us. Bring about good in this situation, like Trish said. Don't let any of the Norths get harmed because of me. Please stop Father's plans. And help Coe and me stay together. I do want to fall in love with him.*

"You have an amazing plan for our lives that far exceeds our thoughts and wishes," Trish continued praying and gently squeezed Skye's hand. "You did a wonderful thing in bringing Coe and Skye together and getting them home safely. Thank You for that, and what You are going to do in their lives in the future."

Had God brought her and Coe together and led them to Thunder Ridge to start a new life together? Being with Coe these last few days had been unlike anything she'd imagined when she hoped to choose a husband. It felt like she was in the throes of a colossal crush on this guy she'd married, a feeling that both confused and thrilled her.

"Dear Lord, please keep danger from our doorstep. Keep Coe and Skye safe by Your angels and unseen power. And, please, give them wisdom which surpasses all understanding." Trish released their hands. "In Jesus's name we pray."

Coe and Skye said, "Amen."

Coe hugged Trish, clinging to her. Skye imagined him doing that when he was a boy and later when he was preparing to leave the country without knowing when he'd return. Seeing them embrace and witnessing their strong emotional connection, she once again felt an ache of longing for the familial ties she'd lost. *I miss you, Mom.*

"I'm glad you are still here with us, Gran." Coe's voice broke, and his tender emotions touched Skye.

"Me too, dear boy. I prayed for you every day while you were away."

"Thank you." Coe wiped his fingers beneath his eyes.

Skye was thankful to have met and married such a kind, tender-hearted man. *He is nothing like Father.* She needed to remember that when she was feeling frustrated with him or overwhelmed by their circumstances. *Coe is a good man who has done everything he can to help me.* How many men would have done the things he did to bring her to safety? Gratefulness welled up in her, and she felt herself giving in to some emotions, too.

"Your prayers sustained me," Coe said.

"Our Lord, in all His goodness and grace, sustained you." Trish nodded.

"I am certain of that." Coe wrapped his arms around Skye. "He led me to you, too." Tears flooded her eyes, and she didn't resist them. "That's why Rhett and Tip's plots won't work." He gazed at her earnestly. "What do you want to do? Do you want us to run again? Or shall we stay here, hold our ground, and not let your father's men bully us anymore?"

She was glad he was asking for her opinion. "If we stay, what then?"

"I will tell those men what I think of their rude actions," Trish declared.

"Now, Gran. I'm Skye's husband. If anyone is going to address their behavior, it'll be me." His fervency made Skye smile.

"If Olivia were here, she'd grab a bullhorn and shout those men off her property." Trish's sentiment made Skye more curious about her mother-in-law.

"Would your mom do that?"

"She calls herself a mama bear, so probably."

"Your husband had two strong women in his life growing up." Trish's eyes twinkled. "His mother and me."

"That's right." Coe clasped one of Trish's and Skye's hands. "Now I have three strong women in my life." He released Trish's hand and gazed solely at Skye. "If you want us to hop in the car and extend our rental, we can head for Montana. Hud and Trista are there. What do you say?"

Feeling thankful he'd asked for her opinion, she spent a moment silently praying and asking the Lord for divine guidance. The lyrics of an old hymn came to mind. *"Where He leads me, I will follow."* She pondered the words, then turned toward Coe. "Do you believe God led us to Thunder Ridge?"

"I do."

"Then, with His help, let's stay and face whatever we need to face together."

"*Together* sounds wonderful."

Chapter Thirty-two

After the emergency text Coe sent his brothers, he expected them to show up in full force and help him devise a plan to order Rhett and Tip to leave their parents' property and never return. He cleaned up the kitchen counters while Skye swept the unfinished floor in preparation for the gathering. Hopefully, they'd get back to painting and tiling the house tomorrow without having to worry about Liam's men. He was ready to be done looking over his shoulder.

He and Skye had worked together on a leftover casserole, which included rice, chicken, veggies, and a soup-based gravy, and slathered it with shredded cheese. Coe wasn't a novice cook, but it had been years since he cooked for his family. When he and his brothers were teenagers, they often made concoctions labeled "glop" or "mystery casserole," using whatever was available in the fridge. Thanks to the melted cheese on top, this one looked especially appetizing.

"How many will be here?" Skye asked as she stacked plates.

"Four brothers, Gran, and us. Maybe Irish."

"I hope she comes. Otherwise, Trish and I will be outnumbered. Don't get me wrong, I think your grandmother can stand up to all of you and win any argument."

"No doubt." Coe chuckled, appreciating the respectful way Skye spoke about Gran. He was already picturing them happily married and bringing home babies for Mom and Gran to make a fuss over. He wondered again how Skye felt about having kids.

Finn was the first through the door. "What's going on? I was nearly out to Lake's when I got your message."

"We'll explain everything when the others arrive." Coe pointed at the food. "Grab a plate and dish up. There's mystery casserole and rolls if you're hungry."

"Thanks. Food makes everything better." Finn grabbed a plate.

"Young man," Gran said from her chair in the living room where she had been dozing.

Finn froze. "Hey, Gran. I didn't see you."

"Have you washed up?" She nodded toward the bathroom. "The same rules apply as they always did."

"Yes, ma'am." Shoulders sagging, he set down his plate and scurried into the other room.

Coe snickered. Even though the youngest North brother was twenty-two, Finn listened to Gran. They all did.

Wilks stomped into the house next, and Gran reminded him about wiping his feet. How often had she prompted them to wipe their feet and wash their hands over the years? A heartwarming sense of how much he loved and appreciated Gran's influence in his life and upbringing rushed through him.

Lake entered with a redheaded woman leading a roly-poly husky pup on a leash. The dog yapped. "Hush, Little Dipper," she said.

"Coe and Skye, this is Irish, my delightful wife." Grinning, Lake draped his arm over her shoulder and kissed her cheek.

"It's nice to meet you," Coe said.

"And you." Irish gave Skye a friendly smile. "Hello. I'm glad to meet you."

"This is Skye," Coe said before she could introduce herself.

"Hello." Skye shook Irish's hand. "I'm particularly glad to meet you since there are so many guys in this family."

"No kidding. And we haven't met them all." Irish bent over and ruffled the dog's fur.

"I hadn't thought of that. How long have you two been married?"

"Three months. We're still newlyweds." Lake smiled broadly.

"Congratulations."

"Thanks." Irish petted the puppy. "We had to learn how to love each other while living in a small cabin with six dogs. After we settled our most important dog issues, things went smoother. Isn't that right, love?"

"We had some disagreements, but nothing that love and compromise couldn't conquer." He gave his wife another kiss on the cheek, and Irish gazed at him adoringly.

"Six dogs, huh?" Skye asked.

"Seven, now." Irish nodded at the pup.

"Wow. Coe told me you two met skijoring."

"That's right. After I kissed Lake, I agreed to marry him." Irish nudged his arm. "I had to make sure he was a good kisser first."

"Which I was. One splendid kiss made all the difference." Lake kissed Irish on the mouth as if to prove it. Everyone laughed, and the husky barked.

Coe glanced at Skye and found her gaze trained on him. Was she thinking one kiss had impacted their lives, too?

"Fill your plates and let's head into the living room. Then we'll get this meeting underway." Once everyone was seated, Coe took a few bites of his casserole, pleased with the flavor, and set his plate on his lap. "I think all of you have heard about Skye's and my flight from Dubai and our race across the country to escape her father's bodyguards. I'll do anything to protect her." He met her gaze, and she smiled tightly.

"Think they'll show up here?" Finn asked.

"Since they're in town asking about us, it's only a matter of time," Skye said.

"They'll likely make their appearance when we least expect it." Coe pushed his food around with his fork, imagining himself lying across the threshold of the guest room door, ensuring Skye's safety.

"That would be after dark, then." Sunday held his dinner roll up like a pointer. "In the movies, bad stuff always happens after the lights go out."

"No bad stuff is going to happen here." Gran shook her finger at Sunday. "The Lord is watching over us."

"Yes, ma'am."

"Then why the emergency text? Why are we here?" Finn glanced between Gran and Coe.

"I need some fresh ideas to stop those guys from pursuing us." Coe met his brothers' gazes, hoping they understood what he was trying to imply without mentioning fighting or doing anything dangerous that would upset Skye or Gran.

Lake nodded. Wilks slumped in his chair. Sunday chewed his food thoughtfully.

"Why not call the police?" Finn asked as if he'd added a "duh" at the end.

"Because I asked Coe not to." Skye scooted to the edge of the couch, set her partially eaten plate of food on the coffee table, and clasped her hands together. "My father acts like a king presiding over his philanthropic work, but he has helped many people in the aftermath of terrible disasters. I'd hate to ruin the good he's done." She drew in a thready breath. "If bad publicity gets out, the Tamarack Foundation might suffer since it's a private enterprise that depends on donations and goodwill sponsorships." Her posture sagged. "However, his security team is relentless and won't stop until they get what they want."

"Which is?" Wilks asked.

"Me. My dad has arranged my marriage to a sixty-year-old billionaire."

"Eeuw." Sunday scrunched up his nose.

"He's manipulative and controlling." Skye toyed with a string on her sweater. "But he is my father."

"Irish and I have dogs who can hang around here." Lake set his plate down, too. "They aren't aggressive, but they look imposing."

"What about the dogs in the shelter?" Sunday asked. "Buster is mean enough to be a guard dog."

"What do you think, Skye?" Irish asked. "Would a tough-looking German Shepherd deter them?"

"I doubt it. And they might harm the dogs."

"We can't have that!" Irish said heatedly.

"No, we can't." Skye shook her head.

"How about if you flip houses?" Wilks nodded toward Lake. "Why don't you guys stay here and let Coe and Skye head out to your property?"

"I don't want Irish to be in a dangerous situation if the hooligans come here looking for Skye." Lake's eyelids closed halfway. "Our place is twenty miles out. If someone were to follow Coe and Skye there, it could be a hazardous situation. You know how isolated it is."

"I sure do." Finn groaned.

"That's sweet of you to worry about me, but I'll be okay." Irish patted Lake's arm. "Aurora and Star wouldn't let anything awful happen to me." She glanced at Skye. "Those are my other babies."

"Her dogs," Wilks mumbled, and Lake elbowed him in the side, which elicited a groan from Wilks.

"What if all of you camped out here in the living room?" Gran asked. "If those rascals dared to step foot in this house, you could send them packing."

"With what?" Sunday asked.

"You boys used to say you were going to send someone packing. How did you plan to do it?" Gran gazed at them with a perplexed look.

"We were a lot of hot air back then. But thanks for the suggestion, Gran." Coe smiled at her. "I'd like to send those guys as far away from Skye as possible, but we must figure out how to do it legally."

"Did they detain you legally?" Wilks pegged him with an intense look.

"No. They didn't." He recapped to the group how Rhett and Tip had dragged him off Liam's property, grabbed him roughly at the airport in New York, and drugged him and Skye in Baltimore, even if they couldn't prove that part. His brothers responded with gasps, groans, and negative comments about his father-in-law's thugs. "I thought you should know what you're getting involved in if we take them on."

"Skye, how do you feel about an intervention?" Irish asked with a serious tone. "Do you want these guys to do whatever crazy idea they drum up to keep you here?"

Skye pressed her lips together, and her face paled like she felt sick.

"We don't mean to put you on the spot." Gran lifted her slightly curled hands toward the group. "This is what we do. We have a family meeting and talk things out."

"Your vote is important." Coe gazed into Skye's eyes, which seemed to appeal to him for understanding.

"Okay, then." She gave him a determined look. "I'd like to face my father's men alone."

"What? That's not happening!" Coe jumped up, all feelings of wanting to listen to her viewpoint evaporating. He had to protect his wife, no matter what that entailed, and no matter what she said she wanted to do.

Chapter Thirty-three

"Come on, Coe. You can't just say no." Skye shot to her feet, her heart pounding, and tugged on his arm, wanting to pull him into another room to have this out with him alone. But he invited his family to this weighty discussion, and she agreed, so she'd have to be bluntly honest with everyone listening. "I have to do this my way. And you can't stop me!"

Yes, I can, the stubborn glint in his gaze said. "You are not facing those criminals alone." His voice was firm, but there was a hint of fear in his expression.

"I won't stand by and let your family fight for me and get injured," Skye spoke insistently, needing to make him understand. "Rhett and Tip are trained combatants. You and your brothers are not. You will be the ones who get hurt. I can't let that happen."

"They will hurt you, too." Coe thrust out his arms like he was exasperated with her. "They already did that."

"No doubt they will try to make me come with them," she conceded. "However, I need to talk to them and convince them that I want to stay here with you. That it's my choice. Please, let me try?"

He groaned and wiped his hands over his face. "I don't see why you feel you must do this."

"I just do. I have to talk to my father's men alone without you interfering."

Coe gazed up at the ceiling, as if seeking an answer or trying to regain calm but struggling.

The others in the room were silent, no doubt, uncomfortable listening to them argue. The puppy didn't even yap. But then, the brothers exchanged rapid glances and head shakes as if passing coded messages. What? Were they plotting how to lock her in a room and take care of Rhett and Tip themselves? They'd better not!

"No one is getting hurt because of me," she said emphatically.

"We're Norths," Sunday said with a louder voice than she'd heard him speak. "We've had a few scuffles. So, we aren't inept at fighting or hauling someone off our property."

"That's right," Wilks agreed.

"I doubt you've gone up against anyone like Rhett or Tip. I'm the only one who can persuade them that I want to stay with my husband. They need to believe we love each other." She met Coe's gaze, realizing that if anyone in the room didn't know they weren't in love, they did now. And if they were in love, this would be an easier sell.

"They'll nab you before you can explain anything," Wilks said in a grumpy tone.

"Wilks—" Coe said.

"What? She thinks talking about your fake marriage will convince those toughs to walk away? Think again."

"Our marriage isn't fake," Coe said grittily.

"Right."

"Even if it doesn't make sense, I must talk with them." Skye could hardly look at Coe and witness the distress written all over his face.

"Skye, please. I don't want you to do this."

She swallowed hard. She respected him but couldn't let the North brothers get pounded by Father's brutish men, who would stop at nothing to get what they came to America to get. If something bad happened to them, it would be her fault. How could she live with herself then?

"She might be right," Irish said.

Skye felt a rush of relief that someone agreed with her.

"How can she be right and wrong?" Wilks shook his head.

"Because my father won't allow them to hurt me." She crossed her arms behind her back, gripping one wrist with the other hand to relieve some stress.

"Yet they gave us a knockout drug and tried to kidnap you. I'm sorry, Skye." Coe turned toward the others. "Let's come up with a better idea and fast."

"Coe—"

"I have a more efficient idea than talking." Wilks ground his fist into his palm.

"For once, I agree with Wilks," Finn said.

"Fighting won't solve anything! Rhett and Tip will pummel you." Skye thrust her fingers through her hair. Coe and his brothers were getting on her nerves.

"There's always calling the police," Sunday said. "Seems like the right decision to me."

"And me," Finn added.

"If it comes to that, I will make the call," Coe said firmly, giving Skye a fixed look as if he was warning her.

"Coe, please."

Just then, the front door opened, and everyone but Trish stood tensely.

"Anybody home?" A black-haired mid-thirties man entered cautiously, peering around at the group. A dark-haired petite woman followed him.

"Hud," Coe said, sounding relieved.

This was Hud? The woman must be his wife. What was her name?

A commotion of greetings, hugs, and backslapping followed the couple's entrance. Skye waited for the laughter and embracing to subside before getting a turn to meet them. What had Coe said about Hud? That he was a cousin-turned-brother after his parents died in a car accident when the boys were young. And that he was one of the three peas in a pod—Lake, Hud, and Coe—and as much a brother as any of the naturally born Norths. With all the hugs and exuberant greetings, she believed it.

The newcomers stopped in front of Trish and hugged her. Grinning, the older woman patted their cheeks. "It's so good to see both of you. Welcome home."

"It's good to see you, too," Hud's wife said.

"How's Aiden doing?" Trish asked.

"He's good. He'll move into one of our artists' bungalows before long." Hud smiled, clearly pleased. "It'll be great having the kid around again."

"That 'kid' is twenty-nine, isn't he?"

"Eh. Who's counting?"

Trish chuckled. "You are a wonderful big brother who's always looked after him. Aiden is blessed indeed."

"Thanks, Gran." Hud's chin dipped, and he shrugged.

"How's the honeymoon going?" Finn asked. "Having second thoughts yet?"

"Hold your tongue." Hud smacked the youngest brother's shoulder. "You know what happens to rude siblings?"

"Yeah, we do." Lake chuckled.

"Coe? Haven't you forgotten someone?" Trish glanced toward Skye.

"Sorry. Hud and Trista, this is my wife, Skye."

Oh, right. Hud's wife's name is Trista.

"So the rumors are true?" Hud embraced Coe and then hugged Skye gently. "I wish you all the best that life and God can give you.

May you have the happiest of marriages, like ours." He stepped back, putting his arm over his wife's shoulder. "This is my bride. Trista, meet my brother, Coe, and Skye."

Trista shook hands with them. "I'm glad to meet you both."

"It's nice to meet you also," Skye said.

Trista slid her hand around Hud's arm and leaned her cheek against him, smiling, and Skye felt a pang of jealousy. If only she and Coe were as comfortable with each other, or at least not arguing and at odds. Where was that colossal crush she thought she had on him now?

"So." Hud gazed around the room at his family members. "Lake filled me in about what's going on with Coe and Skye. That's why we took a slight detour from our honeymoon. Did anyone notice the black car parked outside?"

"What?" Coe yelped.

Skye's first instinct was to run to the window and peer out, but she stayed where she was.

"Two guys are watching the place. One has binoculars." Hud's mouth formed a tight line. "Sorry to be the bearer of bad news." Beside him, Trista nodded grimly.

Wilks strode to the window, but Hud held up his hand, stopping him. "If you look now, they'll realize I spotted them. Let's allow them to live in ignorance for a while longer."

"Good idea," Coe said.

"Fine," Wilks grumbled.

After everyone was seated, Lake took the lead. "How are we going to keep Skye and all the women in the family safe?"

"Since this is about Skye, she should have a say about how it goes down." Irish wagged her finger. "You boys are eager to take control, but don't railroad her. She's the one who must live with the consequences of any rash decisions carried out tonight."

Skye mouthed, "Thank you," to her.

"Is this a fight to the death sort of thing?" Finn acted out sword fighting.

"Absolutely not. And no one is doing anything harmful before I try to talk some sense into them." Skye turned swiftly to Coe before he could argue. "Even Irish agrees with me."

"Up to a point, that is," Irish amended while tugging her puppy next to her legs. "My idea is a compromise."

"A compromise, how?"

"What if you talked to the bad guys from a safe distance while Coe and the others got into strategic positions? If all goes well, great." Irish held up her hands, silencing anyone's rebuttal. "If the hoodlums try anything, the North brothers will converge and stop them from taking you, forcefully, only if necessary." A lump formed in Skye's throat. "Do you want to stay with Coe?" Irish asked.

"Yes. I want to stay with him." A softer look passed between her and Coe.

"Then we aren't going to let them take you," Irish said. "Lake, Coe, and our brothers-in-law will protect you. Right, guys?"

"That's right." Voices chimed in. "We've got this." "We'll show them who's boss."

"We're Norths. All for one," Finn said.

Skye heard their passion for banding together when the chips were down, and something about that commitment and loyalty spoke to her heart. It made her feel like she was becoming more a part of this family of Norths, too.

Chapter Thirty-four

Coe had to accept and respect Skye's wishes to face Rhett and Tip on her own, but he didn't have to like it. He couldn't stop shaking with frustration and fury over the thought of those brutes laying a finger on his wife or trying to kidnap her. If they attempted something underhanded, he would do anything, *anything*, to protect her.

"You okay?" Lake asked from behind the bushes where he and Coe were crouched, trying to remain out of sight.

"Not so great." It had taken all his childhood combat maneuvers to crawl from the back door to this location, trying not to be seen. He scraped his knee on some tree roots, but the pain did nothing to appease the aggravation he felt over Skye facing Rhett and Tip alone.

"It'll be over soon," Lake said.

"Let's hope so."

"This spot is strangely familiar."

"No kidding." Coe pictured how he, Lake, and Hud had often hid here to spy on the front porch when they were young. From this location, they'd listened to grumpy parishioners reprimand Dad for things he said in a sermon or someone reporting a reckless action of one of the North boys. They'd also eavesdropped on Mom scolding one of the brothers for being late, usually Stone. Had any of his brothers watched him getting in trouble when he came home after midnight following a date with Dahlia Lynn?

"Heads up," Lake muttered. "Show's about to start."

Every muscle in Coe's body tensed as Skye strode down the porch steps and two of the black car doors opened and closed. *God, be with her.* He kept an inner dialogue going, asking for the Lord's protection. Rhett squinted toward the location where Coe and Lake were hiding. Was their position compromised? *Lord, please keep Skye safe.*

"I want to talk with you guys." She had a slight tremor in her voice, yet she stood tall, shoulders back, presenting a brave front. Her determination to address her father's men, even though she was afraid, made Coe feel a surge of conflicting emotions of pride and anxiety.

"Get in the car and we'll talk," Rhett said coaxingly.

"No. You have to listen to me right here." *Attagirl. Hold your stance.*

"How about if we listen to you all the way back to Dubai?" Tip said, guffawing as both men strode boldly toward her.

"Stop," she shouted. "Don't take another step."

Ice-cold adrenaline raced through Coe, triggering every protective sensor in his body. Lake's hand on his shoulder barely restrained him. He was ready to leap from his hiding place and face those ruthless brutes.

"Or what?" Tip snarled in his scratchy voice.

"Who's going to stop us?" Rhett asked.

"I am going to try," Skye said. "And my family is waiting to charge out of hiding and confront you." Coe was glad she mentioned that right off.

"Your family?" Tip asked mockingly.

"That's right. My new family is eager to take you boys on."

"I'm so scared." Tip fake shivered.

"He ought to be," Coe muttered through gritted teeth.

"Take this message back to my father—Coe North is my husband. I am staying with him."

"No, you aren't. Mr. Tamarack sent us to get you, and he's getting what he wants." Suddenly, Tip charged toward Skye with Rhett on his heels.

"Stop!" Coe leaped from behind the bush like a ball out of a cannon and sprinted toward her. "Get away from her! You are not taking my wife!"

"Too late." Tip grabbed Skye around her middle, although she fought against his hold.

With a fire burning in his gut, Coe lunged at Tip, grabbing him roughly and thrusting him away from Skye, and at the same time, holding her steady so she didn't fall. Then, with hands clenched and body tense, he stood as a barrier between her and the intruders, ready to take on Tip and Rhett by himself, if necessary. "You're trespassing. Leave this property immediately!"

"We can snuff you out like trash." Rhett took an offensive stance in front of Coe. "We've stopped you before. We'll do it again."

"This time, I'm stopping you."

"And me." Lake strode to Coe's side, positioning himself between Liam's men and Skye, too. Coe felt more emboldened with his brother beside him.

"You Idaho boys think you can clash with us and win?" Tip guffawed and punched the air like he was hitting a punching bag. "Let's fight over your so-called wife. If we win, we take her without resistance."

"That's right," Rhett growled.

"No deal." Hands fisted, ready to fight these two, Coe hoped to get Skye back to the house first. He lifted his chin toward the porch, hoping she got his message about where he wanted her to go. She didn't move. "You aren't taking her anywhere. She's with me. She's Skye North, not Tamarack. You need to respect that."

Rhett and Tip cackled like he'd told a joke.

"Like that will last." Tip used a boxing shuffle, shifting between Lake and Coe like he couldn't decide which one to hit first. The silver tooth shining from his mocking smile showed he was eager for their fray. So was Coe, but he didn't want Skye to get caught up in it.

"Liam has strong opinions about who can marry his daughter, and you aren't it." Rhett spit. "He's fine with her becoming a widow."

"That's not happening today." Six against two seemed like good odds.

"Call my father and tell him I'm not returning, then go back to Dubai," Skye yelled around Coe. He held his arms out, stopping her from advancing toward the other guys. "Just leave, will you? Get out of here!"

"Not a chance. Two against two? No problem." Tip eyed Coe and punched the air a few more times, showing off. "You'll be heading to the hospital before this is over."

Not likely.

"You'll be fighting us, too." Hud marched out from around the corner of the house, his body rigid like a coiled snake ready to strike. Wilks followed, glowering and grinding his fist into his palm. Coe, Lake, Hud, and Wilks moved toward the two muscular men like linebackers ready to defend Skye.

"Is this the best you've got?" Tip's face scrunched up like he'd taken a bite of a lemon. "Wimps. Marshmallows!"

"We might not be buff like you," Wilks said. "But we have something you don't have."

"What's that?" Rhett squinted.

"Class," Finn shouted.

"And decency," Sunday added, stepping into the streetlight.

Tip and Rhett shot glances over their shoulders as Sunday and Finn entered the property from behind them. Their eyes widened as they peered around at the six brothers, and for a few seconds, they didn't look so cocky.

"We can still do this. A piece of cake." Tip glanced at his partner. "Right?"

Rhett squinted intensely at Coe and Lake, then, cursing, stepped back. "Let's go."

"What?" Tip squawked. "What'll we tell Mr. Tamarack? He'll kick us to the curb when he finds out we didn't get the girl."

"We'll get her, just not today." Rhett took a threatening step toward Skye, and Coe held his hands out, stopping him. "Are you married to this farmer boy?" Coe wanted to wipe the sneer off Rhett's face.

"I am married to Coe North." Skye wrapped her arms around his waist. "Go back and inform my father that he'll have to come here if he ever wants to see me again, or his grandchildren."

Internally, Coe smiled victoriously, but outwardly, he kept his features masked with defiance, his eyes locked in a silent battle with Rhett.

After a few moments, Rhett cursed again, then stalked toward the car. Tip followed, complaining and whining about wanting to fight and how they could have easily won. The engine roared as the vehicle took off.

Sighing, Coe drew Skye into his arms, and she collapsed against him, her sigh of relief washing over him like a wave. It was over. He lifted his gaze to the night sky, smoothing his hands over her back, and in a silent prayer, he expressed his profound gratitude to the Lord for resolving a situation that could have ended far worse.

Chapter Thirty-five

Skye sat on a stool at the kitchen island, chatting with Irish and Trista, and munching on snacks while their husbands huddled around a flickering campfire in the backyard. The men's raucous laughter and friendly backslapping suggested that they had outwitted Rhett and Tip. But if that were so, why did Skye have a bad feeling that what happened tonight didn't solve anything?

"Will those guys stop coming after you now?" Trista asked.

"No." Skye heaved a sigh. "They'll be back."

"Why do you say that?" Irish asked.

"My father is a powerful man. He won't allow Rhett and Tip to give up. He doesn't back down once he sets his mind on something." What stopped the duo from trying to get the better of the North brothers tonight? Did Father tell them not to cause injury? Not to hurt her?

"How can you be so composed?" Trista sipped her iced tea. "If I were in your shoes, I'd grab my daughter and run."

"I tried that." Skye twirled a potato chip in a shallow bowl of Ranch dip. "Coe and I left India, crossed the Atlantic, landed in New York, hid in D.C., flew to Seattle, and sped here with those guys following us." She chuckled mirthlessly. "How much farther could we go?"

"I didn't consider all that." Trista pointed out the window toward the men standing around the campfire. "It seems they think they triumphed over them."

"I know." Skye nibbled at the edge of a brownie, picking at the chunks of chocolate chips Coe added, her thoughts flitting to another day when she ate brownies contemplatively. Father had introduced her to Edmund during an awkward dinner at their house. While the men chatted over dessert, she picked at a brownie made by their cook, sulking, and wondering why her father hated her so much as to confine her to a life with an older man with a leering grin. The looming marriage to Edmund had spurred her to flee, seeking solace and safety in Coe's arms.

"Skye?" Irish waved her hand in front of her.

"What?" Skye mentally shook herself. "Sorry."

"You looked half a planet away. Are you okay?"

"Just thinking." She took another bite of the brownie that didn't taste as sweet.

"Are you going to tell Coe you expect to see those bad guys again?" Irish asked.

"Probably." Along with a few other things she needed to talk with him about.

"The North brothers will stand up for you." Irish gave her a meaningful look. "You get that, don't you?"

"I barely know Coe, let alone his brothers. But they proved themselves tonight." Did either of these women who fell in love with their husbands after marriage understand her hesitancy?

"Been there. Done that." Irish smiled.

"Me too." Trista clasped Skye's and Irish's hands. "The ties of marrying North brothers early in the relationship have intricately woven the three of us together."

Skye's heart warmed at her words. She'd always wished for a sister to share secrets and friendship with. Now, she had two almost-sisters.

"That's right," Irish agreed. "I can tell Coe admires you. I'm sure things will work out for you guys."

Trista hugged her briefly. "I'd say he adores you."

"Adores? I doubt that." Skye chuckled, embarrassed.

Irish exchanged a look with Trista. "So, this dad of yours? Is he as awful as he sounds?"

"He was a good father before my mom died."

"What happened?" Trista asked.

"He changed." Skye flinched, wishing she didn't feel a need to be transparent. "Picture the *Brady Bunch* dad morphing into Attila the Hun."

"Yikes." Irish cleared her throat. "I thought my family was bad."

"Yours probably didn't lock you in your room and try to sell you to the highest bidder."

"Nothing so extreme. But I still fear Mom will show up on my doorstep demanding a share of Lake's inheritance." Irish rolled her eyes. "Everyone has someone in their family whom they are embarrassed about or afraid of, right?"

"I don't suppose you had to run for your life, either." The simple statement carried deep emotional weight for Skye.

"No. But I was a single mom, raising my daughter alone." Trista's dark blue eyes filled with tears. "It was hard to go home and confess to Mom that I'd been with a man who wasn't worthy of being a father or a husband. He was a cheating scoundrel." Irish patted Trista's shoulder sympathetically. "Thankfully, Mom and Jesus accepted me with grace, love, and open arms." Trista's smile was a little wobbly. "*He's* here for you, too."

"Thank you for reminding me. I know Jesus is with me." Skye barely got the words out due to the emotions clogging her throat.

Irish and Trista surrounded her in a comforting, sisterly hug she appreciated.

Skye glanced out the window and saw Wilks standing by the fire, gesturing like he was telling a grand story. The others laughed and slapped their knees. Where did all the humor and camaraderie come from when she felt so weighed down emotionally? "What's your love story with Lake?" she asked Irish, seeking a distraction.

"Let's see. A woman needs money to rescue dogs. A guy needs a wife to inherit his money. After an unforgettable kiss, she says yes to marrying him." Her lips spread in a wide grin.

"Instant love?" Skye watched her sister-in-law's eyes sparkle.

"Far from instant, but when true love came, *whoopee!*"

"And you?" Skye turned to Trista. "Was your love *whoopee*, too?"

"Eventually. Hud and I have had our difficulties." She got a far-off look. "My story goes like this—a woman and a man are business partners. Her mom is about to lose everything. He gallantly offers to fix it. But there's a catch."

"Isn't there always?" Skye sighed. "Did fireworks eventually light up the night sky?"

"Oh, yes. Fourth of July fireworks." A relaxed smile crossed Trista's face. "We are deeply in love now. But we still have challenges. Did I mention I have an emotional five-year-old who says everything that pops into her head? She's trying to finagle her way into getting a puppy."

"I vote for giving her a puppy." Irish chuckled. "And love can be complicated and messy, but it's still love. Like, if he says your dog has to sleep outside, that's going to be a problem!"

They all laughed.

"How is the romance going between you and Coe?" Irish nudged Skye's arm. "I saw him gazing at you like you hung a star in place for him. Did you?"

"Well. It's not—"

"Love?" Trista finished softly. "It's okay to say it. Sometimes love comes slowly and achingly sweet."

"I like him a lot. My heart pounds when he enters the room." Skye felt the warmth of their last kiss and stroked her lips. "When we kiss, it's as if fairy dust is falling all over us, and I can hardly breathe. But is that enough to build a life together?"

Chapter Thirty-six

When two days had passed without anyone in the family reporting any sightings of Rhett or Tip, Coe felt optimistic that Liam's men had given up and left town. If they had taken him and his brothers seriously and weren't going to harass Skye anymore, he would be eternally grateful. But doubts followed his confident thoughts. What if the ruffians were still hanging around, but lying low, waiting for an unsuspecting moment to seize Skye when he wasn't looking? What if they planned to incapacitate him and whisk her away? The chance of that happening kept him on edge, glancing over his shoulder, and peering into the shadows.

In addition to his concerns, Skye had been acting more reserved since his family took a stand against Rhett and Tip, and he didn't know why. Did he say something insensitive? Did anyone else? Should he ask her what was wrong or how she was feeling? Their relationship was too new for him to know what she preferred when it came to discussing personal things. If he were feeling disgruntled about something, he'd rather ponder the situation and reflect on his thoughts without having to explain his feelings. But that didn't mean Skye felt the same way.

It had been nice seeing Hud and meeting Trista, even if they were here for only one night. He appreciated the way Hud jumped in and assisted with facing Rhett and Tip. He didn't know when he'd get the chance to catch up with Spur, A.W., or Stone, but he missed the close-knit ties and friendships he'd always felt around his brothers. That's the way it was growing up and moving on, he supposed, but he hoped the whole North family would be together again, maybe for one of his other brothers' wedding celebrations. He smiled at the thought of a big family event like that.

"Ready to lay tile?" he asked Skye, then took a bite of the eggs and bacon burrito he made, enjoying the spicy after kick.

"Ready as I'll ever be." She sighed and stared at her uneaten burrito.

"Is there something else you'd rather be doing?"

"Yeah. I wouldn't mind catching a train to Wyoming. Flying up to Alaska and seeing where Hud and Trista live. Or building a house out of mud." The last one made him smile.

"Are you saying you're bored with our life in Thunder Ridge?"

"I like helping your family. But—" She cringed.

"Is something bugging you?" He wondered again what he might have said or done to bring about her silence or moodiness. "Is it me?"

She pressed her lips together and worked them over her teeth, which drew his attention to her soft lips, and he wished things felt more comfortable between them. Smiling with what he hoped was a friendly expression, he took a risk at rejection and stroked the back of his fingers down her cheek.

Her eyes widened. "Why haven't you touched me recently?"

"Haven't I?" He withdrew his fingers, a mix of confusion and uncertainty clouding his thoughts.

"No. You've been quiet and withdrawn." He had? Here, he thought she was the one who'd been standoffish. "I thought you were mad at me for pushing to talk with Rhett and Tip myself. Were you?"

"Not really." Had he been more introspective lately? "You were stubborn about that. But I tried to accept your decision, up to a point."

"I appreciate that and what you did to keep me safe." She ran her fork over her burrito, still not eating it. "It's not like we know each other all that well. I can't read your moods."

"Nor me yours."

"We haven't been acting like newlyweds, either." She gulped and met his gaze. "Or as if we hope to be like that any time soon." Did she mean she wanted them to be more affectionate? "I've also been worrying about Rhett and Tip coming back. Even though they left like they were acquiescing to our demands, they weren't. You know that, right?"

"I hope they won't come back. But if they do, we'll figure out what to do." He took a breath and exhaled, trying not to get tense about Liam's bodyguards again. "Let's not forget that God is protecting and leading us, even when it comes to your dad and his men's behavior toward us. *He's* always watching over us, even when we don't comprehend it." Realizing he sounded like Gran, he smiled, feeling a glimmer of hope in their shared faith.

"I want to believe that, but I struggle with some what-ifs," Skye said quietly.

"Like?"

"What if they steal me away from you? What if you and I never fall in love?" Her voice broke, and his heart melted.

"Hey, now. Are you that concerned about us not falling for each other?"

"Yes. Doesn't it trouble you?" She pressed her lips together.

"No." Hadn't he told her he had strong feelings for her? Sure, they'd been busy, and he hadn't spent much time showing her he cared for her like a newlywed groom, or even a boyfriend, but shouldn't she realize how he felt about her after five days of marriage and living together? Their struggle with personal expectations for their marital situation was becoming more evident, and he was feeling a bit desperate. Should he address it the only way he knew how? "Skye?" he whispered.

"Hmm?" Her dark eyes met his questioningly, and he brushed his lips softly against hers. Her quick inhalation of breath showed he'd taken her by surprise, another sign he hadn't initiated contact between them enough. But after her first reaction, her lips warmed to his, and she kissed him back tenderly, her hand roaming over his chest like she was feeling his pounding heart.

"Do you feel anything special when we kiss like that?" He cupped her cheeks and smiled, hoping she could read his emotions now.

"Yes," she whispered.

"I'm glad. Because I feel so much wonder and amazement when we kiss and hold each other." He kissed her again, letting his lips say what his heart felt but couldn't fully express. Leaning away, he held her gaze. "When I say we will fall in love, that's because I believe we will." She didn't agree or comment, but her moist eyes trailed his. Scooting back, he picked up his burrito and held it toward her. "Want to taste this? It's quite good."

"Are you bragging about your cooking ability now?"

"You better believe it." Grinning, he offered her the edge of the flaky burrito. "Please?" She opened her mouth slightly. The urge to kiss her again was strong, and he barely resisted as he touched the burrito to her lips, and she took a tiny nibble. He watched her mouth's movements, mesmerized by how her tongue brushed her lower lip as she ate, like she was checking for crumbs, and his heart pounded.

"Mmm. It's delicious."

"See." He took a small bite and chewed slowly, noticing how she watched his mouth like he'd been watching hers. Who knew savoring food could be so romantic? He offered her another bite, and she took a taste, then he ate another piece. They smiled at each other, kissing a few times, and continued sharing food. This was turning out to be a remarkable breakfast.

"I'm glad I married a man who can cook." She ran her hand over his bristly chin, sending shivers through him. "That might come in handy."

"Are you impressed with my culinary skills? My exquisite kissing talents?" he teased, and Skye laughed. He was grateful for this light-hearted moment they were sharing.

"You mean his mediocre attempts at romance?" Wilks sauntered into the room and pounded Coe on the back.

Coe hacked. "You nearly choked me to death."

"Morning, sister-in-law."

"Morning, Wilks." Skye winked at Coe. "You're wrong, though. My husband's romancing is breathtaking." Warmth spread through him. So did his desire to take her in his arms again.

Wilks laughed. "That's why he's never had a girlfriend."

"Not true," Coe balked.

"Oh, right. What was her name? Lily Plant?"

"Dahlia Lynn." He met Skye's glance. "That was eons ago."

"Meaning you're out of practice?" Wilks threw a dish towel at Coe. "If you need advice—"

"You'd be the last person I'd ask." Coe stuffed the remainder of his burrito in his mouth, wishing Wilks had stayed out of the kitchen.

"What about you?" Skye asked. "Do you have a girlfriend?"

"Not at the moment," Wilks replied nonchalantly.

"Yet you're offering relationship advice? Maybe you should wait until you are married or at least have a steady girlfriend before suggesting pointers on how a husband should kiss his wife." Smiling at Coe, Skye smoothed her palms gently across his cheeks and kissed him sweetly—the perfect ending to their meal together.

Chapter Thirty-seven

That afternoon, Lake called while Coe was working on the bathroom floor tiling. He and Skye had been trying to get the white and gray porcelain tiles in place and secure but weren't finished yet. The biggest challenge was trying to keep everyone else out of the main bathroom while they worked.

"What's up?" Coe held the phone between his chin and shoulder, wiping mortar off his fingers.

"I received a call from Dad. He and Gran talked, and she told him what's been going on with you and Skye, and about her father's security team. Looks like Mom and Dad will be back tomorrow."

"What? The place is a disaster. Aren't they supposed to spend a week in Florida?"

"Yeah. I warned them about the mess, but Mom is eager to meet Skye and said they'd been sitting around long enough." Lake chuckled. "Just make sure they have a path to their room. Don't worry about the rest. Dad will pitch in with the remodeling. Mom will help with meals. Everything will be fine."

"Yeah. All right." Coe was looking forward to seeing his parents, but he disliked that they were cutting their vacation short because of safety concerns at home. And they'd be meeting Skye under less than ideal circumstances. "Thanks for the heads-up, bro."

"Of course." Lake cleared his throat. "I want to mention one other thing."

"What's that?" Coe glanced at Skye and saw her yawning. She had been working almost nonstop since they arrived in Thunder Ridge. She probably needed a break. They should do something enjoyable, like going out for dinner or taking a walk by the lake. Realizing his brother wasn't speaking, he asked, "Lake? You still there?"

"Yeah. Awkward conversation alert."

"Just a sec." He mouthed, "Be right back," to Skye, then hurried into Dad's office and closed the door. "Go ahead."

"Irish, Trista, and Skye were talking the other night, and Skye said she doesn't think the deal with her dad's security team is over."

"I heard about that."

"Do you think we should discuss a back-up plan? Talk strategy?" Lake spoke assertively, as if contemplating their next match against Rhett and Tip. "How else can we protect the women from whatever those guys might have up their sleeves?"

Coe hated the constant worry about Liam's men. They would have to call the authorities at some point, and the sooner the better. "Let me talk with Skye and get back to you."

"Sounds good. Everyone's safety is important, so a plan seems wise."

"You're right. I appreciate your concerns. Thanks, man." Coe ended the call, regretful about bringing this trouble to his family in the first place.

"Who was that?" Skye asked when he reentered the bathroom.

"Lake." He carefully stepped around her, appreciating that she'd continued working where he left off. "Great work, Skye."

"Thanks. I love tiling."

Spotting a small blob of mortar on her face, he grabbed a wash-cloth, wet it with warm water, and bent down to wipe the goop from her face. Something clenched in his chest as he stroked the wet fabric smoothly down her cheek. Their gazes met and clung, bringing back thoughts and feelings about their kisses at breakfast.

"Is something wrong? Is that why you took the call in the other room?"

"No." He sighed. "My mom and dad are coming back tomorrow."

"Because of me being here?"

"They want to meet you. But they are also worried about our safety, and Gran's."

"This is all my fault. I'm sorry. We shouldn't have come here. I mean, I shouldn't have come here."

"No, this isn't your fault. And coming here was my idea."

"Because of me. I hate being the cause of your parents ending their vacation." She set the trowel in the mortar bowl and stood, looking shaken.

He touched her arm. "Don't worry about it, okay?"

"How can I not worry? Everyone in your family is at risk." She thrust out her hands. "If I were to leave, this whole mess would disappear."

"No, it wouldn't. And if you left, I'd hunt for you and wouldn't stop looking until I found you." She squinted at him as if questioning the truth of his statement. "You are my wife. I care a great deal about you, Skye." He wished he could say he loved her and reassure her, but he wouldn't lie. "I want you with me always, and to be as close to you as possible." That was the truth. He passed her the wet rag to wipe her fingers, and their gazes held for several moments.

She sighed and nodded toward the doorway. "I'm going to wash in the kitchen and give you this space." She left the room abruptly, and he wondered if she was okay.

Waiting only a moment, he stepped over the recently placed tiles and followed her. He leaned against the kitchen counter and waited while she lathered her arms and hands and rinsed, then handed her a towel. "What would you think of going out with me?"

"As in a date?" She frowned.

"It's not too foreign of an idea, is it?"

"For us, it is." She dropped the hand towel in a bucket of dirty ones. "However, getting out of the house and going somewhere together sounds nice."

"Sure does." He stroked back some strands of dark hair behind her ear, contemplating whether he should mention the other stuff Lake brought up. "Also, Lake thinks we should have a plan in case Rhett and Tip show up and try anything."

Her eyebrows rose. "Were you plotting how to protect me behind my back?"

"No. I agreed we should have a plan. But I told him I'd talk with you first."

"Oh. You did?" Her expression softened.

"Yeah. Is that so shocking?"

"Kind of." She heaved a sigh. "We don't have good communication yet. You and your brothers are close and communicate in ways I don't understand, while I am an outsider."

"You are much more to me than an outsider. You are my fascinating, attractive wife, whom I am beginning to cherish." He wanted to take her in his arms, kiss her slowly, and show her he meant what he said, but one of his brothers could walk in at any moment and he didn't want to make things more awkward.

"Then prove it." She lifted her chin, eyeing him.

"What?"

"Prove that I'm your wife whom you are beginning to cherish, whatever that means." Her cheeks darkening, she gave him an intense look that made him feel like their whole future depended on his response.

"Uh. All right." She wanted proof? Fine. Challenge accepted. With his heart pounding and thoughts of kissing Skye like a husband with a wife scrambling through his brain, he cautioned himself, *Slow down, Coe.* Did she mean what he thought she did? He gazed at her, letting their gazes linger and dance with warmth before he moved closer to her. Then, casting aside worries about one of his siblings barging in, he picked her up and set her on the kitchen counter.

"Coe?" Her eyes widened.

"Shhhh." With ultimate gentleness, he caressed her face with his fingertips, touching her ears, jaw, and neck, and feeling her pulse fluttering. Her dark eyes peering at him drew him closer until his mouth was an inch above hers. "I'm going to kiss you now," he whispered.

"I wish you would." She smoothed her hands over his chest, undoubtedly feeling the rapid beating of his heart.

With all the gentlemanly affection he'd been taught to give a woman he cared for, he kissed Skye softly and intently, their lips brushing each other's like butterfly wings dancing a waltz. He lingered over this phase of sweetness and gentleness with her. And when he wanted more, and it seemed like she wanted more, he kissed his wife with some passion and emotional heat, savoring their kisses like a delicious dessert neither of them could get enough of.

After a few more kisses, he set her on her feet, wrapped his arms around her, and held her close, catching his breath. She sighed, leaning against his chest, like she felt content in his arms. "I hope you will comprehend how much I cherish you and how sincere I am about us falling for each other very soon," he spoke softly, stroking the back of her hair.

"I am starting to believe you," she whispered back.

Chapter Thirty-eight

Skye strolled down the stairs, enjoying Coe's perusal of her from the bottom of the stairway. She had previously felt uncomfortable when a man stared as if he were interested in her. But her husband's earnest gaze and his handsome smile brought back thoughts of their kisses, and her heart warmed to the attention he was giving her. She'd been enraptured and entirely taken by his response to her request that he prove himself earlier. His kisses were gentle yet provocative, and for a few moments she could hardly think, hardly breathe. All she wanted was to be with Coe as his wife. Wasn't it too soon for such personal marital thoughts?

She needed to be careful and not get carried away tonight. Someone had to remind them to slow down and wait for real love before getting too affectionate. Although a warning about taking things unhurriedly wouldn't have chilled her ardor when they were wrapped in each other's arms this afternoon. Would moments like those always be special between them?

Coe brushed her cheek with his warm lips, lingering for a moment near her ear. "You look beautiful, Skye."

"Thank you." She was glad he didn't mention her wearing the same jeans and purple sweater she'd been wearing during non-working hours since their arrival in Thunder Ridge four days ago.

"Ready?" He held out his hand.

"Sure." She linked their fingers, enjoying the familiarity and comfort of holding his hand. "Where are we going?"

"I thought we'd get take-out and head to the lake if that's okay."

"Sounds great." Anywhere away from the house alone with Coe sounded fantastic, as long as Rhett or Tip didn't make an appearance. And since their outing would be casual, she didn't have to worry about what she was wearing.

She gave Coe a once-over. He wore a turquoise button-up shirt and dark jeans and had a sweatshirt slung over his arm. His whiskered face looked trimmed, like he'd used an electric razor to even the facial hairs out, leaving enough for her to run her fingers over his cheeks and enjoy the scruffy feeling during a kiss. She couldn't wait for more of his kisses. *Look how quickly you forgot your slow-down speech.*

Yeah, yeah. She sighed.

When they reached the Sandpoint beach, which Coe said was on the shore of Lake Pend Oreille, they sat on a blanket facing the water with the wind blowing gently against them. Coe was an attentive date, not that she'd had many dates for comparison. But his smile alone was doing crazy things to her emotions, and he was smiling a lot. He touched her hand or arm while they talked, as if he was trying to keep a link between them. She loved the hearty way he laughed, like he was being himself, and their gazes locked as if they were the only two people in the world. In those moments, she couldn't help but wonder what it would be like to have a real marriage and family with this man, one that blossomed from a deep and abiding emotional connection.

They'd picked up bowls of chicken fried rice, eggrolls, and bottles of peach tea. While they ate their picnic dinner, she chuckled as Coe shared tales about his and his brothers' youthful escapades. He was a good storyteller and kept her guessing about the outcomes of some of the boys' mischief-making. With each story, she got to know Coe, the North brothers, and their adventurous natures better.

After a while, she asked, "Do you think we'll stay in Thunder Ridge long enough to get jobs? We can't live off your family forever."

"No, we can't." He gazed along the sandy beach. "When we're done helping at my mom and dad's place, we should look for work. Locally would be nice, since we don't own a car yet."

"What about money in the meantime? You mentioned an emergency credit card. In what situation would you be comfortable using it?" She felt awkward asking, but it was one of those subjects married couples ought to be able to discuss. A man and a woman, both wearing baseball caps pulled low over their faces, strolled by in front of them. They were the only other people she'd seen on the beach. "Or is that a topic I shouldn't ask about?" The thought riled her, and she tried tempering her reaction.

"It's fine for us to talk about anything. I'm not used to sharing personal information about myself or money, so it might take some time for me to get used to doing that."

"Not even with your wife?"

"Well—" He gave her a slow smile. "That's new to me, too. I'm trying to figure marriage out, aren't you?"

"Yes, I am. My dad was the main male figure in my life, and I barely understood him, other than to keep my distance when he was moody." She glanced at Coe and saw that he was watching her as if interested in what she was saying. "It may take some time for me to adjust to you, getting to know your moods and all."

"I appreciate that." He brushed his fingers over her hand. "I'm not that moody of a person, just so you know."

"Is that what your brothers would say?"

He laughed. "No. Lake has called me tight-lipped a few times. I'd say I'm introspective. I tend to think about things before I speak."

"We're similar in that regard."

"About the credit card, I kept it as a backup while I was traveling but rarely used it. If we need to leave Thunder Ridge because of Rhett and Tip, we could use it to get by. But we'd have to be careful with our spending." His words reassured her they were on the same page.

"I understand."

"What kind of job would you like to have?" he asked.

"All I've done is aid work. Whatever job I pursue, I want to do something important in the world. Not that every job doesn't matter in some way, but—"

"Having a regular nine-to-five is hard to imagine after spending your adult life helping people in disastrous situations, isn't it?"

"Yeah."

"It's a view we share." He held his hand out toward her, a softly compelling look in his gaze. She placed her hand in his, the action becoming more natural each time they did it. "I daydream about being back in the field. Do you ever think about it?"

"Sometimes. Lately, I haven't thought about much other than staying clear of Father's men." She coughed around some emotions. She'd thought quite a bit about kissing Coe lately, and beyond what kissing him would be like, but she wouldn't mention any of that. "In the past, I dreamed of making choices about marriage, work, and life. Now, I want to make those decisions, but it's also a little over-whelming."

"It's part of our journey together." Coe's hair blew lightly in the breeze coming off the lake. She thought about how his hair felt against her cheek when they kissed and she strummed her fingers through the strands. She enjoyed how they were talking more openly tonight. If this was how dating Coe was like, she hoped they'd go on many dates in the future. "Helping others has been part of my faith walk," he said, continuing the conversation. "It's my love in action."

"That makes sense. I felt the most like me, more complete, or something, while serving others."

"Me too. I miss being out there, doing good somewhere, you know?"

"I do."

The work they had been involved in with the Tamarack Foundation, where they found a shared passion for helping others, had formed a special bond between them. Skye hadn't even realized how much of a connection until now. Coe draped his arm over her shoulder, and she nestled against his side, relishing the closeness and the shared experiences that had brought them to this moment.

"Working in the mud, repairing a house so a family could live in it again, putting someone's roof back on, all gave my life deeper meaning." He sighed.

"Mine too. Those are good memories." She smiled, feeling at peace with Coe and the way they met. It should be easy to fall in love with this man she'd shared many volunteer hours with if only she let herself. *Wait.* Let herself? Was she holding back from loving Coe? The thought was startling and left her feeling confused. Wanting to refute the notion she might be holding back emotionally, she snuggled closer and kissed him softly. However, he didn't respond as usual and broke the kiss quickly.

"We should, uh, take a walk."

"You want to walk instead of us kissing?" she asked teasingly, hardly believing it could be true.

"I think it's for the best." Was he the one holding back now?

Skye felt a sudden chill that surpassed the windy conditions. She scooted a couple of inches away from him. "Is something wrong? Didn't you want us to kiss during this date?"

"Nothing's wrong." He glanced toward the couple walking by again. "And yes, I want to kiss you. Just not right now." What was with him?

"Is it my breath?" She held her palm over her mouth, and a spicy scent reached her nose. She should have brought some mints.

"It's not that. Don't worry." Standing, he reached out and helped her stand. "Will you walk with me?"

"All right." Perhaps he didn't want them getting carried away with physical displays of affection. Hadn't she thought the same thing before? But considering they were on a date on a mostly empty beach, not kissing or being affectionate seemed odd.

They strolled near the water's edge with gentle waves lapping up on the sand. By the time they reached the dock on the far side of the public beach, Coe had glanced back several times. Was he suspicious of that couple who kept meandering back and forth?

"Do you suppose Rhett hired them to follow us?"

"What? Why would you say that?"

"You keep watching them."

"Oh. You see—" Coe stopped walking, his face flushed. "I have a confession."

"What is it? And why would a newly married man choose not to kiss his wife, even if it is an unusual marriage, when they're on a date?"

Coe pressed his lower lip between his teeth like he was fighting a grin. "Oh, Skye."

"Are you laughing at me?"

"Not at you. But—" He waved toward the couple. "Hey, guys, come here."

"What are you doing?" Why was he calling out to strangers like that? He turned her toward the approaching duo, and she immediately recognized them. "Lake? Irish?"

"Sorry about our subterfuge." Irish removed her hat, releasing her long hair.

"What are you guys doing here?" Skye accepted her sister-in-law's hug.

"Hanging around in case there was trouble. And enjoying a beach walk with my handsome husband." Irish linked her arm with Lake's.

"What can I say?" He chuckled.

"You planned all this?"

"Just trying to make sure you're safe." Coe shrugged.

No wonder he didn't want them kissing. Of course, he wouldn't want Lake and Irish observing them in a romantic embrace. She sighed, relieved.

"Looks like the coast is clear." Lake rocked his thumb toward the parking lot. "No one else is here but us four."

"Thanks, man." Coe shook his hand.

"Anytime." Lake slid his arm over Irish's shoulders, tugging her close. "We're going to head back to the dog ranch."

"I miss my babies." Irish grinned.

"Good night." Lake waved.

Coe and Skye waved and said good night, too.

"We should get back to the house." Coe glanced out toward the shadowy lake. "It's getting late, and we have more renovation work to do tomorrow."

"Wait a second." Meeting his gaze and clinging to it for several seconds, she grabbed hold of his jacket fabric and pulled him closer. "There's one tiny matter I need to address first."

"What's that?"

"Just this." She kissed him slowly, their lips softly brushing each other's, then with some intensity. Coe's soft groan and how he pulled her into his arms and kissed her more heatedly assured her that neither of them was holding back now.

Chapter Thirty-nine

Mom and Dad arrived with exuberant greetings and praise over all the cosmetic changes that had been made to the kitchen, living room, and bathrooms. They were suntanned and looked less stressed than the last time Coe saw them, and he felt thankful for the vacation Lake and Irish had given them.

"It's so good to see you, son." Sniffling, Mom hugged him. "I'm happy and grateful you got back home safely."

"Me too." Coe hugged Dad, and his father clapped him on the back.

"Can't wait to chat and catch up."

"Sure." Coe waved toward Skye. "Mom. Dad. This is Skye, my bride."

Tears filled Mom's eyes and spilled onto her cheeks. "Welcome to our family, Skye. I'm happy to meet you." She embraced Skye like a long-lost daughter. "I'm sorry to have missed your wedding." Mom leaned back and glanced between them. "I realize it couldn't be helped, but my heart is a tad broken about not getting to be there and seeing it all for myself." Her face crumpled into a weeping expression. "Sorry to be so emotional." She turned to Dad, and he took her in his arms, whispering, "It's okay, Livvy."

"I'm sorry." Skye's face visibly tightened. "It's my fault we got married quickly."

"No. It was me who pushed for a prompt marriage." Coe sent a pleading look to his father. "We did what we thought was right, given the circumstances and safety concerns."

"We understand." Dad still had one arm around Mom but held his other hand out toward Skye and shook her hand. "We are delighted to meet you, Skye. We've been eager to meet the person our son chose for his wife and the woman who agreed to marry him." He gave her a friendly smile. "Please be assured, you are already deeply loved and welcomed as a family member."

"Thank you." Skye's voice trembled. "Sorry your house is such a mess."

"That's all right. Look at all the work you guys have accomplished so quickly." Dad nodded toward the kitchen with its partially finished look. "It's coming along nicely. Good job!"

"Yes. It really is lovely." Mom shuffled back, still sniffling. "Sorry. All these emotions have been coming to the surface lately."

"I understand," Skye said.

Coe was concerned with how she might feel with Mom acting so sensitively as he brought Dad up to speed about the renovation. But a few minutes later, Skye sat on the sofa with Mom, both laughing about something, and he felt some relief.

"Got a minute?" Dad nodded toward his closed office door.

"Uh. Sure." Coe hoped he wasn't going to pressure him about the pastorate. As a kid, he thought following in Dad's footsteps or even being like Jack Coe would be cool. Now, he loved the work he was involved in overseas, using his hands to build and help others in practical ways, and would say that was the true calling in his life. He hoped Dad understood that.

"So, you're married now." Dad beamed, dropping into the chair behind his large wooden desk stacked with books and papers.

"That's right." Coe sat in one of the two chairs across from him. "You look happy."

"I am, mostly."

"Mostly?" Dad's dark eyebrows shot up. "Anything you care to talk about?"

"Not really." Since that was private, he wasn't going to confide any personal details about his and Skye's lack of love or intimacy. "Married a week, we're adjusting to life as a wedded couple."

Dad gave him a long look as if peering into his brain and not finding the answers he sought. "My door is always open if you want to talk."

"Thanks." Coe briefly explained what led him and Skye to flee from her father's plans for her and their subsequent marriage, even though Gran had already explained some of it to Dad. "Is Mom okay? She seemed upset."

Dad ran his fingers through his black hair, streaked with some gray. "It's taking her a few heartbeats to catch up with her sons being old enough to choose who they'll marry and where it will happen without her." He tapped his index finger against the desk. "Three sons married in three months? Give her time to adjust. Soon, she'll be planning a wedding celebration for you and Skye."

"Dad—"

"She mentioned it, so be prepared." He held up his hands in a surrendering gesture. "These things are important to the parents, too."

"Sure. But we're trying to lie low for Skye's safety."

"I get that. But a small family gathering wouldn't be too much, would it? Think about it." Coe suppressed a groan. "Any sign of the troublemakers?" Dad shuffled a couple of papers on his desk. "Lake filled us in on the recent activities."

"There might be more problems on the horizon." Coe crossed his right leg over his left knee, eyeing the books on Dad's shelf. "Skye thinks they'll be back. I tend to agree."

"Why don't we call the police and get extra protection here?" Dad stroked his chin with its deep dimple that Coe inherited.

"Skye doesn't want us to do that due to her father's position in the philanthropist community. But if those guys return and cross any lines, I won't hesitate to call the authorities."

"Good. We have Gran and Mom to consider, too." Dad clasped his hands and gave Coe a sincere look. "Are you in love with Skye, son?"

Coe gulped, dislodging his leg from his knee. "I'd rather not discuss the private side of our relationship with anyone but her yet."

"I respect that." Dad tugged his top button loose. "However, if either of you wants counseling or someone to talk with, don't hesitate to reach out to me, Mom, or Gran. Now, there's another matter I want to chat with you about."

"All right." Coe fidgeted in his seat, worried about the upcoming topic.

"William Bradford sent me an email detailing what the church council came up with for the current pastoral requirements. You're married, so that takes care of their main concern, which was previously a problem for them."

"Dad—"

"No matter how hard I tried to get them to alter their stipulation, the board wouldn't budge about a pastor needing to be married." Dad lifted his hands. "So, what do you think?"

"About what?"

Dad grinned like Coe was teasing. "Only what we've talked about since you were four."

"I'm not that kid anymore." Maybe he could make his excuses and check on Skye.

"No. But you still love the Lord and want to follow Him in everything, right?" Dad's voice deepened, like he shifted to his preaching voice.

"Yes." But following the Lord meant different things to Dad and Coe. While Dad had a genuine pastoral heart, Coe felt led to serve in other capacities outside of the church building.

"Then you haven't changed that much."

"I no longer want to be a pastor." He heard the intense tone of his voice and regretted it. "Sorry. I mean no disrespect."

"How—" Dad cleared his throat. "How long have you felt this way?"

"I suppose ever since I experienced serving disaster victims and helped rebuild houses for people who didn't stand a chance at a place to live unless strangers like me assisted them." Coe hoped Dad would read the truth he was trying to convey. "Maybe since I helped a frightened kid locate his parents after an earthquake. Or the time I helped a family barely escape their crumbling home and brought them to an emergency shelter." Coe took a breath. "And since I found out what it's like to depend solely on God, being dependent on Him for everything, I've known this is what I want to do with my life."

"Wow." Dad shivered and rubbed his arms. "I'm proud of you for having that kind of faith and dependency on God." He held out his hands, palms up. "But you have a wife now. A family in the future? How will you provide and be present for them if you are roaming the globe?"

"I don't have that part figured out." He and Skye hadn't fallen in love or even talked about kids, let alone resolve how they'd spend the next few years.

"I'm floundering." Dad raked his fingers through his hair again. "I thought you wanted to be a pastor as a long-term plan."

"I've tried to tell you I didn't. I guess I didn't communicate it well enough." Coe's attempt to speak moderately was a struggle. "I want to follow my heart and how God works in me to reach people's lives right where they're living, struggling, in need, or whatever. All of us are on a unique journey with Him. Isn't that what you always told us?"

"Yes. And that's admirable." Yet Dad stared back at him with an anxious or crestfallen look, reminding him of the expression on Mom's face when she mentioned not being at their wedding.

"I'm sorry if I've disappointed you. I'd never purposefully hurt you."

"I know that." Dad tapped his fingers on the desktop. "You're sure about not wanting to try out for the pastorate here?" Coe heard the longing in his voice.

"I'm sure. Pastoring was your heart's greatest desire."

"That and being a dad." Tears filled his eyes. "It's been a good life."

Coe got a little choked up, too. "I've heard people complain about their dads. But I've always been proud of who you were as a father to nine rambunctious boys." He took a breath and released it slowly. "I always knew you loved me and never felt lost in the group."

"I appreciate your saying that. I love you and your brothers so much." Dad rubbed the side of his finger beneath his nose. "Being a parent has been the highlight of my life."

"I'm sure you hoped one of us would follow in your footsteps as a pastor." Coe felt a knot in his belly. "I'm sorry it won't be me."

"That's all right." Dad covered his face with his palms like he was subduing his emotions or else praying.

"There's always Spur," Coe said lightly.

Dad chuckled. "True. But we may have lost him to Hawaii. He's doing well over there."

"That's great to hear. I appreciate everything you, Mom, and Gran have done for me. If Skye and I have kids, I want to be a good dad like you." He stood, eager to check on Skye.

"Thank you, son." Dad walked around the desk and pulled him into a bear hug. "No matter what you decide to do, I am here for you. Mom's here for you, too. We love you. And we're proud of you."

"Thanks, Dad."

He was a full-grown adult who'd traveled to distant countries, but being back in this office, talking with Dad, and even their hug, made him feel a bit like a teenager again. Yet everything was different because he was a husband now.

Chapter Forty

Skye opened her eyes to early morning light coming through the window and found Coe's side of the bed empty. Was he showering? Making breakfast? She hoped he'd make blueberry pancakes like he did another time this week. She was lucky to have married a man capable of cooking, washing dishes, and doing his laundry. She smiled, feeling content with her new life.

Voices from downstairs reached her, and getting coffee before she showered sounded inviting. She was adjusting to the rhythms of the Norths' household, although not the occasional chaos ensuing when several brothers were in the same room. Their laughter, teasing, and cajoling made her want to escape out the back door and find refuge at Trish's a few times.

Eager for her first cup of coffee, Skye strode down the hall and down a few stairs. But when she heard her name spoken, coming from the kitchen, her footfall froze.

"I'm sure Skye would understand. She seems like a reasonable woman," Liv said.

"She is," Coe said quietly.

Skye released the breath she hadn't realized she was holding.

"Then what's the problem? Would an informal reciting of your vows be so bad? A mini-ceremony would allow Gran and me to watch you get married, Coe. It would mean a great deal to us." Skye heard Liv's tender, motherly tone and wanted to assure her that such a gathering would be fine with her.

"Skye and I had a private ceremony. We don't want any to-do about it."

We don't? They hadn't discussed a reception or family gathering, but why was Coe against it? And why was he deciding about it without talking to her? Her feelings against a man making all the decisions rose in her like a flame gobbling up dry tinder. Was this how he thought their marriage would work, with him calling the shots? Perhaps, he thought she didn't want a big deal made about their wedding and felt he could speak for them. But shouldn't he have asked her first? She wanted to rush downstairs and set the record straight, but Coe was speaking again, and she wanted to hear what he had to say.

"Skye and I chose to marry quickly." His cough overrode something Liv said. "I'm sorry if that hurts you. But let's put the ceremony part of our wedding behind us." Why? Was he ashamed of their courthouse wedding?

"I didn't get to see Hud's wedding," Liv said softly. "So we had a family get-together, and Hud and Trista said some vows so Dad and I could be part of it. It wasn't serious or formal, but it was memorable. Would it be so bad for you and Skye to do something similar?"

Of course, it wouldn't! She wanted to tell Coe her view on the subject, along with a few choice words about him not including her in the discussion. But she waited, hoping he'd say he needed to run this idea by her.

"I'm sorry you weren't at our ceremony. It was brief and without fanfare. And we've moved on." Moved on? In one week? "I promised to protect Skye, and I've tried to do that. It's been challenging, but we're making the best of it."

Seriously? Making the best of it? If that's how he felt, why was he kissing her like they would be together forever?

"Spying, sister-in-law?" Wilks whispered behind her. She clenched her jaw to stop a gasp from escaping her mouth. "What are they talking about so intensely?" He peered over the railing.

Skye grimaced, silently imploring him not to say anything else.

"I think you're underestimating your wife." Liv's voice filtered up the stairway.

"I think I know her well enough."

Skye muffled a groan.

"Ahh. They're talking about you?" Wilks raised his eyebrows, a softer expression crossing his features than she thought him capable of.

"Leave it alone. Please," she whispered, embarrassed about the discussion she'd been caught listening to.

"You're certain there will be no ceremony or party?" Liv asked.

"It isn't a good time. Skye and I are still trying to work things out."

Of course, they were. What did he expect after one week of marriage? Did he mean they might call it quits since they were still in that stage?

"I guess your fake marriage isn't as happy as it appears."

"Wilks—" She gritted her teeth.

Tossing her a mischievous look, he jogged down the stairs. "Morning, everyone."

"Good morning, Wilks. Sleep well?" Liv asked, sounding less emotional.

"Did you know your voices carry up the stairs?" *The rat.*

"Sorry if we bothered you," Liv said.

"No problem." Wilks sniffed. "The food and coffee smells fantastic."

He was right, but Skye was no longer in the mood for coffee or talking to any of the Norths. She pivoted and rushed back to the guest room.

Chapter Forty-one

Skye had been unusually quiet for the last two hours while they were painting window frames and trim on the second floor, and Coe was at a loss. Things had been going well between them since their date two nights ago. Now, every topic he brought up got a one-word, aloof response. He couldn't fathom what was going on. Was she offended by something he said? He couldn't recall saying anything out of line.

If they were fighting, he'd know, right? And if they were fighting, she had asked him to kiss her like they did a few days ago. Thoughts of their previous kisses zinged through his mind, lighting up his sensors and making him eager to try kissing her right out of her funk. But did he dare kiss her like he was imagining without anything romantic leading up to it, just because she'd asked him to? Talk about not understanding women!

"I need more paint." Skye moved woodenly toward the door.

"Do we need to talk?"

She hesitated. "Maybe."

"I'm here if you want to tell me what's going on." He set down his paintbrush, stood without finishing the section of trim, and scrubbed his fingers with a rag. "If I said something—"

"It doesn't matter." By her tone, it mattered a great deal.

"Just tell me what's troubling you, please? I want to know."

"Do you want to know what's bothering me because you care about me, or so you can apologize and not feel guilty?"

Oh. Did she think he should feel guilty about something? "Probably both. Our relationship is too new for me to guess what's happened to make you unhappy with me." He stretched his hands, flexing his cramped fingers. "I'm sorry if I spoke out of turn or lacked sensitivity about something. But it's better if you tell me what's wrong so we can discuss it and resolve the issue. Let's not play emotional games."

She stared at him for several moments, then her shoulders sagged, her chin lowering. "You're right. I don't know you well, either. I doubt you meant to say what you did within my hearing, which makes it worse." *Uh-oh. What did I say?* "When you visited with your mom this morning, I heard your conversation."

He felt an emotional slug to the gut. "What did you hear?"

She heaved a sigh. "You said you had to marry me, like you didn't have a choice. As if your only option was to spend your days bound to a woman you don't love." She pressed her lips together.

"Oh, Skye." His mouth went dry. "I didn't mean it like that. Honestly, I didn't."

"I heard how trapped you sounded. How you felt stuck in our marriage and barely getting through." Her voice broke. "Coe, I know we aren't in a real relationship, but I thought we were trying to have one."

"We are. I'm sorry." He reached out to her, but she flinched, so he pulled his arms to his side. "I was sharing with Mom about how things transpired between us. How we were keeping a low profile. I didn't mean to be so—" Cold? Rude? How could he explain or fix this?

"Is that how you feel? Like I coerced you into marrying me?"

"No."

"Then what?"

"I was trying to do the honorable thing by marrying you. The right thing."

"Oh, Coe." Disdain filled her tone. "I'm not a disaster victim for you to fix. It was noble of you to take on my situation after I asked for your help. But if you want out, you're relieved of your duties and any feelings of being honor-bound to me. We can walk away from this fake marriage today."

"Skye, that isn't what I want. And I don't consider it fake."

"What you want isn't the only thing that matters."

"I know. I'm sorry," he said again, feeling terrible that he had said something that caused such hurt and division. "How can I make this right?"

"You can't. What's done is done." Her words sounded so final.

"I admit I said some regrettable things in my explanation to my mom." He wished he'd spoken more supportively of Mom's viewpoint. And he wished he'd mentioned needing to discuss a wedding reception with Skye before deciding about it.

Skye stared at him with tears swimming in her eyes, and he wanted to promise everything would be better and he'd try harder. Together, they would figure out how to make their marriage work. But empty promises wouldn't be enough. He had to dig deeper within himself to reach her heart. "Skye," he said softly and clasped her hand. The thought of kissing her at a time like this seemed a little bizarre, but she had asked him to do it. He wanted to bridge their emotional gap and try to get them back on track toward falling in love any way he could. He gazed into her eyes, wanting to gauge her response and hoping she'd see the sincerity in his gaze and that he was about to kiss her. He moved a couple of inches closer to her.

She jerked back, eyes widening—not the reaction he was hoping for. "What are you doing, Coe?"

"You asked me to kiss you if we ever argued or our feelings were hurt."

"Well, don't." She shuddered. "Please, don't."

"Okay. I won't." He lifted his hands, feeling more confused and idiotic than ever. "Can we talk some more, then? I have zero experience with what it takes to be a good husband."

"I don't know anything about being a wife, either."

"Then let's make room for each other, allow for some mistakes, and have grace while we try to figure out how to—"

"Fall for each other?" she said, like falling in love was a terrible idea. "Force yourself to love me? Like you were going to force a kiss?"

"Not force. I honestly care for you and have feelings for you. But, Skye, sometimes I'm going to say the wrong thing or do an annoying thing. Like today. Can we please try to help each other figure out what being married means? Let's help each other get better at being loving?" He stroked a few strands of hair back from her cheek and caught a tear on his index finger. "I want to improve at being your husband. I promise I'll try harder."

She stared at him doubtfully, tears trickling down her cheeks, and he wished he were a better husband already.

"Why did you make it sound like we shouldn't have a party? Are you embarrassed about how we got married? Or about us?"

"Heavens, no. I didn't think you wanted a big deal made either."

"How could you know anything I want without asking me?"

"I don't know." He thrust his fingers through his hair, struggling with his thoughts and frustrations. "Have you forgotten we're hiding from Rhett and Tip?" She squinted at him. Maybe that was a touchy subject to bring up in the middle of a tense discussion. "Why were you listening to us? Why didn't you come down and say you wanted all the wedding hoopla?"

"Don't blame me for what you said." She swiped her fingers beneath her eyes. "I should have come downstairs. You're right about that. But you and your mom were talking about me, and I listened. I wish I hadn't. Are you having second thoughts about marrying me?"

"No." He exhaled a sharp breath. "I'm sorry for sounding indecisive. I'm not having second thoughts. But I am still trying to figure stuff out. Do you have marriage all worked out?"

"No." She scrubbed some paint off her nails. "You kiss me like the sun rises on us falling in love. Then you don't kiss me or act affectionate and leave our bedroom without talking to me. What am I supposed to think? How am I supposed to know what you are thinking or feeling?"

But if he stayed—

"I heard you talking to your mom like you were at your wits' end about our marriage, and we've been married a week. A week, Coe!" She thrust out her hands. "Where's the guy who kissed me like the earth shook under our feet in India?"

"I'm so sorry." How many times had he said that in this conversation? "If you want us to do a vow exchange with my family present, I can talk to Mom about it."

"No thanks. You've made your wishes clear. Are we done here?"

"I guess. Skye?"

"You're sorry. I'm sorry. Do you plan to stay married to me?"

"Yes."

"Then I agree with your assessment that we will work out this marriage, eventually. For now, we are all done kissing." She left the room abruptly.

Done kissing? How was that even possible?

Chapter Forty-two

Two hours later, with her nerves taut and thoughts racing with the memory of arguing with Coe, Skye ached to get out of the house, breathe some fresh air, and walk by herself. But the fear of Rhett and Tip waiting for her to make a thoughtless mistake and grabbing her was a barrier to doing what she wanted. She ought to stay indoors. But feeling stuck in Coe's family's house, contemplating her frustrations, only worsened things, intensifying her need to get away.

She paced from the kitchen to the front door and back five times before Trish's invitation to come by whenever she felt like it was too inviting to ignore. She left the house without telling Coe where she was going and strode down the path to his grandmother's cottage. "It's Skye," she called, tapping on the door before entering. "Hello?"

"Skye?" Trish lowered a green throw off her shoulders from where she sat in a rocking chair, blinking, her mouth opening and closing a few times. "I'm afraid you caught me dozing."

"I'm sorry for the intrusion. Should I come back later?"

"Not at all. Are you okay, dear?" Trish peered at her.

"I'm okay. Better now that I'm here." She sat on the edge of the sofa. "I'm sorry for disturbing your rest. I was going stir crazy, pacing and feeling cooped up." It felt nice sitting in this quiet cottage with

Coe's kindhearted grandmother and not feeling all that tension with her grandson.

"No worries." Trish chuckled, her soft-looking blondish-white hair shimmering beneath the lamplight. "I was reading my Bible and fell asleep." A large print book rested on her lap. "I'm glad for the company. There was a time when Liv and Smith's boys tromped through my house at all times of the day, getting cookies, visiting, and praying with me. I miss those days." She sighed and set her Bible on the end table.

"Can I get you anything? Tea? Coffee?"

"I'm fine, thank you." Trish smiled softly. "If you want something, help yourself."

"I'm all right, too."

Trish clasped her hands together, eyes glistening. "How are things going with you and Coe?" It seemed she sensed something was amiss and dove right into the sensitive topic.

What could Skye say? Coe's being annoying? *We're fighting?* Guilt settled in her middle. She hadn't come here to report their personal struggles to Trish. She should have anticipated the strain of new beginnings in a marriage, a feeling many couples could relate to, instead of wanting things to go rosy and romantic with him all the time. So, he discussed their marriage with his mom. Was that so terrible? Why had she reacted so strongly?

"We're doing as well as can be expected, considering our brief relationship and how we plunged into marriage."

"Goodness. That sounds overwhelming."

"It is sometimes," Skye said honestly.

"Is there anything you'd like to talk about? You can tell me anything, and I won't share it with anyone other than the Lord. *He* and I talk about everything." Trish rocked leisurely, a pleasant expression on her face.

Gazing into Coe's grandmother's kind, caring eyes, Skye felt some of her angsty feelings disintegrating. She took a deep breath, and her life story came tumbling out, choppily and out of order, but she felt relieved for the chance to express herself. She shared about her father bringing wealthy supporters of his foundation to their home as potential suitors, her mother's untimely death, the grief and loneliness she felt afterward, and how she found peace and purpose in humanitarian work. She told Trish how she admired Coe's work ethic and caring heart for others, and how attracted she was to him. It felt good to talk with someone who listened, nodded, and seemed to understand her deepest feelings.

Skye gnawed on her lower lip, feeling some turmoil about confessing to something else that was troubling her. She took a deep breath and said, "I used to daydream about ways to get Father to let me marry a man of my choosing. I even devised a plan to get a nice guy to my doorstep and kiss him so convincingly that Father would have to let me marry him." Heat fanned up her cheeks at the admission.

Trish's eyebrows rose. "Is that what happened between you and Coe?"

"Not entirely." Skye took a breath, then exhaled. "However, I thought if Father saw that I cared for a fellow humanitarian, he would have to accept my choice of a boyfriend." Skye replayed the scene in her mind. "But when he found us kissing, he was enraged and became explosive and unreasonable. I should have known better."

"Oh, dear."

"I told him about Coe having a beautiful heart for helping people and how much good he had done in his years with the Tamarack Foundation." Skye groaned. "It didn't matter. Father couldn't see him as husband material for me. No one, other than someone he chose, would ever be good enough for him to accept."

"So, let me get this straight." Trish smoothed her hand over the blanket. "You planned to kiss a man your father would see and approve of, and that man happened to be our Coe?"

"Yes." Skye winced. "But when he offered to walk me home after church and his fingers brushed mine, and our gazes clung to each other's like we'd never let one another go, I realized how much I liked him. And there was no subterfuge in that kiss my father saw."

"Does Coe know all this?"

"He doesn't know about me wanting to set someone up for my father to find me kissing." Her chest tightened with a painful ache. "My scheme failed, anyway."

"Yet, God used it for good, didn't He?" Trish's eyes gleamed. "Thank you for sharing your thoughts with me, my dear. Now, what happened today that troubled you and brought you here, although you're always welcome?"

Skye debated telling her what she'd overheard between Coe and Liv. "I don't want Coe making decisions for me. A man has ruled my life long enough."

"Was he trying to rule you?" Trish sounded aghast at the idea.

"Probably not. But he made some decisions without including me." She huffed. "I might have overreacted."

"There's only one thing to do, then," Trish said.

"We've already argued about it."

"Good."

"Good?"

"Absolutely. You took vows that you would stay married to each other, right?" Skye nodded even though she had been having some second thoughts. "Then you should prioritize your relationship and pray together about your dreams and struggles every day." Trish wagged her finger. "It's been a lifetime since I was married, but I believe communication is vital."

"No doubt." Skye chuckled. "I can see why those boys ran over to chat with you and why Coe loves you so much." She already felt thankful for Trish's wisdom and advice.

A sudden, loud crash sent window glass flying across the room. Skye screamed and dove protectively over Trish. Another crash sounded, followed by two masked men barreling through the glassless frames. *Rhett and Tip!*

"Stay back!" Skye shouted, reaching for her phone.

"What's happening?" Trish asked weakly.

"Come with us now," Rhett ordered in his gravelly voice. "And no one will get hurt."

"Get out of here!" Before Skye could call Coe or 911, Rhett and Tip grabbed her and dragged her toward the door. "Let me go!" Her cell phone fell from her hands. She fought against both men, kicking, jerking, and shoving, but they didn't loosen their hold on her.

"Let her go," Trish yelled, throwing pillows and books at them. "You are trespassing on private property."

"You're coming with us whether you like it or not," Rhett said in his rough voice.

"I'm not going anywhere with you." Skye lunged toward Tip, knocking him onto the couch. She tried doing the same thing to Rhett, but he held on tighter. "Let me go!" She rocked back and forth, squirming and jerking. No way was she letting them take her away without a fight. "Cooooooooe!" Rhett slapped his gloved hand over her mouth. She bit down hard, and he yowled.

"Release her." Trish held up her phone. "My son and grandsons are on their way." *Thank you, Trish!*

"So what?" Tip said mockingly. "No one is stopping us."

"You won't get away with this," Skye shouted. But they continued carrying her toward the door like she was a piece of furniture they were stealing. She grabbed at anything that might delay them taking her, knocking over a bookshelf and a wooden stand that sent a spider plant plummeting to the floor. "I'm not leaving!" *Hurry, Coe!*

"Yes, you are. I'll see you back to your father's house if it's the last thing I do," Rhett said threateningly.

"Let her go!" Coe shouted as he charged into the house. "Set my wife down and get out of here. You are trespassing!"

"That's what I told them," Trish said.

The intruders backed up toward the windows, not releasing Skye, as if they were going to kidnap her right in front of Coe and Trish. But they weren't expecting Smith and Wilks to crawl through the gaping windows, preventing an exit that way. Rhett's and Tip's heads bobbed between the windows and door, as if they were trying to figure out how to fight off the three men and still take her.

"It's over." Coe extended his hands toward them. "Release Skye and leave. The police are on their way. You'll both be arrested and charged if you are still here." He called the police? Or was he bluffing? "If you're here when they arrive, we are pressing charges." He sounded serious.

The shrill sound of sirens approaching was a warning to Rhett and Tip, who immediately dropped her on the floor with a hard thud and fled out the door. Skye moaned and rubbed her side.

"Are you okay?" Coe knelt beside her and helped her into a sitting position.

"I will be. Those scums are out of control."

"I'm sorry this happened."

"Me too." She was thankful he got here in time and hadn't let Father's brutes take her.

Behind them, Smith asked Trish how she was doing. She said she felt energized after hurling household items at the intruders and even bragged about how brave Skye had been. Smith led his mom out of the cottage, explaining that she would be staying at the big house until they got her windows replaced. He called back to Coe that he'd talk to the police. Throughout the exchange, Smith maintained a kind, caring tone of voice that was both comforting and peaceful. *He's nothing like Father, either.*

Wilks took snapshots of the broken windows, then left Skye and Coe alone.

"Why did you call the police?" She didn't mean to sound sharp, but her adrenaline was still spiking, and she had told him she didn't want him to call the authorities.

"This was a violent break-in," he said as if she didn't know that. "You and my grandmother were in danger. Of course, I called law enforcement. Liam went too far this time."

"I still wish you hadn't." She scooted back and stood on her own, some annoyance battling with her desire to understand his decision.

"Your father can't send men to capture you and possibly hurt my grandmother without me doing something about it." He raked his fingers through his hair. "What kind of man would I be, then?"

"I'm thankful your grandmother wasn't injured."

"But she could have been."

"But she wasn't."

"They broke her windows. Flying glass is dangerous." He paced, clearly frustrated. "You could have been hurt, also." Was he angry with her or worried about his grandmother's safety? "You shouldn't have come over here without telling me where you were headed."

"What?" Now he was being unreasonable. "Your grandmother's house is twenty feet from your parents' back door. Hardly dangerous."

"Yet you led the bad guys right to her house."

"No. I. Uh—" She hadn't meant to do that. Was Coe just trying to pick an argument with her? "I didn't know anyone was watching me. How could I?" Her voice trembled with a mix of frustration and hurt. "I needed someone to talk with." *Because of you*, she almost added. "Your grandmother invited me to come by whenever I wanted. So, I did."

Coe heaved a sigh like he was silencing whatever else he wanted to say to her, then marched into the kitchen. He returned with a broom and swept up glass shards. Skye searched for some plastic and tape to cover the windows. They finished their tasks silently and broodingly.

Chapter Forty-three

For a week, Skye and Coe shared a bed with a space between them that felt as wide as a block. The chasm seemed like a mile tonight, since he had thrown some pillows on the floor and was sleeping there. Considering she had the bed to herself, she should have been able to sleep like a baby. Instead, she tossed and turned, dozing intermittently but not falling into a deep sleep. The last time she checked, it was two a.m.

In her restless state, she contemplated everything that had happened with Rhett and Tip's failed attempt to snatch her away this afternoon, including her statement to the police officer who wouldn't leave until he'd asked her some questions, and ending with getting a brush-off from Coe. No doubt, she deserved his cold shoulder. She'd brought trouble and danger to the Norths' house, a fact she couldn't ignore in her self-reflection.

Also, her declaration to him that there would be no more kissing reverberated in her thoughts, a constant reminder of her turmoil and regret. She replayed her request for Coe to promise they'd kiss whenever they were angry or had their feelings hurt and felt terrible for how badly that turned out when he attempted it. What was she thinking, asking him to do such a thing? Of course, she wouldn't want a kiss when she was mad at him. But she shouldn't have gotten upset with him for doing what she asked, either.

She sighed and groaned, then flopped onto her back before returning to her side. What a miserable night. She shut her eyes and imagined fluffy sheep jumping over a short white fence, even counting them, then felt silly for trying the childish trick.

"Skye?" Coe's sleepy voice came from right above her.

"Coe?" Why was he so close to her? She jolted upright, feeling his breath against her cheek, and pushed herself against the headboard. How did he get to her side of the bed without her noticing? His glassy gaze sparkled in the moonlight coming through the window, intensifying her shock at his sudden proximity.

"Skye?" he asked huskily.

"What are you doing, Coe?"

"I, uh, well." He set his hands on the bed next to her.

She gulped, unsettled by his nearness. Did he want to talk or apologize? Did he want to get into bed? Was he cold from sleeping on the floor? Surely, he wasn't going to kiss her.

"I wanted to—"

"Yes?" She smelled his minty breath a second before his lips landed on the corner of her mouth. "Coe!"

"Huh? What?" His weight shifted against the mattress as he stood.

"Why did you kiss me?"

"Did I kiss you?" he asked thickly.

"Yes. You startled me. Go back to sleep, will you?"

"Sorry. I didn't know," he muttered, shuffling away. "I didn't know where I was."

"How could you not—" *Ohhh*. Was he sleep-walking? Skye scooted off the bed and directed him to the other side of the mattress. "Come over here." She pulled down the blankets and top sheet, grabbed his pillow off the floor, fluffed it, then set it by the headboard. "Get in bed, okay?"

"Thanks. You're sweet." *Yeah, yeah.* He probably wouldn't remember saying that in the morning. He stretched out on his side and was snoring lightly moments later. What brought about a sleep episode this time? Was it the stress of their argument? Or his worry about Rhett and Tip trying to kidnap her?

"Good night." She pulled the blanket over his shoulder. "I'm sorry. You don't deserve all the trouble I've caused you and your family."

He didn't say anything or acknowledge her.

She grabbed her pillow, settled on the floor where he'd been sleeping, and spent some time praying before falling into a restless sleep.

Chapter Forty-four

Skye clutched her cell phone with a stranglehold and stared out the guest room window, seeing nothing but the gray clouds and relentless rain. Around four a.m., she'd decided to make this call to Father, a decision made during her struggle to find sleep. Now, wide awake, she was no longer sure she had the courage to interact with him.

Before Coe left their room a while ago, he asked how he got into bed last night, and she explained what happened. He apologized for the unexpected kiss and his part in their disagreement. Since he hadn't heard her apology, she said she was sorry, too. It didn't feel like a romantic reconciliation, but possibly a beginning toward understanding each other better.

Lifting her chin, she tapped the screen. Now or never. *Lord, help.*

"Yes?" Father answered gruffly.

"Why did you send your goons to take me away again? When will this madness stop?" She peppered him with questions, not giving him a chance to interrupt. "When will enough be enough?"

"Are you ready to come home yet?"

"No! I'll never be ready to do that." She tried calming her voice, but it was difficult when she wanted to yell at Father until he accepted her decisions. "I thought you should know the police are onto your guys, and your control of me is about to be exposed."

"How dare you—"

"Speak the truth? Stand up for myself and my husband? Yes, Father. It took thousands of miles and marriage to tell you the truth. Please, leave me alone to live my life how I choose."

Deafening silence greeted her.

"Did you know your brutes broke into Coe's grandmother's house, a woman who has done nothing but show me kindness since I got here, smashing her windows and grabbing me in front of her? Coe had no recourse but to call the authorities when you tried stealing his wife." She clenched one fist around the white curtains, squeezing them. "The officer who took my statement was quite interested in Rhett and Tip's misdeeds."

"Did you mention me?"

"Of course I did. I told them exactly what the Tamarack Foundation's employees have been doing on U.S. soil. How *you* sent them to drag me back to a place I don't want to return to." He cursed, and she winced. "Did you expect this to end well? How could it?"

"I expected you to come home like a loving daughter should, like the daughter I raised would have done before a fool from Idaho brainwashed her." He probably meant to make her feel guilty and obligated to do his bidding, but he no longer had that strong hold over her. She'd broken free of his control, which was liberating, and she had God and Coe to thank for it.

"Coe is no fool. And after the way you've treated me, how can you think I'd come back? If anyone was brainwashing anyone, it was you. At least, your attempts failed." Her words were harsh but needed to be said.

"Is this the loyalty you show me? Is this how you want things to stand between us?"

"I want you to let me go peacefully." She forced her voice to a trained softness, her eyes burning with tears. "Father, if you love me at all, please accept my decision to marry Coe. I fear that is too much to expect, but I'm begging you to let me go. Even though you fought me every step of the way toward my independence, even endangering my life by employing Rhett and Tip to roughly handle me and drug me, I'm asking this of you."

"They chose an extreme path I didn't encourage."

She doubted his innocence where Rhett and Tip were concerned. "They are your well-trained dogs. They bark at your command." She'd seldom spoken so boldly to him. Yet courage rose within her like a sunflower coming into bloom. "Would Mom have wanted you to sell me off to the highest bidder? Would she have allowed you to deny me the inheritance she left for me from her family?"

"We aren't discussing your mother," he shouted.

"Why not?" She also raised her voice. Anyone in the hallway would hear her, but she didn't care. "Her DNA runs through me, too. Why can't you let me live my life how I want? And how I'm sure Mom would have encouraged me to live?"

Father muttered something about her lack of respect and how she didn't appreciate all he'd done for her. At the same time, Coe opened the bedroom door and asked, "Skye? Are you okay?" She nodded and made a go-away gesture, and he quietly closed the door.

"You are all I have left," Father continued. "That's why I can't let you go. Edmund will be good to you. It's safe here. It's where I want you to live."

"Don't send any more criminals after me. I'm warning you," she said firmly. "I'm done protecting your name. I will go to the press if this continues."

"My bodyguards are there for your safety."

"I haven't felt safe around them. They are hoodlums who only want your money and will do anything to get it."

"They have worked diligently to bring you back to my house without harm." He spoke as if he were proud of Rhett and Tip.

"Not true!" She cupped the back of her neck and gritted her teeth. "Just tell them to leave me and the Norths alone. Keep my money for all I care. But call off your hounds."

"Or what?" He really had to ask?

"Or you are creating an uncrossable chasm." She felt a deep pain in her chest, like her heart was breaking. "Someday there might be grandchildren." At least, she hoped there would be. "Do you honestly not want to see them?"

"How do you plan to live the rest of your life without me?" His voice sounded wheedling, like he was still trying to guilt her. "Without my resources? Without my money?"

"I'd rather we got along. Considering your recent actions, I doubt that can happen. Please, let me stay with my husband and walk down the street without fear of retaliation from you."

"Under one condition." She was surprised to hear him concede even one point. "Are you carrying Cole's child?"

"It's Coe."

"Being with child is the only reason I would condone your marrying a man like him without my blessing."

"Unbelievable." He didn't even understand her point about grandchildren being a favorable reason for him to make peace with her.

"Does that mean you are not pregnant?"

If there was a time for a convenient lie, this was it. But she wouldn't do that. "No. I am not carrying Coe's baby."

"Then get on the next flight home," he ordered. "I'll free up your accounts and set the wedding ceremony in motion. Edmond will still marry you."

She groaned, frustrated beyond words. Father hadn't budged an inch and didn't respect her right to choose a life for herself. "I'm not coming back. Goodbye, Father."

"We are not finished!"

"Sadly, we are." She hovered her finger over the disconnect icon. "I love you. But if you are going to be a part of my life, you must accept that I am Skye North and Coe is my choice of a husband."

She ended the call, dropped onto the bed, and sobbed quietly. But even through her emotional tears, her words, *Coe is my choice of a husband,* rang in her ears. If she had chosen Coe, then why wasn't she making more of an effort to stay with him and learn to love him?

Chapter Forty-five

Coe sat between Skye and Gran in the family pew at Thunder Ridge Fellowship, wishing he could bridge the gap between Skye and him, hold her hand, and find peace with her. But their communication hadn't improved since the altercation with Rhett and Tip three days ago. The next day, when he awoke and found Skye sleeping on the floor, he should have insisted they talk more about what happened with her dad's men and about him kissing her in the night. But she acted like it wasn't a big deal, even apologized, and wanting to keep things peaceful between them, he let his concerns go.

Then there was her telephone conversation with her dad he walked in on. He'd left the room and waited in the hallway, catching snippets of her side of the conversation. He longed for the chance to talk with her about it, hoping it would bring them closer. But he got called to check on a problem with the furnace and was distracted for a few hours.

They hadn't discussed Mom's suggestion about a wedding party anymore, either. He'd thought waiting until their emotionally charged differences settled down might be better. But it wouldn't be the first time he was wrong about something concerning their marriage. Probably not the last, either.

The choir sang a modern rendition of "At the Cross," then the congregation joined in on the chorus. Skye's soft alto voice sounded melodic and beautiful. But he couldn't help noticing the foot of space she maintained between them, even when they were standing. He sang a few lyrics, not feeling the spiritual impact he usually did when he sang hymns at church. So many things had gone wrong or were out of sync since he and Skye embarked on this marital path. Why were they struggling to adjust to each other? Why weren't they communicating better?

He silently cried out to God. *Lord, help us. Help me. I haven't prayed like I should have been doing lately. I'm sorry about that. Please, help things improve between Skye and me as a married couple. Help me to know how to be a better husband for her.*

He should have been more understanding about Skye going to Gran's without telling him. Who was he to demand anything from her or tell her she should have talked to him first? What was he thinking, other than being stressed and worried? How could she have known Rhett and Tip were watching his grandmother's house, waiting for an opportunity to abscond with her? He was a fool for overreacting. He'd blown it big time, again.

How was he going to win Skye's heart? He needed to try harder to make this marriage work. But something about that undertaking didn't sound inviting. Why did he keep thinking about making their marriage work like it was an arduous chore, too difficult or exhausting?

He yearned for a heartfelt romantic relationship with his wife, not one that was complicated, forced, or made up. He wanted what Mom and Dad had found—true happiness and a lifelong love. But admittedly, he wanted it to happen promptly. Presto. Easy-peasy. He let out a long sigh that hurt. He had some soul searching and, yes, some work to do in the days ahead.

After the singing ended, a guest minister stood behind what Coe had always considered Dad's pulpit. "Good morning, fellow pilgrims!"

The man was exuberant and loud, and the microphone squawked like it was rebelling against the unusual volume. "Sorry about that." The minister tapped the microphone and cast the crew in the tech booth a grimace.

"I'm Pastor Michael St. James from the lovely state of Indiana. Thank you for letting me share with you this morning. I've been anticipating this trip to the Pacific Northwest and having the chance to meet you and deliver the message on my heart."

"Is that what you would do if you tried out?" Skye leaned over and whispered, her breath tickling his ear.

"Yeah." He was surprised and pleased she was talking to him and felt compelled to engage with her. But Gran would surely elbow him if they continued talking during a sermon, so he didn't elaborate.

"Do you want to do that?" Skye asked at the same time Pastor Michael mentioned where to turn in their Bibles, and Coe missed the verse's location. It was unfortunate that he hadn't explained more about his feelings concerning a pulpit ministry to her before this.

"Not especially." Beside him, Gran moved restlessly. He opened his Bible to Peter, then First John. Where was the preacher speaking from? Ephesians? He felt Skye's intense gaze, like she wasn't satisfied with his answer, but she didn't ask any other questions.

"Let's pray," the visiting minister said.

It was weird to be back in his home church and for Dad not to be preaching. How was he feeling about eager ministers trying out the position he loved?

Pastor Michael preached charismatically and fervently, making the microphone squawk a few more times. Congregants gasped or jerked each time. Coe felt Skye pressing closer to him as the man's volume and seemingly righteous indignation increased. Pastor Michael shouted about the evils of sin in the world, especially in the current political climate, and the unforgettable damnation of hell. With one demonstrative point, he clutched the pulpit so tightly his knuckles bulged, and the whites of his eyes glowed eerily beneath the overhead lights. Leaning forward, grimacing, the preacher bellowed, "If you were to die on your way to a restaurant after church, are you prepared to stand before your Maker?"

The speakers blasted shrilly. And Skye clutched Coe's arm.

It had been eons since he heard a minister speak so fervently. Skye leaned against him like she was trying to escape the noise or the judgment the man was expounding about. At least one good thing came of Pastor Michael's sermonizing. There wasn't any distance on the pew between him and Skye now. Small blessings.

As they left the building following the service, William Bradford, the youngest member on the church board, shook his hand. "May I have a word?" He glanced from Coe to Skye.

"Uh. Sure. This is my wife, Skye."

"Hello." She smiled warmly.

"Welcome to Thunder Ridge Fellowship, Mrs. North. I hope you enjoyed the service."

"The choir was lovely." She met Coe's gaze with a twinkle in her eye. "I'm going to say hello to your mom."

"Okay."

William swayed his hand toward the lawn on the right side of the building. Coe followed him, hoping this wasn't a query about taking the pastorate.

"Your dad has kept us abreast of your good Samaritan travels and deeds. I've been impressed by your faithful efforts to assist people worldwide."

"Thank you." Coe cleared his throat. "I've tried to go where the Lord leads and do whatever task is set before me."

"Exactly. And He led you to your wife?" William grinned.

"I believe He did." Coe didn't want to divulge any personal details, though.

"Doing hands-on work and spreading the Gospel in other countries must have been fulfilling and eye-opening, hmm?"

"Sure." Where was this conversation going? Why was William singling him out?

"Which leads me to my next question." William checked his phone and stuffed it into his gray sports coat pocket. "Would you be available to talk with our council this week?"

"About what?" Coe's stomach tightened.

"Has your father mentioned the possibility of you stepping up to the plate?"

Coe and his brothers enjoyed playing baseball growing up, but he doubted William was referring to stepping up to home plate in a game. "I guess. But you should know, I don't feel the Lord's leading toward a pastoral ministry." Coe tried speaking courteously. "I'm more comfortable with helping others in difficult or trying circumstances like I've been doing."

"Sure, sure." William stroked his clean-shaven chin. "Would you mind chatting with us?"

"I don't see how it would help." He felt blindsided by the man's request, and his first instinct was to say no. He was busy with the remodel, needed to spend more time with Skye, and wasn't interested in pursuing the pastoral position. But even with all that, he found himself acquiescing. "However, I am open to meeting and answering your questions."

"Perfect. Ten o'clock Tuesday morning?"

Just then, he spotted two men who resembled Rhett and Tip, standing beside a jet black SUV. Their backs were facing him, but one had red hair like Tip's. The other was muscular and had dark hair. Had Liam's bodyguards been in the service, watching Skye and him? A chill raced across Coe's shoulders and up his neck. The two guys jumped in their vehicle and sped off, making him feel more certain it was them. A feeling of dread settled in the pit of his stomach.

"What do you say?" William asked, and Coe realized he hadn't given him an answer.

"Uh. All right."

"Thank you for being open to talking with us and praying about a leadership role with the Thunder Ridge Fellowship." William shook his hand vigorously.

Had he agreed to all that?

Chapter Forty-six

Skye accepted Liv's invitation to have breakfast with her at Nelly's the next day and sat across from her in the bustling eatery. The conversation she'd overheard between Liv and Coe four days ago still weighed on her mind, and she hoped for a polite way to bring it up. Would this meeting with Liv give her that opportunity?

Her mother-in-law interacted pleasantly with the wait staff and greeted several customers, asking questions about family members and trips they'd taken. "Do you know all these people?" Skye asked after Liv inquired about the grandmother's health of the woman serving their coffee.

"Not all. But after living in Thunder Ridge for thirty-five years and raising nine boys who participated in sporting events and had friends over, I've met many of the residents." Liv chuckled. "Also, Smith and I are acquainted with a lot of people who attended our church over the years, or ones whose relatives did. Sometimes, the whole town seems like extended family."

"That sounds nice. Father and I never stayed in one place long enough to make lasting friendships, so I don't know what that's like."

"Do you have any family in the States?"

"No. And now I've left Father under bad terms, so Coe is my only family, and I barely know him." Heat bled up her face. Why did she say that to her mother-in-law?

"I can relate." Liv gave her a reassuring smile. "I also left my father's house and business under disagreeable circumstances. I hope you know I'm a part of your family now, too."

"Thank you." Skye felt relieved by Liv's response and hoped she would feel closer to her someday.

When their orders arrived, Liv whispered a prayer. "Thank You for blessing our food and family and for this time of sharing. Amen."

"Amen." Skye took a few bites of her Belgian waffle, but the topic she wanted to bring up kept coming to mind, so she set down her fork. "I've been wanting to talk with you about something."

"All right." Liv set her fork down, too, giving Skye her attention.

"I overheard what you asked Coe the other day about having a gathering in our honor. I'm sorry for how abruptly he declined your idea." She cringed. "And I'm sorry for eavesdropping."

"I didn't know you heard that." Liv lowered her gaze to her plate like she felt embarrassed about it. "I hope you weren't offended or upset by our discussion or my emotional state. If you were, I apologize. I've been adjusting to the idea of Coe being married. He's been away and it all seemed so sudden."

"I understand. And I should have made my presence known or returned to my room." Skye took a sip of water. "But I kept listening, curiously, I admit."

"Don't give it another thought. According to Wilks, we were talking loud enough for everyone in the house to hear." Liv patted her hand. "Thank you for trying to rectify the situation. I've been having a challenging time with my boys growing up and not needing a mama so much." Her smile wobbled. "I miss the days when they sought me out to help solve some dilemma, even if only to mend their socks."

"I thought you might be upset with me."

"Not at all."

Skye sighed, feeling relieved and thankful for this chance to communicate with Liv away from the other family members.

They ate quietly for a few minutes. Then Liv opened her mouth as if to speak, paused like she was contemplating something, then quietly said, "Skye, you are adjusting to life in our chaotic household and big family, but I hope we can become good friends. I mean that."

"Thank you. I hope so, too. And I would have said yes to a gathering, especially knowing how important it is to you. Coe didn't ask for my input—" She gulped, not meaning to speak negatively about her husband to his mother.

"You should have a chat with him about that." Liv's gentle tone held no condemnation.

"I hate causing conflict." The server topped off their coffee, so Skye waited for her to leave before continuing. "I would have enjoyed celebrating our marriage, even if it isn't—" *Ugh*. She said too much again.

"Whatever you and Coe decide about a get-together is fine." Liv turned her coffee cup in a slow circle. "You have to work out your relationship together, and you will. But please, be assured that Trish, Smith, and I are here for both of you, not only Coe."

Skye's heart flooded with warmth at the feeling of family Liv was extending. After the tough conversation she had with Father a few days ago, it meant a lot. "Thank you. I appreciate your kindness."

"You're welcome. Trish has been such a blessing to me. She let me live with her before I married Smith. She helped raise our boys and has been my dear friend through the years." A thoughtful look crossed her face. "I'd love to be like that with my daughters-in-law, too."

"If we have children, I'd welcome your assistance and advice, since I don't have a mom or grandmother."

"You do now."

Skye nearly cried, but she swallowed back her tender emotions. "That's kind of you, especially since you didn't expect Coe to bring a wife with baggage home."

"Sweetie, we all have baggage. Coe is lucky to have you, and you are lucky to have him." Liv gave her an endearing smile, as if she were looking at her as a daughter and not as the stranger her son married.

"I hope that we will truly love each other someday," Skye said, feeling some vulnerability with the admission.

"I'm glad to hear it." Liv's eyes widened like she thought of something else. "What if you embraced the idea that the Lord had a good plan in mind when he brought you and Coe together? What if you thanked Him for the perfect gift of your love?"

"How can anyone be certain if a thing is from God?" Skye felt a twist of anxiety as she sought a way to express herself. "I broke free from my father's plans for my life the only way I could, but I took advantage of Coe's friendship. Did God have anything to do with a part of my journey that seems wrong?"

"Coe felt the Lord was leading him to India. God knew you lived there. You and Coe worked together, right?"

"Yes. Side by side, at times."

"And you liked each other?"

"Yes. And we kissed." Skye felt a tingling sensation sweep up her neck, along with the heat of embarrassment at discussing such things with Coe's mom. "I mean, we really kissed." Why had she told Coe they were done kissing when she enjoyed that part of their relationship so much?

"That's a great starting place for a beautiful story to tell your children someday. And yes, God guides us even when we aren't making the best choices." Liv tugged on her sweater sleeves. "He led me to Trish and Smith when I was seven months pregnant and unmarried. Talk about a situation that seemed wrong. Yet the Lord in His wisdom and goodness made something beautiful out of Smith and me meeting, marrying, and falling in love."

Skye pondered Liv's words. How would it be if she embraced the idea that God brought her and Coe together as a perfect gift for each other? She could never take such a precious gift lightly.

Chapter Forty-seven

Coe sat across from the three council members, wishing he had worn a nice button-up shirt instead of dusty jeans and a paint-speckled flannel shirt. He had been repairing the porch steps right up to the last minute and didn't take the time to clean up properly. He regretted that decision when he saw the others dressed in suits and ties.

He also felt a pang of guilt about not having discussed this meeting with Skye. But why drag her into discussing a pastorate he didn't plan to accept or pursue? Why worry her any more than she already was about Rhett, Tip, and her father? She had enough on her plate. He'd chatted with Gran about today's meeting, and she'd prayed with him. He was glad to be close enough to his grandmother to do that again.

"How's marriage treating you?" William asked.

"Okay." Coe hoped they weren't going to ask personal questions about Skye and him.

"Where did you take your honeymoon?" Mark Cochrane, a middle-aged banker, asked.

"Uh. Well. We've been focused on working at Dad and Mom's place, updating and remodeling. So, no honeymoon yet." Would there even be one? With his short supply of funds, not to mention a honeymoon implied certain aspects of marriage they weren't enjoying, he doubted it.

The others laughed as if he were telling a joke.

Mark shook his head. "Do you mean to say you're making your new bride do repair work during your honeymoon? You'll have a hard time living that one down."

"That's for sure," one of the others said laughingly.

Was it too late to bail on this meeting? "What was it you gentlemen wanted to talk with me about? I have work to get back to." He picked at a spot of dried paint on his nail.

"You and your bride, huh?" Mark snickered.

Coe didn't reply.

William glanced at Mark and the eldest council member, Mr. Peterson. "We want to discuss the possibility of your trying out for the senior pastoral position here."

He'd feared as much. "I haven't changed my mind about that. I don't feel led to a pastoral ministry."

"We want to make sure you understand how eager we are to hear about your life in India and the other countries you've visited. The whole congregation is interested in your spiritual journey." William smiled broadly. "We've discussed how your experiences might inspire our youth to have a deeper walk with Christ and become more service-oriented, too."

"Is that right?" What kind of back-door appeal were they trying to make here? "I thought you needed a replacement for my dad as pastor."

"Oh, we do. We do." Mark rubbed his palms together. "So far, you are the most notable candidate."

"Surely not." Coe pressed back against his chair. "Don't you remember the shenanigans my brothers and I got into when we were kids?" Some of these men were the same ones who knocked on their front door and reported the misdemeanors to Dad.

"That doesn't matter now." William chuckled like he was laughing away embarrassment. "We all sowed some wild oats in our youth. You turned into a man of noble character, that's what counts. We value your input in leading our congregation forward for the next thirty years or so."

Thirty years? Tension rippled across his shoulders and neck.

"What do you think about trying out the pulpit this Sunday?" Mr. Peterson asked, peering at Coe through thick-rimmed glasses that reminded him of a magnifying glass. "Of course, we have to see how you do before moving forward."

Coe heaved a breath. "I can't—"

"We need your help." William peered at him intently. "Since Pastor North informed us of his plan to resign, we've been scrambling to find the right replacement." He sounded desperate. He had to be desperate to make this kind of appeal to Coe. "We've already had four candidates travel here and speak, but none meet our standards. Please, reconsider. To have you continue your dad's legacy in our fellowship would be outstanding."

Coe felt the pressure of three sets of eyes peering at him as if their intense looks alone would coax him to agree, but all he wanted to do was get out of here. "I'm sorry. I can't." He stood and pushed in his chair, his gaze flicking between the trio. "I respect you all and don't want to waste your time. While I'm sure I could speak about my vision for helping people and might inspire someone, that isn't what you need. You are looking for a called-of-God pastor who knows in his or her heart that Thunder Ridge is the absolute place they should minister and shepherd God's flock. That isn't me."

The three men shuffled in their chairs and exchanged glances.

Coe patted his chest. "I understand the toll a pastor's role can have on a family. I consider my dad a great father, but he was often called away from family gatherings to serve others and their families. It takes a special kind of person to do that well. Most of us North boys turned out okay thanks to Mom and Gran's parenting skills, but if it hadn't been for them—"

"How is Stone doing?" William interrupted, a somber expression on his face.

Coe tensed, feeling the burn of anxiety about his out-of-reach brother, then sighed. William's question seemed caring, not judgmental. "We haven't heard from him in a long while."

"We will keep him in our prayers."

"Thank you. Now, I should go so you men can talk about who you should bring on board to pastor this church for the next thirty years." Tempted to run out of the office, he smiled and kept his composure. "Thank you for your time and interest in me. I'm honored."

"Would you be open to speaking this Sunday?" William asked determinedly.

"For what purpose?"

"Inspiration. Direction. So we can hear about the work you've been involved in."

Coe sighed. If he said no, these men he respected might be disappointed in him. Mr. Peterson was one of the people who had generously donated to his original trip. "I can speak on Sunday, but that's all I can agree to."

"Great!"

Each man shook his hand fervently, as if he still might reconsider.

As he walked back home, he pondered how he'd loved hearing stories and reading about Jack Coe's life and dedication to Christ when he was young. He'd even wanted to live up to some of the evangelist's traits and experiences, like selling everything he owned to invest in a tent ministry, dedicating himself to praying for the sick, starting an orphanage, and even pastoring for a while. He'd also wanted a similar drive and urgency for doing good and helping others face challenging situations.

His thoughts flitted over some of the rescues he'd been involved with and how he'd felt selling most of his possessions to go on his first trip to the Philippines. Maybe he still had some deep-hearted passion left to help others. Perhaps that was a conversation he and Skye should have. Did they want to continue working for a volunteer organization like the Tamarack Foundation? Given the situation between them and Skye's father, could they even do that now?

Chapter Forty-eight

Coe picked up his hammer to continue working on the porch steps when the wail of sirens, which seemed to be coming from the south, captured his attention, making his heart pound and the hairs on the back of his neck stand on end. The alarms didn't let up either, which made him want to rush to assist anyone in need. But he couldn't in this situation, right? Even if he wanted to do whatever he could to help his neighbors, he wasn't on duty.

Skye rushed out the door. "What is it?"

"A serious emergency, I'm afraid." Despite the local professionals already in action and possibly in danger, the strong urge to help pounded through his veins and didn't let up. Should he go or stay? *Lord, what should I do here?*

"Aren't we going to see if they need help?" Skye peered at him like she couldn't believe he was standing there doing nothing.

"If we were in India, yes." His phone vibrated in his pocket, and he yanked it out.

Just heard there's a massive collision on the Long Bridge.

Wilks's cryptic text didn't provide much information, but it was enough to motivate Coe like a kick in the pants. "On second thought, let's grab some first aid supplies and water and find out if there's any way we can help out." He dropped his hammer and dashed into the house with Skye close on his heels.

"Do you know what happened?"

"Wilks said there's a large wreck on the bridge coming into Sandpoint."

"I'll gather supplies."

"Thanks."

Upstairs, he grabbed boots and a sweatshirt for himself, and in Mom's closet, he found hiking boots and a sweatshirt for Skye that should fit. He sprinted downstairs to where she was filling two backpacks with water, snacks, and first aid supplies. "Thanks for doing that. Here are boots and something warm to wear."

"Thank you." She tugged on the boots and sweatshirt and grabbed one of the packs.

He snagged the other one and a set of keys off a dish, since they'd returned their rental a few days ago, and Mom said they could use her car anytime. Within five minutes of Wilks's text, they were heading toward the notorious two-mile-long bridge. The Sandpoint traffic was bogged down to a standstill. Was everyone in town heading south or rushing to see what happened on the bridge? By the long lines, no traffic was moving onto the congested thoroughfare.

"How bad do you think it is?" Skye broke the silence.

"Bad enough to cause a traffic jam in Sandpoint." He peered toward the south and saw smoke billowing over the bridge. "That's not good. We'd better hurry and get out there. If it's as terrible as it looks, some folks could be in serious trouble." Coe jerked the car to the side of the road, parked, and jumped out. "Let's go on foot from here." He grabbed a backpack.

"I'm right behind you." Skye exited the car and heaved the other pack over her shoulders.

Coe didn't know what kind of rescues they might be facing or if they'd be allowed onto the bridge, but they were prepared to do whatever they could. He said a quick prayer. *Lord, You are our strength. Be with all those involved in this emergency. Help us help others for Your glory.*

"Ready?" Skye met his gaze with a steady look.

"Ready." They ran side by side toward the smoky bridge.

"Stay back." A uniformed first responder waved at them from the bridge entrance, his posture stiff and expression somber. "This area is off-limits to the public."

"We're humanitarian aid workers. We have experience with offering support in the field." Coe pulled out his Tamarack Foundation ID card and held it out. So did Skye. "If we can help in any way, we'd like to volunteer and be of assistance."

The man peered at their photos, then at Coe and Skye. "Tamarack Foundation, huh?" He nodded like he'd heard of the organization.

"Yes, sir." Coe put his card back in his pocket. "We're here to serve."

"All right." He squinted at them. "Do what you can to help stranded victims, but don't get in the way of emergency personnel."

"We won't."

They hurried onto the bridge, keeping up a steady jog. As they approached the massive collision, Coe's gaze swept over the disarray of mangled cars, scattered metal fragments, the chaotic arrangement of smashed cars, stray metal pieces and tires, and vehicles precariously perched on top of each other, with front ends up on another car's bumper, and his gut tightened. It looked like a twenty-plus-car pileup, a grim sign of the potential victims trapped in the wreckage. His heart ached for every person involved.

Toward the center of the bridge, two large semis lay on their sides, sandwiched and partially charred, spreading from one side of the road to the other. Coe couldn't see beyond the travesty to tell how bad it was on the south side of the collision or how many cars were involved there. But this side looked awful. The first-on-scene EMTs had, no doubt, triaged the worst injuries on both sides of the fallen trucks.

Lord, help all these people, victims and workers. Show us how to help, too.

"Hey." A female law enforcement officer flagged them down. "This area is for emergency personnel only. Please get off the bridge."

"We're here to help," Coe said calmly. "The other officer said we could assist victims."

"Are you medical professionals?" Her glance ricocheted between Skye's and his regular clothes, and she seemed to visually dismiss them.

"We're humanitarian aid workers, fresh off the field." Coe held his card out to her and nodded to Skye to do the same.

"I don't know what good you will do here."

"I also have some nurses training," Skye spoke softly. "We can offer aid, support to victims, and assist however we're needed. Just point us in the direction we should go, and we'll pitch in."

The officer stared at Skye for several seconds, as if considering what she said, then sighed and rocked her thumb toward the area behind her. "There's a child and a pregnant woman in one of those smashed vehicles. Go ahead and offer support. If they can get through the maze, the ambulance will be here shortly."

"Traffic is—"

"A mess. I know." She glanced back at the semitrucks with a worried look.

"Come on." Skye patted Coe's arm. "Let's check on the mom and child."

He had to run to catch up with her. Looking over the crunched cars and trucks, his thoughts churned with ways to help—checking for severely injured passengers, getting folks out of the cars closest to the main collision, and handing out water. However, he and Skye were tasked with one assignment, to assist a pregnant woman and child, and that was their priority.

More sirens sounded. Emergency vehicles were approaching. The air smelled acrid with smoke.

"Here they are!" Skye placed her palm on the back seat window of a blue sedan crumpled between two vehicles. Inside, a child whimpered in a car seat. It was hard to tell if she was hurt or scared, or both. "Hello. I'm Skye. Are you okay? I'm here to help you."

"Mama," the child cried and reached for her mother.

Coe ran around to the driver's side and pulled on the door handle, but it didn't budge. He bent down and saw the pregnant woman inside, tears on her cheeks. "Help my daughter. Please." Her face crumpled, her expression begging for assistance, then she turned and clasped the girl's hand.

"You're going to be okay," he said loudly, hoping she could hear him. "You both are. I'm Coe. I'm an aid worker with the Tamarack Foundation. Can you unlock this door?"

"I'm Rebecca," she called back to him. "They told me to shut off the engine."

"That's fine. See if you can unlock it now, Rebecca."

Her hand shook. Her whole body seemed to be trembling as she tapped the door release mechanism and then the electrical screen. "Nothing is working."

"The sensors are probably smashed."

"I'm pregnant," she said, like he might not know, and ran her hand over her swollen abdomen. "How could this happen?" Her gaze pulsed toward the blackened semitrucks. "We could have died during the crash."

"But you didn't. You're going to be okay. Skye and I will stay with you and do all we can to get you out."

The woman leaned toward the girl again. "How are you doing,

honey?" The child's face puckered into a wail. "Oh, baby. I'm so sorry." She turned back to Coe. "She's Lizzie."

"Skye," Coe called. "The girl's name is Lizzie."

"Hey, Lizzie," Skye cooed. "Everything's going to be okay. We'll get you and your mom out of here real soon. Is that a stuffed doggie you're holding?"

"Yes."

"Rebecca, I'm going to pull hard on the handle." Coe reefed on it with all his might without any success. How was he going to get this pregnant woman and her child out without endangering them? "Are you in any pain?"

"My water broke." Rebecca grimaced like she was having a contraction right then. He hadn't considered that possibility.

"How far along are you?"

"Almost due. I was taking my daughter to my mom's house when—" She lifted her chin toward the wrecked semitrucks, breathing heavily.

"How's that door?" he asked Skye over the vehicle's top.

"Stuck. Yours?"

"Same. Rebecca's water broke."

"What?" She gazed toward town and frowned. "Please tell me there's a hospital in Sandpoint."

"There is. She'll have the baby there if the ambulance can get through in time. Otherwise, here, most likely."

She nodded. "We have to get them out."

The wail of sirens coincided with Rebecca's audible groan.

"Fast," Skye added.

"Is there anything in these packs to break a window with?" It was too bad he hadn't grabbed the hammer he was holding when he got Wilks's text.

"No." Skye eyed him. "But the sound she's making means her time is close."

Coe saw a fire truck inching toward them, moving around the wrecked cars. He waved fervently at one of the firefighters peering out a window. "There's a pregnant woman in this car," he shouted. "We need help getting her out. She's in labor."

The guy nodded and jumped out of the truck, grabbed a prying tool with a fork on one end, and ran to the driver's door. The fire truck continued toward the center of the bridge, its siren howling intermittently.

"Cover your face, ma'am," the rescue worker called. He peered intensely at the door, assessing the damage before he swung with the prying tool, landing it hard in the crack between the door and door jam. He applied pressure to the prybar, groaning as he pulled. After a popping sound, he yanked on the door, and the screeching metal affirmed they would soon have the woman and her daughter out of the vehicle.

"Thank you," Rebecca said between panting when the door opened. "Please, help Lizzie."

"We will." Coe turned toward the rescue worker. "Her name's Rebecca."

The firefighter nodded. "Is this your wife?"

"No, sir. The woman who's talking with the child is my wife, Skye. I'm Coe. We're here to help."

"Okay. Come along, ma'am," the firefighter said as he assisted Rebecca out of the car, and Coe got in position to assist with carrying her. "I'm Wyatt. Coe and I are going to bring you to a safe place to deliver your baby."

Rebecca moaned. "Help my girl. Hurry. Please."

"We will." Skye was already inside the smashed vehicle, so Coe said, "Skye is with her now."

"Thank you." Rebecca let out a guttural groan as they carried her to the side of the bridge where the ambulance would have better access and set her down carefully. Coe took off his sweatshirt and bunched it under her head. "Sorry, ma'am. This isn't much comfort."

"Thank you."

Skye approached them with Lizzie in her arms. "Coe, can you take Lizzie while I help with the birth?"

"Yes." He'd never helped with delivering a child before. But assisting scared kids? He'd done that plenty of times.

"Based on my brief assessment, she seems shaken but otherwise okay. She says nothing hurts." She handed the girl to him, smoothing her hand over her back. "This is Coe. He's a nice man who will sing or tell you stories while I help your mama. Okay?"

"Okay." Lizzie cried, "Mama."

"It's all right. You're safe. Your mama is safe, too." Coe walked a short distance from where Wyatt and Skye were helping Rebecca. Poor woman. What a terrible place to give birth. *Lord, be with her. And be with all these people.* How many others needed assistance? He heard shouts as more rescue teams arrived and were assisting victims. "Let's look over here." He jostled the girl, trying to distract her, and pointed at a boat in the water below. He told her about swimming in the lake in the summertime as a kid, trying to keep her engaged and distracted from worrying about her mom, and Lizzie relaxed against his shoulder.

He sang some kid tunes. She sang along with "Row, Row, Row Your Boat" and "Old MacDonald." A few of his animal sounds made her giggle. When her mom moaned, Lizzie buried her face against his shirt and sniffled.

"Everything's going to be fine," he said, praying it would be.

"Hey." Skye tapped his arm a while later. "Baby's here." Lizzie reached for her, and she took the girl in her arms. "Everything's going to be all right, honey."

"And her mom?"

"On her way to the hospital in that ambulance." She pointed to a rescue vehicle meandering through the maze of cars. "You have a baby sister."

Lizzie leaned back, eyes wide. "Neva?"

"That's right. Neva is beautiful, like you."

Lizzie grinned. "Baby Neva."

"Lizzie will stay with us until the bridge opens and her grandma can get here." Skye met his gaze and smiled. "Her mom was concerned about leaving her, but I assured her that we'd keep her safe."

"Sounds good." He noticed how pleased or relieved she looked. It seemed she had enjoyed helping with the baby's birth even in these dire circumstances.

"Let's grab her car seat before we go. It should be replaced. But I checked it, and it seemed unharmed."

"Will do." He ran back to the car, ignoring the foot traffic of emergency personnel assisting stranded travelers along the bridge, and unfastened the child seat.

By the time they reached the car, Lizzie was asleep in Skye's arms. Coe hooked up the seat, and Skye fastened Lizzie in despite her drowsy state and sat next to her in the back.

The traffic was still clogged as they tried to leave, so it took longer than usual to maneuver from Sandpoint to Thunder Ridge. He caught Skye's gaze in the rearview mirror, and she gave him a weary smile that he interpreted as a sign of relief. Despite the recent strain in their relationship, their shared experience of helping Lizzie and Rebecca through this traumatic ordeal felt like it was bringing them closer, and he was immensely grateful for that.

Chapter Forty-nine

Skye tried to entertain Lizzie and keep her out of Coe's and his brothers' hair while they worked on the tiling and painting in the kitchen that afternoon, but she kept finding her way back to Coe and wanting to help. So Skye took Lizzie and her stuffed dog to Trish's cottage, even though her place was too small to contain the preschooler's energy. Still, it was better than her accidentally touching wet paint or tripping over dangerous tools in the work zone.

"Try this puzzle." Trish handed her a scuffed-up wooden dog puzzle. "My grandsons used to love these. They're a bit ragged but usable."

"They're perfect. Here, Lizzie, take that dog out." Skye removed a few of the other pieces. "Thank you for letting us spend some time here."

"My pleasure." Trish sipped from her teacup. "How's her mama doing?"

"She sounds good on the phone. Lizzie's grandmother, Darla, should be here soon."

"Gamma. Gamma," Lizzie said in a singsong voice.

"That's right. She's coming to get you later."

"Yay!"

"Is the bridge open yet?" Trish gazed toward the new windows Smith and Coe had installed.

"According to the news, it's open but single-lane traffic only."

"See Mama?" Lizzie's eyes brightened.

"I think so." Skye didn't want to make any promises, but she imagined that Darla would also like to see her daughter and new grandbaby.

"You'll miss her, won't you?" Trish tipped her head toward Lizzie.

"I've enjoyed spending the afternoon with her." Skye stroked the girl's wispy hair, feeling a deep satisfaction over how she and Coe got to help Lizzie and her mom. The birthing experience alone was amazing and heartwarming. She'd never tire of watching babies being born and mamas seeing their child for the first time.

"Does it make you want to have children?" Trish asked, looking hopeful. "Or is that too snoopy of me to ask?"

"Coe and I haven't discussed kids yet."

"No? I think you can mention any topic and he'll chat with you about it. He's always been like that."

Skye didn't want to disagree with Coe's grandmother. But in her experience, he wasn't that talkative about personal things, at least, not with her. They still hadn't discussed some topics she considered necessary. When would he mention the pastorate and how he felt about it? She'd heard Liv reminding Smith to pray for Coe's meeting with the church board this morning, but Coe hadn't said anything about it to her, other than there would be one. With his caring attitude toward people, he'd make a terrific pastor. Would he have included her in a discussion about it if she were his real wife? She exhaled a balloon-deflating sigh.

"My dear, you look troubled. Was it something I said? If you want to talk—"

"I have some concerns, but I don't want to discuss them now." She nodded toward Lizzie.

"Of course."

Lizzie switched to a dinosaur puzzle, dumping the pieces noisily onto the coffee table.

"I was wondering, have Coe's brothers tried anything?" Trish asked with some trepidation in her tone.

"None have flirted with me, if that's what you mean."

"Oh, my, no." Trish patted her chest. "I meant, have they tried anything mischievous?"

"As in a prank?"

"Yes. I don't know why those nice boys get the strangest ideas, especially at their age." Trish tsk-tsked. "They were always polite and respectful to Liv, Smith, and me, but they often succumbed to egging each other on through tricks and dares in a way that baffles me still."

Trish was the third person to mention the North brothers' pranks. "No one has done anything weird or mischievous to me."

"I'm relieved to hear it."

The idea of Wilks or Finn playing a joke on her was annoying. If they thought she'd take any of their nonsense without standing up for herself, they were mistaken.

When Darla arrived, Lizzie fell into her arms, clinging to her as if she'd never let go. Skye kissed Lizzie goodbye and assisted Darla with getting the child seated in her vehicle.

"Thanks for helping Rebecca today," Darla said. "She told me about how you assisted with the delivery and offered to watch Lizzie. That was extremely kind of you."

"I was glad to help."

After they said goodbye, Skye felt a tug of emotion, like the young girl had wormed her way into her heart. It was a bittersweet feeling of joy and sadness. Someday, she and Coe might have a daughter like her if they fell in love and stayed together. *If?* Why did she keep adding that disclaimer? But how could she not when things still seemed unsettled between her and Coe?

As she approached the front door, a dark SUV pulled up in the driveway. The passenger window rolled down, exposing Tip's smug grin and his glinting silver tooth. Skye's breath caught in her throat as she froze in place. Then, with a burst of fear and adrenaline rushing through her, she dashed into the house, slamming the door behind her.

Chapter Fifty

"Are you okay?" Coe could tell something was wrong by Skye's pale features and how she stood statue still by the stairway. "Did something happen? How's Lizzie?" He kept his voice quiet so Finn, grouting tile by the back door, wouldn't hear.

"Her grandmother picked her up."

"Are you upset about that?"

"No. But I saw—" She shook her head. "It's him. Them."

"Who?" He stroked his palms down her arms, trying to offer support.

"Tip and Rhett pulled up after Lizzie and her grandmother left."

"You're sure?" Adrenaline shot through him.

"Positive."

Coe strode to the door and peered out, checking the driveway and along the road. "It looks like they're gone." *Thank God.*

"Good. I knew they might still be around, but seeing them again scared me."

"I'm sorry." He shut and locked the door, then went back and drew her into his arms, his protective instinct kicking in. He smoothed his hand down the back of her hair, trying to comfort her. "It's going to be okay. We'll figure this out." They hadn't been this close in days, and he enjoyed the sensation of her strawberry-scented hair sliding between his fingers, ticklishly soft. "What do you think we should do?"

She stepped back, frowning. "Are you asking for my input?"

Why did she look so surprised? Hadn't they worked as a team, volunteering at the emergency today? Didn't their gazes meet significantly afterward, like she was as thankful as he was that they'd done something important together?

"I am. You want us to face every situation as partners, right?"

"Yes." She squinted at him like she was assessing him. "Okay, then. I should go somewhere and lure Father's men away from your family." He admired her bravery, but he couldn't let her do that.

"That's not happening."

"You can't say no right off." Huffing, she marched to the couch and dropped onto the middle cushion, arms crossed.

"In this instance, I can." He followed and sat as close to her as he dared. "It's my job as a husband to keep you safe and prioritize you."

Finn clapped in the other room. Coe gritted his teeth, tempted to put his kid brother in his place, but this wasn't the time.

"I don't expect you to act like a husband already," Skye said in a defensive tone.

"You mean since we haven't—"

Finn snickered.

"Finn—" Coe warned.

"Sorry." Too bad his brother was within hearing range of this conversation.

"Not just that." Skye cast him a wilting glance. "We aren't familiar enough with each other to act like spouses. I'm willing to go away to protect those you love. It might be for the best."

"The best for whom?"

"You. Me. Your family."

"Not me. Don't include me in your list of who would benefit from your leaving." He raked his fingers through his hair, feeling more agitated. "I don't want you wandering off alone. Tip and Rhett are like hungry vultures, waiting for the chance to take you away from me. I can't let that happen. I made a vow to you, and I intend to keep it."

She groaned again. "Then what will we do to protect Trish and Liv if I don't leave?"

"Let's look for other solutions. Any other solutions." Keeping his gaze fixed on her, he scooted a tad closer and spoke quietly, "Skye, listen. I want us to stay together and face whatever needs to be faced as a married couple. And I want you to feel safe. We could go to Lake and Irish's. It's far enough out of town to lose Tip and Rhett's scent for a while. But—"

"They'd find us. And we'd put Lake and Irish and their dogs in danger."

"Maybe. So what can we do other than you resorting to leaving?" She stared at him like she doubted he'd listen to her viewpoint even if she offered one, reminding him that he had to try harder to treat her like an equal partner. "I'm sorry for saying no to your suggestion without hearing you out." He swallowed against the dryness in his throat. "Your ideas are of value to me, even if we disagree. But it's hard for me to hear you talk about leaving."

"All right. Thank you for that."

Finn came into the kitchen and ran water at the sink, creating a momentary distraction.

"I need to ask you a question, but not here." Skye nodded toward the stairs.

"To our bedroom?" Coe coughed. He'd been avoiding interacting with her in their room, even leaving before she woke, since he was determined to keep his word about waiting until she was ready for physical closeness. "Can't we keep talking here?"

"With Finn eavesdropping?"

"Not trying to," Finn muttered. "Gotta wash up somewhere."

"Talk to me," Coe said persuasively.

"All right. It feels like you're making all the decisions. I've had enough of that."

Finn chuckled.

"Finn!" Coe and Skye said at once.

"Okay, okay." He strode through the kitchen and shut the back door hard.

"You have to allow us to toss around ideas and figure stuff out, no matter how long it takes, even if you don't like my suggestions." Skye scooted to the edge of the couch. "Either we're married, or we aren't." She stood with her hands on her hips, her posture exuding confidence. "I'm not your little sister for you to boss around."

"No, you aren't." He stood, too, unable to stop his grin. "I've never once thought of you as my sister, Skye. And I am trying to act like your husband."

"Are you?" She tipped her head, almost challenging him with her look. "Have you been treating me like a wife since our marriage twelve days ago?"

Her implication made his pulse race. "Meaning?"

"What do you think makes any couple feel like a husband and wife?"

"Beyond their vows?" Coe narrowed the gap between them, thinking kissing her would make him feel more like a newlywed husband.

"And beyond romance or sexuality."

Oh. She wasn't implying what his mind had leaped to. "What does this have to do with Rhett and Tip?"

"Everything has to do with everything." She strode to the base of the stairway, then pivoted back toward him. "Can you answer my question, please?"

He followed her contemplatively. "Other than marital vows, I suppose—" What would make him feel more like a husband to her beyond kissing? "Communication. Working toward a common goal. Shared experiences."

"Are those things essential to a happy marriage?"

"You weren't asking about a happy marriage. If it were up to me, I'd want those things *and* the other parts we aren't talking about." He wasn't discounting their need for romance and intimacy, eventually.

"Are you communicating with me one hundred percent?" She crossed her arms, implying he wasn't.

"No. Have you been communicating with me one hundred percent?"

"Not really." Her shoulders sagged. "While I don't feel like you're a stranger, I don't think of you as my husband, either."

"How can I do better?"

"I don't know. But when you take charge—"

"It reminds you of your dad?" An intuitive light bulb went off in Coe's brain.

"Maybe." She tugged her fingers through her hair in agitated movements he longed to still. "When we rushed to the wreck and helped Rebecca and Lizzie, it was like we were our old selves, racing to help people and fix things. I felt a close bond with you, then."

"I felt the same way. But life isn't always a rush."

"No. It isn't." She shook her head, looking sad.

"I'm sorry you haven't felt like we're getting closer since we've been working here on the house. And I'm sorry for not including you more."

"I don't mind working beside you as long as we're also moving toward our future." She gazed at him with a pleading look. "Are we working toward something meaningful, Coe?"

"Absolutely."

"What, exactly? I want to know what you're thinking."

Taking her hands in his, he smoothed his thumbs over her knuckles. He was thankful she didn't pull away. She had small hands. Cute hands. "You are beautiful, Skye."

"Coe—"

"You said you want to know what I'm thinking. You worked hard in India, and you are doing that here. You have beautiful hands that have served God and His people through hundreds of hours of challenging work." She squirmed like she was uncomfortable with his praise. "Your hands are soft. I like it when you touch my face with them when we're kissing."

She went still, her moist gaze locked on him, and his heart pounded ferociously. He let go of one hand and stroked some of her hair back behind her ear, gazing into her dark, shiny eyes. "You have luscious eyes that make me feel like I'm drowning in their beauty."

"Coe—" She hurried across the room and stopped behind the couch. He followed her, unwilling to let this part of their conversation go.

"Your mouth makes me want to—"

"You will not discuss my mouth."

"Why not?" He leaned closer, setting his hands on the couch at her sides. He felt her breath on his lips and yearned to kiss her like the husband she doubted he was and the one he longed to be. He remained still for a few moments, his mouth inches from hers, his eyes staring languidly into her dark pools of chocolate. "May I kiss you, Skye?" The pull between them became enticingly magnetic, and he could hardly bear waiting for her reply.

"Yes," she whispered.

Softly, he claimed her lips, hoping to dispel any doubts about whether they were meant to be together. Soon, she wrapped her arms around him, and things heated up quickly. This was their first kiss in days, and Coe wanted to relish every second of Skye being in his arms, her fingers playing through his hair, and her mouth dancing a slow, tantalizing dance with his. He wanted so much more and—

The front door creaked open. "Am I interrupting something?"

Mom? Coe froze, his mouth a hair above Skye's. "Later?" he whispered.

She winced and nodded.

Chapter Fifty-one

"I don't know how to show her how much I care. I don't love her like I'm crazy about her yet, but I'd still like to—" Coe stared at the wall beyond his father's head in his office. Dad didn't say anything, so he kept talking, primarily to himself. "I jumped into marriage like nothing would hold us back from finding love. It felt like the right thing to do, the only thing to do, at the time. But how long will it take for us to fall for each other? How long will I have to wait for—"

A grin crinkled Dad's face with laugh lines.

"What's so humorous?"

"You. You have been married to a woman with whom you fled from India and wed because two bad guys were hunting you down for all of what, ten days?"

"Twelve."

"Okay. And you expect her to fall at your feet so soon?"

"I wouldn't say I expect it. Wish for it, maybe." Coe heaved a sigh, trying to relieve some of his frustration.

"Perhaps you want to leap through the hoops at breakneck speed, so she'll fall into your bed, hm?" Dad lifted his chin, giving Coe a look he'd seen many times as a kid, getting lectured about being respectful, keeping his hands to himself instead of punching his brothers, or kissing girls he shouldn't be kissing. Heat bled up his neck. Dad had always been direct regarding integrity and honor in manhood and taking responsibility for his actions.

"I can't say it hasn't crossed my mind."

"That's normal. But you've acted honorably with Skye, right?" Again, with the look.

"I've tried to be honorable and patient. But it would be a lot easier if we could move forward like a married couple instead of—"

"Waiting for love? Waiting for her feelings to catch up to yours?" Dad eyed him contemplatively. "Do you want to rush a relationship because you're in a hurry to have the benefits of marriage without love and commitment?"

"Dad—"

"Am I off base?"

Coe squirmed like he did as a sixteen-year-old after being caught kissing Emilie Whitefield behind the church. His brief kissing session with the deacon's daughter hadn't been worth the trouble he'd gotten into or the embarrassing apologies he had to make to Emilie and her parents.

"Not far off base," he admitted. "I want to believe Skye and I will fall in love and have a satisfying marriage someday. But a part of me thinks, why not sleep together like a married couple should be doing and jump-start a deeper relationship?"

"Should be doing?" Dad asked incredulously. "Are you hearing yourself?"

"Isn't intimacy what a regular married couple would expect?"

"Are you a regular couple? Have you courted Skye and given her time to fall in love with you?" Dad's words hit like a well-aimed dart hitting the bullseye.

"No. I haven't." Coe rubbed the back of his neck. Why did he even come to Dad's office? He should have known it would turn out like this, with him feeling like an adolescent all over again.

Dad was silent for several seconds, moving a penny around on the surface of his desk. "Have you spoken with Skye about taking your marriage to the next level?"

"No." Coe groaned. "She says we need better communication. And she has authoritarian issues because of her father. I'm the one wishing we could move forward and forget the rest."

"Your feelings are understandable. But patience is key. Are you being sensitive to your wife?" Dad crossed his arms over the desk.

Was he? Or did he just want his own way? "I thought I was. But anything I say or do might seem insensitive considering all we've been through in a brief time."

"Exactly. Have you been praying with Skye?"

"Not much." She'd asked him to pray with her on their wedding day, and he felt closer to her afterward. Why hadn't he done that more? "I don't know how to keep that vulnerability and openness between us. Or what to pray about, exactly."

"Perhaps, pray with her about her father." Dad nodded thoughtfully. "Or about whatever you both want to have happen in your marriage. That would be a way for Skye to feel assured you care about her and for you to draw closer together before the fireworks start."

Oh, he'd felt plenty of fireworks. That's why he tromped into Dad's office. He swallowed what felt like a lump of peanut butter. "I've been praying about our relationship myself."

"I'm sure you have. You are a sincere man of God who is caring and compassionate." Coe detected a "but" coming. "But you haven't been a husband before."

"True. It's a tougher role than I imagined."

"Give it time. Talk with your wife. Pray with her about anything either of you is troubled about." Dad waved his hands upward like prayer was his solution to a fulfilling marriage. "As a married couple, praying together strengthens your connection and love for each other." Was prayer the missing piece of their marital puzzle? Along with communication and patience?

"Thanks for talking with me, Dad. I appreciate your wisdom and experience." He twiddled his thumbs, his thoughts churning, his feelings still unsettled.

"Is there something else you want to discuss?"

"Did you mean that I should talk to Skye about my desire for intimacy before we've fallen in love?" He heard the doubt in his tone. Did Dad?

"Have you two kissed?"

"Yes. Mom walked in on us doing so a few minutes ago."

Dad chuckled. "That must have been awkward."

"Monumentally. I don't know what I was thinking, asking a woman to marry me who I haven't fallen in love with." Coe raked his fingers through his hair.

"Like father, like son?" Dad grinned. "Listen. You believe God is working everything out for your good, right? And that your time in India was part of His will for your life?"

"Yes." Coe sat up straighter.

"Then don't give in to doubts. Skye is a part of the journey God is leading you both on. Embrace her as your partner. But be careful about pushing for too much physically or emotionally before she's ready. Help her prepare for life as your wife and prepare yourself as the husband she needs you to be." Dad clasped his hands, looking calm and peaceful. "Son, you asked if you should talk with her about what you want. What does your wife need?"

How was he supposed to know? He sighed again. *What does Skye need from me?* "Communication," he said, even though Dad's question didn't require an audible answer. "She wants to feel like she's an equal part of our marriage and that I'm trying to understand her viewpoint."

"See. You're doing better at being a husband already."

"Not there yet, but thanks." Coe stood.

"My door is always open." Dad stood, too. "Do you mind if we pray together?"

"I'd welcome it."

Dad walked around the desk and put his hand on Coe's shoulder. "Lord, thank You for bringing my son home safely. His journey has been challenging, but You have been with him every step." As Dad prayed, Coe felt a rush of emotion. They'd stood like this many times throughout his teenage and young adult years, praying and talking, him gleaning advice from his dad, and Dad leading him closer to their Heavenly Father. "Thank You for Coe's heart to serve others and how he has used this calling for good. Help him to be a loving husband. It's a mystery to Coe as it was to me for a long time. Please, lead him in this new adventure of marriage and starting a family."

He heard his dad sniffle, and another wave of emotion hit him. It felt like a mantle was settling on his shoulders about what being a good husband and a good dad meant, like Dad had been and still was.

Chapter Fifty-two

Coe looked handsome and confident standing behind the pulpit on Sunday morning. Back at the house, Skye had asked him if he was nervous about speaking, and he shrugged and said, "A little." His reserved response concerned her, but she stored it alongside her other uncertainties about him and their marriage. She longed to understand Coe's thoughts about the pastoral situation and wished he'd confided in her about why he felt compelled to speak today. Did his father pressure him? Did it have anything to do with the church meeting he attended on the day of the bridge emergency? Was he considering being a pastor? She could have asked him any of those questions, but she'd kept her curiosity to herself, waiting for him to talk about it, and regretted it now.

His slicked-back hair and morning scruffiness made him look alluringly handsome, like a model on the cover of a magazine. Her heart pounded as she perused him, her awareness of Coe being her husband rushing through her. He wore a light blue button-up shirt and a navy tie. Did he wear her favorite color on purpose? Her thoughts skimmed back to their last kiss five days ago. How could she forget that epically embarrassing moment when Liv walked in and found them in each other's arms, kissing like they might die if they didn't? Coe had acted reserved ever since, and no wonder. There wasn't any privacy in the North house. How long were they going to stay there?

Sitting beside her, Liv whispered, "He looks nice in a tie and dress shirt, doesn't he?"

"He does. He's an attractive man," Skye whispered back, smoothing her hand over the pink dress she was wearing for the first time since their wedding ceremony.

"And a good man?" Liv clasped her hand and squeezed gently.

"That, too." Skye swallowed back some emotions. Even though she and Coe had terrible skills when it came to talking about personal matters, she'd married a thoughtful man who'd given years of his life to helping others. Then there was how he helped her escape Father's marriage plans for her and was trying to keep her from danger. He was selfless, gentle, patient, kind, and far different from Father, which was a really good thing.

So what if they had a few hiccups in their first seventeen days of marriage? They had enough chemistry to light up a darkened room. And when he touched her cheeks, gazed deeply into her eyes, settled his hands on her waist, and pulled her close for a romantic kiss, a roaring flame spread through her senses. *Ugh*. She shouldn't be daydreaming about kissing Coe while he was talking to the congregation, right?

Sighing, she tuned into his sermon. As she listened to him describe the sights and scents of India, she was mentally transported to working beside him and doing all they could to help people in desperate situations. Would she ever experience that feeling of commitment and community with him again?

Even Father had been a kinder human when he assisted the injured and offered sanctuary to people in crises. But he became a tyrant when they were home, and he got lost in his sorrows and memories. She should have left his household years ago. However, it wasn't for lack of trying. He was good at catching her, or rather, his men were. Fortunately, they failed this time. Would there be a next time? Agitation whisked through her that she tried to subdue.

She noticed how Coe's face seemed to glow as he shared stories of rescues and the courageous workers who ran into disastrous conditions to assist victims. She heard her name mentioned and became more alert, listening closely. "When I met my wife"—he chuckled—"or before I met the woman who would later become my wife, we were shoveling out ditches of flood waters. Skye worked as hard and determinedly as any of the men there." Their gazes locked across the crowded church, and she felt a surge of warmth. This man, who said he cared for her and kissed her like he meant to fall in love with her, made her feel seen and special.

"We were co-laborers who became friends before anything serious happened between us." He nodded in her direction and smiled tenderly. "Meeting Skye was one of the greatest things that happened to me on the field."

He thought she was one of the greatest things that happened to him? She gulped, feeling giddy and stirred emotionally.

"Many of you contributed to my journey initially," he continued. "For that, I am profoundly grateful. Every dollar you gave helped me to be there when people needed assistance. I will forever be thankful for the opportunity. If I had the chance to do it again, I would."

Did he mean he wanted to return to humanitarian work? Would he consider volunteering with the Tamarack Foundation again?

"I hope to be a better man because of what I experienced as an aid worker. A better husband and dad, too, since what I learned about compassion is life-changing. It's a voice that calls to me at night, a yearning to follow the Lord and be His vessel in the middle of chaos, a light amid darkness, wherever He leads." He ended with prayer and then stayed around to answer questions.

After the service, while Skye and Coe were walking back to the house, she told him how much his sermon had meant to her. "You are a natural at speaking, Coe."

"I don't know about that. But thanks."

"Seriously. What you shared was thoughtful and inspiring."

"Skye?" He tugged her to a stop. "Are you flirting with me?"

"No." She batted at his arm. "I'm telling you how I felt while you shared your experiences in India. I wanted you to know I liked hearing how you felt and what you liked best about aid work." Some of the time, it had seemed like he was speaking right to her heart.

"And me? Did you like me?" He gazed deeply into her eyes and smoothed the cool edge of his index finger down her warm cheek, sending chills through her, making her long for his kiss.

"Yes, Coe. I liked you, too." She kissed his cheek quickly, disguising her yearning for more.

"While I was speaking, I noticed you were wearing your wedding dress." He smiled. "You looked so beautiful, it took my breath away. I could hardly talk for a few seconds."

"Really?" She was glad he'd noticed and been affected.

"Really and truly." He clasped her hand, and they walked the rest of the way to the house, his words about her taking his breath away and being the greatest thing that had happened to him echoing in her thoughts.

Chapter Fifty-three

"Surprise!" "Congratulations!" "Welcome to the family!" Four of Coe's brothers leaped out from behind kitchen doorways and around living room furniture, shouting greetings and extending gifts toward Skye the next day.

"What's this? What's going on?" She tried to wipe her hands free of the pizza dough she was working on. Since her husband's siblings had a reputation as tricksters, she felt leery of them clustered around her. But soon their happy, carefree expressions put her more at ease, although not entirely.

"It's a hearty welcome from the North brothers," Lake explained.

"You're lucky to be a North!" Wilks grinned and threw confetti around the kitchen and some fell over her. The others joined him, tossing the messy stuff around. Their silly smiles and expressions were hilarious despite the disaster they were making and how the confetti was getting stuck to her gooey fingers.

"We're pleased to have a new sister-in-law, and we wanted to welcome you properly." Lake held a pink floral gift bag out to her. "This is for you."

"Thank you. I don't know what to say. I'll just—" She wiped her hands on a dishtowel before realizing that made the sticky problem worse.

"Even though we'd rather toss you in Lake Pend Oreille, Lake convinced us to go easy on you." Wilks held up a black bag, his grin mischievous.

"Thanks, I guess." Was there a trick in the bag?

"At least we get cake out of the deal." Sunday nodded toward a delicious-looking fudge chocolate cake he was holding.

"You aren't going to throw that at me, are you?"

"No way. This cake is too good to waste on a prank," Sunday said as he set it on the counter.

"I'm relieved to hear it."

"But when you least expect it—" Finn rocked his eyebrows and held out a gift card envelope with a coffee shop logo on it.

"I'm surprised and grateful for all this. Thank you for the gifts. Let me clean my hands better." She turned to the sink, slathered her hands with dishwashing soap, and rinsed. But recalling Trish's and Jazzy's warnings, she kept an eye on Coe's brothers. She trusted Lake. The others? Not so much.

"I could think of a better way to initiate Skye into the family than giving her presents," Wilks's voice rose silkily, reinforcing her worries.

"How about sprinkling pepper on her pillow?" Finn laughed.

"Or locking her in the bathroom," Sunday said.

Where do they come up with this stuff?

"We don't want to leave Skye without a North family memory to cherish." Wilks stared at her with impish mischief written all over his face.

"Now, now." Lake stood by her while she dried her hands, and she was thankful for his implied protection. "We're going to start a new tradition beginning today."

"Who made you the boss of—"

"None of your shenanigans are going to play out here." Lake set down his gift on the counter with a thud. A dust cloud of flour rose around the pizza dough.

"Says you," Finn muttered.

"That's right. Says me. It's true that your older brothers weren't stellar examples when it came to horsing around. So, pulling pranks on us is one thing. We deserve it." Lake cast a stern glance at the others. "But leave the women out of this. We are doing this my way from now on."

God bless Lake.

"We should have taken a vote," Wilks grumbled. "Why should this be any different—"

"Because you took things too far with Trista." Lake settled his arm over Skye's shoulder. "You will show respect and kindness to the women who are brave enough to join our family and take on eight brothers-in-law. Got it?" No one spoke. "Got it?"

"We've got it." Sunday lifted his hands.

"Fine. Welcome to the family, Skye." Finn bowed dramatically.

"Thank you."

"Wilks?" Lake said testily.

"I apologized to Trista. But is this how we're going to welcome wives from now on? With cake and confetti?"

"That's right."

A playful idea sparked Skye's thoughts. "Or perhaps with something more like this?" Spinning around, she grabbed two handfuls of white flour and tossed them right at Wilks's face. He gasped and sputtered, shouting his outrage. Flour covered his hair and cheeks and speckled his clothes. He looked like a snowman! The others guffawed and pointed at him. Rapidly, Skye flung handfuls at Finn, Sunday, and Lake, too.

"What are—"

"How—"

"Stop that!"

Boisterous laughter and an epic flour fight ensued as everyone threw fistfuls of flour at each other. When the bag was emptied all over them and the room, Wilks shook the remaining particles over Skye's head. All five were coated in fine white dust by the time the playful skirmish ended. A layer of flour and confetti covered almost everything in the kitchen and living room, including the cake. But despite the mess that would take hours to clean, it had been an enormously fun and exhilarating activity.

Lake hugged her. "Welcome to our family, Skye."

Even Wilks one-arm hugged her. "I'm surprised you had it in you." He swept a pile of flour into his hands from the counter and rained it over her hair. Laughing, she spit the taste of it out of her mouth.

Sunday and Finn also gave her hugs. Then they grabbed paper plates and divvied up the cake. A fudge chocolate cake had never tasted so good, even with the extra layer of flour.

Coe strode into the house and stopped, his mouth open wide as he gazed around the room and at Skye and his brothers. "What happened here?"

Skye and the others looked at each other and burst out laughing. And strangely, she felt more like a North than she did before.

Chapter Fifty-four

"How would you feel about going on a date with me Friday night?" Coe asked Skye two days later. The anticipation of an evening out with her filled him with excitement for another chapter in their romantic journey. He was hoping to spend more time doing things as a couple, and with Finn's play coming up, that seemed like the perfect event for a date night.

"Another date already?"

"Yeah. I thought we could dress up and go somewhere nice." Despite the potential threat from Rhett and Tip, Coe was determined to create a special moment with his wife. They couldn't remain hiding forever, and he was torn between caution and wanting to show Skye a good time.

"That sounds lovely." She looked cute, her hair wet from showering and her face free of makeup, as she put on the walking shoes Lake had given her for a welcome-to-the-family gift.

"Finn's play opens then, too."

"Oh, right." She winced like she'd forgotten. She put on a pink baseball hat with the words "Okay Sister-in-law" on it that Wilks had given her, and Coe inwardly chuckled at his brother's sense of humor.

"We could go to dinner, watch the show, and hang out together. What do you think?"

"I'll need something to wear." She cringed. "Or I could use my wedding dress again."

"While your pink dress is lovely, why don't we go shopping and find something new?" He glanced at the work clothes she'd been wearing for three weeks without complaining. "I still have some money left."

"An outfit from a thrift shop would be great. Thanks."

"I appreciate your willingness to keep our expenses minimal." He gazed deeply into her eyes, wanting to connect with her emotionally. "The important thing is that we spend time together, right? Dinner and a play seem like a good starting place."

"They do. I'd like that."

She gave him a soft look, and he wished he could buy her everything she ever wanted. He also wished he felt the liberty of taking her in his arms and kissing her with some husbandly affection. But ever since he talked with Dad a week ago, he'd been trying to let their romance come more naturally and wait patiently for Skye's feelings to catch up with his. However, keeping a restrained distance from the woman he enjoyed kissing was more challenging than he anticipated.

Skye clasped his hand and brushed a kiss against his cheek. Could she hear his heart pounding like a drumbeat at her slight touch? "There are some things I'd like us to discuss, too, if you're okay with it."

"Sure." Did she want to talk about deepening their relationship? Was she starting to fall in love with him and wanted to tell him? "We can discuss anything you want. I like hearing what's in your heart, Skye."

"I want to know your heart, too. Like, what are you thinking right now?"

"That I'd like to kiss you and spend more time alone with you."

"Why, Mr. North. I'm surprised to hear you say such things." She grinned like she was enjoying their exchange, and he was even more tempted to kiss her.

"You'd be surprised by my other thoughts, then."

She gave him such an adorable look that he couldn't help himself. He kissed her gently, planning to keep things light. But the kiss deepened fast. Skye wrapped her arms around him, stroking her fingers through his hair and scalp, electrifying his senses. He smoothed his hands around her waist, pulling her closer, loving how she fit perfectly against him. He longed for everything in a real marriage and wished for it to happen sooner than later, until he recalled his father's words. *Patience is key. What does Skye need?*

Sighing, he lowered his hands and set her back from him. "I'll look forward to our shopping trip and date later in the week."

"Me too." She smiled, her cheeks dimpling. "Did I tell you I'm visiting Irish at the animal shelter today? Some of the cute puppies might tempt me." She winked.

"You wouldn't consider picking one without me, right?"

"Promise." She headed for the door, then paused. "Would you mind terribly if I did?"

"Uh. Well." His heart was taking its time returning to normal after their kiss. "We should hold off until we figure out what we're going to do before we make any major changes or take on any new responsibilities."

"You're probably right." She got a far-off look, which made him wonder what she was pondering.

It seemed they had a lot of things to find out about each other without the complication of a cute puppy who might win their hearts before they figured out how to win each other's.

Chapter Fifty-five

"I love this adorable puppy," Skye said, cradling the black border collie puppy as she sat in Irish's cozy office next to the reception area. "He's so sweet."

"I wish I could keep them all." Irish sighed, gently caressing the husky pup resting on the floor beside her. "I fall in love with every dog who comes through our door or is born here. But with seven dogs at home and the hope of raising more, Lake insists we can't have more pups for now. Little Dipper is my baby."

"He's a darling, too." The puppy in Skye's arms licked her chin, and she giggled. "You're full of sweetness, aren't you? That's what I'd call you. Sweetness. Or Sweetie Pie."

"Already picking out names?"

"Yeah. But I can't keep him. Our lives are too unsettled."

"Does that mean no babies, either?"

"It's hard to do when—" She shrugged, embarrassed over what she almost admitted.

"I get it." Irish patted her arm like she might do to comfort one of the dogs. "I've met those North boys. And happen to be married to one." A nostalgic look crossed her face. "But when it comes to love and tenderness, it's hard to imagine any man being better than my Lake."

"Kissing Coe is—"

"Out of this world? Think it runs in the family?"

"I don't know. But it got me into trouble when my father saw us kissing like a wildfire was happening and we were the combustible fuel."

"And you say there's no chance of babies?"

"Not for a while, anyway."

"No doubt, Liv and Trish are praying up a storm for you and Coe and are available for all the heart-to-hearts you want." Irish's green eyes sparkled. "I have never met a wife and mother-in-law duo like theirs. Lake loves them both so much. Goodness. So do I."

"Is there a but coming?"

"*But* if you need a semi-neutral listening ear, come and chat with me."

"Okay."

"How you took matters into your own hands with the brothers the other day was brilliant." Irish shook her head. "When Lake came home with flour all over his hair and clothes and told me what you did and how shocked the guys were, I roared with laughter."

"It was spur-of-the-moment. Wilks and Finn were acting dejected about not getting to pull a prank on me, so I turned the tables on them."

"Good for you!"

"It was fun and broke the ice." The pup wiggled in her lap, and she smoothed her hand over its back. "It was challenging to get everything cleaned up before Liv got home. But the guys pitched in, even Coe."

"That's great."

"And Wilks gave me this." She pointed at her hat. "Apparently, he thinks I'm okay."

"Well, that's something. Speaking of the North brothers, I've been thinking about us starting a sisters-in-law support group. We could FaceTime with Trista. What do you think?" Irish gazed at her expectantly.

Skye took in a breath that hurt. Would she still be a North wife in a year? In six months? Was she being unfaithful to Coe by even thinking like that? Her sigh came out like a moan.

"What is it? What did I say that brought about such a look of pain? Do you want to talk about it?"

"Yes. No. Maybe." Skye stared at a wintry photograph on the wall of Irish and two dogs crossing a snow-packed finish line. Irish's red hair flew freely behind her, and the dogs were moving in tandem, straining forward, a look of indescribable joy on their faces. Had Skye ever felt such exquisite happiness?

Irish's phone vibrated, and she scanned the screen. "My receptionist is running late. But everything is quiet, and the dogs have eaten, so I have a few more minutes to visit."

"Sometimes I question whether Coe will ever love me," Skye said abruptly.

"Oh, Skye."

"He can be bossy. It's probably because he had all those younger siblings, but I don't like that about him." The words came out in a rush, and she didn't take time to sort out what she shouldn't say. "Father was the ultimate authoritarian, and everything had to be done his way. Sometimes, Coe is introverted and doesn't talk with me like I think spouses should. I don't know what he's thinking or feeling or what he expects of me. What if he has to control everything like Father?" She grimaced. "Like the pastoral stuff. Why doesn't he just talk to me about it and include me in whether he will accept the position? I'm sorry. I didn't mean to ramble."

"You're doing fine. Go on."

Her thoughts shifted to another topic. "Coe and I kissed in India, which changed everything. But I don't know if that's enough to build a relationship. An exuberant, passionate kiss?"

"It worked for me." Irish's cheeks flamed red. "I told you I kissed Lake first."

"And did you wait until you were in love to do everything else?"

Irish's jaw dropped, and Skye felt awkward for asking. "I don't discuss my love life with anyone other than my husband. That's private between us."

"I'm sorry. Forget I said anything." She buried her face against the puppy's soft fur, wishing she hadn't bought up such a personal question.

"However, I'm also the type of person who says what needs to be said." Irish stroked Little Dipper's ear. "So, while I'd like to tell you that Lake and I waited until we were deeply in love, we didn't. We were married, and I'd told him I was falling for him, but he wasn't ready to say the words." Her voice softened. "Still, he'd shown me he was falling for me in a million ways. And we are very much in love now."

Skye exhaled the breath she'd been holding in.

"Have you and Coe considered moving to the next level in your relationship before you're certain you love each other?"

"I think so. I don't know much about men, but I melt into oblivion when he holds me tenderly. And when his lips touch mine, I'm a goner." She felt relieved to talk about this with another woman, but was also embarrassed. "If this is too weird, I'll stop talking."

"We're sisters-in-law. So, we can discuss anything." Irish tapped the arm of her chair. "I take it you're getting mixed signals from Coe?"

"Yeah. Even my feelings about him are mixed up. One minute, I'd like him to follow me to our room and throw caution to the wind. And the next, I think we should forget our vows and go our separate ways." Skye closed her eyes momentarily, a deep sigh escaping her lips. "But then, I feel guilty for having such traitorous thoughts."

"Oh, Skye. That's quite the diversity. Do you view Coe as someone you could love?"

"Sometimes I imagine us falling in love, starting a family, and being amazingly happy."

"If he did what?" Irish eyed her.

"Probably if he talked with me and included me more." Was that all that held her back from loving Coe? There was something else. "I'd like him to fall for me first. Does that sound silly? I don't want to fall completely in love with Coe and then find out he's changed his mind or decided I'm not what he wants in a wife."

"Actually, I felt that way too."

"Really?"

"Mmhmm. But when true love came?" Irish hugged herself. "That's all that mattered."

Skye pondered that for a moment. "I wonder if Coe would rather be married to someone who doesn't need to be involved in every discussion like I want to be." Her yearning for mutual feelings with her husband was a deep ache in her heart that seemed unresolvable.

"Or maybe he does but doesn't know how to make that happen or explain himself yet." Irish gave her a sympathetic smile. "He's probably trying to figure out how to be a husband like you're trying to figure out how to be a wife."

"That's what he says."

"You doubt him?"

"Maybe."

"Is it possible your uncertainty stems from the situation with your dad?" Irish grimaced. "Sorry to bring that up."

"It's okay." Had she thrust her distrusting feelings toward Father onto Coe without meaning to or realizing it? Tears pooled in her eyes, and her throat felt tight.

"I'm no psychologist. But anyone with a dictatorial father like you must be churning inside about starting a relationship, even with a great guy. And especially when you've been thrust into marriage before falling in love." Irish nudged a tissue box closer to her. "Give yourself time to adjust. Coe, too, for that matter."

"You're probably right." Skye took a tissue and dabbed it beneath her eyes, then sighed. "Sorry. I needed someone to talk with more than I realized." She pressed her lips together and stared at a spot on the carpet.

"What are you contemplating?"

"That I know diddly-squat about marriage or being in love." She huffed. "I've been living in a fairy tale world of wanting Coe to be my dream husband while I am no Princess Skye."

"I was no Princess Irish, either. I was the bossy one. Lake and I found our bond of love through a lot of missteps and learning to pray together." Irish's gaze landed on something beyond Skye. "Now, I am so much in love with that man I can't imagine a life without him in it."

"I envy you."

"You and Coe will have a loving relationship, too. Keep praying and believing God for it."

"I hope you're right."

The outer door opened, and Jazzy bustled in, holding a dark-haired baby girl with an adorable smile and sparkling eyes. "Sorry, I'm late. This is going to be a bring-your-daughter-to-work day. I hope that's okay. My babysitter is sick."

"Of course, it is." Irish held her arms out, and Jazzy passed her daughter to her. "Hey, beautiful girl," she cooed.

"Hello again." Jazzy smiled at Skye. "This is Jasmine."

"She's so cute."

"Thanks. I see you've got one of our latest puppies. Is Irish trying to convince you to take him?"

"She wouldn't have to do much convincing." Skye snuggled the puppy closer again. "I'm sold."

"What's the problem then?" Jazzy tipped her head one way, then the other, her short, dark hair bobbing.

"A new marriage. A chance we might not stay here."

"Really? Isn't Coe considering taking the pastorate? I thought he must be after his sermon on Sunday."

Skye didn't want to admit that she didn't know what her husband was planning to do. "You heard that, huh?"

"Sure did. I would be thrilled for him to be our next pastor. Even my grandmother is excited about it. Of course, she is loyal to the North family."

Skye swallowed hard. Did everyone in Thunder Ridge think Coe would become the pastor? Why hadn't he talked with her about it?

Chapter Fifty-six

When Lake burst into the house on Friday afternoon, saying, "Sorry, man, they put me up to this," Coe knew he was in trouble. He'd assumed his brothers spent their mischief-making energy on the flour fight. Boy, was he wrong. Despite his attempts to flee out the back door, Wilks, Finn, Sunday, and Lake chased him into the backyard, caught him, wrestled him to the ground, grabbed him by his limbs, and hauled him toward Lake's truck.

"Put me down!" He shouted threats, kicked, and tried to jerk free, but being outnumbered, there wasn't much he could do but go along with this ridiculous rite of passage.

"You brought home a wife without telling us," Wilks proclaimed with a scowl.

"That was three weeks ago!"

"So? Remember all those tricks you pulled on us when we were younger? It's payback time."

"Grow up. We're adults!"

"When did that make any difference?" Finn asked.

Coe groaned. If he could escape, he'd run like crazy, find a hiding place, and wait for his brothers to calm down. But knowing them like he did, they'd see a prank through to the end once they got wound up about it. Hadn't he been the same way in the past? "Where are you taking me?" he asked resignedly.

"We heard about this great dunking spot." Sunday snickered.

"Lake Pend Oreille? You're kidding me." The water would be cold, probably fifty degrees. He shivered at the thought of being submerged in those temps. "I didn't tell Skye where I'm going. She'll be worried." He threw out excuses, not caring if they sounded lame. "She's expecting me."

"Are you saying you have more important plans than getting tossed in the lake?" Wilks asked tauntingly.

"That's right. We're going on a date tonight."

"Sorry, bro. You're about to have a chilly bath first." Finn cackled.

Coe groaned again, regretting all the pranks he'd ever pulled.

His brothers dropped him into the back seat of Lake's truck and buckled him between Wilks and Finn, even though he wrestled against their attempts to restrain him. Sunday squeezed into the crawl space behind the seat and held his shoulders tightly. The three younger brothers laughed and cajoled as if they were pulling off the greatest coup ever. And Lake wasn't innocent in this escapade, like it seemed in the beginning, since he drove the getaway vehicle and cast frequent grins at Coe.

The hyped-up quartet bellowed nursery rhymes en route to the Sandpoint beach, where Coe and his brothers had performed many of their dunking pranks, chanting unique lyrics to "Old MacDonald." "Poor Coe North deserves a prank—E-I-E-I-O," was followed by "We're the ones to throw him in—E-I-E-I-O," and "He's going to get soaking wet—E-I-E-I-O." They howled the last "O" of the verse like a pack of wolves, making Coe shudder with dread over the dunking to come.

When they pulled into the parking lot at the public beach, he clenched his jaw, determined to get this over with and then focus on his date with Skye. None of this childish stuff mattered, he tried convincing himself.

But when his brothers carried him down to the beach and the spring wind hit him full in the face, the thought of getting dumped in the water renewed his desire to break free. He yanked against them, jerking and pulling. Sunday lost his grip on Coe's ankle, and Coe twisted his leg around himself like a pretzel, then kicked hard, taking the others off guard with his swift movements. He fell to the ground with a thud and, realizing he was loose, raced down the sandy beach, hoping to outrun his pursuers. For a few moments, he thought he might get away. But all too soon, Lake and Wilks caught up and grabbed him, lifting him off the ground, and hauled him to the water. This time, they clung to him even tighter.

"Come on, guys. Have a heart."

"We have lots of heart," Finn shouted.

With them holding his ankles and wrists like handcuffs, Coe braced himself for the chilly waters. However, he was also determined that someone was going with him if he was going in.

"One. Two. Three," the guys shouted, swinging him back and forth like a porch swing. Suddenly, they let go, but he held firmly to Wilks's wrists, dragging him into the lake. The cold splash was a shock, even though Coe knew it was coming.

He burst out of the water, spitting and sputtering, and so did Wilks, yelping and shouting for revenge. Coe splashed Lake, Sunday, and Finn as hard and fast as he could, using his hands like paddles. The guys yelled their disapproval, but then plunged in, dunking and splashing each other repeatedly. They all got soaking wet. By the end of the fiasco, they were laughing, and his brothers were patting his back and congratulating him on his nuptials.

"In the future, we can tell our kids about this." Finn puffed up his chest and lifted his chin.

"You're going to have kids?" Wilks asked incredulously.

"So what? Unlike you wimps, I'm going to wait for true love."

"Who are you calling a wimp?" Water dripping off his face, Coe grabbed Finn by the waist and, with Lake's assistance, hauled him back to the water.

"No, guys. I was teasing. You aren't wimps." Finn tried to wrestle free, but Coe wasn't letting go. "I'm in a play tonight, remember?"

"All the more reason to throw you in again," Coe shouted.

And that's what they did.

Chapter Fifty-seven

"This was a thoughtful idea. Thank you for bringing me here." Skye glanced around the dimly lit restaurant with tables for two covered in burgundy tablecloths and a white candle shining from the center of each. At the next table, a twenty-something couple gazed at each other, their eyes sparkling with attraction as if they couldn't stop staring into one another's eyes. Skye felt a longing for that kind of bond with Coe.

"You deserve a night out," he said.

"I don't know about deserving anything." She forced her gaze away from the other couple and back to him. He looked handsome in his dark blue sports coat, navy tie, and pastel pink shirt.

"You've been working hard since we arrived in Thunder Ridge. It's my way of saying thank you." He shrugged like he didn't know if that was the right thing to say.

She had questions she hoped to ask him tonight but didn't want to bombard him right off. What if a deeper discussion ruined their evening? What if she was right about him not wanting to be married to someone who had to be involved in all his decisions? What if he had been a bachelor so long that he wasn't adjusting well to being married? She squelched a groan over the questions swirling in her thoughts.

"Is something wrong?" He gave her a soft look.

She felt caught and decided to be honest about her feelings. "I've been pondering some things. Worrying a little. Troubled, you know?"

"Oh?" He held her gaze, his expression compassionate.

Why couldn't she just enjoy the restaurant's ambiance and the companionship with this attractive but reticent man sitting across from her, and let her apprehension about what they weren't saying to each other go for one evening? She could talk to him about vexing topics some other time, right? She remembered what Irish suggested about giving themselves time to adjust. But wasn't three weeks long enough to figure out how to talk to each other about potentially emotional topics?

"You look lovely."

"Thank you. I appreciate the clothes, especially this dress." Some might call the vintage ruffle at the bottom old-fashioned, but she liked the fabric's comfortable feeling, and baby blue was usually her first color choice. "It might be my favorite for years to come."

"You are something, Skye."

"What do you mean?" She watched him closely, wanting to know his thoughts.

"How can you not mind living without luxuries when you were used to wealth and ease in your father's house?"

"Ease? Did you forget our humanitarian efforts already?"

"No." He waved his hands toward her dress. "However, you don't seem to mind thrift store shopping or wearing—"

"Gently used clothing? I don't mind. But if Father were here, we'd argue about it, and he'd fill my closet with a new wardrobe of clothes that he deemed appropriate for Liam Tamarack's daughter." She groaned, hoping she hadn't offended Coe. "But none of that matters to me. I gave in to his opinions because I didn't want conflict and walked on eggshells around him." She stirred her lemon water with a spoon. "Not anymore. Otherwise, I wouldn't be married to you." *And I won't walk on eggshells around you.*

"You burst out of your cage and—"

"Leaped into your arms." Their gazes met and held like dancers. Skye's heart pounded, and for a second, she yearned to lean across the table, kiss Coe like she was already falling for him, and forget about asking him anything troubling. Instead, she took a sip of her bitter-tasting water. "After working among the poor and getting our hands filthy with things we don't want to discuss and building make-shift houses neither of us would care to live in, we are living like a king and queen in your parents' house." *We've been through so much together, and yet, it feels like we're living separate lives under the same roof.* Would it always feel that way? Or would they slowly discover how to talk to each other, love each other?

"True. It is a matter of perspective. But you are special, and I'm proud you are my wife."

His words struck her like a bolt of lightning, igniting a fierce emotional battle within her, and she didn't know how to respond. Father never praised her, only gave orders, and expected compliance. Was Coe's pride in her genuine?

"I didn't know what kind of woman I'd want to marry. Someone who loves the Lord, of course, and a woman whose focus wasn't on material things but on making sure others were taken care of, too. I am thankful you are like that," he said huskily. "I'm intrigued with you and devoted to you, Skye."

Devoted to her? Warmth radiated through her chest. It was like he was saying he would have chosen her even if their marital arrangement hadn't transpired. Was he saying that?

"I've admired you from afar and should have acted on my feelings sooner." He smudged his fingers over the condensation on his water glass, teasing her with his glances. "Maybe then, your dad would have accepted me as a suitor for his daughter. If I called and tried to get him to see reason, do you think I'd convince him that I'm an acceptable husband for you and a decent son-in-law for him?" He gazed at her with so much vulnerability she wished she could say yes.

"I'm sorry, Coe. My dad won't accept anything he doesn't have control over."

"God can change his opinion, right?"

"True." Sometimes she forgot the spiritual impact of declaring such things. "*He* can do anything. But until God alters Father's attitude, he won't accept you or my decision to choose you."

"Then we'll have to keep praying about that."

"I'd like that." Maybe she and Coe would pray together more and move toward a closer relationship. Would spending time together this evening and talking resolve some of the challenges they'd experienced?

When their food arrived, Coe quietly said a blessing. He didn't include anything personal, so Skye added a silent, desperate plea. *Lord, if we are meant to stay together, help us learn to talk and pray together and do all the things that come with marriage. I feel unsettled, and our future together seems uncertain, even though we have made promises to each other. Please, help us.*

She ate her delicious steak dinner, occasionally glancing at Coe, who seemed to be enjoying his meal, too. Did he want them to become closer as friends and marriage partners, sharing and conversing about everything? Should she ask him about that?

He set his fork on his plate abruptly. "I'm sorry for rushing you."

"Were you?" She glanced at her partially empty plate. "I didn't feel hurried. The food was delightful."

"I don't mean the meal." Coe nudged his plate forward, crossing his arms over the empty space. "I meant I'm sorry for rushing you about romance and intimacy before you were ready."

"Were you doing that?"

"Maybe." His cheeks darkening, he stared at his plate like he felt awkward or regretful. "Just because we exchanged vows doesn't mean we're ready for the next step."

"I agree." It seemed like he was trying to be more open with her, even if the conversation wasn't the one she'd hoped to initiate.

"I want to be honorable with you." He glanced at her and his eyes shimmered with moisture. "How we proceed and decide to come together emotionally and physically matters to me. As a husband, I want to be sensitive to you and your needs."

She didn't know what to say. The clink of dishes and muffled chatter rose around them, and they stared at each other as if asking a dozen questions with their gazes but not their lips. Skye drummed her fingers nervously on the table while Coe reached his hand out toward her, hesitated, then withdrew it.

"It seems like you've given this a lot of thought," she finally said. "Why haven't you mentioned it before?"

"I guess because it's hard for me to bring up things that might cause conflict between us."

"I get that."

"I'm sorry about not being better at this." He didn't say what he meant by "this," but she figured he was talking about their marriage and communication. "I want us to find our way together."

"That's nice to hear." Maybe now was a good time to bring up the pastorate. "There are some things I was hoping we could talk about, too."

"Of course." His shoulders sagged like he dreaded whatever was coming.

"You took a risk to get me back here despite Rhett and Tip's herculean efforts to stop us," she said, detouring slightly from what she hoped to discuss. "I appreciate everything you've done for me. Thank you, Coe. That you went the extra mile to marry me means a lot."

"You're welcome. I don't regret marrying you, if you're worried about that. I would do it again in a heartbeat."

It was kind of him to say that, but how could he articulate something so appealing and profound when he hadn't mentioned whether he was planning to become a pastor? That issue dangled over her head and heart like a heavy weight about to drop, and she needed to hear his thoughts on the subject.

"What did you want to ask me?"

"Maybe we should talk somewhere else." Should she even mention his lack of communication when he seemed to be trying to improve that tonight?

"Finn's play starts in forty-five minutes. We'll have to head to the theater soon. So, please, tell me what's on your mind."

"Okay." She scooted forward and tried to speak calmly, despite the tension creeping up her neck. "Why haven't you talked to me about the possibility of you pastoring your dad's church?" She gulped. Did that come out too accusatory?

"Haven't I?" A frown creased his forehead.

"No. You said you were going to a meeting about it, then spoke in church on Sunday. But you didn't tell me about the offer. Wouldn't that decision impact me, too?"

"If I planned to say yes, it would." His jaw dropped. "That's what's been bothering you?"

"Yes." Annoyance rose in her. "It bothers me that my husband hasn't talked with me about a possible major life change for us, if we stick together."

"If?" His eyelids nearly closed. "I didn't mean to leave you out or hurt your feelings."

"But you have hurt me," she admitted, exhaling. "Don't you think you should have brought up something this important?"

"You could have asked me about it."

Yes, she could have. But was he blaming her? Guilting her like Father had done so often?

"Don't you think I'd want to know my husband's thoughts on the subject?" Her attempt to modulate her voice was failing. "Don't I deserve a chance to voice my opinion on matters that affect our marriage?"

"Of course." He looked at her directly. "But this isn't that big of a deal."

His words felt like a slap, a dismissal of her feelings, like what she had been struggling with emotionally wasn't valuable or of any consequence to him. "Not that big of a deal? How can you say that?"

"It just isn't. I meant to talk with you about the meeting I attended, but we rushed to the bridge accident that day, and we've been preoccupied with the remodel ever since." He lifted and lowered his hands. "I told you being a husband is new to me."

"Don't use that for an excuse, Coe." How long would he rely on the cop out? There had to come a time when he took responsibility for his actions. "Even though our marriage is new and different, shouldn't we work at communicating and praying about stuff?" She tried to sound reasonable, but some heated emotion crept into her voice.

"I do, actually." His admission surprised her. "I meant for us to pray together, but I've been forgetting about it. Once we head to our bedroom, I try to focus on falling asleep." He gave her a meaningful look. "Nothing else."

His softly spoken explanation almost made her regret her next question, but it was something she had to know. "Did you speak with your dad about the pastoral position?"

"Yes."

Something painful and foreboding swelled in her chest. "And your mom. Did you talk with her about it?"

"Uh. Yes." His face turned a gray pallor.

Tension squeezed her throat like it was choking her. Her heart pounded, a strong drumbeat reverberating through her body, but she forced herself to ask, "Did you talk with your grandmother and ask her to pray with you about becoming the pastor?"

He tugged on the neck of his tie, his voice strained. "Yes."

Tears flooded her eyes. It felt like her heart was breaking into pieces. "Now do you see why I'm bothered about this thing that isn't a big deal to you?" She stood and gathered her sweater and purse before her silent tears turned into a wail she couldn't stop. "And why I think this marriage isn't working?"

"Skye, please."

She hurried to the exit with emotional agony burning through her. How could she stay married to a man who prioritized communicating with everyone in his family but her?

Chapter Fifty-eight

Coe couldn't believe what just happened. How had their date, which he carefully planned and put thought into, and where he tried to initiate honest conversation with Skye, gone downhill so rapidly? All because he hadn't discussed with her about taking a pastorate he didn't want? He met the sympathetic glances of a few people he knew from around town or church. How many heard their disagreement and watched his wife flee from the restaurant?

He sighed and waited impatiently for the server to bring his check so he could pay their bill and find Skye. Was she waiting for him outside? Did she mean what she said about their marriage not working? Was she thinking of getting a divorce? *That isn't happening. Please, God.*

As soon as he paid for their meals and left a tip, he dashed out of the restaurant and checked both ways along the sidewalk. Not spotting her, he jogged out to his car in the parking lot. She wasn't there, either.

Way to go, North. You are already a lousy husband.

He sprinted to the end of the block, then turned around and ran the other way, spending some of his frustration with physical effort, but not all. Was she walking home? Where else would she go? He jogged to the car again, started the ignition, and pulled into the street. He drove to his parents' house without finding her, made a U-turn, and drove back, peering into the darkness, searching every street corner and sidewalk for her. How fast was she walking? Where was she?

Why couldn't they have had a calm discussion without her getting offended and stomping off? Why was she so upset about him discussing the church's offer with Mom, Dad, and Gran? That's what he'd done his whole life. It was second nature for him to talk with them and ask for prayer about situations he was facing. They'd always been his prayer warriors and support team.

While Skye was … *my wife. My bride, who wants to build a trusting relationship with me, one where she feels like an equal partner.* He groaned.

A wretched feeling of being at fault and hurting someone he deeply cared about coursed through him. He hadn't purposefully meant to exclude her. But he hadn't intentionally included her, either. He breathed and exhaled slowly, trying to release some of his irritation and regret, but it squeezed tighter in his chest. Acid rolled up in his throat, making him feel sick.

Lord, I've made some foolish mistakes. What do I do? Where is my wife? I have to find her!

It was nearly time for Finn's play to start. Coe promised he'd be there for the opening show since he missed his brother's plays for the last two years and didn't want to let him down. But he made promises to Skye, too. He couldn't attend Finn's play and ignore his wife's disappearance. What if she was in danger? What if she planned to leave him?

He circled the area between the restaurant and the high school where the theater company would be performing. On his second pass, he spotted her. Skye stood in front of the school building, her arms crossed over her middle like she was either cold or still mad. Her words replayed in his thoughts. *"Now do you see why I'm bothered about this thing that isn't a big deal to you? And why I think this marriage isn't working?"*

"I'm sorry, Skye," he said as soon as he ran up to her after parking the car on the far side of the packed lot. "I mean it. I'm sorry for everything."

"Let's watch the play, okay?" She pivoted toward the entrance without meeting his gaze. "Then we can talk."

Each second of silently walking to their seats and waiting for the show to begin was excruciating. Whenever Robin Hood entered a scene, Coe paid close attention to Finn's lines. The rest of the time, his mind busily replayed everything he and Skye had said or done since they kissed in India, ending with the fiasco at the restaurant.

Why had he thought he was doing all he could to bring them closer in their marriage? Why hadn't he talked with her about the pastoral thing? Even if it wasn't that important to him, why was it simpler to seek out Mom and Dad and explain his feelings to them, instead of talking things out with the woman he pledged his life to? *Man.* He messed up. He reverted to acting like one of the bachelor North brothers instead of a husband who wanted his wife to love and trust him.

Lord, I confess my failings and faults, and they are many. Please help Skye and me work things out and find love and forgiveness for this mess. Help us before it's too late.

Would she even stay with him after this?

Before tonight's disaster, he thought he might be falling in love with Skye. But his recent actions denied that lofty idea.

He thought of the vow he'd heard in other weddings about the groom loving the bride above all others, and he'd thought that meant loving and honoring her above other women. But when he returned to Thunder Ridge and fell into his old rhythms with his parents and grandmother as confidantes, and his brothers as friends, he'd put his whole family above his bride and the intimacy that should have been developing between them.

She was right. He was to blame. He hadn't involved her in discussing fundamental aspects of their life together. He'd decided about the pastorate without praying with her, asking her thoughts on the subject, or telling her his views. He had a lot of apologizing to do, and a lot of praying.

At intermission, Skye stood and eased out of their narrow row without saying where she was going. She was probably heading to the restroom, but her cold shoulder was difficult to bear.

He should talk with Dad about the husbandly things he'd been neglecting and devise a plan to get back on track with Skye. Dad would understand the awkward stage they were in and give him godly advice. Gran was a great listener and would pray with him and tell him how much she loved him. Mom would—

A mental spotlight as bright as the one trailing Finn on stage hit him between the eyes. The first thing he should have done when the church board asked him about being their pastor was to talk with Skye about it and ask her to pray with him. Why hadn't he? Was he afraid of being vulnerable with her? Exposing that he wasn't always the confident guy he tried to portray?

"A man shall leave his father and mother and cling to his wife," ambled through his thoughts. Had he been clinging to his wife since their wedding? *No, I haven't.*

His phone vibrated silently.

I found a seat at the back.

Thanks for letting me know.

He sighed as the curtain came up. Robinhood and Marion's love story hurt more poignantly in the second act. Finn did an excellent job of playing the part of a sensitive yet brave woodsman trying to win his leading lady's heart. He had Coe convinced he was smitten with the woman. Their ending kiss was enthusiastic enough to make him look away, embarrassed to be watching his kid brother kissing someone so passionately. Mom and Gran were in the audience, for goodness' sake. What must they think about Finn's amorous performance?

As applause erupted, Coe's thoughts fell solely on Skye and how he'd offended her. What could he do to make amends and make better choices about their marriage in the future, if she was willing to give him a second chance?

Chapter Fifty-nine

Skye slipped out of the theater and sent Coe a text. *I'm tired. Walking home.* She'd watched enough romantic interactions between Robin Hood and Maid Marion. Every time they spoke endearingly or kissed, she felt a wave of inadequacy wash over her. No matter how hard she and Coe tried, how often they kissed, or how frequently he said he cared for her, she felt like she was falling short, that their chances of a happy marriage were falling short. What did caring mean to him, anyway? Was it something below loving? A notch above friendship? The questions gnawed at her, increasing her angst and doubts.

She thought she heard footsteps and glanced over her shoulder. *It's no one. Everything is fine.* The air smelled of spring with new blooms on the trees and bushes. If she were staying in Thunder Ridge, she'd love to help Liv with her garden and small orchard. What would it be like to have access to an outdoor space like hers? But her in-laws were going to sell their place, right? And after tonight, who knew what she and Coe would be doing?

The crunch of tires rolling over something set her on edge. She increased her walking speed and looked back. No headlights. Was it only her imagination? Rhett and Tip hadn't made a threatening appearance in two weeks, which she was glad about. *I'm jumpy, that's all.*

Her phone vibrated in her pocket. Was Coe trying to reach her? It buzzed again. *Give it a rest, Coe. We'll talk later.* She walked faster.

Suddenly, the thunderous roar of an engine and the blinding brightness of headlights sent fear rocketing through her. She recoiled as a vehicle skidded to a halt before her, coming right up on the sidewalk. Her breath caught in her throat. For a moment, she felt petrified, unable to move. Rhett and Tip lunged out the doors, and she bolted, trying to flee, but her high heels hampered her escape. Rhett was swifter, and his arms wrapped around her tightly, stopping her.

"Leave me alone! I'm not going with you!"

"Yes, you are," he said in his gravelly voice. "We've been waiting for an opportunity like this."

She wrenched her body left and right, ramming her elbows like a hammer against his ribs. Rhett groaned, loosening his grip, and she kicked him hard in the kneecap with the heel of her shoe. He buckled, calling her vile names. She sprinted down the sidewalk, desperate to outrun this brute her father had sent after her, but his shoes pounded the cement behind her. She sped up; so did he. Breathing hard, sides aching, she pushed herself to keep running, trying to stay ahead of the kidnapper's intent to capture her. But how long could she keep up this pace?

How foolish she'd been to walk home alone. *Lord, help me.*

The same sedan careened recklessly along the sidewalk again, stopping ahead of her. Tip leaped out and came straight for her. She ducked and dodged him. But both men were chasing her now. She continued sprinting, pushing herself, determined not to let them take her. Still, with their physical advantage, they seemed equally determined and more capable of running fast and outmaneuvering her.

Her high heels made getting away difficult, but she wasn't giving up or slowing down. She was a fighter. She'd battle for her freedom as long as there was breath in her. *If I'm such a fighter, why am I giving up on my marriage?* The thought hurt. Why wasn't she fighting, doing everything she could to stay with Coe? Battling for their love? *I'm sorry, Coe,* repeated in her brain with the rhythm of her heels hitting the sidewalk and her noisy gasps for air.

Rhett's growl alerted her to his nearness a second before he knocked her over, taking her down to the ground, both rolling and scraping along the cement. She moaned and twisted, elbowing him in the gut, then shouting hoarsely for him to let go as she kicked and shoved him. Tip jumped into the fray, grabbing her legs, even with her kicking and squirming. Nothing she did stopped them from lifting her and carrying her like an old rug toward the vehicle.

Game over. She'd fought her hardest. And lost. Some things weren't meant to be. Like her and Coe. Like love. *Goodbye, Coe. You are a beautiful man. Thanks for trying to keep me safe.*

However, when they reached the car, Skye felt a surge of energy. The game might be over, but she wasn't entering these reptiles' cave without resisting. She writhed back and forth, clawing at her captors, struggling to stop them from putting her inside.

"Get in the car!" Tip ordered.

"I won't." She wrestled an arm loose and punched Rhett in the face. He swore and flung his hand over his nose, groaning. He still held her with his other arm, but as soon as he moved his hand, she punched him again.

"You little wretch!"

She kicked Tip as he half-dragged, half-pushed her head into the car. She shouted at him to leave her alone and yanked against his grip on her. Her cries seemed to infuriate Rhett. He held up his fist threateningly, like he intended to knock her out to silence her, but she didn't flinch or cower. Blood was smeared across his swollen nose and cheek. Was he even seeing straight? He swung at her with a roar, but she ducked, and he rammed his fist into Tip's face, who bellowed and toppled backward, releasing Skye.

She fell to the sidewalk and rolled, moaning. Then she scrambled to her feet and sprinted down the street again, barely staying upright in her haste to escape. She was free. *Thank God.* But for how long? A car screeched to a stop beside her. She didn't glance at it since she assumed it was Tip. Rhett was still pounding the cement behind her. If she made it to the convenience store up ahead, she'd run inside and call 911, or yell at the clerk to do so.

Car doors opened and slammed. Running footsteps. *God, help.* She was utterly spent, her burst of energy gone, her breaths coming in irregular gasps. Her feet throbbed with each step, a relentless reminder of the pain her feet were enduring. Yet she kept running, not daring to look back.

Thud. Thud. Thud.

Was that Rhett? Had Tip joined him?

Thwap. Thwap. Thwap.

Wait. Those sounded like punches, not footsteps. Were Rhett and Tip fighting each other? She glanced over her shoulder and gasped. *Coe? Lake?* Her footfall stumbled. She nearly toppled over. How did Coe and Lake know to come after her? How had they found her?

Breathing raggedly, tears burning her eyes, she bent over and watched her husband and brother-in-law belt Rhett and Tip with surprisingly powerful punches. They were stronger than she realized, or the thugs' attempt to kidnap her had upped the ante on them winning this fight. Wilks and Sunday ran over and stood close to her, fists clenched, their bodies taut and straining forward, like they were ready to fight to protect her.

"Are you okay?" Sunday asked.

Still gasping for breath, she nodded, wincing as Coe took some hard punches. Wilks and Sunday moaned or huffed with each hit, like they were in the scuffle with their brothers. The air crackled with tension as Coe and Lake, bloodied but undeterred, appeared to be winning the brawl. Yet, Rhett and Tip threw some heavy punches, too.

Skye clutched her middle, her sides hurting from rolling and scraping against the sidewalk. Her hands were sore from the impact of slugging Rhett. She longed to soothe her feet in cool water and sleep for a week. But seeing her husband and brother-in-law locked in a fight for her with Rhett and Tip was a revelation. Coe and his family had taken significant personal risks and pain for her, and she felt extremely humbled and grateful.

After more scuffling and groaning, and with Rhett and Tip spread out on the grass, whimpering like children after a playground fight, Coe ran over and picked Skye up. He held her tenderly and close to his chest, and she clung to him, feeling safe, a stark contrast to the panic she'd felt and the violence that had just unfolded. "Are you okay?"

"I'm okay thanks to you and Lake." She nodded toward her brother-in-law, who stood over Rhett and Tip threateningly.

"I was so worried when I got your text." Coe's voice broke. "Please, stop running off like that."

She wanted to tell him to put her down and stop telling her what to do. But she was too tired and so grateful he'd come for her and stood up for her. "I'm not going to live in fear of being captured anymore. And you don't talk to me. So I will do whatever I must to survive."

"Okay. But listen." He gazed into her eyes, and for a second, she thought he might kiss her or break down crying. She felt a surge of fear and hope, not knowing what his next words might be. "Starting now, things are going to be different." He inhaled and exhaled a few times as if he was also trying to catch his breath. "Everything is going to be better between us."

"Really?" Her voice broke. "You promise?"

"I promise." He nodded toward Rhett and Tip. "What about those scoundrels? What are we going to do with them?"

Was he letting her decide their fate? She remembered what he'd told her about his brothers' prank today. "You know how you guys threw each other in the lake?"

"Yeah."

"You could do that to them about twenty times or drop them off at the police station. Either way, I'm done protecting my father's name and the jerks who work for him." She turned and yelled at Father's bodyguards, "Never chase me or follow me again. You hear me?"

"But your dad—"

"I don't care what Liam Tamarack told you or how much he promised to pay you. His choices for my life don't count on American soil. Leave the country, or you will spend the next decade in prison for kidnapping and assault. Got it?" Coe chuckled like her ferocity amused him. "Got it?" she shouted louder.

"Yeah, yeah. I need a doctor," Rhett spoke nasally.

Tip's face looked bruised, and he gave her a departing glare as he limped away.

"Let's go," Lake said, dragging Rhett toward the vehicle. "Wilks and I'll take care of this, Coe. Get Skye home safely. Love you guys."

"Thanks, bro. And ditto." Coe jostled her slightly. "I never want to be apart from you again, sweetheart."

Sweetheart? Did he get hit on the head, or something? She gazed at him in the moonlight and saw some bruising under his left eye and a crack along his cheek. "That looks painful. I'm sorry they hurt you."

He winced. "It was worth it."

She slid her arms around his neck, gazing into his moist eyes, trying to see into his heart. "Do you mean it about never wanting to be apart from me?"

"I mean it," he said huskily and tugged off her shoes.

"What are you doing?"

"Making sure you don't run again."

Too weary to complain, she rested against her husband's chest and let him carry her home.

Chapter Sixty

Coe invited Skye to join him on the bench beneath one of the apple trees in the orchard the following day. This wasn't any ordinary spot on his parents' property, but one with special significance, and that's why he chose it for this important talk. It was here where he and his brothers had spent countless hours playing and climbing, where he read adventure books and biographies, and where Mom and Gran shared their love of gardening and knitting and often prayed together. Gran had always said sitting on this bench beneath the beautiful fruit-bearing trees was the best place for connecting with God and each other.

Skye had been resting and took a long soak in the tub after the previous day's ordeal, and Coe wanted her to take it easy, but he also hoped to clear the air. This morning, he talked with the Lord about how much he needed His help to be a better husband and partner for his wife. He'd taken so much for granted about their three-week-and-two-day marriage and hadn't given as much effort as he should have to communicating with Skye. He had some honest confessions to make and prayed she would listen and understand.

"I want you to know how sorry I am for not talking with you about the pastoral offer," he said as soon as Skye sat down. "I don't know why I didn't, other than I like to ponder things before speaking. But not talking with you about it was a mistake I regret."

"Thank you." She smiled softly. "I've thought about it and prayed about it, too. I'm sorry for getting all worked up instead of trying to figure things out with you."

He stroked her hand lightly beneath her sore-looking knuckles. Her bruised skin was a painful reminder of what she went through and what might have happened if he and Lake hadn't found her in time last night. "I fell back on what I've always done when I needed to talk to someone and turned to my parents and Gran. I'm sorry for not including you."

"I forgive you. And I get it." She lifted one shoulder in a shrug. "If I had a loving family like yours, I might do the same thing. We haven't been married long, but I expected everything to go smoothly, and our misunderstandings would be instantly resolved. That wasn't fair. I should have asked more questions. Or at least asked why you weren't talking to me." She heaved a sigh. "So, do you want to become the pastor here?"

"No. For about a minute, wanting to be like Dad was tempting. I'm embarrassed to say, it felt good for the board members to seek me out and want me as a spiritual leader." He winced, and his sore cheek tightened up in pain. He covered it by rolling his eyes. "Me, can you believe it? It was prideful to be impressed, and I repented about it."

"I guess you're human, after all." She nudged his arm. "So, did you tell them no?"

"I did as soon as they asked. But I wish I'd talked about it with my wife first."

"Is that so?" She eyed him loftily.

"I told you things were going to be different." He gazed into her eyes. "I mean that, Skye. You and I are married. We are a team now. Besides my faith in God, you are my priority. Every day, I will strive to be a kinder, more understanding husband, and eventually, a good dad for our family."

"You are already a kind man and a sweet husband." Her words touched him, but he still wanted things to improve. "Are you saying from here on out, you're going to include me in *all* your decisions?"

"You bet. You will be the first person I confide in." He leaned closer and whispered in her ear, "And the last person I tell my thoughts to at night."

"I like the sound of that." She smoothed her fingers down his cheek, touching lightly around his bruise, and gazed dreamily into his eyes, making his heart flip-flop.

He smoothed some hair behind her ears and played with her soft earlobes. "I vow to pursue a loving relationship with you, which means having honest discussions where we both have a say about everything."

"Even things that don't seem like a big deal to you?" She tipped her head, eyeing him.

"Even those."

"Even when we disagree?"

"Even then."

"Thank you. And I promise to listen and support your thoughts and ideas, too."

"I appreciate that. I value your trust, and I want you to feel comfortable sharing your concerns with me," he said with some emotion tugging at him. "I want us to talk about and pray about everything. And even when it feels awkward to reveal personal thoughts or secrets, I want to understand your heart and for you to understand mine."

"I feel the same way." Her cheeks turning rosier, she swiveled on the bench until they were sitting face to face. "Can we take our talk a tad deeper?"

"Absolutely." He continued gazing into her eyes, loving how they sparkled back at him.

"Why don't you want to be a pastor, despite the boost it would be to your ego?" She winked, and he chuckled.

"Even if I can draft a three-point sermon, I don't feel a deep call of God toward being a pastor. If I did, we would be having a different conversation."

"You have a good heart." She brushed her hand over his shoulder. "You've helped many people, sacrificing your time and money, and working hard for others."

"But it isn't a pastor's heart."

"Some might say it is."

"But I know the truth."

"I've seen you running through a flooded area, carrying children to safety." She clutched his hands, holding them between them. "I've seen you weeping over a person we didn't get to in time." Her eyes glistened with moisture.

He nodded slowly, their gazes meeting and clinging, and he felt a rush of tender emotions for this woman he already cared for so much. Those experiences they shared on the field, combined with their conversations and things that had happened since arriving at Thunder Ridge, were building a stronger link between them every day, and he thanked God for it.

"Is this one of those things we should pray about together?" she asked.

"Absolutely. Let's pray about everything as a couple."

"Okay."

With their foreheads nearly touching, he prayed, asking for wisdom and direction about their future careers and their lives as married couple and a family. Then Skye spoke softly, asking the Lord to bring genuine love to their hearts so they could be open and trusting of each other, and that Coe would know God's will for his life and their lives together. He felt a deeper bond with her as they prayed and shared their hearts beneath the apple tree, with the birds singing above them and the warm spring sun shining down on them.

After their prayer, Skye said, "You have a big, loving family who is always there for you. But I'd like to be your—"

"Wife? Love?" Warmth spread through him.

"Yes." She smiled, and her cheeks darkened. "I don't want to replace your family bonds. What you Norths have is beautiful and unique. But I want to be the one you search for when you want to talk to someone. I want to be your special person."

"You are my special person. I could sit here for hours with you like this." He hugged her gently. "I am eager to engage with you in conversations, kissing, and becoming a husband and wife who adore each other."

She leaned back, a twinkle in her eye. "You think I'm going to adore you?"

"I hope so. I adore you already." He kissed her cheek and caught the scent of her strawberry-scented shampoo, which made him want to bury his nose and face in her hair.

"Aww, Coe." She sighed. "There is something else I've been meaning to ask. How many kids do you hope to have?" She looked so apprehensive he almost laughed.

"I haven't given it much thought, other than imagining Mom and Gran being involved in our children's lives."

"They will make an amazing grandmother and great-grandmother duo. But you don't want a big family like yours, right?"

"Are you worried about that?"

"Yes."

"How many kids do you want to have?"

"More than one, but much less than nine." She gave him a cute, cringing look.

"Deal." He shook her hand.

"Are you still okay with us not rushing anything?" She gazed at him with so much trust, and what he interpreted as possibly a bit of falling in love, that he longed to kiss her and make some new memories under this bower of apple trees.

"There's no rush. Let's fall madly in love together, Skye." He was already halfway there.

Chapter Sixty-one

"That was an amazing dinner." Skye set her scrunched-up paper towel on her empty plate at the small kitchen table in Lake and Irish's cozy cabin. "The roast was delicious. I can't believe what great cooks you North brothers are. You're quite impressive." She was speaking to Lake but noticed Coe grinning, too.

"We lucked out, didn't we?" Irish said laughingly.

"Definitely."

"Thank you, ladies." Lake bowed his head. "With our large family, we were taught how to cook and encouraged to explore recipes at a young age."

"Must have been nice." Skye glanced around the compact kitchen and living room combo. She loved the homey ambiance of the fire burning in the woodstove and could imagine her and Coe living happily in a secluded place like this. "I experimented when I could, but our cook wanted me to stay out of her kitchen and not mess anything up. Still, I watched her sometimes."

"Were you pampered?" Irish asked teasingly.

"I don't know if I was pampered or excluded from doing something I would have enjoyed."

"Lake and I have fun cooking together." Irish winked at Lake. By her blushing cheeks, she was thinking of something romantic.

"Most of the time." He grinned back at her.

"Are you referring to our water fights?"

"Occasionally, my wife gets playful during kitchen duty."

"Lake—"

"I'm not saying that's a terrible thing. I'll water fight with you any day of the week." Lake kissed her lightly, and Little Dipper frolicked around their chairs, yapping.

"Settle down, baby," Irish purred. A couple of other dogs woofed in another room.

"Sorry about the racket." Lake rocked his thumb toward the back of the cabin. "They're excited to hear your voices."

"No problem. I like hearing their yowls," Coe said.

"Pretty soon, we'll be in our big house, and all the dogs will be welcome inside." Irish thrust out her hands like she was encompassing all their animals.

Lake coughed. "Well, I wouldn't say—"

"That gets him tongue-tied every time." Irish giggled.

"So, which dogs are allowed inside?" Skye asked, enjoying the banter at the table.

"My dogs." Smiling, Irish collected the dirty plates into a pile. Lake coughed again. "Why don't you fellows feed the dogs while Skye and I get things tidied up?"

"That pie looks delicious." Coe nodded toward a creamy concoction on the counter.

"It's banana cream, compliments of yours truly. But feeding the dogs comes before dessert." Lake stood and stretched. "Want to come out and see the gang?"

"Absolutely." Coe jumped up, and Skye welcomed his brief kiss on her cheek. "See you in a bit, sweetheart?"

"Mmhmm." She held his gaze, liking how he'd been calling her endearments lately.

"Looks like you two are warming up to each other," Irish said after the guys left with Little Dipper and two bigger dogs.

"You could say that." Skye collected the leftover bowls and silverware. "Things are progressing in our friendship."

"Friendship is important." Irish tossed her a cheeky grin. "So are certain other aspects of marriage."

"Irish—"

"Just saying."

Skye felt the heat of embarrassment on her cheeks and changed the subject. "Do you like your life out here?"

"As in this cabin with our dogs? Or being all alone with my handsome husband on twenty acres?" Irish chuckled, her red hair shining in the lantern-like lights above them. "I love it here. It's like Lake and I are living a daily idyllic adventure together."

"Sounds incredible."

"It is. I will love our new house, too. Did I tell you I'll have a one-room shed for me and my dogs to hang out?" She wrapped a couple of bowls in plastic and tucked them in the fridge. "It was something I asked Lake about, and he agreed. It will be my minimalistic retreat."

"I'm happy you guys are so in love and agree about stuff after such a short time of marriage."

Irish laughed. "Believe me, we don't agree about everything. We are still competitors and into training our dogs how we want to."

"How is that going?" Skye pushed the chairs around the table.

"My girls and I won a dryland race recently," Irish said matter-of-factly. She set out plates and a knife by the pie. "Lake encourages me to do my best, even if that means he loses."

"And does he win sometimes?"

"Oh, yeah. Then I cheer him on like a wild fan." She poured two cups of hot tea, and they took them into the living room and sat down. "Marriage is like that, isn't it? Sometimes, things go his way, and other times, my way. Sometimes we fight. Other times we fight for each other."

"I get that." Skye smiled. "In our case, it's me who wants to have a say about what we're going to do. And it's an adjustment for Coe to run things by me, having been a bachelor for so long."

"Tell me about it." Irish hooted. "North guys want things their way."

"Coe has been doing much better about including me in conversations and decisions." Skye sipped her tea. "Every time he asks me what I think about something I'm grateful."

"That's terrific." Irish sat quietly, clasping her steaming cup. "I spoke with Trista yesterday."

"How is she doing?"

"She and Hud are back in Alaska, settling into married life with parenting."

"Sounds like a lot."

"Sure. Someday, we'll all have to work on our parenting skills, right?"

Skye's eyes widened. "You aren't—"

"Not yet. Lake and I are busy with our dogs and races, building a house, and working at the shelter. But in a year or two?" She shrugged. "We're talking about it."

"So I'll get to be an auntie?"

"And a mom?"

Warmth rushed up Skye's cheeks, which had nothing to do with her hot tea. "We'll see. First, I have to figure out how to be a wife."

Chapter Sixty-two

Skye had never been in love before, so she was in uncharted territory. Unsure whether her feelings for the man walking beside her were love or the deepest friendship she'd ever experienced, she wanted to bravely pursue the hope that she was falling for Coe. Since they'd spent more time talking and praying together over the last two weeks, she felt the truth growing inside her. She was on the brink of telling her husband she felt more than friendship or caring for him, but there was a private, somewhat embarrassing matter she still needed to address and felt some conviction about.

Why had she put off talking with him about it this long when she was the one who'd pushed them to talk about everything and be honest about their feelings and struggles? Was it because her confession might ruin the steps they'd taken and the progress they'd made in their relationship? Did vulnerability require her to reveal everything she'd thought of doing leading up to their first kiss, even though that took place before they exchanged marriage vows? If the Lord was nudging her, she should explain it to Coe, right? Wouldn't she want him to be open with her if their roles were reversed? Still, it was difficult to initiate such a discussion.

With a whirlwind of emotions and mounting tension, she grappled with whether to share her thoughts and struggles during their predinner walk or wait until a more opportune moment. This might be their only chance for a private talk tonight. Coe wasn't a fly-off-the-handle type of guy like Father, for which she was thankful. He was kind and compassionate. And she had trusted him with some of her deepest thoughts lately. He wouldn't get mad, right?

"Coe?" She swallowed a cotton ball of dread and tugged on their linked hands, slowing their walking pace.

"Hmmm?" He asked languidly as if his thoughts were far off.

"I need to tell you something that's a little hard to discuss."

"All right. Did I do something wrong?"

"No."

"Did I say something stupid?"

"No. It's something I did or tried to do a while ago." She expelled a breath. "I don't even know how to start."

"Hey, now." He drew her to a stop. "We've shared a lot of things about ourselves recently. Just tell me. It'll be okay."

She took a deep breath, gathering courage, and said the next words quickly. "When we first kissed, I mean, before we first kissed, I wanted to kiss you, but—"

"That's nice."

"No, Coe. It wasn't nice."

"You didn't like our first kiss?" He stepped back, his jaw dropping.

"I loved our first kiss," she rushed to assure him. "But let me get this out, okay? Before we kissed, I wanted Father to catch us kissing, but I also longed to kiss someone I liked, which was you. But I also needed him to see me standing up for myself and making my own choice about kissing a man, so ultimately, he'd let me marry who I wanted."

"You thought this all out before we kissed?"

"Sort of. I mean, not necessarily about you, but someone." She cringed, hating to admit that.

"Like any guy would do?" He looked mortified.

"No. But when I recognized I had feelings for you, I wanted it to be you who I kissed."

"Okay." He scratched his scalp, his gaze flitting toward the yard they stopped in front of. "So, are you saying you plotted to get me to kiss you that day? Did you act attracted to me so I'd kiss you, and your father would see us?"

"That sounds awful, doesn't it?" Heat crawled up her neck. "I couldn't have plotted how wonderful I'd feel in your arms or how your kisses set my skin on fire. I couldn't have arranged to have strong feelings for a man I would marry on the run. But the rest?" She rushed through the next words lest she chicken out and whitewash her offense. "I wanted to kiss someone passionately so Father would see and recognize I was taking charge of my life. I wanted to steal his power over me." She swallowed a lump in her throat. "I'm sorry for using you, even though it wound up being the best ruse I could have imagined, because I was so attracted to you."

"But you were using me?"

She hated being the cause of his emotional distress or doubt, but she had to speak the truth, no matter the outcome. "Kind of. I'm sorry. And I'm sorry for not telling you about this sooner." She twisted her hands together. "I've asked you to talk with me about everything and include me in all decisions about our future. But I wasn't transparent with you about my past."

He gazed at her for a long while, his eyes reflecting a deep contemplation of her words. She felt a mix of apprehension and anticipation, unsure of how he would react or what she could say to make things better. So she remained silent, giving him time to consider everything.

"When you came to my bungalow that night—" He grimaced like the memory hurt.

"I desperately needed your help, but I also wanted the person I left India with and would possibly be forging a life with to be you, Coe."

He thrust his hands over his hair, linking his fingers on his head, pacing about six feet away and back. "Were you faking that you wanted my kisses?"

"No. That was real. Every kiss has been real."

"Then I'm confused." He lowered his hands but didn't clasp hers. "If I was the one you wanted, what's the deal?"

It would be easy to agree and drop this. But as spouses, as lovers, eventually, she wanted transparency and authenticity between them. "It's about my need to be honest and face my mistakes. If I don't express myself now, you might find out and be more hurt. I've struggled with guilt for trapping you in our marriage." Tears flooded her eyes, but she refused to give in to them. "I'm sorry for forcing you into—"

"Hold on. You didn't force me into anything. I wanted to kiss you."

"And I craved your kisses." She was desperate to make him understand. "I was so drawn to you that I could barely trust my feelings that night I spent in your bungalow." She took a shaky breath. "You were honorable and considerate, and I felt a deep sense of security with you, but I had feelings for you that ignited fast. When the topic of marriage arose, I wanted to be with you and only you, Coe."

"Oh, Skye."

"Thank you for being a gentleman with me. I'd never met a man as nice as you are. Thank you for promising to marry me, never backing down, and never taking what I want to give to only one man, my husband." His silence made her feel unsettled. "What are you thinking?"

"That I need time to ponder what you've shared."

"I understand." She clenched her hands behind her back to hide their shaking. Coe hadn't raised his voice or said anything demeaning, yet her body trembled, a reaction to even perceived dominance. But that wasn't his fault. That had to do with Father, and it was something she needed to face and pray about. The trust she'd built with Coe over the last six weeks of marriage kept her from wanting to run away or pull deeply into herself. But knowing she might have hurt the man she was falling in love with was difficult.

She was falling in love with him, right? All these feelings, and even her willingness to tell him the things that were difficult to express, had to be love.

"This doesn't change anything between us." Coe swept some strands of hair off her cheek, his cool fingers barely brushing her skin. "When I say I have to think about stuff, that's all it means. I'll ponder what you said and get back with you. Can we discuss this again later?"

"Sure. Whenever you're ready."

He held her gaze, his face displaying a raw expression of tenderness and compassion, and she felt a ray of hope that they were going to be okay.

Chapter Sixty-three

Coe asked Skye to meet on the bench in the apple orchard after lunch the next day. He'd spent some time praying and thinking about what she shared with him. And while her explanation about plotting a kiss with a guy didn't make complete sense to him, she had apologized for something she did or thought of doing that she felt bad about. He needed to forgive her as he would want to be forgiven. There would, no doubt, be many instances where they each needed the other's forgiveness and grace. Isn't that what Mom used to say? That marriage was all about loving, forgiving, and giving grace to the person you married and the family you built together?

"I've thought a lot about what you told me," he said when they sat beside each other on the wooden bench. Skye twisted her hands together, and he wanted to put her at ease. "I have a question for you."

"Okay." She heaved a sigh.

"Did you pick anyone else for your father to see you kissing?"

"Someone other than you?" She gave him a blank look.

"That's right."

"No. I didn't pick anyone else. I was attracted to you. I liked you and hoped you liked me."

"I did." He clasped her hands. "I still do, Skye."

"That's a relief." She shook her head, causing her hair to fall forward over her eyes. "I wanted to kiss you that night and didn't mean to use you falsely."

He brushed the hair off her face. "Our first kiss was authentic and perfect to me."

"And to me," she whispered.

"Yet you felt remorseful about scoping me out?" It was silly to ask, but it helped with processing his feelings. "And picked me above all the other available men?"

"You stood way above the others, Coe. But the more I cared about you, the more guilty I felt about my plan."

"Even with your minor scheming, I'm honored and proud to have been the guy you chose and kissed." He made a heart shape with his thumb against her cheek, encircling her dimple. "I'm delighted it was me because that unforgettable kiss led to our marriage, this moment, and the blessing of all our tomorrows together." He drew her to him, enfolding her in a gentle hug, and she snuggled closely, leaning her cheek against his chest and sighing.

"Thank you for understanding. I couldn't resist your charms then. Still can't." She leaned back and touched his neck, smoothing her fingers across his skin, which sent an electrical current rushing through him. He brushed his lips hungrily against hers, delighting in her soft, supple lips and how her palms moved ticklishly over his cheeks and chin. "Does this mean you forgive me?" she whispered.

"If there was anything to forgive, I do." He kissed her from her lips to her earlobe, then whispered, "Do you like my kisses now, Skye?"

"Oh, yes."

He kissed her longer and more tantalizingly, letting his lips speak of what his heart couldn't say yet. But soon, he vowed, he would tell her everything he felt for her.

Chapter Sixty-four

Skye and Coe held hands, laughed, and chatted on their walk, as they'd been doing for the last week since she'd confessed her kissing plan and he graciously forgave her. Each day, they talked about various aspects of their lives with more emotional depth and detail than before, and it felt like Coe was trying to be more transparent with her, letting her see into his heart and his hopes for their future, and she tried to do the same thing with him.

She loved their prayer times in the apple orchard and before they slept at night. How he held her hands softly, praying for their lives together, and even prayed for Father and her feelings toward him, touched her heart. Each moment spent together, each whispered prayer, and every kiss they shared brought Skye closer to falling in love with Coe.

They still didn't know what they would do when the remodeling project was finished. They'd been painting his grandmother's cottage for the last week, and the task was nearly done. They were tossing around ideas about going to Montana or Alaska, but that depended on them finding jobs and raising some money quickly.

They both agreed that their hearts still compelled them to do all they could to help people in troubling circumstances. God had surely put that desire and calling within them, so they continued praying about it, believing in His time, He would show them what they should do next. Coe asked if she minded updating their information with the Tamarack Foundation, and she agreed. Since Rhett and Tip were in jail, she didn't have to worry about anyone knowing where she was staying. One day, she might be open to volunteering with Father's projects again.

Her phone vibrated. Father's name crossed the screen. Why was he contacting her? She stopped walking. "My dad is texting me, but I don't want to read it."

"Why not?"

"I don't want any negative reactions to whatever he's going to tell me to alter how happy I feel with you right now." Even though they'd been praying about her feelings toward Father, she still felt some anxiety about interacting with him.

"Ah, sweetheart." Coe stroked his fingers down her cheek, and tingles of romantic feelings swept through her. "I'm right here. Let's face whatever it is together, okay?"

She inhaled deeply, then sighed. "Yeah. Okay." She held up the phone so he could see the screen, too.

My lawyer got Rhett and Tip off.

"What? Already?" She groaned. Had it been premature of her to think she was safe?

"We knew this might happen, right?"

"Yeah. But—" Her phone vibrated again.

They are heading home now.

"Oh. Coe, look. Rhett and Tip are on their way back to India. Do you know what this means? They won't bother us anymore. They're gone for good." She wrapped her arms around his waist and hugged him tightly.

"So, even if it's awful that he got them off the hook, it's a relief, too?"

"Yes!" She started to put the phone away, but it pulsed again. *You are free to marry Cole.*

Skye let out a squeal. She didn't need Father's approval for her marriage, but there was a part of her that had wished for it. "Do you see this?" She held the phone near Coe's face. "Do you see it?"

"I see it." He chuckled. "This is great news. I don't even mind him calling me Cole." He lifted her and twirled her in a circle, both laughing. The phone vibrated again, and he slowly set her down.

I hope to see you again one day.

Tears flooded her eyes. She still had emotional stuff to unload about Father and the way he'd treated her, but he was still her dad, and she desired peace with him. Hadn't she and Coe been praying for a breakthrough in their relationship? She didn't know what had led Father to reach out like this. Were his texts an olive branch?

Coe held her close, stroking her back, and whispered a prayer, "Lord, thank You for this amazing answer to our prayers. Touch Liam's heart and continue working in his life, in Jesus's name."

"Amen," Skye said, then quickly replied to Father's text. *Thank you. I'd like to see you again, too. I love you.* There was no reply, but that didn't dampen her feelings of happiness and gratitude. And even though everything wasn't resolved with Father, and there would still be hurdles to cross in their relationship, God was working in him and their situation. All the way to the house, she silently thanked Jesus for this turn of events and His blessings in their lives.

When they entered the darkened living room and Coe flipped on the lights, his brothers, Liv, Smith, and Irish jumped out from various places around the room, shouting, "Surprise!" "Congratulations." "It's party time!" And the one dearest to Skye's heart, "Welcome to the family," that Granny Trish said as she shuffled toward them.

Finn broke into a rousing rendition of "For He's a Jolly Good Fellow" with the words, "For they're a jolly good couple." Everyone laughed and joined in.

"Did you know about this?" Skye nudged Coe's arm.

"Not that it was happening today. I talked with Mom about having a gathering." He met her gaze. "I hope you don't mind."

"Surprises are always okay with me." She kissed his cheek. "Thank you."

He leaned close to her ear. "I'll have to remember you like surprises."

A chill skittered up her neck. "You do that." They exchanged warm, meaningful smiles.

Liv rushed forward, hugging them. "Congratulations, you two!"

"Welcome to our family." Smith hugged Skye and then Coe.

"Thank you." Tears rushed to her eyes. These Norths were impressively genuine, kind, and supportive, and even with their pranks and quirks, she was growing to love them all. After spending the last month and a half around Liv, Smith, and Granny Trish, she understood why Coe turned out to be so kind and sensitive. She especially loved his incredible grandmother and claimed her as her own now. She had her favorite brothers-in-law, too. Lake showed her kindness from the moment she met him. And even with Wilks's initial attitude, he came to her rescue and got punched in the jaw in her defense, which connected her to him like a good friend, or in this case, a good brother-in-law.

"God bless you both." Granny Trish hugged Skye and Coe and kissed their cheeks.

All the brothers and Irish hugged them. The younger guys teased Coe about how he and Skye should be the first to start a family. Skye enjoyed Coe's blush and the way he told his brothers to mind their own business, a reaction that brought a smile to everyone's face.

Liv led Skye and Coe over to a large chocolate sheet cake with the words "Coe and Skye Forever" written across the top in light blue. Beside the cake, an enlarged photo of them, that Coe took on their wedding day, was displayed in a wooden frame.

"Aww. Look, Coe. It's us."

"Yeah, it is." He put his arm around her shoulders. "Mom asked for a photo of us."

"That was sweet of her." She turned to Liv and clasped her hand, noticing how happy she seemed. "It was so thoughtful and generous of you to put all this together. Thank you."

"You're welcome, sweetie." Liv hugged her. "Now, let's eat."

A buffet-style taco dinner was spread out on the kitchen island, and everything smelled spicy and delicious. Once they were all seated at the dining room table, Smith said grace and included a prayer for Coe and his "beautiful bride." Coe squeezed her hand beneath the table.

"Dig in," Liv said.

While everyone ate tacos, they chatted about the renovation's success, Finn's play that had just closed, and the positive reviews published in the *Coeur d'Alene Press* and the *Spokesman-Review*. Liv raved about how well Finn performed, even if the kissing scenes were a tad embarrassing.

"Now, Livvy," Smith said. "He had to do what the director required."

"I know. But still."

The conversation transitioned to Rhett and Tip, and Skye explained the news she received about them leaving the U.S. Some groans followed, along with questions about how two lowlifes like that could get off without a worse penalty. However, Granny Trish praised the Lord for the work He was doing in keeping them all safe. *She's right. Thank You, Lord.*

"Something cool happened at the coffee shop this week." Wilks grinned.

"You got your job back?" Lake asked.

"That was a minor misunderstanding." Wilks waved it off like it was nothing. "A customer told me I made the best-tasting latte this side of the Rockies and gave me an extra tip." He rubbed his knuckles over his shoulder. "One day, I'll own a coffee shop that's popular for my exclusive coffee blends." He nodded toward Lake as if commenting on a discussion they'd already had.

"We've heard that before." Finn rolled his eyes.

"You'll see."

"What are you going to call this place?" Sunday asked. "Wilks's Bitter Brew?"

"Hey, now." Wilks frowned.

"How about the North Café?" Skye suggested.

"I like that." Coe smiled at her.

"I'll take all ideas into consideration." Wilks returned to the buffet.

"How about a hundred bucks for the best title?" Finn asked. "Or coffee for life?"

"Maybe a ten-dollar coffee card," Wilks muttered.

"That's not any enticement." Finn scowled.

Skye's phone buzzed, and she peeked at it in case Father was texting her again. *I've given you access to your mother's funds.* She suppressed a gasp and could barely breathe for a few moments. Between this and the other texts from him, she wanted to shout and dance around the room, giving thanks and praise to God. Instead, she set her palm on Coe's arm and held the phone discreetly below the table for him to see. His eyes widened, and they both grinned, sharing the information privately. Maybe now they'd get to have a honeymoon and buy matching wedding rings.

"I have a question for the newlyweds. What are your plans? I think Skye would like a certain puppy at the shelter." Irish winked in her direction. "If you guys stick around, you should get it for her, Coe."

"Have you been dog shopping without me?" Coe's eyebrows rose as he met her gaze.

"Would I dare look for a puppy without my husband's input?"

The room went strangely quiet, and everyone seemed to be awaiting his answer.

"You have been rather daring lately," he said cheekily.

"Coe North!"

Chuckling, he leaned in flirtatiously, and she anticipated his kiss until she recalled everyone at the table was watching them.

Finn tapped his fork against the table. "Kiss. Kiss. Kiss." The chant got louder as others joined in.

"Come on, Coe. Show us what you've got." Wilks returned to the table with a full plate. "Kiss the girl already."

Coe quirked a look at her as if asking her permission. *Like he needs it.* She craved his tender kisses like she needed her next breath. Although she'd rather be alone with him to receive the amorous kiss she was imagining, she leaned toward him for a modest one. He pulled her into his arms, met her lips tenderly, then deepened their sweet lip-lock with much more enthusiasm than she anticipated. *Goodness.* This romantic interlude should have been reserved for private, but she wouldn't be the first to pull away.

Everyone clapped and cheered good-naturedly.

Coe broke the kiss and gazed at her. "You okay?"

"I'm okay. It was a nice kiss, husband." She caressed his whiskered chin, her fingers tracing the path of his stubble. Noting how the bruises on his cheek had faded, she reveled in her freedom to touch him.

"Just nice? I can do better, wife," he said for her hearing alone. She smiled back at him, thinking she couldn't wait to discover what that kind of kiss would be like.

The rest of the celebration was a blur. They ate chocolate cake with delicious fudge frosting and danced like they were at their wedding reception. The brothers all had tales about Coe and their mischief-making days growing up. According to Wilks, the brothers' pranks were all Lake, Hud, and Coe's fault, since they were the ones who schooled the younger guys in paybacks and how to celebrate occasions the North way, which she didn't doubt.

Skye and Coe danced a couple of slow dances. His heart played a gentle rhythm in her ear as she rested her cheek against his chest, and she wanted to stay like that forever. Feeling the tenderness of being in Coe's arms, and knowing she was where she belonged, she planted the golden memories in her heart. Every touch sparked a cascade of feelings within her and ignited hopes for a long and happy marriage with her husband.

Chapter Sixty-five

Skye said good night and gave Coe such a captivating look that he yearned to jog up the stairs after her and find out if he was getting her message correctly. Was she silently telling him she was ready for their next phase of marriage? Was she in love with him? She'd kissed him like she was, but was she?

Was he ready to proclaim his undying love for her? He had strong feelings for her, no doubt about it. Heat filled him with the memory of their kiss at the table. After tonight's celebration, dances, and kisses, he felt so drawn to his wife, so knitted together with her, he couldn't imagine much more time passing before they exchanged the words that would tie their hearts together for the rest of their lives.

I love you, Skye. He imagined saying the phrase softly, whispering it in her ear. *I love you.* He felt a tug of emotion flaming in his heart. He loved Skye. He loved his wife! *Oh, man.* He had to tell her tonight. But what if she didn't feel the same about him? What if she still wasn't sure? If that were the case, he'd have to continue being patient and wait for her love to catch up with his. Isn't that what he'd promised to do?

But Skye had given him such a wooingly intense look when she walked up the stairs. Didn't that mean something? Maybe it meant she wanted to talk. *Right, talk.* He gulped.

He said goodnight to Mom and Dad, who were going to walk Gran back to her place. Lake and Irish had left, and the younger brothers were somewhere out of sight. Wilks was wiping down the kitchen island with a wet washcloth, and Coe paused to get a glass of water. If he went upstairs right this minute, would he be able to refrain from kissing Skye?

"Why'd you do it?" Wilks tossed the washcloth in the sink and eyed Coe.

"Why'd I do what?"

"Marry a stranger." Wilks crossed his arms. "Our pact notwithstanding, and even with how nice of a person Skye is, why would you ask a woman to marry you just to keep her safe?" Doubt and betrayal shadowed his face.

"I didn't ask a stranger to marry me, Wilks. We worked together for two years." Coe leaned against the counter and crossed his arms, too. "I was attracted to Skye when I kissed her and suggested we get married."

"But you weren't in love with her?"

"No," he said honestly. Although he didn't have to explain this to his brother, he wanted Wilks to understand. "I cared for Skye. I knew God was directing my footsteps, even in how I felt about her. Life doesn't always turn out in a neat little package like we talked about when we were kids."

"No kidding. Do you regret not falling in love the normal way? You know, first comes love? I still hope for that." Wilks shuffled his shoulders. "Even pray about it sometimes."

"That's good. Just be open to how God leads you, whatever path that might be. And for the record, I don't regret marrying Skye." Warmth spread through him, heating his face, ears, and brain cells.

"I love her." He heard the awe in his voice. A wide grin crossed his mouth, and it felt like his heart was smiling too. "I *really* love her."

"Whoa, dude."

"I want Skye by my side for the rest of my life. She's sweet, amazing, and perfectly right for me." Fireworks like the ones that lit up the sky over Lake Pend Oreille on the Fourth of July shot through him. "I need to go tell her how I feel." He patted Wilks's shoulder. "Let's finish this chat in, say, two years?"

"Why so long?" Wilks shook his head like he couldn't believe Coe was ending the conversation like this.

"Maybe you'll have your own love story to tell by then."

"What? Coe, wait!"

But he was already sprinting up the stairs. He couldn't wait to share his heart with Skye. *I love you. I love you.* He flung open the bedroom door, ready to shout the words from the rafters. The room was empty. "Skye?" He checked the bathroom. She wasn't there. "Skye?" Panicking, he raced through the house, calling her name.

Chapter Sixty-six

Skye crept down the stairs, wanting to get Coe's attention so he'd come up to their room because she had something important to tell him. While they were kissing at the table, she realized beyond any reservation or doubt that she loved him with all her heart. Previously, she thought she might be falling for him. But after that impassioned kiss, an undeniable awareness of her feelings for Coe rushed through her like a wave, sweeping her into a blissful state of love and desire for her husband.

Something else spoke to her heart, too. She remembered Liv's question that day at the diner. *"What if you thanked Him for the perfect gift of your love?"* Skye was so grateful for everything that had led her to Coe, their new life together, and even Thunder Ridge that she felt ready to express her deepest thanks to the Lord. *Thank You, Lord Jesus, for giving me a perfect love with my husband. Thank You for working in our hearts and preparing us to be together."*

She heard voices coming from the kitchen and paused on the step. Listening from the stairway had gotten her into trouble before. Should she return to her room? She started to turn around, but when she heard Coe say, "I really love her," she couldn't retreat or move. *He loves me!* Her heart overflowed with amazing joy and delight, a myriad of emotions that made her want to dance, weep, and dive into his arms and kiss him with more passion than she'd kissed him before. But Wilks was in the kitchen. Why was Coe expressing his love for her to his brother? Shouldn't he be telling her how he felt?

Instead of heading back upstairs, she silently hurried down the stairway, opened the front door, and slipped outside. The cool night air felt wonderful, and she relished the freedom of being outdoors and no longer having to worry about Father's men coming after her. She dropped onto a step, waiting for Coe to look for her, because surely, he would find her and tell her the words she longed to hear him say. Sighing dreamily, she pictured their previous kisses and the equally romantic kiss she'd like to give him in a few minutes.

The door burst open. "Skye?" Coe said in a panicked tone.

"I'm right here. I'm fine. Will you sit by me?" She patted the step.

"Thank God." Huffing, he closed the door and dropped beside her. "I'm relieved to find you." He clasped her hand, peering at her. "Are you okay? Is everything okay between us?"

"Yes. But when I was coming downstairs, I heard what you told Wilks. You said you love me." She felt the wonder of his declaration again.

"You heard that?" A soft smile crossed his lips.

"I did. And I love you, too."

"Aww, sweetheart." He stroked her face, gazing into her eyes. "I love you so much."

"I love you as my friend, fellow humanitarian, prayer partner, and most of all, as my incredible husband." She kissed him before he had the chance to say or do anything. As their lips danced a sweetly familiar dance, she observed him watching her while she touched his mouth and cheek with her lips. She adored his kisses and touch and loved being affectionate with him. He was such a precious gift to her. "I love you, Coe."

"I love you, Skye. You are my beautiful, beloved wife, whom I absolutely, truly love."

She snuggled closer and kissed him with all the fervency and love she felt. "Coe?"

"Hmmm?" he answered, his voice a murmur against her lips.

"Will you be my husband for all my days and nights?"

"Nights?" He went still.

"Mmhmm."

"I will. I do," he said like a vow. Standing, he picked her up in his arms, his adoring look saying he loved her over and over. "May I carry you across the threshold since we didn't get to do that on our wedding day?"

"If you want to." She giggled, her laughter echoing in the empty living room as he carried her into the house.

He paused, and they kissed softly, their lips tenderly exploring each other's. Then he whisked her up the stairs and into their bridal suite for the beginning of the rest of their forever.

Chapter Sixty-seven

The scent of bacon, eggs, and coffee lured Coe and Skye out of their room the following day. Otherwise, he would have preferred staying upstairs for the next twenty-four hours. He paused on the stairway and kissed his wife slowly. "Did I say I love you today?"

"Not yet. But I like hearing you say it."

"I love you," he whispered, kissing her again.

"I love you, too." She kissed his cheek. "A lot."

"I'm glad to hear it."

"Good morning, you two," Mom said as they approached the kitchen island that was laden with bacon, scrambled eggs slathered in cheese, toasted English muffins, and steaming homemade applesauce.

"What's the occasion?" Coe waved toward the delicious-looking spread.

"Dad and I are putting the house on the market today." Mom leaned her head against Dad's shoulder, and he hugged her.

"It's time." Dad nodded.

"I'm happy for you guys. I know it's a big decision." Coe glanced around the room that held so many memories of their family cooking together and sharing meals and felt a mix of pride and sadness. He was glad for the work he and Skye had helped with, but some melancholy strummed through him at the thought of having to say goodbye to his childhood home.

"We appreciate everything you all have done. The house looks great. Now, we can move forward with getting a smaller place." Dad gave Mom a warm, timeless look that Coe related to now that he had such strong feelings for Skye. "It's a new season for us. I'm sorry about how it will affect you. Gran will stay with us, but the rest of you are on your own." Mom and Dad chuckled, looking both amused and emotional. "Thankfully, Lake and Irish can host our family dinners and Christmas get-togethers at their house once it's finished."

Wilks and Finn, sitting at the table, mumbled about having to hunt for an apartment.

"Don't worry about us." Coe clasped Skye's hand. "We haven't figured out what we'll do next, but Lake and Irish's cabin will be available soon. We might move out there after we take an extended honeymoon." He shared a look with Skye, and she nodded.

He was glad they'd discussed what they wanted to do last night. Their honeymoon was first on their wish list, along with wedding bands, smartphones, and clothes for Skye. Since she had access to her mother's funds, she'd offered to pay for a romantic getaway, which sounded perfect for celebrating their marriage. They were also tossing around the idea of starting a local foundation to help people in crisis. The idea would take more exploration and research, but Coe thought Lake would also be interested in contributing to it.

Before breakfast was over, Coe's phone buzzed. Even though he respected the no-phone rule at the table, he glanced down and recognized the caller. Why was Effer Dickson, the placement director for the Tamarack Foundation's volunteers, calling him? "Sorry. I should take this." He showed Skye the screen, and her eyes widened.

"Yeah?" He took the phone out onto the porch, hearing Skye's footsteps behind him.

"Hurricane Gabrielle hit the East Coast last night," Effer rattled out, no doubt, saying the same explanation to dozens of volunteers. "I saw your name and location in the database and thought I'd give you a call. If you are available, we could use your help. You'd be flying into Richmond, then taking a bus to Virginia Beach. Can you get there ASAP?"

"Oh. Uh. Just a sec." Coe met Skye's gaze. He didn't want to leave her when their honeymoon phase had just started.

"What is it? What does he want?"

"A hurricane hit the eastern states. They need help immediately."

"Tell him I'm here too. I want to go with you."

"Are you sure?" He gazed deeply into her eyes, wishing he had hours to continue doing so.

"Yes." She squeezed his hand, looking so happy and hopeful he wanted to freeze the moment to memory. "Do you believe this is God's will for us?"

"I do," Coe said with conviction. They'd been praying for this kind of direction, and he wanted to go where he was needed. Having Skye with him would make the experience even more meaningful.

"Then let's go together. We can be ready to leave in a few minutes."

Coe couldn't resist kissing her briefly, appreciating her heart to serve others. He told Effer about his and Skye's marital status and how they could get on a plane today. Effer said he was pleased to hear it and explained their travel arrangements.

Dazed at the rapid changes, Coe pulled Skye into his arms for a hug after the call ended. "Are you sure you want to spend this part of our married life helping hurricane victims?"

"What better way for us to live than helping and loving people with all the energy and hope God has given us? I love the idea of doing this with you, Coe."

"I want us to do this together, too." He clasped her hand. "I love you."

"I love you." She tugged him toward the door. "Let's hurry and get ready."

"First this." He pulled her back into his arms for a husbandly kiss before they became aid workers again. Her kiss was sweet and answered every move his lips made with hers.

"And Coe?"

"Hmmm?" He continued kissing her, even though they had to pack.

"When we return, I want a special honeymoon with you to Alaska, Hawaii, New Zealand, or somewhere so fantastic we will never forget it."

"You've got it." He smiled, feeling a powerful surge of gratitude and love for his wife. As she made her way inside, he pulled her back for another kiss. "This one has to last us."

"What do you mean? I'm going to kiss you on the airplane." She smiled, her eyes sparkling like the stars in the night sky, and he wanted to take her in his arms again.

"I'm looking forward to it already."

"Good."

They kissed once more. Then they hurried upstairs to pack their duffel bags and prepare for their next great adventure *together*.

Epilogue

Six months later

Dear Mom.

The words pained him to write. It had been almost two years since he'd seen Mom, Dad, Gran, and his brothers. Two years of misery. Two months of sobriety. The weight of his past actions hung heavy on his heart. Writing Mom a text instead of calling her was the coward's way out, but it was a start.

I'm sorry that I hurt and disappointed you and Dad. I'm heading home, but taking the first step is difficult.

Maybe telling her this in a text was a bad idea. He deleted the words. What if he contacted Lake and asked him to talk to Mom? That would be the chicken's way out. He was different now. A better man than when he left Thunder Ridge, he hoped.

Someday, he would apologize to Mom and Dad and face his family to explain how sorry he was about his choices that had affected them, but not via texting.

Someone outside the family also deserved his apology. He sighed, his chest hurting. His journey into despair had cost him and others he cared deeply about. However, he was rising from the ashes to face his mistakes. *God, help me.*

Gran and Mom were probably still praying for him under the old apple trees. They didn't know the depths he'd crawled into or how their prayers had led him out of misery and onto a homeward path, although that trail was laden with pitfalls. Mom's and Gran's forgiveness and love were a beacon of hope, drawing him toward Thunder Ridge. But how had he walked away from such love in the first place?

What could he even say to Mom? He shut his eyes, praying for strength and clarity.

I hope to see you next month. He deleted it.

I'll be home next week. He held his thumb on the cursor, obliterating the words.

Was he brave enough to face what he left behind? Was he honorable enough to apologize and make amends to everyone he'd hurt or taken advantage of?

I hope to see you soon. That brief explanation would have to suffice. Yet one more thing gnawed at his conscience, tugging at his heartstrings until he felt like he was bleeding from his heart. *I love you, Mom.*

Stone

Thank you for reading *Coe*, Book 3 in The Preacher's Sons series!

The Preacher's Sons series is a spin-off from *Liv & the Preacher*. If you haven't read Liv and Smith's story yet, try it today!

Special Acknowledgements

Paula McGrew … Thank you so much for helping me with another story! Coe and Skye's tale is better because of your help with deepening their characters. I am *so* grateful for your assistance, encouragement, and friendship.

Jason Hanks … Thank you for encouraging me to keep writing and cheering me on to the finish line. I appreciate you taking the time to read this book and offering valuable feedback. Thanks for all those long walks and coffees while we talked about storylines.

Mary Acuff, Beth McDonald, and Joanna Brown … Thank you *so* much for saying yes to reading another book! Thank you for being thoughtful and enthusiastic readers. I appreciate all your comments and thoughts about the North family. You are amazing!

Suzanne Williams … Thank you for another wonderful cover! And thank you for sharing your time and artistic abilities with me. I appreciate you!

Debby Hanks … Thanks for the chats about international flights and airports. Thanks for helping me figure out some pertinent details for this story.

Thank you to all the readers who have been waiting for Coe's story. I hope you enjoy it.

(This is a fiction work. Any mistakes are my own. ~meh)

* Thunder Ridge is a fictional town near Sandpoint, Idaho.

Christian fiction by Mary Hanks:

Liv & the Preacher

The Preacher's Sons:

Lake, Hud, Coe

Restored Series:

Ocean of Regret, Sea of Rescue, Bay of Refuge, Tide of Resolve,
Waves of Reason, Port of Return, Sound of Rejoicing,
Shores of Resilience (finale)

Basalt Bay Series:

Callie's Time, A Touch of Blue

Second Chance Series:

Winter's Past, April's Storm, Summer's Dream,
Autumn's Break, Season's Flame

About Mary Hanks:

When Mary isn't exploring the world through her characters' eyes, she's singing toddler songs, playing in the sandbox, and having fun with her grandchildren. Vanilla lattes, gardening, and taking long walks with Jason, her husband of *almost* fifty years, are also high on her list of favorites. Telling stories is a deeply rewarding part of Mary's life, and she hopes to continue writing heartwarming tales of grace, mercy, and love for a long time.

Thank you for reading The Preacher's Sons series!

www.maryehanks.com